DEATH ON A BUDGET

AN EMERSON WARD MYSTERY

DEATH ON A BUDGET

MICHAEL W. SHERER

FIVE STAR
A part of Gale, Cengage Learning

GALE
CENGAGE Learning™

Detroit • New York • San Francisco • New Haven, Conn • Waterville, Maine • London

GALE
CENGAGE Learning™

LIBRARY OF CONGRESS CATALOGING-IN-PUBLICATION DATA

Sherer, Michael W.
   Death on a budget : an Emerson Ward mystery / Michael W. Sherer. — 1st ed.
     p. cm.
     ISBN-13: 978-1-59414-891-0
     ISBN-10: 1-59414-891-0
     1. Ward, Emerson (Fictitious character)—Fiction. 2. Chicago (Ill.)—Fiction. 3. Journalists—Fiction. I. Title.
    PS3569.H3993D46 2006
    813'.54—dc22   2010014206

First Edition. First Printing: August 2010.
Published in 2010 in conjunction with Tekno Books and Ed Gorman.

Printed in the United States of America
1 2 3 4 5 6 7 14 13 12 11 10

S

For Brendan, Morgan, Megan and Anne

ACKNOWLEDGMENTS

The business of writing is a solitary affair, but I could not complete a book like this without a lot of help from others. A few of the many who contributed information and ideas so I could get the details right were the people of Huntley, Illinois, especially, Chuck Sass, Margo Eckerly, Carl Tomaso, and John Ciomber, and librarians Liz Steffensen and Scott Lindsey. Thanks to Jeff Lovell, at the Parkside Pub, and Steve Grechis, at Huntley Dairy Mart, for being good sports. John Marynell explained some of the intricacies of financial deals on large commercial real estate projects. McHenry County Coroner Marlene Lantz provided helpful background on death investigations. And I'm indebted to Leo West, retired FBI explosives examiner, and Stephen Miller, explosives expert, for information on how to blow up an RV without loss of life. The rest is fiction, and the mistakes are mine.

Finally, I couldn't continue to write one book after another without the unflagging support and inspiration from my beautiful wife, Valarie.

CHAPTER 1

If George Saunders had been lucky that Tuesday, he might not have ended up lying on the pavement, an ever-widening pool of his own blood oozing from beneath him like primordial pitch, black under the leaden sky of early morning. Then again, maybe no amount of luck could have saved him. Whoever had gotten to him had wanted him badly.

His body—most of it—had been found in Montrose Park, near the lake. A shotgun blast had turned his knee to hamburger. Another had torn off his right arm at the shoulder. Probably ended up as fish food—it wasn't found anywhere near the body. The third load of shot had blown away most of his face. It was several days before the body was positively identified.

I know you're not supposed to love two people at the same time, but sometimes you don't have a choice. I was madly in love with Nell Reilly. And I was in love with our two-year-old daughter Emily. Still am. The problem was we weren't together. Nell insisted on maintaining her independence, which meant we led these separate but equal lives that to my mind suited neither of us.

After a lifetime of bachelorhood, of drifting in and out of love and casual affairs, I'd fallen hard for Nell. Hard enough that I was ready to give up the comforts of my solitary existence for a life with someone, a partnership. Hard enough that in my early forties I suddenly became a father, happily mired in a sea of dirty diapers, bottles, books and baby toys. But we weren't together. I was alone, sitting on my bricked garden terrace with a cup of coffee and the paper.

I knew a George Saunders, so the story on a back page of the metro section of the Sunday *Tribune* caught my eye. My stomach grumbled indignantly as I read the rehashed particulars of his death. Every once in a while, stories of adversity stir up something inside of me. Call it moral outrage. Righteous indignation. Call it being just plain pissed off. Sometimes the hard luck tales make me want to do something to fix it, to make the world a better place. If nothing else, it makes me want to better myself, be a little more compassionate, take a little more time to anger at bad drivers and inconsiderate shoppers. And maybe that's the good side of bad news.

That Sunday was sunny. One of those rare, warm March days designed to make me forget the rain of the previous week and the inevitable early April snowstorm yet to come. A day too beautiful to contemplate tragedies. But my curiosity was piqued. The name in the article had tried knobs and opened some cupboards of memory. I wondered if I'd known the man who'd died on gray pavement under a gray sky. Hard to picture the George Saunders I'd known finding himself in the awkward position of staring down the muzzle of a shotgun.

Shrug the shoulders, turn the page. Look at all the pretty pictures in the travel section. Turn up a corner of the mouth in wry amusement at something in the entertainment section. Think sunny thoughts on a sunny day. Anything to keep from wondering what my baby girl and her mother were doing without me.

The tinkle of the bell on the back gate disrupted all that sunshine. Brandt Williams let himself in and pointed at the mug in my hand.

"Got any more of that?" he said.

"Pot's fresh." I waved the mug in the direction of the house. "Help yourself."

He passed by without further comment, and reappeared a few moments later with an identical mug in his hand. This time he gestured toward the paper in my lap.

"You saw the news? About George?"

I glanced up and saw him wipe his mouth uneasily with the back of his hand, his complexion pale. The bits and pieces of flesh and gristle and bone the medical examiner's office picked up in Montrose Park five days earlier *had* been the remains of the George Saunders I'd known. Brandt's expression said it all.

"Poor sum' bitch ended up in the park like Texas road kill." He shook his head sadly. "Who'd want to do a thing like that? It's a sick human being could do that to another man."

"I didn't realize you were that close."

He seemed puzzled for a moment. "I don't know that we were. Just seems a damn shame when someone you know gets killed that way. Bad enough when folks you know pass on. But this . . ." He sat next to me, picked up the metro section of the paper and stared at it glassy-eyed.

"Paper doesn't even tell the whole story," he went on. "Man was taken apart piece by piece."

"How do you know?"

"The widow Saunders asked me to go down to the morgue with her to identify the body. Cops asked if she minded answering a few questions while she was there. She asked me to sit in instead of waiting for her lawyer. I guess they don't really think she's a suspect 'cause they let slip a few details they held back from reporters."

"So, it wasn't a robbery?"

"He still had his watch, a ring."

"He must have pissed off somebody pretty bad, then. Did he have enemies you know of?"

11

He shook his head. "Not that kind. He had lots of enemies. Banking is cutthroat. Businesses don't make it. Banks foreclose. But those enemies would have tried to ruin him financially, not kill him. I think someone wanted information."

"They went to pretty drastic lengths to get it. Looks to me more like someone was in a rage. I mean, who carries a shotgun around in the city? This wasn't some punk-ass kid with a Saturday Night Special. Or some homeboy with a MAC-Ten."

He waved a hand. "What the papers didn't say is that George's T-shirt was tied around his leg, above the knee. Like someone was trying to stop the bleeding." He watched me digest this new information. "Widow says he was skittish as a foal on a frozen pond the past six, eight months. When she pushed him, alls he'd say was he was worried about a deal he was trying to work on a condo. He was looking at a high floor of the Bloomingdale's building. Tough gettin' jumbo loans with this mortgage mess."

"I don't follow."

"I talked to Whit Piedmont, George's lawyer. George barely had two nickels to rub together when he died. No, that's not quite true. He'd put a stock portfolio into a trust for his ex-wife and their son. Left the widow a life insurance policy and the mortgage payments on the new condo. But his bank accounts were bare as a beggar's cupboard."

"Weren't he and Mitzi having 'marital difficulties'? Seems to me I recall hearing something about that."

Brandt nodded. "She doesn't deny it."

"Could be he was trying to hide assets in case of divorce."

"Could be. Doesn't seem like the George I knew, but people change." He didn't sound convinced. "Thing is, he was doing well at the bank. No business problems that I heard tell. And he was certainly pulling down a good salary. But something spooked him, according to the widow. He didn't even leave her the house. He'd already sold it. Leased it back from whoever bought it."

"So, what bothers you?" I said.

"There was nothing else. No cash, no nothing. No debts, either. It's just too damned neat. Like he was tidying up loose ends for some reason. I'm almost ashamed for thinking it, but I can't help wondering if he was into something risky or dirty. Something crooked. All three. And that just doesn't square with the George I knew. Lord knows Mitzi can be as mercenary as a Dallas debutante. And could be things soured enough between them to curdle the cream, make him want to start over somewhere else. But I don't think so. Somebody got to him. Maybe figured out what he was into and tried to get him to talk."

I wondered about the tourniquet. It could be someone wanted to give George hope, then take it away. Or, like Brandt laid it out, someone let George know he was in some seriously deep crap, then kept him alive long enough to talk. I met his gaze.

"It still could have been a robbery gone bad."

His brow furrowed. He wasn't buying.

"Chalk it up to bad luck, Brandt. The police have any ideas who killed him?"

"Nope. Not according to Mitzi. And neither do I."

I felt annoyed suddenly that he'd interrupted my Sunday solitude. "What do you want from me?"

"Just poke around some. For Mitzi. You've done it before. And you're usually lucky."

"The police will handle it," I said firmly. "It's what they do. There's nothing more I can do that they won't already have thought of."

He was right, of course. I'd done it before. Like I said, usually because my sense of righteous indignation compelled me to do foolish things. Sometimes because there was an added incentive that would increase my retirement fund substantially enough to warrant risky behavior. But this wasn't a good time for me.

I considered his eager expression. His face was weathered by the years, but the clear blue eyes and lopsided grin still held boyish charm. The close-cropped, wavy hair had gone steadily grayer until it had turned mostly silver, shaded with streaks of the original charcoal. Bandy legs and a barrel chest along with the leathery, rugged face made him resemble one of the cowpunchers that populated his father's side of the family. But Sunday casual to him was wearing no socks with the Italian leather loafers, no tie with the Brooks Brothers button-down oxford shirt, no blazer or suit coat with the lightweight wool slacks.

Mutt and Jeff, I thought looking at him, noting pink scalp under the thinning hair for the first time. I suddenly noticed the stiffness in my knees from a hard run up the lakefront the day before, the crick in my neck from sleeping too long in one position. If two people were more unalike, I wasn't aware of it. Yet we'd been friends for twenty years or so.

"Are we going to do this again?" I said wearily.

Eagerness turned to innocence. "What?"

"The dancing bears routine?"

Now he looked miffed and a little hurt. It evoked the requisite amount of guilt. I wondered if I could have kept a little of the bite out of my voice.

I sighed. "You know. You playing my Sancho?" He didn't answer. I changed subjects. "You ever think about what you're going to do when you retire?"

"I *am* retired. You know that."

I snorted softly. "You work harder than just about anyone I know. Between sitting on all those charity boards and managing the family fortune, you're awfully busy for a retiree."

He flushed unexpectedly. "Labors of love. Doesn't seem like work to me. Well, all but the family business."

I smiled. "My point is someday I may want to slow down, goof off some more, enjoy life. You ever think that maybe this business of getting up on that horse and charging off, lance in hand, is dangerous to my health? Seems like every time things get a little slow for you, you want me to take on a little more excitement in my life. I've got plenty right now."

He stroked his chin and looked at me for a long time before speaking.

"I do what I do because I'm good at it," he said slowly. "I like it. You ever stop to think that you do what you do for the same reasons? You're good at it." He waved away my attempt at protest. "You are. You're like a pit bull with a pork chop." He watched the words sink in.

"I've got a family to think of now, you know, not just me."

"I know." He sat immutable.

I tried to read the thoughts rolling around in his head. "I still say you're bored again."

He fell silent and started studying the bricks again, elbows resting on his knees. I remembered he'd come through the gate a little tentatively earlier. Not like him.

"Something else wrong?"

He looked up soberly. "I'm not quite sure how to tell you this."

I tried not to let him see me stiffen. "There's not much we haven't told each other over the years." I kept my voice light. "How bad can it be?"

He twisted his fingers. "I really screwed up. Remember that market index play we talked about?" he said softly.

A while back, Brandt had gotten excited about derivatives, investments that are more akin to playing the tables in Vegas than purchasing ownership shares in a Fortune 500 company. He'd been studying the market, he said, and the timing was perfect for making a killing. Derivatives were counter to his usual investment strategy, but he was so excited I told him to take a shot.

"What about it?" I asked.

"It went south," he said softly.

"How far south?"

He sat up and jerked a thumb over his shoulder. "*Way* south, partner. Spanish-speaking south."

"What, Nuevo Laredo?"

He shook his head. "I'm talking Southern Hemisphere. You lost a little less than half."

"Half of what? What you put in?" I heard a ringing in my ears.

He shook his head, looking miserable now. "A little less than half of your retirement fund."

My jaw worked, but nothing came out at first. "*Jesus*, Brandt!"

He kept nodding. "I know, I know. It was about the dumbest thing I've ever done. Dumber than trying to rope a dogie with a coontail."

I stood and paced the short distance to the gate and back. "What the hell went wrong?"

He winced. "I got greedy," he mumbled. "On your behalf, of course. Sorry."

"A 'no-brainer,' you said. 'Easy as gettin' dirty in a pig sty,' to use your exact words." I put my hands in my pockets so I wouldn't be tempted to take a swing at him. "What happened?"

"In a nutshell? Bad timing. I've been meaning to tell you for a while now. I just . . ." He pressed his lips together and shook his head. "You remember the deal?"

I sat down. "A technology stock index. You said signs were good for a turnaround in certain segments of the industry. It's been long enough since the dot-com bubble burst that some stuff was poised for a comeback."

He nodded. "Right. But we bought warrants on the index, not the index itself."

I rolled my eyes. "Which is kind of like doubling down at the blackjack table."

He looked hurt. "I thought of it as a way to leverage the funds you had available. You know, buy more with less. Anyway, it worked beautifully. The market had been advancing pretty steadily. The index performed pretty much as I figured. I just left your funds in a little too long."

"What do you mean?" I felt my anger rise again, held my clenched fist against my thigh.

He squirmed before answering. "Look, the index was doing great. I figured why exercise the warrants until the expiry date if they're doing so well?"

"But . . . ?" I pressed him like a parent trying to get a kid to 'fess up.

"The market dipped, week before the warrants were due to expire."

"Why the hell didn't you get out? Call me? Do *something?*"

He threw up his hands. "I thought it was a market correction, a one-day sell-off. It wasn't. The index started tanking, and on the expiry date your warrants were worthless."

He looked at me glumly, his expression as forlorn as a child denied candy.

"My warrants?" My brow furrowed. "I thought you were in this with me."

He wouldn't meet my gaze. "I got out a few weeks before," he said softly. Finally, he looked at me. "Something came up that I needed the funds for. I didn't have that much in it to begin with, but I want you to have everything I made on it. I know it won't make up for what you lost, but I want you to have it."

"I don't want your money, Brandt."

He flinched as if struck.

"Look," I said, gritting my teeth, "it's not your fault the market fell. I knew there was risk involved." I was angrier with myself for letting him talk me into it in the first place. We both knew better.

CHAPTER 2

There wasn't anything wrong with the arrangement Nell and I had to raise our daughter. Lately, there didn't seem to be much right with the arrangement, either. I remembered how I'd overlooked her all those years I'd known Brady. She was a fixture at the photo studio, quietly efficient, gracious and soft-spoken, unpresuming yet self-assured. Those who'd known Brady well had known that Nell was largely responsible for the studio's success. Brady's talent would have been squandered without someone to run the business. Nell had been a lucky choice for Brady. She ran a tight ship. Still did. Marty Hopkins had moved up to fill Brady's shoes after Brady was killed, and he'd put Nell in charge of managing the studio.

She was so unlike all the women who littered my past, like so much human detritus the morning after a frat house toga party. So unlike even the one or two—Jessica, and even Cat, came to mind—who might have brought me out of myself if they'd been given the chance. I remembered how, when Nell had finally gotten my attention, she seemed to blossom in front of me. How the conservative dress and quiet mannerisms hid a passionate and earthy creature with simple needs. She hadn't changed. I'd just noticed, finally. She was sturdy, strong, grounded. And she was sensual, captivating, enchanting. Pretty faces had turned my head all those years, but when I'd taken the time to see Nell—really *see* her—I'd discovered how beautiful she was, inside and out.

That I loved her so completely, without reservation, almost from the first, surprised me. She'd taken a chance on me, a reclusive bachelor unlucky in love. She'd planted a seed that had taken root, filled me with her essence, crowding out thoughts or desires for anyone but her. She was everything I wanted, ever could have hoped for. She was kind, considerate, sensitive. She thought of others before she thought of herself, and went out of her way to make life easier for those around her.

The little gestures she made unconsciously a dozen times a day were the most endearing. Like hanging up clothes that had been pulled off in frantic haste when we had a rare moment alone for intimacy. Not because she objected to the mess, but because she wanted them to look nice when they were put back on. I never saw her do it. They were just there, on a hanger or a convenient hook, in the morning or after an episode of love-making. Or like noticing when the toothpaste was almost gone and putting a fresh tube out on the bathroom counter. Or putting out a clean towel every time I stayed at the apartment, even though I might have used it only once before.

It's easy to be critical. Almost as if we have a built-in early warning system to counteract the intense biochemical rush of physical attraction. In almost every relationship that had soured for me, the worse it got the more annoying I found my partner's habits. The way she brushed her teeth or chewed her food. The sound of her laugh. Her habit of putting on eyeliner while driving. Any one of a hundred irritating things would give me pause to wonder why I was with that person. Not Nell. I loved everything about her. What I might have found vexing in others was winsome in Nell.

I liked the way she ran her fingers through my hair when she came up behind me in the kitchen while I fixed dinner. I liked the way her cheeks dimpled and her eyes crinkled at the corners when she smiled. I liked the way she smelled when she came to bed at night, a faint mixture of mint and talc and Chanel Coco. Even after a hard day at the studio when her hair smelled dusty and the musk of dried perspiration was part of the mix. I liked the way Nell held Emily when she fell asleep after a bedtime story, cradling her tenderly as if she was a delicate and fragile baby bird, yet with a fierce, protective strength that could defy legions.

I liked the short, utilitarian cut of her hair, the clear coat of polish on her nails, the subtle, neutral colors she chose for the minimal makeup she wore. She was most beautiful, in fact, when she first awoke each morning, devoid of anything that wasn't naturally hers. I liked the feminine, yet practical clothes she wore. She felt good in my arms. I liked the way our bodies melded together when we made love and fell asleep nestled like spoons. She fit neatly into the spaces of my heart and soul that were meant for a companion, partner, lover.

I was pretty sure she loved me the same way. What I couldn't figure out was why we weren't together. If we loved each other, if we were raising a child together, why wouldn't she marry me? What was it in me—or herself—that she feared?

The voice on the phone was familiar, but it took me a moment or two to place it. When I finally did, I flashed back to a time when I spent hot, humid Midwestern summers with my best friend Lou Barrett playing pick-up games of softball on the high school athletic field. Or riding bikes through town to the drug store to get a cold bottle of Green River soda. Or playing army games in a tall field of alfalfa, pretending to sneak up on enemy positions. And inevitably, the memories included a little tomboy who tagged along like Lou's shadow.

"Meg *Barrett?*" I asked, a note of incredulity in the words. She'd said Meg Brodsky, but I knew that voice. Even after almost twenty-five years, I knew that voice.

"Right," she said. "Sorry. You remember Phil Brodsky, don't you? He was the class behind you."

"Of course." I had a vague recollection of a tall, thin, serious-looking kid with a lock of dark hair flopping over one eye. "You married him, I take it."

"Sixteen years now."

"Hey, that's great, Meg. I'm happy for you. Kids?"

"Two. Boy and a girl." She didn't volunteer more.

I stepped in inanely before the silence got awkward. "Gosh, what a surprise to hear from you after all these years. How's Lou?"

"Truth is, that's why I called." She hesitated. "He died yesterday."

I wasn't prepared for it. News that she was organizing a high school class reunion, maybe, but not that. I tried to get my mind unstuck.

"I thought you should know," she went on.

"Yes, of course," I managed to get out finally. "I wasn't aware . . . was he ill?"

"No, it was quite sudden." She hesitated again, making me wonder what she wasn't saying. "It's been quite a shock."

"I'm so sorry, Meg. It *is* a shock." In the picture in my head, Lou Barrett was still nineteen or twenty, stocky, red-headed, freckled and fearless. "Is there anything I can do?"

"The funeral's on Friday. It would mean a lot if you came."

My gut clenched, and a storm of emotions from out of nowhere buffeted me. It had been half a lifetime since I'd seen Lou Barrett.

"You were best friends, Emerson." Her voice was soft, almost a whisper.

"That was a long time ago, Meg."

"It has to count for something."

I still hesitated, but not for reasons she may have believed.

"Please, Emerson? For me? Please come. I'd really like to see you." Again, her voice revealed more than the words. She didn't just want to reminisce about the good old days.

In the end, I'm not sure what it was that made up my mind for me. But the words were out before I could take them back. "What time?"

"Ten. Come a little early. You can meet me at the house and go to church with Phil and me and the kids. Parking will be tough. It's looking like we'll have a good turnout."

I quickly calculated how early I'd have to leave downtown to get out to the country by then. Friday morning traffic on the Kennedy and Northwest Tollway, even at that hour, would be horrible.

"All right. I'll do that."

"You remember how to get to the house?"

"Your old house? You still live there?"

"I know, I know. Sad, isn't it?" She didn't sound sad.

"I'll find it."

I tried to talk Nell into going with me, but she begged off, saying she couldn't leave the studio while a major client was in shooting ad photos.

"This is your big chance," I told her, "to see where I grew up."

"I can't," she said. "You'll just have to take me out there another time."

That she felt obligated to work didn't surprise me. The studio ran like the Swiss Railway when she was there. Clients were happier, the crew was more productive, and Marty was more relaxed. But it irked me, too. I knew that Marty would gladly give her a day off. And the studio would survive, though squeakily, without her. Marty would manage just fine.

23

The surprise was that she passed up a chance to find out more about my roots. We'd never talked much about our past, at least our childhood years. We talked about everything but, it seemed. For me, life began when I became an adult and was out on my own. I shared that part of my past with her. Even then there were things I couldn't tell her. Things she didn't need to know. Things I wanted to shield her from. She knew about the darkness there. After all, it had been Nell who had saved me from Brady's killer. There was no reason to worry her about all the other times.

She'd asked a few times about my family, especially around the holidays the first year we were together. I waved her off with a vague explanation that my family had never been close. She never said much about her family, either, and I never asked. She was very modest. I accepted that. It was part of what had drawn me to her—quiet, reserved in public, passionate in private. She was always honest with me, emotionally open, yet still mysterious. I knew she'd married young, gotten pregnant with Darlene who was now in college, and divorced somewhere along the line. Other than that, I knew little about where she came from or who her family was, if she even had any.

In a sense, it made it easier. We took each other at face value with a what-you-see-is-what-you-get attitude. Almost as if the tip of the iceberg was all there was to either of us. We had no hidden agendas, brought no baggage into the relationship. I know—not possible. I sensed in Nell depths, guarded places I might never plumb. No doubt she was curious, too. She never let on.

Early Friday morning I put on my best dark suit and set out in a nondescript rental car the color of the forlorn, monochromatic April sky. My car—the little red Alfetta GTV I bought used when I got my first job out of college—was in the shop. The rental sedan lulled me into a false sense of security. It was

re like sitting in a living room easy chair than driving. No
:k, no clutch, no tach, little engine noise, decent stereo, cruise
ntrol and one-finger steering. Too easy to forget that I was
irtling down a ribbon of cement.

I glanced at the occupants in the cars around me. A man in
n SUV on a cell phone over there. A woman in a minivan wav-
ng one arm at two kids in the middle seats, head swiveling
from road in front to kids behind her to see why she hadn't hit
one of them yet. Another man with a map spread out across his
steering wheel. I sat a little straighter, checked my mirrors,
gripped the wheel with both hands. No sense making it two
funerals.

CHAPTER 3

We don't always get to pick our friends. Sometimes they pick us. I was eight when I first ran into Lou Barrett. New kid in a new town, exploring shady, tree-lined streets on a hand-me-down bike used by both of my older brothers. It was still a toe-length too big, and the front wheel had a tendency to wobble. I made it to town unscathed, pumped full of adrenaline from keeping the bike steady on the gravel shoulder of the two-lane highway as pick-ups and an occasional big rig blasted past.

The noisy rush of highway traffic faded on the side streets in town, replaced by the twitter of birds, a child's laugh, the high-pitched growl of a distant lawnmower. A hot August sun shone brightly in a cornflower sky dusted with cotton-ball clouds. Big oaks and maples lined the streets, their thick, green leaves dappling the pavement with dancing shadows as they rustled ane-mically in the faint stirrings of humid air. It was an adventure, I reminded myself, a new place to explore.

I even started humming to myself, some catchy tune I'd heard on my brother Will's transistor radio in the dark after bedtime. All of a sudden a bike came around the next corner from out of nowhere. The handlebars lurched in my hands as I tried to turn away from catastrophe. Out of control now, I smashed headlong into the other bike. Momentum launched me over the handle-bars. Before I hit the hard pavement I caught a glimpse of the kid as he went down, flashing me a look of pure annoyance under a thatch of flame-red hair.

I scrambled to my feet, mumbling "Sorry, sorry," turning around to look for the kid I ran into, worried about how mad he might be. With three brothers, I had a lot of experience.

"You gotta watch where you're going, kid." He got up slowly, rubbing his shoulder. He was almost a head taller than me, with pale skin nearly covered in places with freckles. Unruly red hair hung over his forehead. He brushed it back with a forearm, leaving a streak of dirt on his forehead. It flopped right back into place.

"Sorry," I said again. "You okay?" As the words came out of my mouth, pain hit me like a dog gnawing on bone. Hot knives stabbed at my knee, my elbow, the side of my face. I blinked back tears and clamped my teeth shut.

He shrugged. "No big deal." He screwed up his eyes and took a step closer, looking me up and down. "Man, you got tore up pretty good."

"Nah, I'm okay." I shook it off.

"No, I mean it. You're bleeding."

I looked down at my knee. A trickle of red had already made its way down my shin and was turning claret. I crooked my arm. Tiny red droplets welled out of a grimy patch of skin on my elbow.

"I'll be okay." My lip started to quiver. I sucked it between my teeth and bit down.

He cocked his head and squinted at me. He shrugged again and turned, bent down to grab his bike by the handlebars. Setting it upright, he walked around it, inspecting it, moving his hand from chopper-style handlebars to low-slung banana seat to keep it steady. I would have given a year's allowance for that bike.

"No harm done," he said. He toed the kickstand open and leaned the bike onto it. "Let's check yours out."

Grateful he wasn't going to deck me, I followed him over to

my bike. Watched as he picked it up off the sidewalk and gave it the same onceover.

When he completed his circuit, he grunted. "Front wheel's bent, but not too bad. Might be able to straighten it."

"Think you could show me how to fix it?"

"Sure. I'll give it a shot. Come on. There's tools in my garage."

Side by side, we walked the bikes around the corner.

"You just move here?" he said, glancing at me.

I nodded.

"Thought so," he said. "What's your name?"

"Emerson."

"No, I mean, like, what's your first name."

"That *is* my first name. Emerson. Emerson Ward."

"Oh, man, are you going to catch it when school starts. You better stick with me, kid. What grade you in?"

I looked at him like he had to be crazy. "Fourth."

"No way. How old are you?"

"Almost nine."

A big grin split his broad, freckled face. He punched me lightly on the shoulder, but hard enough to hurt. I willed myself not to rub the spot.

"Gotcha," he said. "I'm gonna be ten on my next birthday. But that's okay, 'cause we'll be in the same class. Anybody gives you a hard time about your name, you let me know and I'll take care of it, okay?"

Lou Barrett was good to his word, but I never had to go far to find him. More like he stuck with me from that day on. At least until our last day of high school.

The Barrett—now Brodsky—house had been caught in a time warp. The brick foursquare on a quiet side street a couple of blocks from the center of town looked exactly the same as the first time Lou brought me there, dirty, hot, sweaty and bleeding from multiple abrasions. At the top of the cement walk, stone steps led up to a porch that ran the width of the house. A juniper hedge concealed the brickwork around the base of the porch. A bushy Austrian pine that I remember not quite reaching the porch rail now rose above the roof and shielded the whole left side of the porch. The porch pillars and second story facade had a fresh coat of beige paint that contrasted nicely with the salmon brick.

A girl of about ten in a floral-patterned frock with poufy sleeves and black patent leather shoes answered my knock. She looked at me solemnly with wide eyes that self-consciously followed my gaze.

"You dress is very pretty," I said. "Is your mother home?"

She blushed and wordlessly swung the door open. I stepped inside. Voices sounded from somewhere in the back of the house, one of them—Meg's—coming closer.

". . . isn't that big a deal," she was saying over her shoulder as she rounded the corner of the living room. She stopped at the foot of the stairs and looked up. Familiarity stirred up something long buried inside me. A rush of indeterminate feelings flitted past in a dark blur like bats in a cave. For a moment I was yanked back in time and space. I gripped the door frame tightly. Shook off the shadows of the past.

"Mom?" Meg called. "Where did you put that purse you borrowed? You know, the black one?"

"That one?" I said, pointing to a handbag on the hall tree.

She started, one hand going to her throat as she whirled around. "Emerson," she cried. "You scared me half to death."

She glanced in the direction of my finger and waved testily at the bag. Taking both my hands in hers, she leaned in to give me a kiss on the cheek. Then she stepped back, holding me at arms' length to look me up and down.

"It's so good to see you. I can't believe how long it's been."

She turned to the girl who still stood next to me silently. "Dana, this is Mr. Ward, an old friend. Well, not old, exactly. Just, well, just someone we've known a long time. He and Uncle Lou were best friends when we were growing up."

Meg's eyes misted and she swallowed hard, trying to put the smile back on her face. Dana studied her shoes, then glanced at me surreptitiously to see my reaction.

I smiled and nodded, hoping I looked vaguely reassuring. "Nice to meet you, Dana."

Meg sniffed and let go of me to swipe at one eye with the back of her hand. The fingers of her other hand tightened around mine.

"Dana, run up and tell your brother we're leaving in five minutes. Make sure he's brushed his teeth."

Dana scurried past her and up the stairs. Meg stepped back toward the living room and tugged on my hand.

"Come on. Phil's back in the kitchen. I'll get you some coffee. We don't really have to leave for about fifteen minutes yet, but the kids will never be ready on time if I don't set artificial deadlines." She stopped the patter long enough to give me a sidelong glance. "You really do look great."

The living room looked the same as I remembered. The boxy color console TV had been replaced with a flat panel screen, the overstuffed couch with the rounded and nubby fabric by a sleek brown leather one. It was different, but I knew some of the older pieces in the house—like the hall tree in the entry—had belonged to Meg's parents.

Maybe living in the house she grew up in had caught Meg in the same time warp. Despite twenty-five years and two kids, time had been kind. The long strawberry-blond hair I remembered was rolled and pinned into a chignon at the back of her head, revealing tasteful diamond studs in her earlobes. A few stray wisps curled down her long graceful neck like delicate orange streamers against milky, rose-tinged skin. Toward her shoulders and the top of her décolletage before it disappeared beneath the black silk of a simple dress, the smooth skin was lightly freckled. Clear blue eyes framed her pert nose. Her face was unlined. It was more mature somehow, but not visibly aged. In jeans, with her hair down and no makeup, she would no doubt be carded in any bar in the country.

She released my fingers as she led the way into the kitchen. The sleeveless cocktail shift complemented her slender figure, and black heels lent definition to her shapely, athletic legs. I'd always marveled at how she managed to be so incredibly feminine and seductive while exuding the no-nonsense confidence of a sportswoman. She wasn't the sort who was afraid to break a sweat or chip a nail, but she was all woman. In high school, she could whip almost guy I knew in tennis, or just about any other sport for that matter, and make them smile while she did it.

"Phil, look who I found," she said as we walked in.

They'd built an addition on the back of the house. I remembered a square kitchen in one corner of the house with a heavy, white-enameled steel gas stove, white refrigerator with a rounded top, a chrome-legged table with a yellow Formica top in the center of the room. Now the kitchen was expansive, modern, with an island in the middle trimmed in cherry wood and matching cupboards on the walls. Beyond was a multipurpose room with large glass windows that looked out onto the backyard, made even brighter by two skylights cut into the ceiling.

The kitchen counters were littered with serving platters and bowls of all sizes, some already containing food. The room was silent except for the sounds of food being prepared. A tall man stood at the sink with his sleeves rolled up to the elbows. He turned at the sound of Meg's voice, looked first at her, then me, his face solemn. Close-cropped thinning hair couldn't hide the widow's peak. Like Meg, though, his face was youthful. I vaguely recollected a younger version of it, but it didn't conjure specific memories. He was slim and wiry, the tendons and ropes of muscle in his forearms standing out as he gripped my outstretched hand.

"Good to see you again," he said.

"Likewise," I said, imitating his familiar tone. "It's been a long time."

Two other women in the kitchen stopped what they were doing to watch our exchange. The expression on the face of a willowy blond over Phil Brodsky's shoulder reflected fleeting disappointment.

"Emerson, you remember Sue Ann, don't you?" Meg said.

I wondered if Meg had seen me looking. I tilted my head slightly now as I took in the blond. "Sure. Sue Ann Kolnik, right?"

Phil turned to let me reach past him. The blonde squeezed the tips of my fingers with a smile that came and went like an express train.

"It's Anderson now," she murmured. "Nice to see you."

The name knocked a bubble loose from the sediment deep in my memory. Meg moved on before the bubble broke free.

"And this is Sarina Thomas." She gestured to a dark-haired woman standing on the other side of the island. "She was in my class, too. She was Sarina Ahmed then."

"Of course," I said. I leaned over the island to shake her hand. Her grip was firm, dry. "How are you?"

"Fine, thank you, given the circumstances."

"I've got to get going," Sue Ann said loudly. She flashed Meg an impatient look. "I promised I'd get home in time to go with the boys." She started for the door.

Meg looked at a small, black-strapped watch on her wrist.

"Oh, my, of course. Shoo, both of you. All this can wait until after the service."

Sue Ann gathered a purse and coat from a nearby chair, and made her way out. Sarina gave me a sad look, then turned away to drape a scarf over her hair and tie it under her chin before putting on a coat. She put a hand on my arm as she was leaving.

"I hope we'll have a chance to talk later. Nice to see you."

When she was gone, I turned to Meg and Phil. "Anything I can do?"

"Not just now," Meg said. "I'm sure we'll find plenty for you to do later." She turned to her husband. "We'd better get moving. Would you see if Todd's ready? I sent Dana up after him, but now she's disappeared, too."

He nodded and moved for the door, rolling his sleeves down as he went. An elderly woman appeared in the doorway and he twisted sideways to ease past her, not missing a step. She paused, startled, when she saw me.

"Goodness, is that you, Emerson?" she said.

"Yes, Mrs. Barrett, it's me." I gave her a quick hug. "I'm so sorry about Lou. It must be a terrible loss."

She held me by the shoulders and gave a shuddery sigh. "Thank you, Emerson. And thank you for coming."

Her eyes were rimmed with red, and her face was splotchy under the makeup from crying. Once upon a time, Mary Barrett had been like a surrogate mother. Now, short white hair in a loose perm framed a face that was beginning to resemble aged parchment. She was a grandmother now. Strange how we become our parents and then our grandparents as we move through life. I didn't *feel* like I'd turned into my father, even with a young daughter of my own now. Not yet.

"Is Doug here?" I asked to fill the silence.

"Oh, my, no. We moved to Florida ages ago. Meg and Phil

took the house off our hands." She nodded toward Meg with a small smile.

"He couldn't come?"

She shook her head. "No, dear. He had a stroke—oh, five years ago now. It left him unable to get around much. It's best he stayed where he is."

"I'm so sorry. Give him my best."

Meg had moved around behind her mother and was drawing a circle in the air around her ear. She mouthed the words "Tell you later."

Phil reappeared in the kitchen doorway with his suit coat on, a small child on either side of him. A little boy about six had the fingers of one hand jammed down his shirt collar pulling it away from his neck. He twisted at the waist, trying to scratch at the back of his leg with his other hand. His hair was plastered wetly against his head, combed back slickly. He was quite handsome, though uncomfortable, in a miniature blazer and tie. His sister rolled her eyes at him.

"Ready?" Phil said quietly.

He and the kids led the way out the back door to the garage. Meg shrugged into a black silk jacket, and helped Mary with her coat. We walked her out between us.

CHAPTER 4

The service at St. Mary was crowded. Lou Barrett was well known, if not well loved. I sat with the family up front. The Barretts had always attended St. Mary, the Catholic church, but now the parish was housed in a new church on Huntley-Dundee Road instead of the old building in town I remembered. The number of eulogies made the full Mass longer. Each one reminded me how little I'd known Lou Barrett, the man. My best childhood friend. I didn't know what he'd chosen to do with his life, how he'd earned a living or what his hobbies had been. I didn't even know if he'd gone to college, gotten married, had children, joined the Rotary Club, played golf on weekends, vacationed in the same place each year.

The speakers commended him, said his was a life well lived, claimed he was generous, kind, the sort of man who gave back to the community. But the anecdotes they related held little frame of reference for me. They were about unfamiliar times and places. I'd known one Lou Barrett. They'd known another. I listened closely, tried to learn if he was still the man who'd been my friend all those boyhood years.

In the middle of the family sitting across the aisle from us was a woman veiled in black under a broad-brimmed hat. Features well hidden, it was impossible to tell if she was young, old or somewhere in between. Her erect yet graceful carriage suggested youthfulness. The deference paid her by priest and eulogists—glances and gestures meant to include her—indicated she was Lou's wife. Odd how weddings and funerals divide people into two camps, his and hers.

When the service finally ended, Phil slid out of the pew and joined five other men around the casket in front of the altar. I vaguely recognized one or two, but couldn't put names to their faces. They led the procession out of the church, rolling the casket on its stand as far as the curb outside the door. Then shouldered the heavy load into a hearse.

The gravesite was close, in St. Mary Cemetery near the center of town. By the time the pallbearers pulled the casket from the hearse and set it on a stand next to a freshly dug grave, most of the procession of cars had reached the cemetery and parked. The congregation quickly spread out on three sides. I helped Mary, Meg and the kids get seated in folding chairs, but declined one myself, melting back into the crowd. The priest waited at the grave for people to get settled. I stood at the back, taking in the faces of those I could see.

A pallbearer, his face vaguely familiar, quietly slipped through the crowd and stood next to Sue Ann. In context now, his name immediately popped into my head—Pete Anderson. Life had been good to him, but not necessarily kind. Rich food and too little exercise had filled out his face, making his starched collar look a size too small. The broad chest and shoulders succumbed to gravity, settling some of his bulk around his belt, an athlete gone to seed. He still had the same flattened nose, wide-set eyes and too-small ears that reminded me of a boxer. Not unhandsome, but tough-looking, dark, brooding. The same shock of dark hair still fell over his forehead as if trying to maintain his boyish look. It was out of place on the florid face.

Pete had been in Meg's class, two years behind Lou and me. I was surprised now that I hadn't recognized him. He'd been named starting quarterback of the varsity football team his sophomore year, the year Lou and I were seniors. That was the year we'd voted Lou, a guard, captain of the squad. The year I'd won a partial scholarship to Colorado State to play tight end. The year I'd left and never looked back. Until now. I'd run several hundred million miles from this place since, this place where I was born, raised, nurtured, shaped. But like sunlight reflecting off Saturn's rings, I'd ended up only an hour away.

I recognized others now, too. For every two strangers' faces, one conjured up the past. A family friend here, a classmate there, someone from a village business. I tried to put names to them, but in many cases too much time had passed. I hadn't accessed the memories in so long that the neuronal pathways were weedy and overgrown. Most didn't feel the scrutiny, paying attention instead to the priest, looking for meaning, consolation in his words. Some saw me looking. A few glanced away in embarrassment. One or two recognized me, acknowledged me with a nod.

I found Meg in the milling throng afterward. Phil stood several feet away deep in conversation with some other men. I told her I felt like walking, that I'd meet her at the house. She nodded and turned away to help her mother. The rain held off, but it was still gray and a chilly breeze was gusting in spurts, flapping black dresses and suit coats like ravens' wings. I turned my collar up against the cold and sauntered away from the church in the opposite direction of mourners heading for their cars.

Off to one side, a man stood alone next to a tall tree, watching me. Recognition made me falter and stop. He was older, far older than I remembered, but it had been a long time. He still looked fit, trim, but the years hung in folds on his tan, weathered face, his hair now white everywhere but the thickest parts on top of his head. He appeared shrunken somehow, as if the suit he wore was a size too big. He looked at me intently, but made no move, nor gave any signal that he wanted to speak to me.

There was no curiosity on his face, nothing that suggested we were anything but strangers. I matched his gaze, wondering why he'd come. After a moment, he turned away without a word.

Half of the big cemetery belonged to the parish, the other half to the village. I wandered over to the village side, wondering if I would still be able to find the markers. It took a while to get my bearings, but there in a familiar row stood the simple black granite headstone marked "June Simmons Ward, Loving Wife and Mother, August 22, 1933–March 25, 1974."

I wouldn't let memories of that day back into my consciousness. I remembered instead my mother in the kitchen of our house in the country, alive, vibrant, happy. Standing at the stove in front of a huge, steaming pot of fresh-picked strawberries, sugar and Knox gelatin being readied for Mason jars and a sealing layer of paraffin. I remembered her being most content doing simple things, comforting things. Like quietly darning socks or knitting a sweater in front of the fire on a cold winter evening. Or shucking fresh sweet corn for dinner on the back porch, brushing away lazy flies, copper highlights in her dark hair lit up like veins of smoldering coal by a summer sun still hanging high above the horizon.

"I miss him." The voice behind me startled me out of my reverie. "Don't you?"

A man a few years younger than me stopped not far away, looking at the ground at his feet. He was dressed in dark gray slacks, navy blazer, white shirt, tie. One of the mourners. He turned to look at me.

"Tommy?" I squinted at him, looking for a boy inside the man standing there. "Tommy Burke?"

He stuck out a hand. "How are you, Emerson? Been a long time."

"Yes." I matched his grip. Clarified. "Yes, I miss him."

In that moment I missed him something fierce. Next to my

mother's headstone was another one that simply said, "Henry David Ward, 1963–1979." My little brother. The baby of the family.

Tommy Burke shook his head slowly. "I come out here every so often."

I looked at him in surprise. When he saw my face, his turned pink and he looked away. He turned back and shrugged.

"No big deal." He looked around expansively. "It's quiet here. A good place to think. I come here sometimes just to clear my head or think something through. I seem to find myself most times right here in this spot. You know, just talking to him. Well, not to him. More like to myself. But it feels like I'm talking to him sometimes. You know. Like I'll sound him out on something that's bothering me. Try and figure out what he'd say. Figure if I listen hard enough, I might hear him tell me what to do, you know?"

He glanced at me fleetingly for a reaction, scuffing the toe of his shoe in the grass.

"Yeah, I know, Tommy. Been a long time since I thought about him, but I bet he hears you when you talk to him. I always thought he was pretty lucky to have a friend like you." I paused, looked at the headstone, remembering. "I kind of wish he'd stuck a little closer to you."

He shook his head again. "I'm not sure there's anything anyone could have done. He always made up his own mind, no matter what anyone else said."

"I suppose." I felt an old familiar twinge of guilt, like a long unused muscle reminding you it's there with a dull ache.

"I still don't think we really know what happened that night."

I looked at him sharply. "What do you mean?"

He drew back a little. "I—it's just that I can't believe he would have done that on his own."

"Henry didn't have too many boundaries."

His expression turned placating. "Look, you don't have to tell me. He ran wild. But you weren't here, man. Not that last year. Hank did some crazy shit, but he always knew his limits. He might have stepped over everyone else's line, Emerson, but he knew where to draw his own." His lips tightened and he rubbed a hand across his mouth.

After a moment he started again, quietly. "I can't tell you how many times I've been here, playing that night in my head."

I looked at him curiously. "Why would you do that, Tommy? He's been gone a long time."

He shrugged. "He was my friend. My best friend. He always took me at my word, always stuck up for me. Kind of like you and Lou, I guess."

"People change. They grow up. Move on." I heard the harshness in my own words.

"Maybe for you. Don't get me wrong. I've got plenty of friends. But Hank was about the best, most loyal friend a guy could ask for. You don't forget a guy like that easy."

Funny how people can carry the past around with them like it happened yesterday. He'd had twenty-five years to forget. I stared at the grave and thought about Brandt. I thought about Lou all those years ago, despite what had eventually happened to us. With a sigh, I looked at Tommy and nodded.

His eyes flicked across my face, made a decision. He shifted, relaxing his weight onto one leg. "I let it go a long time ago. What's done is done. And as often as I talk to Hank out here, he's for sure never told me what happened. But I know someone put him up to it."

I didn't pursue it, didn't want to go there. It was ancient history. Bad juju. No sense dredging up the past. Like Tommy said, what was done was done.

CHAPTER 5

Mourners overflowed the house onto the front porch. Either Lou had a lot of friends or a bunch of folks were itching to take a Friday off work. The siren call of smorgasbord right about lunchtime probably swelled the crowd by a body or two. I dug my contribution out of the trunk of the rental car—a Caesar salad to counterbalance all the casseroles people bring to these things—and walked it around through the back door.

Several women in the kitchen rebuffed my offer to help. Shooed me away as if a male presence might somehow spoil the food. I steeled myself and waded into the crowd, making my way to the living room to pay my respects. It was slow going, like swimming upstream only to be swept aside into a quiet pool before gathering strength to try again.

The woman in black from the church held court in the living room. Mary sat close by, and I realized they were receiving a line of well-wishers that started near the door. Meg and Phil greeted people as they entered. I slid into line before a couple at the door got past them, and patiently waited to pay my respects. The woman had doffed her hat and veil, but I wasn't able to catch a glimpse of her face until the line moved much closer. I don't know why I was surprised, but I stood flat-footed for a moment while more memories flooded through me.

She still had a face that made men do double-takes and women suspicious. A certain look that said she was unattainable. Wild even, like a mustang running free on the Texas plains.

41

A blond, blue-eyed beauty who exuded a natural earthiness so sensual that even back in grade school prepubescent boys wished they were old enough to ask her out and old men wished they were young enough to still get it up. The schoolgirl bangs were gone, her long hair now brushed back, some of it pinned into a ponytail. The innocence in her eyes was gone, too, replaced by a hardness, or maybe sorrow, that looked earned. I always wondered, sensed she was too self-aware to be as ingenuous as she affected. The effects of her spell, intentional or not, weren't always pretty. She ended up with Lou by the end of our senior year. She was a freshman then.

The line moved. My turn.

"Tish," I murmured, clasping her outstretched fingers between my hands even as she let her eyes follow the woman ahead of me. "I'm so sorry for your loss."

She looked at me, and for an instant, I thought I saw more than surprise in her eyes.

"Emerson. I'm so glad you could come. Lou . . ." She tried a smile, but her eyes brimmed with tears. She dabbed at them with the handkerchief in her free hand. "I keep thinking how much Lou would have enjoyed this, enjoyed seeing all these people. I keep expecting him to walk through the door."

"I'm sure he's here in spirit, Tish. Probably miffed he's missing a good party."

She let out an awkward laugh that was part sniffle. "Oh, I'm sure. He really would have missed seeing you. God, how long's it been?"

"A long time." I swallowed uncomfortably, and gave her hand a shake, ready to move on.

Her eyes moved to the person behind me then back to my face. "Are you in town for a while?"

"Probably not. I planned on driving back this afternoon."

"If you have time, please come by the house later. I'd love to catch up." Something in her eyes suggested she wasn't just being polite. I wondered why.

"Thanks. I'll try."

She gave me a last earnest look, then shifted her gaze to the next person in line. I stopped briefly to exchange a word with Mary, then broke free and made my way back to the kitchen. Braving the wrath of the neighborhood ladies was preferable to trying to find words to cheer the bereaved. Dodging hands that reached out to swat me for grabbing a few nibbles off trays, I wended my way through the kitchen to the big room at the back of the house.

It was quieter there, though the loud babble from the front of the house filtered back and the activity in the kitchen was plenty noisy. An animated movie flickered on a big-screen television in the corner, the volume too low to be intelligible. A half-dozen kids of various ages sprawled across a couch and chairs. Some watched the TV, a few others played a board game on the floor. Most of them looked as if they'd rather be back in school. This wasn't the day of hooky they'd bargained for.

A little girl with the round, flat face and slanted eyes characteristic of Down's syndrome sat on the couch watching the television with a big grin. My niece, Harriet. I sat on the arm next to her, glanced at what she was watching. When the show broke for a commercial, I looked at her.

"Hello, Harriet." She turned at the sound of her name. "How are you? Do you remember me?"

The girl next to her swiveled her head. She was several years older. "She was too little to remember," she said.

"Hello, Rachel." Harriet's sister. "Nice to see you again."

Harriet turned to Rachel and tugged at her sleeve. "Who's that?" She pointed at me.

"Uncle Emerson," Rachel said. "He's Mommy's brother."

"Oh." Harriet looked at me and smiled, then giggled and

blushed. She turned her attention back to the TV.

"How's school?" I asked Rachel over Harriet's head.

"Fine." Rachel's attention had wandered back to the TV, too.

"Oh, there you are," another voice interrupted before I could think of a way to extend the conversation.

I turned to see my sister approach with her usual expression of impatience. It wasn't directed at me.

"Yes, Mom. We're right where you told us to go." There was no mistaking the sardonic tone in Rachel's voice, but Elizabeth chose to ignore it.

"Where's John?" she said.

"Right there." Rachel pointed to the kids on the floor without looking away from the TV.

Elizabeth's gaze followed her finger, then turned to me. "Come help me," she said.

She turned and walked away. I stood up slowly and followed, shaking my head. It was as if the years vanished without even a flash or puff of smoke to veil the trick. Not just the few since we'd last seen each other, but all of them since I'd left home without looking back. She led the way out back and gestured toward some boxes on the ground. Cases of wine.

"We need these inside," she said. "I knew Meg wouldn't order enough. I'm glad I brought more."

I stacked one on top of another and hefted them both. She didn't move to help. I waited, motionless.

"I saw you in church," she said. "Why didn't you sit with us?"

"Well, hello to you, too, sis. Long time, no see." My brow furrowed. "Meg invited me to sit with the family."

"Frankly, I'm surprised the church let her hold a service at all," she went on, unfazed.

"Why?"

"You know." She looked around furtively.

"No, I don't."

She had her impatient face on again. "Everyone knows it was no accident, Emerson. You can't be that naïve."

"What are you talking about?"

She saw my confusion. "You don't know how he died?"

I shook my head.

"I can't believe no one told you." Her eyes glinted with grim delight. She leaned in conspiratorially. "Your old pal Lou blew his brains out."

Lucky thing I was holding two heavy cases of wine. I might have forgotten my manners and wiped the smirk off her face with the back of my hand.

"You can't tell me getting a shotgun stuck in your mouth is an accident," she said.

My knees trembled with anger. "He did what? How the hell would you know that?"

She took a startled half-step back. "Well, I don't, of course. But they found the gun in his hands."

"Why? Why would he kill himself?"

She shrugged. "I heard he was depressed," she said innocently.

"It still could have been an accident." My mind raced, trying to comprehend the news.

She gave me a skeptical look. "Oh, please."

"What does that have to do with church, anyway?"

"Suicide's a mortal sin. Don't tell me you don't know this. Catholics aren't allowed a funeral Mass or church burial if they kill themselves. Father Pat must be a real softie to buy the 'accident' story."

"You would have told the family to get lost, I suppose."

"Rules are rules."

"Why so hard-assed? The man's dead."

Her shoulders rose and fell an inch. "Are you going to take

those in or not?" She gestured at the boxes in my arms. "I'm not going to stand here all day. It's cold out." She crossed her arms and shivered for emphasis.

I wrestled the door open and set the boxes on a counter where she indicated, eager to get away. Before I took a step, she handed me a corkscrew.

"Help me open these."

I sighed quietly, spread the flaps on the closest box and pulled out a bottle. She stepped up to the counter and opened the other box. High heels put her nearly shoulder to shoulder with me. I glanced at her, saw my own face reflected there. Felt the twinge of an old resentment that we'd sometimes been mistaken for twins. We couldn't be more different.

"I'm sorry," she said after uncorking a bottle and twisting the cork off the screw. "I know he was your friend."

"It's okay." She didn't understand. My anger had little to do with someone who hadn't been a friend for longer than he had been one. "You just surprised me, that's all."

She started in on another bottle, no doubt determined to see that all the guests had a good time. Or at least got good and drunk.

"Did you see him this morning?" she said. She saw my puzzled look and let out a *tsk*. "You know. He came. Don't tell me you didn't see him?"

I nodded, seeing where she was going. I looked at the bottle in my hand and slowly turned the opener again. "I saw him. At the cemetery."

"Well? Did you talk to him?"

I set the bottle down on the counter and managed to keep my voice even. "No."

"Why not? Why won't you talk to him? He wants to see you, you know."

Some of the old anger started burning inside again, hot

magma bubbling up from unseen depths. "If he wants to see me, or talk to me, all he has to do is call and tell me."

"You could do the same thing, Emerson. Call him. Talk to him."

"I don't have a damn thing to say."

"He's family, for God's sake."

"Then he ought to act like it."

"Speak for yourself." Her eyes hardened. "You're the one who left, Emerson. You just took off and never gave us a second thought."

"I . . ." I closed my mouth. She knew just which buttons to push. She always had. Retreat had always been a better option than any defense.

An hour later, Elizabeth's plan was working just fine. Passing acquaintances had paid their respects and left. Friends, family, most likely a few enemies and those who couldn't pass up free food and booze, were all that remained. The crowds had thinned. But the noise level, if anything, had increased. Wine and liquor loosened tongues and hardened opinions.

I found Meg, made excuses. She looked disappointed, asked me to stay. Said we hadn't had a chance to really talk. I felt bad, but didn't see the point. I gave her a chaste peck on the cheek and she stepped in for a clinch that seemed long, even given the circumstances. When she let go, her eyes brimmed. Her mouth was set firmly, as if afraid that opening it would let loose the tears. I said an awkward good-bye and she just nodded.

Raised voices in the front of the house saved us both from embarrassment. They quickly escalated to shouts of anger. I moved in that direction, Meg at my heels. By the time we reached the living room, several people had stepped in to take control. A ring of bystanders made room, anticipating a spectacle.

On one side, Tommy Burke and another man each held one of Pete Anderson's arms. He strained against their grip. Just enough for show, it looked like. Pete glared at a short balding man across the room Phil restrained with a lanky arm thrown like a seat belt across his chest. Phil gently pulled him toward the front door.

"You're just messing things up!" the man said heatedly, but not shouting now. He waved his arms and struggled a little more forcefully than Pete but let Phil slowly pull him away. "You can't keep doing this. You're screwing up this town."

His voice faded a bit as Phil backpedaled him out the front door. Pete shrugged himself free, and turned away, scowling.

"What a shithead," he said, the words loud enough to carry.

Sue Ann pushed her way through the throng, dispersing now that the excitement was over. She wore her coat, Pete's draped over her arm. She held it for him, tried to get a sleeve hooked onto one of his hands. He shrugged her off, snatched it away, clutching it in one big paw as he headed for the door. She trailed in his wake, a mixture of resignation and annoyance on her face.

I felt Meg at my shoulder. "Who was that?" I asked, moving after Sue Ann.

She stayed with me. "Danny DeHaan."

"Danny?"

"Yep. Hasn't changed much."

"You kidding? Where's his hair?" I glanced at her, saw the look she threw me.

We stopped on the porch. Pete and Sue Ann were halfway down the walk to the street. Phil stood in the yard, hands on the smaller man's shoulders, towering over him. Talking to him in low tones, like someone soothing a horse. Danny looked at him, caught a word or two, and craned for a look around him at the departing Pete.

"You're next, asshole!" He flung the words at Pete's back.

Sue Ann turned, her face beaming a ray of pure hatred Danny's way. Pete just raised his hand above his shoulder and flipped Danny the bird. Then they were in their car and gone. Danny nodded reluctantly now, staring at the ground as Phil talked to him in the same soft voice.

"I've got to get back inside," Meg said.

I watched Danny turn and walk the opposite direction Pete and Sue Ann had gone.

"Yeah, sure," I said. I focused on Meg's face, tried a small smile. "Thanks again for thinking of me. It was great seeing you again."

"You, too." She looked like she wanted to say something else. She bit it back and went inside.

I met Phil coming up the walk. "What was that all about?"

He shrugged. "Danny's old school. Doesn't like all the growth."

"And Pete's responsible?"

"Partly. Pete and Lou both." Another shrug. "If not them, though, would've been someone else." He saw my puzzlement. "Right. You *have* been gone a long time. Lou was a developer. Pete's a contractor. They did a bunch of deals together."

I nodded. "Lot of changes." I swung my gaze from one side over his head to the other.

"Enough for a lot of developers."

"And Danny takes offense?"

His head bobbed once. "Danny'd rather see time stand still altogether."

"So would I, if I was losing hair like that."

He chuckled quietly. I liked the way he'd handled the situation, liked his quiet reserve. I'd wondered about Meg wearing the pants in the family, but had seen how well they paired up, how they complemented each other's strengths. Made me wish

I'd known him better in school. He could have been a friend.

"Danny works out at the railroad museum now," he said. "Tends to keep him stuck in a time warp. Makes him wish we lived in simpler times."

"Simpler maybe. A lot harder in some ways."

His face turned wistful. "Lot of people wish we could hold progress at arm's length a little longer. Slow it down, at least. It's why we stayed."

I smiled. "Clean air. Safe streets. Good place for kids."

He nodded. "Still something to be said for that."

Hard to argue. I let it hang a beat before I asked, "So, what'd Danny mean, 'You're next'?"

Phil's brow furrowed. "I'm not sure." He chewed on it. "Danny's part of a group wants to slow the growth. Stop it outright, if they can. Change the zoning. Save farmland. That sort of thing. Been putting pressure on people."

I nodded. "Lou was one?"

A cloud passed over his face. "Lou had his own problems, but yeah."

I let that hang, too. Shifted my weight from one foot to the other, awkwardly sticking out a hand. "Well, I'm heading out. Sorry again about Lou."

He looked at my hand, gripped it, then looked me in the eye. "Not your fault."

"Right. Well, nice seeing you again."

He let go, his gaze following me out to the car. In the rearview, I saw him still watching as I turned the corner out of sight.

CHAPTER 6

Spring. In Chicago. An oxymoron to anyone who's spent any time here. There are usually a couple of weeks in May that are representative of spring, a week or two in October that could be construed as fall. Hard to call them seasons, exactly. Those who live here know Chicago has only two seasons—winter and construction. Metaphors for life.

Winter, that time of darkness, decay and death, beneath which lingers a fierce vitality. Life that, while dormant, gathers strength. Not in spite of, but because of winter's cold womb. And construction, when we create order out of chaos, impose structure, expand, improve. We spend a lifetime constructing ourselves, our surroundings. Fashioning them into pleasing and comfortable edifices, refuge against the elements and foreign invasion. We use materials at hand, adding, enhancing, each year shoring up and building upon what came before. Throw on a deck here, a room addition there. Soon it begins to look a little random, if not ramshackle.

Little did I know that what lay ahead was a season of *decon*-struction. Like a remodeling project, an extreme home make-over, life would be stripped bare, down to the studs. Examined for structural defects, mold, gaffes in design, adequate plumb-ing and electric. Then the question becomes rebuild? Or tear it all down and start anew?

My daughter liked to go for walks. Rain or shine, warm or cold, it didn't matter. As an infant, she was my motivation to get outside. Even before I gave up cigarettes for good years ago I tried to get a run in a few times a week. After Emily was born, it became a more regular habit. I'd bundle her into the stroller with the big wheels and push it at a jog through Lincoln Park.

Now, she eagerly looked forward to our outings. Some days she wanted to ride, urging me to push faster as the sights zipped past. More often, now that she was more mobile, she wanted to get out and push the stroller herself. Or walk alongside me, her little hand snug in mine. Sometimes we stopped to watch the ducks or the crews in their shells on the lagoon. Every once in a while we took a path through some part of the zoo. She never wanted to leave the elephants or the penguins. I could never decide which I liked best.

She let me stuff her arms into her pink down parka and zip it up. She pulled a knit cap with ear flaps over her curls. I tied it under her chin. I suggested mittens. She shook her head. They went in my jacket pocket. The wind off the lake would be raw. She'd want them later. I picked her up and opened the kitchen door. The bell at the front door rang. Emily looked up with a start.

"I wonder who that could be," I said. Her eyes widened. "Let's go see."

She smiled and clapped her hands together. "Let's see, Daddy."

I cracked the front door a foot or two and stepped into the opening. A Jehovah's Witness would have been more expected.

"Meg," I said. As if she had forgotten her name.

She looked uncomfortable, searching my face. "I'm sorry. I shouldn't have come." She started to turn.

"Wait. Please." Her eyes met mine. "This is Emily." I looked at my daughter's face. Couldn't help but smile. "Emily, this is my friend Meg."

Emily waved one of her chubby hands. A tiny Michelin Man in pink. The doubt on Meg's face retreated. Hard to focus on the negative in the presence of a cute kid.

"We're about to go for a walk," I said. "Join us?"

She tilted her head. "Sure."

I led her through the back, out to the carriage house on the alley. Where there was barely room for things like a stroller squeezed in with the hulking old GMC RV and the rental sedan in the bay where the Alfa usually sat. I strapped Emily in and we headed up to the park.

Meg seemed content just to tag along in silence. I glanced at her from time to time. She seemed in no hurry to explain why she'd come. She took in buildings, people, traffic, head swiveling like a tourist gawking in Las Vegas. I took her in when she wasn't looking, trying not to gawk. She was casually dressed in jeans and bush jacket over a turtleneck. Her ponytail was threaded through the back of a baseball cap. She looked younger than she had a few days earlier. She'd grown into a handsome woman, but still reminded me of the tomboy she once was. We were well into the park before she said a word. When she did, it wasn't what I expected.

"Been ages since I got away from the kids like this." She smiled and took a deep breath. Stretched her arms wide. "I forgot what it's like to take a personal day."

"I like your kids," I said. "They're great."

She nodded, assessing. "They are. I love 'em to death. But they're a lot of work." She glanced at the stroller. "Well, you know."

Four steps later she asked, "You have her all the time?"

I shook my head and explained what Nell and I had worked out. Since I freelanced from home, I watched Emily during the hours Nell spent at the studio.

She looked at me sidelong from under the brim of her hat.

"Why aren't you two together?"

"Long story." Her gaze didn't waver. I told her.

We talked all the way up to Fullerton and halfway back. About kids, small-town life, city life, her volunteer jobs, my freelance business. Everything except why, out of the blue, I'd seen her twice in a week after all this time.

Emily started to get restless. I scooped her out of the stroller and let her walk. She reached for one of Meg's hands, turned to look for one of mine. Content, she waddled along, leading us down the path.

"This is a great age," Meg said.

I caught her smiling broadly down at the little girl between us.

"Time goes too fast." Wistful now. "It seems like ages since Todd was in a stroller." Then a minute later, "He didn't do it, you know."

"Who didn't do what?"

She kept her eyes on the ground in front of us. "I know you heard. How he died. What they're saying." She still didn't look up. "He didn't do it. Couldn't have."

"Why not?"

That brought her up. "You knew him," she said. As if I had to be kidding.

I shook my head. "I knew a boy named Lou a long time ago. He had a lifetime to change. A lifetime of disappointments, maybe."

Vehemently, "No." Then her voice softened. "Lou had it good. I'm not saying he didn't have problems. We all do. But life was good to him. He had no reason to do what they're saying."

She saw the doubt in my face. "What? What did you hear?"

I could feel my face twist in annoyance and waved off the question. "A lot of people were talking. Not saying much. But talking. About how they saw it coming. Wondering why someone didn't do something."

I paused, saw her thinking. "What *did* happen, Meg?" I said softly.

"An accident. That's all."

"But you're here."

She gazed off into space, seemed to work it out in her head. "After graduation, Lou was kind of lost. He saw all his friends moving on. Going to college. Getting jobs." She looked at me. "You left."

I shrugged. "Like a lot of people."

She sighed. "I know, I know. Grow up. Leave the nest. It's just some of us didn't fly that far. Or want to, I guess." She considered that. "You remember how big F.F.A. was when we were still kids? Don't know if there's even a chapter anymore."

It took me a moment to pull it up from memory—Future Farmers of America. Must have been thirty or forty kids in the yearbook photo senior year.

"Anyway," she said, "Lou kicked around some. He didn't get a scholarship like you did." She saw my look and went on quickly. "Not that he couldn't go if he wanted. Dad would have paid. Just that he didn't have any purpose. No direction. Football was all he really had in high school."

"He had a lot more than that."

She drew back, blinked. "Well, yeah. But he didn't see it that way. He was something on the team. Captain. Big man. Off it, he always felt like he had to prove himself. He sure couldn't compete on grades."

I started to open my mouth, irritated again. Thought better of it. Lou wasn't stupid. Or slow, that I remembered. He just didn't want to put in the work.

"He ended up taking classes up at McHenry," she went on. "Got a job selling insurance for Ed Jarvis. Made a little money and eventually got a degree in business from Rockford.

55

"When Dad sold the business and retired down in Florida, he gave Lou and me each a small stake. Said if he didn't give us a little something now, he'd spend all our inheritance in retirement." She waved a hand in front of her face. "Like I ever wanted his money. I know he was kidding us. I don't think he ever imagined it'd be true. You have no idea how expensive assisted living is."

"Your mom mentioned his stroke. I didn't know it was that bad."

She nodded. "She needs a lot of help with him. He's in a wheelchair. Lost most of his memory, speech."

"Sorry to hear it."

Emily stopped and tugged on my pant leg. "Up-py," she said.

I turned her around, lifted her over my head and sat her on my shoulders. After we stepped off again, I gave Meg an expectant look.

"So, Lou took his stake, bought a house and flipped it," she went on. "Made some money. Did it again. Saw the suburban sprawl headed our way—God, you should see what happened to Algonquin. Anyway, he developed a little subdivision east of town. Snowballed that into a bigger development."

"Is that when he threw in with Pete?"

She nodded. "Pete had been doing mostly single homes at that point, but a lot of high-end custom builds. They both saw the potential in doing bigger volume. They were right. Growth exploded. They couldn't keep up—well, Lou couldn't. He didn't have the financial leverage. So big development companies moved in and took over some of the growth. But Lou and Pete were doing just fine." Her face darkened.

"What happened?"

"Lou saw how much housing he and the other developers were building." She stopped and turned to look at me. "You remember how small it was when you left?"

I shrugged. "Fourteen, fifteen hundred?"

She nodded. "We're up to nineteen *thousand*. They say thirty thousand in the next decade."

I gave a low whistle. Emily chirruped on my shoulders, trying to imitate me.

"So Lou's thinking it's time for retail development," she said, walking again. "He gets it in his head that he can bring big-box stores to town. Not discounters, either. Upscale stores. You know, Nordstrom, Saks. Like that."

"Isn't there a big mall out by you anyway?"

"Springdale. In West Dundee. Lou figured we're far enough away. And what with growth going the way it is, he could draw from Rockford suburbs, too, as they spread east."

I looked at her. "Didn't pan out that way?"

"Oh, no. It started out great. Lou pulled some investors together, bought the land, did the impact studies, got permits." She smiled at some memory. "Heck, he had retailers signed up. Convinced them the state would pay for tollway on–off ramps on the west side of Forty-Seven. Then convinced the state he had retailers signed up so they'd cough up the money for the ramps. Pete's company got the construction bid and they started to build."

She fell silent.

"What went wrong?"

"That's the point. I don't know." I heard the frustration in her voice. "Next thing I hear, the deal's coming apart and Lou's selling everything he owns to cover the bank notes. He won't tell me what's going on. Eventually some of his friends tell me that he's gone into bankruptcy. Well, you know Tish is too proud to admit it. And Lou's not talking. I just felt, so . . . helpless."

I let it rattle around some. Hoped she heard it the way I did. "People get depressed, Meg," I ventured. "Heck, if I was doing the biggest deal of my life one minute, filing for bankruptcy the next, I'd feel pretty lousy. Don't know what I'd do."

"I get all that," she said, impatience in her voice. "But it wasn't Lou's style to give up. He was stubborn. You know that. He hit a wall, he'd hit it again a few times. Then take his time trying to figure out how to go around it. Or over it, under it. Whatever. He wasn't depressed. He was angry."

I peeled Emily's fingers off my left eye and repositioned her hand on my forehead. Took a couple of bouncy steps until she giggled. Then slowed.

"We must be talking an awful lot of money," I said. "That means an awful lot of a guy's pride."

She heaved a sigh. "It had to be an accident. I just can't see him doing something like . . . *that*." She shuddered. "Even so, that's not the point."

She went another step or two before she realized I stopped. She turned, saw my confusion. "Look, you'll never convince me he killed himself. Whether he did or didn't, what I want to know is how he got screwed out of the deal."

"What do you mean? Deal's dead, isn't it?"

Her head wagged. "Oh, no. Pete's crew is out there throwing up buildings as fast as they can. There're new investors. A new bank deal." Her voice trailed off.

The light was finally beginning to dawn. "And you want me to figure out what happened?"

She didn't have to answer.

"Aw, he—" I caught myself. "H-E-double-hockey-sticks, Meg. I can barely balance my checkbook. You don't really want me to stick my nose into some business I know nothing about? A deal like this? Must be talking, what, a couple hundred *million*? This is so far out of my league I never even heard of the game. Probably way out of Lou's league, too."

Her eyes sparked. "Hey! We don't live in the big city, doesn't mean we're stupid."

I let go of one of Emily's ankles to hold my hand up palm out. "Sorry. I didn't mean it like that." I shook my head. "I just can't comprehend numbers with that many zeroes. He had something going that big, I have to give him a lot of credit."

She said nothing, tension in her neck and shoulders easing as the anger seeped away. "You don't have to know the business. You know Lou. You know Pete. You know the town."

"Knew." I corrected her. "Things change. I don't belong there. Probably never did."

"Maybe that's the point. You know the history, but you're an outsider now. You've got a different perspective. Some distance."

I mulled it over and slowly shook my head. Thinking it was a game, Emily pressed her hands against my temples and waggled my head back and forth.

"What's the point?" I said.

"The *point?* The point is my brother—your friend—lost everything. Yet everyone else seems to be doing just fine, thank you. The point is, maybe if he hadn't he would have been out hustling, not sitting at home playing with a shotgun, accidentally shooting himself. The point is, my brother's dead, and some- one's laughing all the way to the bank."

"No matter what, it won't bring him back."

She squared off in front of me, hands on her hips. "You're not listening. He got screwed. I want to know who did it."

I stared at her. She flared like a kitchen match with the same heat that had burned in the Lou I remembered. Their dad had the same smoldering temper, ready to flame at any moment. My thoughts jumped like drops of water in a hot skillet. Two people, including this woman from my past, had come looking for me in two weeks, asking for help—*my* help—when I had to beg the woman I loved to make me her helpmate, her partner. Something wasn't right.

"I can't," I said.

"What?"

"I don't know what you expected coming here, Meg. I've got a life. I can't just up and leave. I have a child. Work to do. Nell." I shook my head "Let it go."

Her mouth still hung open in disbelief.

"Look, is Tish taken care of? I assume he had life insurance if he worked for Ed."

She nodded.

"Then let it go. If I start asking questions, it'll just put people's noses out of joint. Life happens, Meg. I'm sorry he got a bum deal. But he must have known the risks going in. Could be he was just overextended. Project that big, I wouldn't be surprised."

I wanted to convince her. The more I talked, the redder her face got. I could feel the heat coming off her like an infrared lamp on an "El" platform in the dead of winter. Her eyes narrowed, mouth turned down at the corners.

"You owe me." She said it so softly that I got the gist from reading her lips. "You owe Lou."

Suddenly, I felt the heat from inside. Emily went still and dead quiet on my shoulders. I tried to stop it, but it bubbled up and spread like hot tar poured on a pitched roof. It started somewhere in my gut and crept up my face and out to my ears.

"We were *kids!*"

She stood her ground, but the force behind the words squelched any reply. Emily squirmed now, anxious to get away from me. I swung her off my shoulders. Tried to repair the damage with a kiss on the cheek and a smile on her way down.

"Push, Daddy," she said. "Push the 'troller."

Her hands reached halfway up the handles. She started off down the path, stroller weaving from side to side. Some of the stiffness eased from Meg's stance. The strain was still taut between us as we fell in behind Emily. Not once had Meg ever mentioned that day. Not to me. I hated her for playing that card now. Hated myself for grudging her advantage. It was a long time before either of us spoke.

"You won't give this up, will you?" I gave her a sidelong glance. Saw her shake her head.

When she turned to me, her eyes were pleading. "He was my brother."

The words hit a hollow spot somewhere inside. Clanged loudly in the emptiness. Echoes filling me with so much sadness and regret I bit my lip to fight off sudden tears. I looked away, feigned interest in a passing tree. Swallowed the lump in my throat.

"What did you do with yours?" I finally asked. "Your stake?"

Her mouth formed an O. "Put Phil through dental school."

"You two seem good together."

She hesitated, saw me raise an eyebrow. "We are. It's—I—" She paused to rethink it. "This whole mess got me thinking, that's all."

"About how things might have been?"

She nodded.

"Only natural at this stage in our lives."

"You wonder, too?"

I shrugged. "Only every other minute. Gets tiresome, second-guessing myself."

Idly, I watched my daughter push the stroller a few steps ahead. Saw the back end rise and fall as the wheels went over a bump. Felt my heart leap into my throat when the toe of Emily's shoe caught on the jutting pavement. Knew that two big strides were too late to stop her from going down. Hard. Face first. I scooped her up and held her to my chest.

Time stood still while the nerve endings sent messages to her little brain. Meg froze, hand over her mouth, eyes wide. The whir of traffic on Lake Shore and all other sounds disappeared.

I pulled Emily away from my shoulder to assess the damage. Watched as her face screwed up tight, turned red. Saw her mouth open wide and the tears flow at the same time her wail rent the air like a buzz saw through butter.

"Oh, my God! Oh, my God!" Meg hovered. "She's bleeding."

I handed her the diaper bag hanging off the back of the stroller. "Should be spit-up towels in there."

I stroked Emily's face, her hair. Made cooing sounds. Told her everything would be all right. None of it helped. She had a set of lungs to rival any diva's. Blood poured out of her mouth, staining the front of her parka. A red welt rose on her forehead. Passersby gave us cold looks that accused us of child abuse, if not attempted murder.

Meg put the towel in my hand. I tried to wipe Emily's mouth. Daubed the blood on her chin instead. She pulled her head away, wailed some more. I held her close again and rocked her gently. Meg paced, and I imagined her every instinct urged her to snatch Emily out of my arms, make it all better somehow. Gradually, the wailing lessened in intensity, trailing off in a series of hiccups.

"You went bump." I smiled at her.

She looked at me seriously. "Big bump."

"*Ker-flump, ka-plump,*" I said.

She nodded and giggled. The bleeding had stopped. A dark red dash on the inside of her lower lip appeared to be the source.

"Open up and say 'ahh,' Like this." I showed her. She imitated me perfectly. One of her front teeth had broken off near the gum line. No doubt the cause of the cut on her lip.

"Beautiful," I told her. "You'll be just fine."

"Just fine," she repeated.

"How about riding in the stroller now?"

"Okay." She wriggled out of my arms, walked around to the front of the stroller and climbed in. I fastened the straps. No sense tempting fate twice.

"You're good with her," Meg said as we started off again.

I looked at her to see if I could detect any sarcasm behind the words. "Right. Bring her home with a broken tooth, a concussion, blood all over her clothes. That's good."

"It's not a concussion. It's a baby tooth that'll fall out anyway. The blood will come out with peroxide. And a little ice will get rid of the bump. I mean it. You really handled it well. Not the way I would have, but . . ."

I wasn't so sure. Her unfinished thought spoke volumes. I brooded silently the rest of the way home.

Nell was on the stoop when we came up the walk. Her gaze flicked from me to Meg, then back to me, questioning now. I gave her a smile, willing Emily silent. The longer Nell was distracted by Meg's unexpected presence, the longer my sentence was deferred.

"Hello, love," I said. I introduced them.

Meg bounded up the stairs two at a time, hand outstretched. "Pleasure, Nell. Emerson's told me so much about you. The man's definitely in love."

"Nice to meet you," Nell murmured, looking nearly disarmed. She flashed me a fierce look, though, intensifying the flush creeping into my cheeks. Then smiled sweetly at Meg. "He hasn't told me nearly enough about you."

Meg laughed. "Not much to tell. It's been so long. We were just trying to catch up."

I was beginning to feel a spring thaw coming on when Emily piped up.

"Mommy, I got a bump!"

Nell smiled broadly. "You did?" She froze halfway down the steps, her smile fading fast. "Oh, my goodness!"

She rushed down the remaining steps, undid the straps and

lifted Emily onto her hip. "Are you all right?" She gently turned Emily's face side to side to get a good look.

"Just fine," the little mimic said cheerfully.

Nell whirled on me. "What on Earth happened?"

I shrank several inches under her glare. "She was pushing the stroller and tripped."

"She's supposed to be *in* the stroller. With the seatbelt on."

"She likes to push. Besides, she needs to get out and walk sometimes."

"Walk, yes. Push, no. It's too big. I can't believe you let her do that. You should know better."

"It was an accident," Meg said quietly. "It could have happened whether she was pushing the stroller or not."

Nell turned the look on her. Meg should have dropped dead instantly.

She shrugged. "It's true. A piece of buckled sidewalk tripped her up. Could have happened to anyone."

"She's not just anyone." You could scrape frost off the words. Nell turned to Emily and nuzzled her. "You poor sweet'ums. Got a *big* bump, didn't you?" She brushed the hair out of Emily's face and winced when she saw the bruise.

"I need to take her home and put ice on this," she said to me.

"We were about to do that. She fell just as we were leaving the park. We came straight home." The protestations were meek. Humble, even. And fell on deaf ears.

"We're going home," she said firmly. She slung the diaper bag over her shoulder, muttered "Golly, what a mess," and left us standing there with the empty stroller.

"Gosh," "golly" and "oh, my goodness" to Nell were tantamount to swearing.

"I am in so much trouble," I muttered.

CHAPTER 7

"It's been nearly a week. I don't know if I can take this much longer."

Brandt watched me pace the living room, his face impassive. I stopped, turned. "You're not helping any."

He shrugged off the accusatory stare.

I tried again. "I'm dying here. Nell refuses to talk to me. Won't let me take care of Emily. I don't know if she's pissed about Meg being here or Emily getting hurt."

"Both," Brandt said. "Probably can't decide which burns her up worse."

I frowned at him. "You're still not helping."

He shrugged again. "Sorry, partner. Just callin' 'em like I see 'em."

"That's not fair. Emily could have gotten hurt no matter who was with her. A few bumps and bruises. Part of being a kid."

"Happened on *your* watch. You're supposed to protect her."

"I *do*. I'd throw myself in front of a bus for her. You know that."

He held up his hands. "Don't look at me. I'm just trying to tell you what Nell's probably thinking. Consolation is, something like that happens when Mama Bear's on watch, she'll beat herself up way worse'n what she's doing to you."

"Gee, thanks." I gave it a few seconds. It still didn't feel like consolation. "Well, I don't know how she can be mad about Meg. I didn't even know she was coming. And she's certainly no threat as far as Nell's concerned."

"Nell doesn't know that." He saw my mouth fall open. "A woman you grew up with—a looker from what you told me—drops out of the clear blue sky. Comes lookin' for you four days after her brother's funeral. You don't think that'll make Nell wonder?"

"If she has to wonder at this stage, she hasn't been paying attention."

He cocked his head, gave me a strange look. "You sure, partner?" He let me stew a bit. "Women are funny creatures, God love 'em. They get a whiff of something a little off, it won't matter what you say. They're all about what you do. Not what you say."

I tried the wide-eyed innocent look. "What've I done? Send her love notes? Bring her flowers? Hell, I even clean her apartment when she's at work."

He took a breath, let it out. "Don't know what to tell you. You best talk to her, though."

"She won't return my calls."

"Get your butt over there. Give her a chance to get it off her chest, whatever it is. Be humble. Grovel. Beg her forgiveness, even if you don't know what for. If she's feeling charitable, she'll let you know. Then you can beg some more."

Didn't sound like fun to me.

I took Brandt's advice anyway. I cornered Nell at the studio around lunch time the next day. Offered her flowers. She hesitated, slowly stretched out a hand and took them.

"I know this doesn't fix anything," I said. "At least let me say I'm sorry."

She thawed some. "Thank you."

"Can you get away for a short walk? We need to talk."

"All right," she said. "I'll get my coat."

We walked from Ohio up through River North where the streets were a little quieter. Nell was silent, putting it on my shoulders. Time to beg.

"I can't tell you how sorry I am about what happened to Emily," I began. I put all the sincerity I could muster into it. "You were right. I need to be more careful about what she can and can't do."

"You don't watch her carefully enough. You can't let yourself get distracted. You have to keep an eye on her all the time."

"I know. I will. Promise."

She put a hand on my arm, stopping me. Her eyes searched my face. "I know you love her as much as I do. I know you'd never intentionally let her come to any harm. But I have to know when she's with you you're focused only on her."

I nodded. Apparently satisfied, she started walking again. I kept pace.

"I know we have to let her stretch," she said. "Grow. Try new things. I know we can't protect her from everything. But she's so little. We have to hold her back a bit. She doesn't know what's dangerous. We do."

We walked half a block in silence.

"Something else is bothering you," I said. "Is it Meg?"

She didn't reply at first. "I can't trust you," she said finally.

"I didn't ask her to come." I said it too quickly, heard the defensiveness in my voice. "Until the funeral, I hadn't even heard from her since we were kids."

She shook her head. "It's not Meg." She reconsidered. "Well, it is, sort of. It's a pattern."

"What pattern?"

"You're a very private man, Emerson. I respect that. I know you think I'm very reserved, too. And I appreciate your patience with me. I like that we don't have to explain ourselves to each other all the time. That I can be quiet around you and not feel funny for not talking. But you're *too* secretive. You keep things from me. It makes me think you're hiding something."

"I don't understand. I wasn't trying to hide Meg. She showed up. I had no idea she was coming."

She put up a hand. "I must admit I was very surprised when you walked up with a strange woman. I understand why you couldn't give me any warning. But this has happened before. Last time it was a runaway. Ellen. Whom you hadn't seen in, what, a few years or something? And now Meg? Twenty-five years? Am I the only one who sees a pattern here?"

"Ellen was just a kid. Her mother asked me to help find her. You know all this." I felt sucker-punched, woozy. I flailed, feeling my way. "Look, I have a past. There's nothing I can do about it. So do you. You don't see me questioning yours. Because I trust you. Implicitly." I couldn't keep the edge out of my voice.

"Men from my past aren't suddenly popping up in my life," she said calmly.

"What do you want me to do, Nell? I'm not prescient. I don't ask them to pop back into my life. I wish they wouldn't. I don't need their problems."

The head-shake again. "It isn't just the fact that people—women—seem all too comfortable coming to you with their problems. Goodness, I suppose I can't blame them, in a way. The problem is that you're not being truthful with me."

"I've always been honest with you."

"To a point. You withhold a lot. I need you to be completely open and up front with me, Emerson. I can't trust you otherwise."

I took a breath, shoved aside the panicky feeling, stayed calm. "You're right. I just assumed that my past didn't concern you. Concern us. I should have called you when Meg showed up. I'm sorry."

She still didn't look happy.

"Look, Nell, I've done a lot of things I'm not proud of. A lot of things that weren't smart. A few things that were pretty dangerous. I try to protect you from that. So you won't worry. And maybe so you won't think less of me. But I love you. I'd never keep anything from you if I thought it affected us." I paused. "I understand what you're saying about being more up-front. But have I done anything to make you distrust me?"

She gave me a look that said I didn't want to know the answer. I felt cold inside.

"Don't go there," she said quietly. "Please?"

She knew, I realized suddenly. Or at least suspected. It wasn't possible, but somehow she'd found out. My face suffused with blood. I worked my jaw, thoughts racing.

"I—"

"Don't." She wouldn't look at me, didn't want to see what my face might reveal. "It's better this way. Not knowing."

The sudden relief didn't wash away the guilt. Whatever she did or didn't know, she may have harbored for the past three years. It would explain, in part, her reluctance to move in.

"There's no one in the world more important to me than you," I said. "You know I want to spend my life with you. I'll do whatever it takes."

She stopped, put two fingers to my lips. "Time." Her voice was soft. "It's just going to take time, that's all."

It wasn't what I wanted to hear. I didn't have much choice. "So where does that leave us?"

"I'm not sure." A long pause. "I do love you, Emerson. Let's just leave things the way they are for a bit. Let me work through this."

"I'm not sure what there is to work through." Calm had settled back in. "I love you. We have a child. I want to marry you. Seems to me not much else matters. But take whatever time you need."

"Thank you."

I heard her sincerity. It meant things were better. Not back to normal. But better.

I called Meg two days later. Told her I'd thought about it. Decided it wouldn't hurt to ask a few questions, see what I could find out. I'm not sure why. For lots of reasons, I suppose. I had time on my hands, for one. I didn't have any active projects. Susan, the *au pair* we used when I was too busy to watch Emily, kept an eye on her full time now at Nell's. I felt restless. I could have filled time with projects around the house. Trolled for work. Neither held any interest.

There was the debt Meg had hung over my head. I could have ignored even that. Like I told her, it'd happened too long ago to be worth much now. Despite the guilt I still carried around. And it was a lot more complicated than she knew.

Then there was all that stuff Brandt had said—about me being good at poking at a problem until it spilled a solution like a busted piñata. I'd already turned him down, he and the widow Saunders. Anger still simmered inside over what he'd done, and I wasn't quite ready to forgive him completely. Maybe Meg's cause was a viable alternative for testing Brandt's theory. And a way to rub his nose in it.

But Meg had a point. Lou had been my friend once. My best friend. Maybe I did owe him. Not in the way she meant. But on some level I wouldn't be who I was if I hadn't been Lou's friend. He'd shaped me, molded me in ways he never would have expected. Ways that I would only begin to understand during my summer of deconstruction.

So I drove to Huntley on a sunny day in April for a dental appointment. Phil Brodsky housed his practice in a new office complex south of town, not far from the tollway exit. The small

office park contained a series of nondescript, two-story buildings along a curved drive. Phil was on the second floor of the
"C" building, which was haphazardly wedged between "A" and
"E." Without the signs, I might have wandered indefinitely,
caught in a *Twilight Zone* episode.

A bell chimed softly when I stepped into the office suite. The
receptionist looked up, smiled. She had blond hair cut in a bob,
a pert nose on a cute face. Taut skin above her cheekbones suggested an eye job, if not a complete lift. Made it tough to tell
her age.

A patient emerged from the hallway next to the desk, shrug-
ging on a coat. Phil followed right behind.

"Take care now, Miz Warren," he said to her back. He stopped
at the desk. "Who's up next, Diane?"

The receptionist gestured at me. He started, noticing me for
the first time.

"I made an appointment," I told him.

He looked confused. "You need to see a dentist?"

"I need to see you, figured this would be the best way. You
can bill me for the time."

Annoyance flashed across his face, but he hid it quickly.
"Come on back."

He led the way past two or three exam rooms to a small office at the end of the hall. I stepped inside. He closed the door
behind me and rounded the desk. Motioned me to sit. I took
the only chair, looked around.

"Nice," I said.

"Better than what we had. We just moved here last year from
that space north of town. Near the grocery store?"

"Sure, I know it. Doc Abel was up there."

"I went into practice with him. Took it over when he retired."
He tapped the desk softly with a forefinger, tired of small talk.

I looked him in the eye. "You can guess why I'm here."

He nodded. "Meg put you up to it." A weary look crossed his face. "How can I help you?"

"What'd you think of Lou?"

He looked as if it wasn't the question he expected. He sat back, appraising me. Came to some sort of decision and leaned forward, elbows on the desk. "I think he was mostly bluster and bullshit. But he got things done. And I never knew him not to be good to his word." His voice held no animosity.

I smiled inwardly. I liked him more every time I talked to him. "Except that last time, maybe?"

He frowned.

"Meg said you two put up some money for Lou's mall development."

"Right." His face lightened. "Sure. We did, but it wasn't Lou that went back on his word. Not that I could tell."

"So how did it work, exactly? How did you get into the deal?"

"I'm probably not the best person to talk to about that. I don't know much about these things." He lifted a shoulder, let it fall. "Lou was making money. When he told us about the mall, it seemed like a good idea."

"You never put money into one of his projects before?"

"He never asked. Managed to put them together on his own. This one was big. He needed a lot of help. Went to most of the big money in town. Put together a 'syndicate,' he called it."

"So, Lou asked you to be part of the syndicate?"

He shook his head. "Meg said he needed help to put the deal together. Convinced me that we'd make money. We came in late. We were small time anyway. Didn't have that much to put into it in the first place."

"So, what went wrong?"

"Hell if I know. Like I said, I don't understand that stuff. Things just started going wrong. I wasn't paying much atten-tion. I was too busy with the move, keeping the practice going. I just heard the project wasn't developing the way it was supposed to. Next thing we know, Lou's in bankruptcy, and we're out in the cold."

"You're not mad about that?"

"Sure I am. But if I stayed mad at Lou it would have just made things worse with Meg. She feels guilty enough. And getting pissed off won't get the money back."

"You lost it all?"

"We thought so at first. The way it worked, the syndicate put up the money for the land, the impact studies, the permits, architectural fees, that sort of thing. All the upfront stuff."

"Where all the risk is."

He nodded. "Then the bank came in with the first construction loan based on the retailers that told Lou they were coming in as tenants. Whatever went wrong, the bank called the note. That meant the bank was first in line. We were last in line."

"Lou came up with enough money to pay everyone off?"

"Not hardly." He grimaced. "That's why he went bankrupt. He sold everything else off just to cover part of the loan. Figured bankruptcy would save the house, at least. For Tish. No, eventually some other bank came in and bought out the note. Or that's what I was told."

"Why? What changed?"

"You're asking the wrong guy. All I can tell you is someone, some other investor, came in and took over the project. We were offered fifty cents on the dollar for our shares in the syndicate. Better than nothing. We took it."

"And the project is back on."

"Apparently."

I was silent for a moment. "Who was in the original syndicate?" I asked finally.

He gave me a funny look. "It wasn't like we held regular poker games. I really couldn't tell you. I could probably guess at some of them. So could you." He paused, watched me start to make a mental list. "We really were on the fringe of this. And only because Lou was family. Tell the truth, I think he wanted to keep Meg out of it. She was the one who kept pushing it with me. Now that I think of it, I doubt he ever asked her for money."

"Sounds odd."

"I don't know." He shifted in his chair. "Seems to me that family and business don't mix well. A deal going sour like this always creates bad blood. I should have known better. Meg's hard to say no to."

"You think maybe Lou felt bad about what happened to his family and friends?"

"Bad enough to kill himself?" He looked surprised. Then thoughtful. "I doubt it. He might've felt put out he didn't protect himself well enough. I never knew Lou to care enough about anyone else, though, to be bothered much by something like this."

The summer I met Lou, Mom was happy I'd made a friend so quickly. She had her hands full with Henry, who was just five. Having a playmate meant one less child to watch, one less thing to worry about. First time Lou rode out to the farm with me on our bikes, he wore this grin the whole way. Like he knew something I didn't.

I gave him the grand tour—the big, drafty four-bedroom farmhouse; the old dairy barn, empty now except the hayloft and a single Case tractor my father had bought used; a cement-block silo, a few feet of sour-smelling corn still lining the bottom; the tool shed with the small pump house attached that chugged to life every now and then when someone turned on a tap in the house.

He loved it all, eagerly exploring each new stop on the tour.

Drinking it in as if he'd never been on a farm before. Maybe he hadn't. I hadn't until a few weeks earlier. But now *I* felt a little superior, like I knew something he didn't.

Tour over, the first place Lou headed was the hayloft. Dusty bales filled only a quarter of the cavernous space. A wooden track ran the length of the loft at the peak of the roof. A rope and pulley contraption with long-rusted hooks hung from it. Once used to move bales from one end to another, it now hung in limp disrepair. Robbie, though, had discovered how to use the rope to swing across the loft. Had stacked bales along one side. Sometimes he played Tarzan, sometimes a pirate. That day, I think Lou and I took turns being Spiderman.

Soon we were hot, itchy and covered with scratches from the dried hay. Shafts of sunlight slanted through cracks in the old wood siding, lighting up drifting motes of alfalfa like pixie dust. Filling our nostrils with a musty, earthy scent that made me think of ancient bones and secrets turning to ash. A rustle and coo from the rafters loosed a lone feather. It floated gently, spinning in and out of the sunlight.

Lou was the first to call it quits. "Come on," he said. "I got something to show you."

He gave a conspiratorial wink and ran for the ladder. I scrambled down after him. At the bottom, he dug into his pocket and pulled out two small cardboard tubes and a pack of matches.

"Rocket engines." He grinned.

I stated the obvious. "We don't have a rocket."

"Let's see what you do have."

He led the way on a search of the barn. A few smaller rooms adjoined the main barn where the milking stalls had been. One for the milk tanks. Another for tools and machinery. Dusty now, and filled with cobwebs, some still guarded by spiders as big as a silver dollar. Lou found a tool bench there with a vise bolted to it. As he brushed past the table leg, a dark shape darted from hiding onto a web near his knee. Retreated just as quickly when it sensed no prey.

"This'll do," Lou said, oblivious. He stuck a tube in the vise and cranked it closed.

"I don't know," I said, nervous now. Feeling imaginary spiders crawling up my leg, down my back. "I'm not sure this is such a good idea."

"What's it gonna hurt?"

I didn't have an answer. "I just don't think you should, that's all."

"You wanna see what it'll do, don't you?"

I shrugged. He took that as a yes, turned back to the vise and struck a match. The rocket engine went off like a Roman candle. Pretty cool, I had to admit. I'm sure the grin on my face matched the one I saw on Lou's. Until I saw the little tendrils of smoke drifting up from the loose hay scattered on the floor. Before I could say a word, it sparked and flamed.

"Holy crap!" Lou said. He stomped on the flame, spreading it further. He stomped some more, sparks flying each time his sneaker hit the floor.

"Stop!" I yelled at him. "Are you crazy?" He didn't listen. I spotted an old saddle blanket on a wall hook and grabbed it. Shoved Lou aside and dropped the blanket on the flames. Stomped on the blanket. Saw Lou just staring at me.

"Don't just stand there! *Now* you can stomp!"

He joined me. We danced around on that blanket until the fire was out. The barn reeked with the acrid smell of smoke and gunpowder.

"That was so cool," he said.

"We are in so much trouble."

His grin barely faded. "Why? Nothing happened."

"Geez, we almost set the barn on fire. My dad is gonna kill

us for sure."

"Us? Hey, leave me out of it."

My mouth hung open in disbelief. "They're *your* rocket engines."

"Not exactly. They're my dad's. I just borrowed a couple. Anyway, you wanted to see it just as much as me. Your dad asks, I'll tell him you said I should do it."

"Help me clean up, at least. Maybe nobody'll notice."

We kicked the burned hay into a pile, scooped it into an old coal shovel and carried it out behind the barn.

"You there?" Phil peered at me.

I shook my head, looked at him. "Sorry." Saw him check his watch. "I'll get out of your hair."

He rose, waited for me at the door. I stepped into the hall, then paused.

"One more thing," I said. "Which bank gave Lou the construction loan? Do you know?"

"Huntley National."

"Harry?"

He nodded. I was afraid of that.

CHAPTER 8

The car drifted slowly into town. I noted all the changes I'd missed the last time. Across the highway from Phil's office complex gold lettering on brick pillars announced the entrance to a huge Del Webb retirement community. A landscaped waterfall out front suggested rolling hills and idyllic dells beyond the gate. A low stone wall backed by a rising knoll shielded the homes and golf course from view. The wall stretched north half a mile toward town before taking a left turn and ending abruptly.

Plowed fields and farm land extended east of the highway, still undeveloped up as far as Kreutzer Road. On the opposite side, a business park was being carved out of a big plot where the retirement community's houses marched west at the end of the wall. Off in the distance stood a domino maze of cookie-cutter houses in a subdivision east of town just the other side of Kreutzer. As if the farms had been sitting too long in the sun, structures now sprouted from the soil like basal cell carcinoma.

The center of town looked the same, the gazebo in the park outside village hall spiffed up like it hadn't aged a day. Main Street was quiet compared to the parade of traffic on Route 47. A spot at the curb beckoned just past Church Street. I pulled in and locked up, wondering why I bothered. Couldn't imagine anyone in this sleepy town wanting let alone taking the drab, generic rental car.

Ed Jarvis still worked out of the same storefront office he had when Lou and I were kids. We'd see him wave through the plate-glass window as we rode past on our way to the Dairy Mart for fries and chocolate malts. I thought he might have retired. He seemed old back then. But old to a kid is anyone out of their teens. The office had changed some. A receptionist manned a desk in the space inside the door where Ed used to sit. An open door off to the right revealed a small conference room. Two other doors led to small offices. The last door was closed.

The woman at the desk coolly and efficiently elicited my name and purpose. Sensing I wasn't a prospect, she dampened hopes of seeing Ed without an appointment. Suggested another agent might be free soon if I could wait, just in case. I shook my head, persisting. Told her I could come back if she would check his calendar, let me know a convenient time. She started to reply, not bothering to look. Paused when the door behind her opened. Our heads turned in unison.

A large man emerged and stopped just past the doorframe. Slicked-back gray hair held in place with gel helmeted a craggy head. The long, jowly face seemed to sink into the broad shoulders with no sign of a neck. He'd buttoned a voluminous sport coat over girth the size of an octogenarian oak. He trained pale blue eyes rimmed in red on the woman.

"Carol, you get your hands on that Jankowski file yet?" The eyes flicked away, took me in. Registered recognition. "I'll be switched. That you, Emerson? I heard you were in town last week." He took a step toward me.

I met him part way, gripped a large hand. "How are you, Mr. Jarvis?" Saw the receptionist's frown of displeasure.

"Ed, please. Don't make me feel older than I am. You here for me?"

"If you've got a minute."

He checked his watch, looked at the desk. Spoke before the receptionist could protest. "Hell, for you? Sure. Let's go next door and get a quick bite. It's almost lunch time."

He put a hand on my shoulder, steered me toward the door.

"Mr. Jarvis," the receptionist called, "don't forget—"

He waved without looking back. "I know. My twelve-thirty with Mrs. Huxtable." He reached around me, gave the door a shove to let me through.

On the street, he caught up to me and wrapped an arm around my shoulder.

"Sorry I missed you last week," he said. "Felt bad I couldn't make it to the funeral. Had a conflict." He glanced at me. "Hard to believe it. All grown up. Time flies. Even have a baby now, I hear."

I nodded, opened my mouth.

Ignoring me, he went on before I could speak. "Lot of changes here since you left. Lots of growth. About time, too."

He guided me up to the door of the Parkside Pub. It looked untouched by the years. Inside, he scanned the room, found a table he liked and gestured toward it. I took a seat. He eased his bulk into the one opposite, looked for a waitress. The pub was nearly empty, still early for the lunch crowd. Those who already had a stool at the horseshoe bar wouldn't be eating anyway. He caught someone's eye, raised his arm.

"Still the best burgers in town here," he told me.

I laughed. "I wouldn't know. Only burgers I ever had were at the Dairy Mart."

He wore an embarrassed grin. "Guess you would have been a bit young for this place."

A woman with a hard face came up to the table dressed in black jeans and a hunter green polo shirt a size too large. She pulled an order pad out of the apron tied around her waist and waited silently. No specials, apparently.

"Vodka rocks," Ed said. "Tomato juice on the side. Burger, rare. Bacon. Blue cheese." He turned to me, raising an eyebrow.

I looked up at the waitress. "Iced tea. Ditto on the burger." I tipped my head toward Ed and caught his small smile.

When she left, he kept up a steady patter about town progress. How great the growth was for the local economy after all the years of having to depend on good crop prices and the Union Special plant where they made parts for industrial sewing machines. The waitress was back a few minutes later with drinks on a tray. Jarvis gazed reverentially at the tumbler of vodka as she placed it in front of him. He waited, watching her make her way back to the bar. Splashed some Tabasco sauce into the glass of tomato juice. Took a big sip of chilled vodka, chased it with half the tomato juice.

"So, what can I do you for?" He leaned back, swiping a paper napkin across his mouth.

I shrugged, deciding how to play it. "Been a long time. Coming back after all these years brings back memories. Hard to tell which are real and which have changed." I smiled.

"I know what you mean."

"Meg was pretty thrown by this whole business with Lou."

His head bobbed. "A shocker, for sure. A real shocker."

"She's having a hard time accepting it. You know. Lou being depressed enough to kill himself."

"Hell, son, I was in his shoes, I'd have been depressed, too."

"What do you mean?"

"You must've heard about the mall development." He took another swallow of vodka, chased it with the rest of the juice. Looked thoughtful for a moment. "Plain and simple, Lou was in deep financial doo-doo. He—a lot of us, really—had serious money tied up in this mall. The deal went sour."

"You were one of the investors?"

"Sure. Lou made me a lot of money when he worked for me. Figured the least I could do was put some of it back in one of his developments." He frowned. "Hell, *I* was depressed when

81

things didn't work out. Stood to make a lot of money on that deal. Ended up losing half what I put in. Can't imagine how Lou felt losing everything."

He looked over my shoulder, paused while the waitress put plates in front of us. She waited a half-second, then turned on her heel when no one spoke up. Ed lifted the bun off his burger and slathered it with mustard. He flattened the sandwich with the heel of his palm, picked it up in both hands. Worked it into his mouth and bit. He chewed a few times, moving the food into his cheek like a plug of tobacco.

"Thought he could weather it at first," he said through the food. "Didn't seem to faze him much. Last few times I saw him, he looked pretty desperate."

I swallowed a bite of mine, no mustard. "What was to weather? How'd the deal go sour?"

"Don't know for sure. Seemed like there were labor problems on the job site. I heard talk of a strike." He gnawed off another hunk, chomped on it. "Project got behind somehow. Lou was just stretched too thin."

"He didn't come back to the investors for more money?"

He snorted. I thought burger might come out his nose. "What do you think?"

I took it as a yes. Figured no one bit second time around. "Who all was in on the original deal?"

His eyes narrowed, his jaw stopped. "Why the questions, son?"

I put on a disarming face. "I told you. Meg's upset. She wants to understand why. She can't get her arms around the fact that he could have been depressed enough to do this."

"Take my word for it. Lose that much money, you're gonna feel like shit." He appraised me. "You know, for a minute there, I almost thought you might've been sent to investigate the claim."

My surprise was genuine. "The insurance?"

He didn't answer the question. "I figured an old friend wouldn't do that," he said, taking another bite. "And anyway, it's clean. After all, I sold him the policy."

"Why would anyone investigate?"

"Lot of policies don't pay if death's a suicide. Some pay, but only after the policy's been in force a certain period. Two years, usually."

I shrugged. "Whatever. Not my business. But I'd still like to talk to a few people. Try to convince Meg what everyone's been saying is true."

He ran his tongue along his front teeth, sucked out bits of food. "Makes sense. She should move on. Frankly, I'd think Tish'd be more upset." He paused. "So, you want to check in with folks close to Lou?"

"Well, family and friends have one opinion. Investors tend to have another perspective."

He rubbed the back of his hand across his mouth. "I don't know everyone, but it's probably no secret. Tim Crandall's one. Bill Caruthers. Poor guy's got Alzheimer's. Barely knows his wife anymore." He licked a spot of mustard off his hand then turned his palm up and ticked the names off on his fingers. "Frank, of course. Me. Jerry McKenna. You might not know him—lawyer in Marengo. Harry—Senior, not Junior. Duke Anderson—Pete's uncle. What's-his-name, the guy that owns Data Transfer. Probably after your time. Klaus Pohlmann. Hard to forget a name like that. Got a patent on some computer storage thing-y. Hit it big."

His eyes rolled up. As if more names might be scrawled on the ceiling. Looked at me again. "Probably a half-dozen, maybe a dozen more. Some in it big. Some for loose change. Lou was on the line for the most I'd say. Had to use everything he owned for collateral."

It sounded like Lou. Put everything on the line. Yet it didn't. I'd never known him to risk anything of his own that wasn't a sure bet.

Ed looked at his watch, pulled out his wallet. "I gotta get back. Been nice seeing you, Emerson. You talk to Frank yet?" He dropped a bill on the table, saw me shake my head. "You should. Something else you should do if you know what's good for you. Leave this business with Lou alone. It won't do anyone any good to stir it up."

I stared at him. Hostility shone through his slick salesman's veneer, all buddy-buddy joviality gone. "You have something to hide, Ed?"

"Me? Nah. I don't mind talking to you for old times' sake 'cause I like you, kid. Always did. But a lot of people here feel they got screwed over in this mall deal. You can ask your questions, but they ain't gonna raise Lou from the dead, and sure as shit ain't gonna put bank back in people's pockets. More like you'll just piss people off. Cover the tip?"

He strode off without waiting for a reply. Left me wondering if mention of Lou's insurance policy had struck a deeper nerve than he'd let on. Still stewing over his sudden change of heart, I reached over and picked up the money. A ten. Turned over the check the waitress had left with the burgers. Pulled a twenty out of my pocket and put both bills on top. I was about to turn and look for the waitress when I felt a hand on my shoulder. Made me nearly jump.

"How was the burger?"

A bearded man stepped into my vision, stood at the side of the table.

"Great," I said. "Haven't had one in ages. Really hit the spot."

"Yeah, they're good here." He eased into the chair Ed had warmed and grinned at me.

I straightened. He was about my age, I guessed, though the

beard made him look a little older. Dressed down in jeans and plaid shirt. Rolled-up sleeves revealed ropy muscles on long, thin arms. A tattoo on the right forearm. He was familiar, but nothing was coming to me. I waited him out.

"Alzheimer's?" he said.

I felt my face redden. Forced myself to look at him more closely. Hazy images floated in my head. I took a stab.

"Jake?"

He extended a hand across the table and gave me a gap-toothed smile I instantly recognized. "Would've been sad to think you're losing your marbles already. How are you, man?"

"Good, thanks. Jeez, you had me going. The beard, I guess. Makes you look different."

He laughed. "Yeah, I'm incognito now."

I looked around. "So, what're you doing here? In for lunch?"

"No, man. I'm working." He nodded off to my right. "I tend bar. Look after things."

"You stayed, then. Always thought you were going to take off. See the world."

"I did." He grinned. "Courtesy of Uncle Sam."

I glanced at the tattoo again. Wings. *"Semper fi?"*

"Army." he shrugged. "Eighty-first Airborne. It was all right. Not sure the Marines would have taken me. Didn't get around like those Navy guys, but saw a few sights anyway."

"How long?"

"Fifteen years. For a while thought I'd end up a career grunt. Didn't work out."

"Sorry to hear it."

He waved it off. "Don't be. I got no regrets."

"What happened?" I thought better of it. "Unless you're not comfortable talking about it."

"It's no big deal. Iraq happened. The first one. Desert Storm." He sighed. "I was in Grenada, too. What a joke. You're in this place, right? You're thinking you should be on the beach with a rum punch and a babe in a bikini. Instead, there're bullets flying all over the place. Weird, man."

He looked over at the bar, nodded as if acknowledging some signal. Got out of the chair.

"Come in some night if you're going to be around," he said. "We'll catch up if it's not too busy."

"Sounds good. Nice to see you." I stood.

He took two steps. Then stopped even with me, the smile gone. "You been away a long time, man," he said quietly. "Careful about rooting around in the past. Might not like what you find."

He was gone before I could begin to think of how to respond. I left the money and the check on the table and walked out. Wandered up the street and climbed behind the wheel of the rental. Turned the key, and stopped. Realized I didn't know where I was going next. I sat back and thought.

Jake Reynolds was the second kid I met the summer we moved. Lou and I rode our bikes over to Deicke Park one day. Lou was in the lead as usual, thick, freckled legs churning the pedals. He hunched over the raked handlebars, willing the bike faster. With each little twist of the path he gained on me. Sunlight bored holes through the canopy of leaves, dappling the dim forest floor in green leopard skin. The spots of light were so bright they hurt the eyes. Ahead, Lou's white T-shirt blinked on and off like a semaphore.

"Come on!" He tossed the words over his shoulder, not bothering to see if I was following.

My bike was bigger, heavier than Lou's. With the seat as low as it could go, I still had to stretch for the pedals. Even when I pedaled fast, the bike moved sluggishly, lumbering down the path, front wheel wobbling in the dirt. The air was thick, laden with moisture, hot as a sauna. My shirt clung damply to my skin. I panted, taking shallow breaths, afraid the air might somehow scald my lungs if drawn any deeper.

The white shirt ahead winked out and disappeared. The handlebars flashed in the shafts of light. I didn't see the bend until I was nearly on it. Gripping the handlebars tightly I rounded it and heard a whoop of excitement ahead. The path rose slightly to a crest and dropped steeply. A yell of triumph followed Lou's rear tire as it fishtailed around a sharp curve at the bottom, narrowly missing a big tree.

Fear clutched at my stomach. I longed for the thrill of speeding down the slope in free fall, skidding into the turn like my friend. I knew better. The bike was too big. I stood on the brakes before the bike got up too much speed and eased the rest of the way down looking for Lou. The dense forest canopy threw everything into dim shadow. My breath caught in the sudden silence. Around the next bend, Lou's bike lay on the side of the path.

I pulled up next to it and hopped off. Looked around. No Lou. I laid the bike down next to his and guardedly ventured a step or two off the path. Called his name softly. No answer. Heart pounding, I waited for him to jump me from the brush, scaring the pee out of me. Nothing. I followed a narrow trail and pushed through the bushes. I heard moaning, muffled and distant. Hairs stood up on the back of my neck.

"Lou?" It came out a whisper. He was having fun with me. Another groan from somewhere ahead quickened my pace. Maybe he'd been hurt. "Lou?"

Hands wrapped around my ankles and yanked them out from under me, scaring the breath out of me. I fell hard and struggled for air. Lou's face, framed in red, hovered over mine.

"Shhh!" He put a finger to his lips. His face disappeared.

I worked my jaw, belly heaving, swallowed hard and finally

sucked in a big breath. Lay there for a second or two letting my pulse rate settle back into double digits, glad to be alive. I rolled onto my stomach and found myself next to Lou. Pulled my elbows up beneath my chest and wiggled forward under some bushes until our heads were even. He barely acknowledged me.

I followed his gaze. Through a small break in the undergrowth, we had a clear line of sight to the pond fifty yards away. No one swam there. The mosquito-infested water was thick with muck and algae. It had other uses apparently. In a clearing near the cattails at water's edge was a tangled heap of clothing. Something moved and someone moaned.

I froze, breath leaving me yet again. A tangle of bodies wrestled and grappled in the mud. Until they rolled over. The person now on top pushed into a sitting position. A woman—girl, more likely—naked from the waist up, her skirt bunched around her hips. She threw her head back. Long, wavy brown hair cascaded down her back. She arched, thrusting bare breasts skyward. A hand reached up and cupped one of them. She rocked back and forth. There were two moans now, one high, one low.

I don't know how long we stayed and watched, mesmerized by the sight, the sounds of the couple's lovemaking. I'd never felt stirrings like that inside me before. Didn't really understand them. They weren't physical. More like a yearning. I looked at Lou, saw the eager excitement, the flush on his face. Knew that somehow we saw and felt different things. I felt ashamed, embarrassed. Not by the act itself. Because I was intruding on their privacy, sharing something that was meant for them alone. They were two high school kids letting hormones get the best of them. But at the time, nothing could have seemed more magical, more beautiful.

I fell in love that day for the first time. Not with the girl we watched, but with women. With their form, their grace, their sensuality. And when I was old enough, the way they looked and smelled, the way they felt and tasted, even thought.

Lou nudged me in the ribs.

"Come on! We gotta get out of here." He scrabbled backward out from under the bushes.

The couple pulled on their clothing. I hadn't even noticed they'd stopped making love. I backed out the way I'd come in. Then stood and started to turn.

A voice came out of nowhere. "Nice, huh?" The bushes next to us parted.

Lou jumped. "Holy crap!"

My heart leapt into my throat. A skinny kid with brush-cut hair emerged from a thicket. I eyed him warily. He flashed a quick grin, revealing a chipped front tooth. For a brief moment I started to relax.

An angry voice echoed through the woods behind us. "Who the hell's out there? Somebody spyin' on us? I swear I'll get whoever's out there."

"Holy crap!" Lou said again, this time in a fierce whisper.

The girl's voice floated through the trees, distraught, the words unintelligible. Then the guy's again. Loud enough to be distinct.

"Kids, I'm telling you! I'm gonna pound their skinny asses." Then louder still, for our benefit. "You hear that! Gonna kick some butt!"

Lou beat feet up the trail, the skinny kid and me right behind him, crashing through the brush. With chests heaving, the three of us burst onto the path next to the bikes Lou and I had left there. We stopped to breathe, bent nearly double, hands on our knees, listening for sounds of pursuit.

Lou straightened and cocked his head. "I don't think he's coming." He turned to the kid. "Jeez, Spook, you nearly made me pee my pants."

The kid smiled.

"Where's your bike?" Lou asked.

"I hid it up the path."

"Were you there the whole time?" The kid nodded. Lou turned to me and jerked his thumb over his shoulder. "This is Jake. We call him Spook."

Jake looked at me. "What's your name?"

"Em—"

Lou punched me hard on the arm. "Ralph," he said, looking at me defiantly.

"Ralph?" Jake tilted his head, eyebrows furrowing.

I nodded, rubbing my shoulder.

Lou picked up his bike and swung a leg over the saddle. "Come on. That guy's likely to show any minute."

He shoved off and started pedaling away. I picked up my bike and shrugged.

"See you around," I said, wheeling it past him. A quick glance showed Lou already out of earshot. "It's Emerson, by the way."

His sharp look changed to a smile of sudden understanding. He nodded. "See you."

CHAPTER 9

Huntley National Bank was in a square, two-story traditional brick building on Main Street. Other banks had built newer structures on the outskirts of town. Even some of the big Chicago banks had started to add branches this far out. Huntley National's only nod to modernization was a drive-through ATM in the parking lot behind the building.

The interior still reflected hints of rural small-town opulence—polished granite counters, cherry-paneled walls, brass fixtures, high stucco ceiling, barred windows. The slate floor had been carpeted in waiting areas occupied by plush but institutional-looking furniture designed to soften the banking experience, all of it dated. The contrast was jarring. Bonnie-and-Clyde meets Ozzie-and-Harriet.

I asked a teller where I could find Mr. Hammond. She called over a severe-looking woman in a gray wool suit who introduced herself as the customer service manager. I asked her the same question. She made some excuses about how busy he was. I persisted gently, asking if she'd mind checking to see if he could spare five minutes for me. She stared at me a moment, mouth set, eyes impatient, but finally relented. After getting my name, she walked to a desk, picked up a phone and punched some buttons. I followed slowly, watched her speak tersely, then nod. She hung up and turned to me.

"He'll be with you in a moment," she said, and gestured at the waiting area. "You're welcome to have a seat."

Hammond kept me waiting long enough to give the impression he was as busy as his manager claimed. Several minutes passed before he appeared through a door at the back of the lobby and strode across the floor like he owned the place. He did. He looked the part—conservative but expensive suit, crisp white cotton shirt and striped silk tie, black wingtips, neatly coiffed salt-and-pepper hair.

I stood. He extended a hand two steps before he reached me. Put a beaming smile on his face that made me wonder where the cameras were. In-laws are never that happy to see each other.

"Emerson. Good to see you."

"Hello, Harry. Been a while."

His shoulders rose and fell a fraction of an inch, but the smile remained. "You're always welcome." He paused, eyes flicking over my face. "So, what can I do for you? Need some money?" The smile broadened at his own joke.

"Spare a few minutes to chat?"

"Of course." He didn't move.

"Privately?"

The smile faltered for an instant. He checked his watch, pasted the smile back on and put a hand on my shoulder.

"Certainly. Let's go to my office."

He led the way back through the door he'd entered and up a flight of stairs. From across the room he'd looked tan and fit. Up close, the healthy glow was a face florid from high blood pressure or booze. Maybe both. Good tailoring, not workouts, trimmed his figure. A good haircut and careful comb-over disguised how much his hair had thinned. I reminded myself that he had a dozen years on me.

He preceded me through a door marked with a brass plaque that read "President." Gesturing me to have a seat, he rounded the large cherry desk and eased into the leather swivel chair. I remembered being in the room once as a kid. Harry's father had sat behind the desk. The room looked the same. Same desk, same credenza, same chairs. It had seemed bigger then.

I leaned forward. "What can you tell me about the mall development?"

He frowned, surprised that I'd skipped the small talk.

"Not much, I'm afraid. We're not involved in it." He straightened a pen on the desk.

"Lou's development deal. You *were* involved in that."

"Well, yes." He hesitated. "But I can't tell you much about that, either, to be honest."

"Because?"

He looked uncomfortable, but shrugged it off. "You know. Confidentiality and all that. I really can't discuss particulars."

"General terms, then."

"Why are you asking? What are you looking for?"

"Come on, Harry. It can't be that tough to figure out. I'm not looking for bank irregularities, if that's what you're worried about. You know me better than that."

"Family gatherings around the holidays every few years?" The mask disappeared entirely. His face darkened and some of his self-assurance came back. "I don't think I know you at all. Sure, people around town know your name, but you've been gone a long time. I'm not sure you have much credit here. Better spend it wisely."

I shrugged. "Always the banker. Probably good advice." I paused. "Lou was my friend once. Meg just wants to understand how he could have done this. This isn't about you, Harry."

He sat up straighter, rolled his head on his neck. "Look, I feel terrible about Lou. If any of us had known he was that depressed, we would have intervened, gotten him help. But he was a big boy. He'd been doing this a long time. He knew the risks. I just think the less said about the matter, the better. It pays to be cautious."

My brow furrowed. "And *I* worry you?"

He hesitated. "I hear things."

"Such as?"

"You . . . help people."

I waited him out, curious.

"Maybe you came back to help someone. Tish Barrett, maybe."

My turn to be nonplussed. "Does she need help? I never got the impression Tish needed help from anyone. What would she want from you?"

"Nothing." He waved dismissively. "People sometimes get it into their heads that the world owes them somehow." He'd evaded too many questions.

"So, what did happen here?"

He flushed. "Some deals work. Some don't. This one didn't. Simple as that."

"You weren't cautious enough?"

His flush deepened. "All investments involve risk. Whenever you lose money, you always think you should have been more conservative. Was this deal risky? Sure. But I don't want anyone to get the wrong idea. Lou had a good track record. The financing was sound. Above board."

"But people lost money."

He nodded. "Unfortunately. I did, too. That's no reason to take legal action."

"To recover the investment?"

He spoke hesitantly, choosing his words. "There were rumblings about a suit."

"Why? Everybody was in the same boat."

"Not exactly. As you might expect, the bank was in a more favorable position than the individuals involved. The bank more or less broke even."

I shrugged. "No surprise there. I didn't think you were in on this. I heard the old man put money in, but you didn't."

He sighed and looked out the window. When his eyes met mine again, he seemed to shrink somehow, look smaller in the chair. "I gave Dad money to invest. To avoid any appearance of impropriety."

"A lot?"

He nodded. For a moment, I felt sorry for him. If my sister knew her husband had pissed away a small fortune on one of Lou's deals, she'd be making his life hell. I never knew her to pass on an opportunity to make someone else as miserable as she was. The only girl in the family, she got special dispensation growing up. Preferential treatment. She never saw it that way, always casting herself as a victim. She must have known about Harry's lost investment, I realized, thinking back on what she'd said about Lou at the wake.

"What went wrong?" I asked.

He shrugged. "Timing. The deal was sound, but squeaky. Lou collateralized everything. He had just enough seed capital to pay interest only on the loan for a certain period. The project was supposed to be completed in stages. The loan covered the first phase. Lease income from initial tenants was supposed to start coming in at the same time principle payments on the loan kicked in. The first phase didn't come in on time. Lou missed payments. Prospective tenants got nervous. Some pulled out. We had no choice. We did what any bank would have done—we foreclosed."

"Must have been a few angry investors."

"Of course. A few saw it as a great write-off. And most got over it pretty quickly."

"Any who didn't?"

"Not really. The loss hurt, but didn't put anyone on the street. Except Lou." He frowned and looked at me, eyes widening.

"Why? You don't think . . . ?"

I shook my head. "Just wondered if someone could have been angry enough to wear him down, make him feel guilty."

He steepled his fingers and touched them to his lips. "Not that I can think of."

"That's it?"

"Not much to it. Lou was overextended and just didn't have enough time. I tried to give him as much as I could." He put both palms flat on the desk. "Anything else?" Interview over, apparently.

"I guess not."

He stood. "Hope it was helpful. Good of you to stop by. I'll tell Elizabeth you said hello."

"Don't bother." No sense giving her a chance to shift her sights from him to me.

A convoy of cement trucks lumbered through a field off Route 47 south of town like a procession of elephants. They sluiced their cargo into a jumbled gray structure that unfolded and expanded with each fresh load of slurry like a blow-up toy. From a distance it was a shifting, shapeless blot on the landscape, blurred by dust. A Midwest mirage.

I pulled in behind one of the behemoths and bumped along the rough road. Swirling clouds of dirt obscured the construction until the road curved, letting a cross-breeze clear the way ahead. The trucks rumbled across an expanse of gravel dotted with pickup trucks and the occasional car, all coated with a thick layer of grime.

The line slowed as the trucks eased through a break in a tall chain-link fence held in place by posts set in concrete blocks. Trailers lined the fence for fifty yards in either direction. Beyond, the trucks split off to the right and the left, circling the site to find repositories for their contents. I swung the wheel hard left and peeled away from the convoy, pulling the car into an empty space on the gravel. I locked up and strolled through the gate.

Workers swarmed over the structure, all apparently with a set of instructions. None, probably, with any idea of what the whole would look like. Most confident that if they kept their heads down and did what they were told, they'd get a paycheck and the thing would get built.

I picked my way carefully, dodging trucks and workers carrying heavy loads. The roadbed around the immense building was mud mixed with rock. Cranes twirled slowly overhead in a blue sky, swinging materials from one side of the site to another. Welders' torches sizzled as they worked on the steel skeleton. The high-pitched whine of power saws pierced the air, backed up by the basso rumble of the cement trucks and the staccato rhythm of nail guns. Over it all men's voices shouted warnings and orders.

The space closest to the entrance was unfinished. Empty shell still being formed. As I walked around the circumference, the building began to look more finished. Gravel gave way to smooth blacktop with crosswalks marked by paving stones. Bare concrete walls enclosing empty space still open to the sky became a colorful facade for glassed-in retail stores fitted with counters and shelves. Carpenters and carpet installers replaced welders and masons. Delivery trucks and tradesmen's panel trucks took the place of cement trucks.

Behind the end of the building stretched an expanse of graded earth, tall light poles standing like sentinels guarding empty fields beyond that. Incongruous, somehow, that this new mecca of American consumerism rose out of a cornfield. I scanned the horizon, getting my bearings. The landscape looked strangely familiar.

Over the din I heard someone call my name. In a loading bay

between sections of the mall, a man in a hardhat sat on a stack of drywall with his arm raised. Tommy Burke. I nodded and headed in his direction. He was with half a dozen other guys dressed in jeans or coveralls and hardhats, all in various stages of repose. A few held cigarettes smoked nearly down to the filters. On my approach, the men stirred, stood, drifted away like tumbleweeds.

I walked up to Tommy. "Something I said?"

He followed my gaze to the backs of the receding men and chuckled. "Your breath, more likely." He hopped down from the sheetrock, his beer-gut jiggling when he landed. "Nah, they're just being careful about watching the clock on break."

"I didn't know you were working out here."

He shrugged. "Pay's good. Steady, too."

"You work for one of the contractors?"

"*The* contractor. The G.C.—Pete." He shrugged again as if to apologize. "Usually, I'm my own man. Do a lot of projects for people. Decks, room additions, remodels. Done a lot of work for Pete over the years, though. This came along, seemed like it was too good to pass up. Union wages, big project."

"No job security, though."

He cocked his head, gave me a funny look. "You mean when the project shut down?"

I nodded. "Must have been rough."

"I've seen it happen before. House gets half-built. Builder runs out of money."

"That what happened here?"

"Far as I can tell. The project slowed down. Paychecks started coming late. Just once in a while at first. Then all the time. Finally stopped. I heard Lou couldn't make the bank payments. That was all she wrote."

"Why the slowdown? Did somebody hear the project was in trouble?"

98

He looked surprised. "Not that I know. Things were hum- ming along just fine." He paused. "This is a big deal for this town. We're not blind. At least not most of us. We seen it com- ing at us for years. And development's been here a while now. All those new subdivisions. Heck, it's what keeps my kids in clothes. But this . . ." He looked right, then left. "This is differ- ent. A retail development like this and we're not just some bedroom community. This puts jobs here. I was real proud of Lou for pushing this through."

I followed his gaze. Had to agree it was pretty impressive.

"I still don't get it." I looked at him again. "What happened?"

"It's no big secret." He shrugged, but lowered his voice anyway. "The union pushed for more money. Said wages here weren't on a par with projects in Lake or Cook County. Asked us to follow union rules to the letter."

"That slowed things down?"

He snorted. "Practically had to get forms in triplicate to hammer a nail, take a stopwatch to the can."

"That what those guys were worried about when I walked up?"

"Hell, no. They got what they wanted. Some of it, anyway. Went on strike to do it. Now, they want to look industrious. Prove they're worth the extra sixty cents an hour."

"You don't care?"

"Sure, I care. I care about doing a good job and going home to Wendy and the kids. I'm not turning down the extra money, but I was plenty happy with what they were paying us. The strike just put us all out of work for a couple months. Gotta work a lot of hours for sixty cents to make that up. Good thing I was able to pick up some projects on the side."

"But no problems since then? It's okay working here?"

"I guess." He hesitated, thinking it over. "Like I said, good, steady pay. Lot of things I'd do different." He looked as if he wanted to say more. Whatever it was, he swallowed it.

His face suddenly went on alert as his eyes caught sight of something over my shoulder.

"Speaking of trouble," he murmured. He straightened and put a smile on his face. "Hey, boss."

I turned to see a short, grizzled man in a hard hat walk up to us. He looked me up and down, then turned his attention to Tommy.

"Friend of yours?" he asked, jerking his thumb toward me.

Tommy nodded.

"He doesn't have a hard hat."

Tommy's head bobbed, sun reflecting off the sweat on his face. "He didn't know."

I put a smile on my face and threw my two cents in. "I'll keep an eye out for falling objects. Promise."

The man turned and stepped in close enough to tell he smoked menthol cigarettes and ate garlic for lunch. He wasn't smiling.

"This is a closed site," he said. "You had permission to be here, you'd have a hard hat." He pointed a finger at my bare head. "No hat."

He stood his ground, waiting. Behind him I glimpsed Tommy nervously signaling me with a jerk of his head.

"Ah, you want me to leave," I said.

"I figured you for a smart guy." He turned back to Tommy. "Break about over, big guy?"

"Sure, boss," Tommy mumbled. His face became suffused with red.

I was well away before I looked back over my shoulder. Both Tommy and the foreman had disappeared.

A bunch of contractors had trailers at the front gate. Two of the trailers were marked "Anderson Construction." I picked the closest one. Inside, a woman nearly decked me with a right cross as she shrugged into a coat.

"I've got to go, Carla." She spoke over her shoulder. "Time to pick up the kids."

The one she called Carla looked up from a desk with a smile and nodded. Saw me and the smile turned to a look of alarm. She raised a hand in warning, too late. Sue Ann Anderson turned and walked right into me.

"Hey!" She bounced off and gave me an accusatory eye. "Oh, it's you."

I put out a hand and steadied her. "You okay?"

She nodded, her face softening. "What are you doing here?"

"Looking for Pete. Is he around?"

"Yes, actually. He's usually out on the site somewhere putting out fires, but he's around. Carla will get him for you. Right?" She glanced at Carla and back at me. "Sorry. I've got to get going. I'm late picking the kids up from school."

She brushed past me out the door. Carla was already on the phone. When she hung up, she looked subdued.

"He's on his way out," she said. She went back to the work in front of her. I watched her for a moment. Young, not long out of high school, I guessed. Attractive in a wholesome Midwestern way, but not pretty. Dark curly hair, sallow complexion, figure rounded by too much comfort food and too little exercise.

Besides Carla's, there were two other desks in the room. On the far side near the door was a reception and waiting area with a couple of mismatched chairs and a table laden with magazines. I wandered over and thumbed through the disheveled pile— mostly old copies of *Popular Mechanics*, *Field & Stream* and *Sports Illustrated*. Artist's conceptions of different house styles hung on the walls, faded and worn. In the center of the floor was an easel on which stood a large rendering of the mall. A fantasy land where the sun always shone, the flowers always bloomed and the salespeople were always nice. Huntley Hilldale

Mall. Have a nice day.

I meandered back to Carla's desk. She looked up, flashed me an apologetic smile.

"Sue Ann works here with you?"

She looked furtively at a door behind her, then back at me. "She handles most of the bookkeeping. Takes care of accounts payable."

"Guess that doesn't leave much for you." I smiled. "So what do you do?"

She shrugged. "Answer phones. Whatever they tell me to."

She stiffened and lowered her head at the sound of the door opening behind her. Pete pushed through it, hardhat in hand, a scowl on his face. His eyes took us in, and the scowl inverted to a smile. He took two big strides toward me, pumped my hand and clapped me on the shoulder with the hardhat.

"Emerson. Good to see you. Missed chatting with you at the wake. How are you?" He turned to Carla before I could answer. "Carla, did I ever tell you about how we almost missed the playoffs my sophomore year—first year I broke the rushing record—because a crappy tight end with a sissy name dropped a perfect pass? No? Well, some other time." He gripped my arm above the elbow and steered me toward the door, still talking over his shoulder. "I'm taking this guy on a tour of our fabulous project. Then I have to meet with Joe about some screw-up in C module. Beep me on the cell if you need me."

He gave me a slap on the back that sent me out the door. It slammed behind us. Pete headed for the building without a sideways look, screwing the hardhat onto his head. I took a few long strides and fell in step.

"What do you want?" he said, eyes straight ahead, all pretense gone.

"Still charming. Always liked that about you."

"You gonna tell me you want to go for a beer and share locker room stories? Reminisce about the snatch that got away?" He snorted, turned and spat. "You didn't come here for old time's sake. What do you want?"

"To find out why Lou killed himself."

He didn't hesitate. "Because he was a big chickenshit baby, that's why. Didn't have the balls to face up to what he'd done."

"What was that?"

"Screw up the biggest deal of his life and end up losing millions of dollars of other people's money. Lot of people got hurt. Instead of making it right, he took the easy way out."

"Yet here you are." I made a sweeping gesture with my arm.

He pulled up short. "Yeah. So?"

"From what I hear, the one who pulled the short straw in all this was Lou."

"Like I said, a lot of people got hurt."

"What? Some investors lost a little money? Take it from a guy who knows. It stings. You get over it. Lou lost everything. And then he lost his life."

He huffed, turning red, and growled in a low voice. "He damn near took us all down with him. I can't tell you how many times I pulled his butt out of the fire. I warned him about this one. He wouldn't listen."

He started walking again, making me hustle to keep up.

"What do you mean you warned him? What happened to screw this deal up?"

"None of your business. Go home. There's nothing for you here. Never was. Go home."

"I'll find out somehow. I'm not letting this go."

He stopped again and swung around to face me. "Let me see if I can explain this so even you can understand. It's simple. This is a union project. The union wanted more money. I told Lou to pay it. He said we couldn't afford it. The union went on strike, deal went bust. Got it?"

"Yet here you are," I repeated.

" 'Cause I worked my ass off to save this deal. Found new investors, a new bank deal."

"You?"

"Don't look so surprised. You think this company got this big because I don't know my ass from a hole in the ground? Jesus, I swear it must be the smog in the city does that to your brain." He turned away in disgust.

"No disrespect, Pete, but I thought Lou did all the deals you two worked."

"I didn't need Lou." His lip curled up in a sneer. "I never needed him. We just saw ways to help each other."

"Why didn't he find a way out of your problem? If you found one, surely he could've, too."

"He bet it all, that's why. He had nothing left to bargain with."

"You don't seem sorry he's dead."

"I'm not breaking out any violins. Doesn't mean I'd wish it on anyone." His shoulders rose and fell. "I outgrew him."

He turned and left me there trying to think of a response.

CHAPTER 10

Meg's kids quietly occupied themselves in the family room. Dana flopped on the floor in front of the couch, hard at work on a geography assignment from school. She stuck the tip of her tongue out of the corner of her mouth as she concentrated on the map in front of her. Todd sat in an easy chair with a book, content for the moment to read. I couldn't imagine that lasting for long. Meg motioned silently, leading the way to the living room.

"Sure I can't get you something to drink?" she asked.

"I'm fine, thanks. I have to head back soon. I wanted to check in first, let you know what I've been up to." I gave her the rundown on my day.

She listened without comment. Looked thoughtful when I was through. "Doesn't tell us much."

I shook my head slowly. "Look, I'll make the rounds. Get everyone's take on where his head was at. No promises."

She nodded gratefully. "I know it's silly. Holding out hope. Not like it's going to change anything. It's just . . ." She paused, eyes filling. Swallowed hard.

"You two always were close."

She nodded. "Hard to believe everything you know about a person is a lie. I'm not ready for that."

"What he did doesn't take away from who he was," I said softly. I didn't know if I believed it. People change. I didn't know the man who found the view of a shotgun muzzle more inviting than the view of his future.

Meg fell silent. My thoughts drifted.

"Can I ask you something?" I said. "What do you remember about the night Henry died?"

Her eyes slowly focused, but she looked confused. "Your brother, Henry? Why?"

"Something Tommy Burke said at the funeral. It made me think of him."

"I don't know." She picked at a thread on her jeans. "I don't remember much. Don't think there's much to remember." She looked away. "It was a long time ago."

"Please. Anything you can think of is fine." She wasn't convinced. "I wasn't here, Meg. I should have been."

"You were away at college," she protested gently. "There wasn't anything you could have done."

"I know." I tried a smile. "But there's part of me that still doesn't believe that. I was supposed to watch out for him. He took it hard when Mom died. Went a little crazy."

She looked at me blankly. "He was always a wild kid. Your mom's death was rough on all of you. But rougher on Henry? Because he was the baby? I don't know. If you ask me, he didn't change much. Just got older. Braver. Dumber." She looked at me and quickly put a hand on my arm. "No offense."

I felt my ears redden. Maybe she was right. So why did the memories still nag at me?

Meg took her hand away. "You remember what Tish used to call him? 'Wild Child.' "

Memories slowly came back to me, incomplete pictures obscured by tendrils of mist. "I used to wonder if half of it wasn't put on just for her."

"He had it bad for her."

"So did half the guys in school."

She cocked her head. "Not you."

I shrugged. "Not my type." I waited a beat, then prodded gently. "So?"

She shifted position, stared at the hands in her lap. "What's the point? After all this time . . ."

"I don't know. Peace of mind? Maybe it's no big deal. I feel guilty that I never wanted to know before. It was bad enough I wasn't here. Figured if I never knew what really happened, it wouldn't feel so bad."

The loose thread on her jeans was getting a workout. "I don't know if anyone knows what really happened." She met my gazed and sighed. "All I know for sure is what I saw. And that wasn't much. Whatever else you've heard is probably a story. And there've been a few of those floating around over the years."

She stared out the window as if conjuring up the memories. "Henry was working that night. A bunch of us went up to the Dairy Mart to hang out. You know how it was. We kept Henry hopping, but I know he enjoyed the company. He always liked it better when it was busy.

"I don't remember how long we'd been there, but most of us had finished eating when Tish and Pete showed up."

"Pete? Where was Lou?"

She shook her head. "I don't remember. Doing something for Dad, maybe. I just remember when we decided to go out he said he couldn't go with us. He was ticked off about it." She paused, saw my face. "You know they always were friends."

"Yeah, but—"

"I know, I know. That's what set Henry off that night. He and Pete had words. They almost got into a fight. Pete shoved a hamburger in his face, and told him to, you know—'ef off.' Got in his car and left. Took Tish with him.

"Next day we heard about the accident. Police said Henry stole Pete's car sometime later that same night, and went for a joyride. Car stalled on the tracks over on Seeman Road. You

107

know the rest."

I rubbed my forehead. "I never got why he didn't try to get out before the train came."

"Maybe he didn't have time."

"Jeez, Meg, I can't believe he didn't see it coming. How much time do you need?"

"Maybe he panicked. Realized there's a big difference between a joyride and totally trashing Pete's car. Maybe he was trying to get it started, move it off the tracks. He was drunk, remember? Who knows what he was thinking? Maybe he passed out. Asleep at the wheel. It's over and done with. You can't bring him back. And you can't blame yourself."

Questions still roiled the surface of my mind like a school of feeding fish.

"He didn't even have a driver's license." It wouldn't have stopped Henry. Nor would the lack of car keys. He'd always shown a keen aptitude for how things worked. Hotwiring Pete's car—a black '68 Chevy Impala SS—would have been no problem.

Meg sighed. "Only the good die young."

I've never seen a guy fall as hard for a girl as Henry did for Tish Miller. I think the crush began around fifth grade. By freshman year, he was flat out smitten. Goo-goo-eyed in love. Enthralled. Acted like a lovesick puppy any time he was within fifty feet of her.

Lou nudged me in the ribs with an elbow. "So what's the deal?"

I looked up from my plate and followed his gaze across the lunch room. "Says he's in love."

Hearing the comment across the table, Elizabeth turned to look. Henry and Tish sat side by side, heads tipped so they touched. His dark, hers light. Yin and yang. She laughed at something he said.

"I think it's disgusting," Elizabeth said, turning back to her food.

Lou snorted. "Love? Come on. He just wants to get into her pants. Like everyone else."

Elizabeth looked at him in shock, fork halfway to her mouth. "You're disgusting, too." She slammed her fork down, shoved her chair back, grabbed her tray and moved to another table. Lou paid no attention, eyes still riveted on the couple across the room. He leaned in and spoke in low tones.

"So what do you think?"

I blinked. "About what?"

He drew back, looked at me. Laughed. Leaned in again.

" 'Tish the Dish.' You know. Think the stories are true?"

"What stories?"

"God, you're thick, Ward. Does she put out or not?"

I swallowed hard. "Hell if I know."

"Well, shit, what does Hank say?"

"He's not talking. You know that." I wouldn't have told him even if Henry had confided in me. Not likely to happen—not too many people you can trust at that age—but he was my brother, after all. "Anyway, I bet the rumors are just bullshit."

He nodded automatically. "She could have her pick of any guy in school. Is Hank hung, or what?"

My face felt hot. "Hey!"

He turned, smile dissolving quickly. "I'm kidding. Jeez, Ralph, get a grip."

"It's that 'Wild Child' shit," I said, still defensive. "She likes that bad boy routine." Fact was, I'd watched Henry make a concerted effort to court Tish Miller. Almost like he had a strategic plan to make sure she picked him over any other guy. Away from her, he was a wild man, a risk-taker. In her presence, he was more romantic than Cary Grant.

109

Lou nudged me again. "Hey, get a load of this."

I rubbed my ribs where his elbow landed. Watched as Pete Anderson approached Henry and Tish. Felt my face grow hot again at the sight of his swagger. Saw Henry's face slowly darken while Pete spoke. Wondered about Tish's detached expression, the faint droll smile, her lack of concern. Felt Lou's arm across my chest like a six-by-six oak beam, restraining me when Pete shoved Henry back into his chair as he tried to stand.

"Wait," Lou whispered hoarsely. "Let it play out."

Henry shoved his chair back and scrambled to his feet before Pete could get close enough. Their voices rose, enough to carry over the lunch room din, but not enough to catch the words. Heads turned and the room slowly went quiet. Henry went toe-to-toe with him. Gutsy for someone six inches shorter and sixty pounds lighter. Boy versus man-child.

"He'll get creamed," I said.

"And he'll hate you for the rest of your life if you even think about it," Lou replied.

Pete punctuated each word with the stab of a finger to Henry's chest, rocking him back on his heels each time. Henry grabbed Pete's finger, twisted it to one side and planted his other hand on Pete's chest, returning the favor.

"Oh, shit," I murmured. "This is going to end badly. I just know it. Jeez, I gotta do something."

Lou patted my knee. "Sit tight. I'll take care of it."

He was halfway across the room before I could stop him. His movements showed no hurriedness, only confidence. Pete's hands clenched and unclenched. It was only a matter of moments before he hauled off and decked my little brother. I sucked in my breath, steeling myself for the blow that Henry would feel. Suddenly, Lou's hand was on Pete's shoulder. Pete turned, surprise turning to anger then slowly melting into an ugly mask of something resembling contempt.

Lou's mouth kept moving. Gradually, some of the tension in their bodies eased. They backed off a half-step. Finally, Pete turned and walked away with a dismissive wave. Lou leaned over the table and said something to Tish. She nodded, didn't reply. Henry sat back down and leaned in to say something, too. She nodded again, but her eyes were on Lou as he made his way back to our table.

Some idiot trying to cut across four lanes of traffic from the Edens Expressway to the Irving Park exit brought me back to the present. Henry had been special. Gifted. Bright. Too smart for a town like Huntley. Not that Huntley didn't have smart people. Just that there'd been no challenge for Henry in a small town like that. Not at his age. So, he'd made his own challenges. Took risks. Did things some people thought were over the top. Like jumping off the school roof with a patio umbrella for a parachute. Or drafting a semi-trailer on his bike out on Rte. 47. Or sneaking up behind a car at a stop sign on his skateboard and hanging on to its bumper when it took off.

But Tommy was right. Henry had known his limits. His risks had been calculated. I wondered when he'd completely lost control. And why.

CHAPTER 11

Emily Alycia sat in my lap turning the pages of a large picture book. She pointed to each picture, earnestly telling the story as if reading the words. I murmured encouragement, snuffing the scent of baby in the fine dark blond hair that hung in loose ringlets from the top of her head. Watching my child grow filled me with delight and a gnawing sense of mortality, as if time had suddenly started hurtling past at breakneck speed. Despite the fact that I finally had roots, a family, the love I'd always yearned for, life still felt like it hadn't begun.

"Busy week?" I asked.

Nell sighed. "You've no idea." She didn't elaborate.

"Everything okay with your client?"

She looked pained, but nodded. "We got through it. No one died." She waved a hand as if brushing away a gnat. Her face lightened, but the wan smile looked forced. "How about you? How was your trip home?"

"Home?" I bounced Emily on my knee. She smiled. "This is home."

Nell's pale skin pinked. "You know what I mean."

"Going back was a little weird after all these years." I gave her a quick summary of the day I spent in Huntley. She nodded in the right places, asked a few questions to be polite. I kept my answers short, sensing her heart wasn't in it. The thread of conversation petered out quickly, leaving only silence.

"You're somewhere else," I said after a moment. "Everything all right?"

She sat straighter, hands placed primly in her lap, looking as though she sat on a thumbtack. "There's no easy way to say this. I'm leaving."

"Leaving?" Nell had once saved me from a madwoman with an ice pick. Now it felt as if she'd shoved cold, hard steel into my heart. "Look, if this is about—"

She cut me off sharply. "No!" Then more calmly. "This doesn't have anything to do with us. My mother is ill."

I blinked. "I'm sorry. I didn't know."

"You didn't ask," she said quietly. "That's the problem."

"Whoa. I did ask. Not directly, maybe. But when I express interest in how your day was, how your week went, don't you think that would be a good time to slip it in?"

"It's not something you just bring up in casual conversation. 'How was your day, dear?' 'Fine, sweetheart. My mother's in the hospital.' "

"Jeez, Nell, it's not as if you've made it easy to see you, let alone talk the past few weeks. Maybe if we lived under one roof it would be easier to find time to tell me something like that."

She didn't waver, but her eyes filled with tears. "I'm not going through this again."

"How can we work it out unless we talk about it? We don't talk because you won't move in. You won't move in unless we're married. You won't marry me because you don't trust me. I can't read your mind. I only know what you tell me."

Emily squirmed on my lap. "Down now, Daddy," she said emphatically. Her rejection deflated me like a punctured tire, heat and anger dissipating into thin air like a breath in a gale. I let her slide to the floor and watched her totter off to play with some toys in a corner.

Several moments passed before I could look at Nell. "Will

she be all right?" I asked tentatively.

She sniffed, swiped away a tear before it spilled down her cheek. "I don't know. That's why I have to go."

"What is it? Do they know?"

"Lymphoma. Non-Hodgkins."

"How long does she have?"

"Who knows? A while, I guess. They say it's stage two, so it's already started spreading."

"But it's treatable, right?"

She nodded, choking back more tears.

"You've known for a while." It explained some of her preoccupation, her distance. Something about us, about me, though, was still the root cause.

"There wasn't anything I could do. There wasn't much sense in flying out until we knew what was wrong. So, we had to wait until she got the results of a biopsy."

"I'm sorry, Nell. I'm so sorry. You should have told me. Of course you have to go." I paused, not wanting to ask. "When do you leave?"

"She starts treatment Tuesday. I have a flight out on Monday."

"Emily . . . ?"

"She's coming, too, of course."

"If you think you'll have your hands full . . ."

"It will be fine." She paused, saw something in my face. "Goodness, I couldn't possibly leave her for that long. Besides, she's never met her grandmother. Who knows how many chances she'll have?"

"You're sure?" I saw her hesitate, then nod. "Do you know when you'll be back?"

"I can't say for sure." She became all business, tears forgotten. "I've already told Marty I'm taking my two weeks of vacation now. Sarah is going to take over bookings and most of my duties. She knows all the clients and how to keep things running. Marty will bring in a temp to answer phones."

"And us?" I had trouble getting the words out.

She didn't answer at first. "It's not forever."

"No, I suppose not. You know I'll be here for you."

Later, long after Emily had been bathed, read to, given good-night kisses, when the two of us fell exhausted into bed, Nell let me hold her. There was still too much unresolved between us to think of making love, but she curled into me contentedly. I felt her slowly go lax in sleep. I lay awake a long time listening to her steady breathing, feeling the regular beat of her heart. We hadn't been this close for weeks. I wondered when we would feel this close again.

"You still talking to me these days?" Brandt's disembodied voice sounded across the patio.

"Just the man I wanted to see, actually." I straightened, looked around, saw him come through the gate. "Get that hose on your way." I pointed to his right.

Wordlessly, he picked up the coiled hose and brought it over. I attached it to a faucet, screwed a nozzle onto the other end and walked to the garage, uncoiling it as I went.

"Grab those buckets, would you?"

Brow furrowed, Brandt did as I asked and ambled slowly after me. My garage originally housed carriages and the horses that pulled them. A cavernous space with high ceilings and dusty, unused coachman's and footman's quarters above, it now contained a mismatched pair of vehicles. Where the bug-like Alfa usually squatted was the small gray rental sedan I'd been driving. Hulking over it was the GMC motor home that had been responsible for my change of career twenty years earlier from modestly successful stockbroker to freelance writer. I'd never regretted the choice. Wondered, on occasion. Never regretted.

"Set them over there." I waved toward the RV, and pushed a button on the wall. Motors hummed overhead and the oversized garage doors slowly rose, curling over the tops of the vehicles. Sunlight spilled into the openings, dispelling gloom and ghosts.

Brandt's curiosity got the best of him. "What are we doing?"

"*You* are washing. I've got maintenance to do."

"And I'll do this thankless scut work because . . . ?"

"You're paying me back for all the tequila and vodka you've drunk out of my liquor cabinet."

He looked like he was about to protest. Thought better of it. Closed his mouth and brought a bucket over to be filled. For the next couple of hours, we immersed ourselves in the work, disinclined to chat when elbow grease and simple companionship were enough. Brandt worked his way around the bus with a step ladder, a bucket of suds and a hose until it sparkled. I flushed and filled the fresh water tank, topped off and recharged the batteries, checked all the fluids, filled the tires to the proper pressure, checked the propane tank.

When Brandt finished, he found me inside cleaning. He tacitly picked up a rag and started in on the small galley. I threw a mixed bag of jazz CDs in the changer—Diana Krall, Al Jarreau, Yellowjackets, Madeline Peyroux—and started polishing, dusting, vacuuming. We worked in opposite directions, trading tools and cleaning solutions as each of us shifted tasks. A couple of times I caught him looking at me curiously, as if he wanted to ask me a question. Each time he looked away as soon as our eyes met.

I finally peeled off the rubber gloves and walked back to the house to get a couple of beers. Brandt had organized the cleaning supplies and thrown the dirty rags into an empty bucket by the time I got back. I passed him a cold bottle. He wiped it across his brow, took a big swallow and sprawled on the couch. I swung one of the captain's chairs around to face him and eased into it.

I raised my bottle. "Thanks."

"Sure. Planning a trip?"

I gave a short nod, too busy sucking down several ounces of cold, amber liquid to talk.

"Fishing?" he asked.

"Figured as long as Nell's going to be out of town, I might as well spend some time out in Huntley."

He frowned. "Proving Nell right?"

"About what? Me?"

"Weren't you the one told me you and Meg were sweet on each other once upon a time?"

"When we were kids. Puppy love. Give me a little more credit. She's happily married. I'm happily committed." I ignored his widening eyes and incredulous look, plowing ahead. "Well, sort of. And that was a lifetime ago. If anything, I'm proving how trustworthy I really am."

"Whatever you say, partner. Just something about you and vulnerable women. And you know how vulnerable a woman can get when someone close has died."

I winced. "Ouch. Below the belt. And I thought you were my friend."

He shrugged. "Friends tell it like it is. They don't pull punches."

"Hey, I'm just going to see what I can find out about Lou." I heard the defensiveness in my voice and sighed. "You don't think I beat myself up enough? I made a mistake. A long time ago. I was hurt, confused, angry. Vulnerable myself, as a matter of fact. It didn't happen again. It won't."

"*I* believe you. Does Nell?"

"I've given her no reason not to. You know that."

"But she knows."

I thought back to the day I'd brought her flowers at the

studio. "Probably. She just doesn't want me to confirm it. Which is fine with me. Water under the bridge."

Three years before I'd stayed too long at a wake for a young woman—a girl, really. Ellen, the runaway. I'd promised Audra, her mother, I'd find her, but she'd been killed before I could. Her death had been as devastating for me in its own way as it had been for Audra. I'd never lost a child like Audra had, but I could empathize with her pain. We found each other that night, recognized a need in each other, comforted each other. Period. End of story. I didn't regret it. But in hindsight, life would have been easier if I'd made a different choice. Nell and I had taken a break of sorts from each other at the time, but no matter what problems we'd had or how I justified it, my night with Audra had been selfish.

I glared at him. "Why are you giving me such a hard time all of a sudden?"

"You're a mite crusty today. Sort of like an armadillo ain't had a bath." He paused for a smile he didn't get. "Just want you to be clear on why you're doing this."

"I don't have any projects right now, and sitting around here moping because I can't be with Nell or my daughter won't do me any good. I might as well see this thing through for Meg. Figured this would be easier than commuting. Cheaper, too."

"You could do the same thing here." The words came out tentatively. "You know, look into what happened to George?"

"You sure you want to go there, partner?" I glared at him. "Besides, what's the incentive?"

He chewed on the question for a while without an answer. Washed it down with beer. "Anything I can do?"

"No. Don't look so forlorn. I'm sure I'll figure out something."

"You're still mad."

"Hell, yes." He flinched. "I'm mad that Nell's leaving. Taking my daughter with her. I'm mad that I'm broke, don't have any prospects and don't feel like doing a damn thing about it. I'm mad that I got myself roped into another one of these no-win situations where nobody comes out happy. But get over yourself, B. I'm not mad at you. I'm done being pissed with you."

Relief crept over his features, but he still sat hunched like a dog expecting another blow. "How long you going to be gone?"

"Long as it takes, I suppose."

"Want me to look in on the place from time to time?"

"That'd be nice."

The yard looked empty, desolate. Not abandoned, for there were signs of life. But old and tired, superfluous. The main lumber shed was gone. Inadequately trying to fill its footprint sat a trailer with a sign above the door that read "Office." The trio of three-sided umbrella sheds lining the perimeter of the property still stood, roofs sagging like sway-back nags. They held pallets of hundred-pound bags of cement mix, mounds of gravel—pea and crushed—stacks of cinderblock. A couple of flatbed trucks idled in the middle of the yard, riding low. Two men traversed from sheds to trucks in funereal procession under the weight of materials they added to the loads. They ignored me as I walked to the office, gravel crunching beneath my shoes.

Inside, a wiry man with a vulpine face stood behind a makeshift counter. I looked around for something, anything, familiar.

"Help you?" He barked the words, reedy voice a match to his mien.

"Lumber yard's gone?"

He didn't answer, expression suggesting I ought to have known better than to ask.

"Any idea where Bill Caruthers went?"

"Retired, I guess." He peered at me, alert. Sensed I was no

danger—no customer, either—and looked down at some paperwork on the counter.

"This your place?" I stepped forward, spotted a small stack of business cards and picked one up.

He looked up, huffed through his nostrils as if catching a scent. "Yep. Bought it three, four years ago."

I glanced at the card—Midwest Concrete Co. "I used to work here. In the lumber yard. When I was a kid." I took a step forward, stuck out my hand. "Emerson Ward."

He looked reluctant, but extended his own. "Chuck Redman."

"You took the main shed down?" My home away from home for two summers. The place that had helped put some money in my savings account and muscle on my lanky teenage frame lifting a ton-and-a-half of building materials a day.

He snorted. "Not hardly. Burned down a couple years ago."

"You're kidding."

He shook his head. "Had it all set up for loading trucks. Lightning, they say."

" 'They?' "

"Fire department." He shrugged. "Probably right."

"Sorry to hear it."

"Life." He attempted a smile that made him just look hungry. "You know anybody needs concrete, though, you tell 'em we do good work."

"Lot of construction going on around town, looks like."

"Sure. We get some small projects here and there."

"Nothing big? Like that shopping mall going up?"

"We put a bid in on it." He raised his palm up, nodded at the window. "The fire put us out of the running. Been trying to rebuild ever since."

"No insurance?"

"Not enough." He shrugged again. "Like I said, life. We're

doing okay. Sorry I couldn't help."

I waved off the apology. "No problem. Good luck with the business." At the door, I thought of another question. "You know who got the contract for building supplies over there?"

He shook his head. "The yard over in Crystal Lake, maybe?" One of the lumber yards Frank used to own.

CHAPTER 12

Meg pulled the big SUV out of the driveway, kids buckled into car seats in the back. I waved from the curb. Dana stared at me blankly, but Todd waggled his arm cheerily. Neither one of them understood why their mother had invited me to visit, nor why I brought my own sleeping quarters. Todd, however, had immediately asked for a tour of the RV when I'd arrived the day before. He thought it was the coolest thing ever, and pestered his mom to get one.

The SUV disappeared around the corner at the end of the block. I unhitched the rental car, stowed the chains, and locked up the RV. Saw a ticket stuck under the wiper blade, tugged it out and stuffed it in a pocket. Wondered when the town had become hard up enough to issue parking tickets.

I could have walked—the day was crystal clear with a softness that promised some warmth later. But I'd already gone for an early run and showered in the tiny head. Afterward, I sat on the banquette eating a banana and cold cereal out of the box while I looked out the big picture windows and watched the neighborhood wake up. Phil had driven off to work a half-hour earlier. I hadn't waved. He hadn't seemed in an amiable mood.

First stop after breakfast, a gas station out on the main drag for a cup of convenience store coffee. Services in town hadn't caught up with the population boom yet. A new supermarket sat across the road from the retirement community. There was an outlet mall next to the tollway, a few other new businesses.

But still no decent coffee. Another five years and there would be a Starbucks on every other corner.

I resigned myself, figuring this early in the morning the coffee might still be fairly fresh. A loud chime sounded as I crossed the threshold. A dark-skinned man a few years younger than me looked up from behind the cash register. He gave me a broad smile full of teeth that looked like they would glow in the dark. I nodded. Pakistani, I guessed. Nearly smacked myself in the forehead when I realized where the guess had come from. Stopped and turned to look outside for confirmation.

Pumps were new, just like the facelift the store had gotten. At one time, though, the gas station belonged to Aazim Ahmed, Sarina's dad. Probably still did. Judging from his age, the fellow behind the counter could be one of Ahmed's sons. Or nephew. Cousin, maybe. Certainly related to the extended family somehow.

Voices emanated from the back of the store. A small older man in a dapper suit almost pushed a younger, much larger fellow in front of him toward the door.

"I don't care if they come in wrappers or not," he said in lilting heavily accented sing-song. "I will not allow that filth in my store. Do you understand?"

He escorted the younger man out the door and walked to the counter. He tugged the corner of a gray brush-cut mustache that stood out from his dark skin.

"Fahd, you must watch him next time he comes in to check the magazine stock," he told the clerk. "It's one thing to sell wine and beer. But I won't have those magazines in the stores. You hear?"

"Yes, Uncle." The clerk's head bobbed.

"Mr. Ahmed," I said. "Hello." He faced me, features fixed in a disgruntled expression. "Emerson Ward. I went to school with Sarina."

He ignored my outstretched hand, saying something in Urdu to the man behind the counter instead. Fahd responded in the same guttural tones, flashing a quick smile at me that looked less certain than his earlier greeting. After a rapid exchange, Ahmed grunted, apparently satisfied, and gave my hand an apathetic squeeze.

"Yes, yes, good to see you." His voice held impatience, not enthusiasm.

I maintained a polite smile. "How have you been?"

"Busy. Very busy."

"Of course. I won't keep you."

He nodded and turned to Fahd, exchanging a few more words of Urdu before he hurried out. Fahd looked at me and shrugged. I headed for the coffee.

The Ahmeds had moved to town in the early '70s, from Pakistan by way of Chicago after the secession of Bangladesh. Sarina was the oldest of the kids. The first ethnic person I'd ever met up close and personal. Ahmed had bought a gas station south of town, going into competition with Elmer's Disco "Gas For Less." A few years later, the place had gone up in flames. Rumor had it that the station had been torched to encourage the "foreigners" to get out of Dodge. Ahmed had stubbornly rebuilt. A matter of pride, since it was his first in a chain of stations across northern Illinois and eastern Iowa.

Sarina and Meg had always been friends. Meg even helped Sarina lose her accent. The girl assimilated into small-town life faster than I had. Good thing, too. Being Meg's friend had been like playing with cobras. Not that Meg wasn't genuine, loyal. Just that I remembered their dad, Doug, being one of the most vociferous bigots I've ever known. The invective that came out of his mouth was pure poison. Meg somehow remained immune. Not Lou.

★ ★ ★ ★ ★

"Get you a soda or something? Punch?" I tugged at the too-tight collar of the rented tux. Wondered if it was obvious the shirt was soaked through with sweat, thankful the lights in the gym were dimmed almost to the point of needing flashlights.

"No, thanks, Ralph." Meg fanned herself with a hand. A few tendrils of red hair stuck to her damp neck. The emerald satin gown with tulle accents made her look grown up. Adult, not sixteen. Definitely the best-looking girl in the crowded room. "Think they could open a window?"

"We could go outside. Get some air."

"Not now. They're about to pass the scepter."

"Dumb tradition," I grumbled.

"Why? I think it's cute."

"The king and queen name successors. So? What if the kids they pick aren't popular next year?"

She glanced at me pityingly, then turned to scan the room.

I leaned in closer so I wouldn't have to raise my voice above the music. "I wish you wouldn't call me that—Ralph."

She swung around, surprise on her face. "Lou does. I didn't think you minded."

I shifted my weight. "I don't. Well, I do, but that's Lou, you know?"

"What? We're not good enough friends?"

"I didn't mean that. Don't be mad. It's just . . . we're a different kind of friends."

Her smooth, freckled face suddenly wrinkled in consternation. "You're not thinking we should try that boyfriend–girlfriend thing again, are you?"

I flushed, turning warmer, if possible. "No, no," I said hastily. "Not after that . . . well, you know."

"Fiasco?" she said, relief flooding her face.

"Your word, not mine."

Meg looked away. "Here comes Sarina," she said.

Sarina wound her way toward us through the throng, Tony Pollastrini in tow. They looked good together, like they'd just come back from a month in Florida. Tony and I acknowledged each other with a nod. The girls immediately started chattering excitedly about the impending ceremony. We stood with our hands stuffed in our pockets, looking around, avoiding eye contact. That would have obligated us to talk. We didn't have to worry.

The crowd to our left parted as if by an unseen force, clearing a path for Lou, Tish and entourage—Pete, Sue Ann, a couple of other guys from the football team and their dates. All smiles, Lou bulled his way between Tony and me, knocking both of us off balance.

"Hey, kids," he said expansively. "Everybody having fun?"

His voice held a note of belligerence. I smelled beer on his breath.

"Yeah, great time," I said.

He looked at Meg and punched me on the arm a little hard to be called friendly. "So, sis, this dude treating you right?"

She frowned. "Of course. Why wouldn't he? It's been fun."

"Should come with us. Dump these losers. You'd have a better time."

Laughter tittered from the group gathered around us. I shifted uncomfortably.

"Yeah, you should come," Tish echoed, nodding at Meg. Then she looked directly at Sarina, face turning to stone. "Not you."

Sarina's polite smile vanished. Tony tensed, a worried look on his face.

Lou shrugged. "No offense." His tone was nonchalant. "We just don't want to smell camel jockey all night."

Anger flashed across Sarina's face, but she quickly replaced it with a smooth mask of composure. "Stupid," I heard her mutter under her breath.

"What's that?" Lou snapped. "You got something to say to me?"

"Lou!" Meg said. "What's your problem?"

"You must be thinking of people from the Middle East," Sarina said politely.

"Whatever." Lou shrugged again. "You're all ragheads."

"Give it a rest, Lou," Tony said angrily. He took a step forward.

Pete and the other guys tensed, their ears perked, faces hungry. Lou ignored them.

"Gonna do something about it, wop?"

I got between them, kept my voice low so the others wouldn't hear. "Don't. Take it somewhere else, Lou. No one here's doing anything to you."

He stared at me, anger twisting his face into something ugly. Adrenaline made my knees tremble. I hoped he wouldn't notice. Two years, even a year earlier, I wouldn't have dared get in his face. But I'd had enough of his intolerance. And the past year had put height and meat on me. I now towered over his stocky five-ten. It made him think twice, even drunk. Something in his eyes relented. It wasn't our friendship. Lou was Lou, but lately he'd been copping this attitude.

"This party's a drag," he said loudly, still looking me in the eye. I didn't blink. Finally, he looked away. "Come on, let's go have some fun."

The boys loosened up. They jostled each other, laughed a little too heartily. Lou started to turn away, but looked at Sarina again. My hackles went up. Tony went on alert.

"You ought to tell your dad to be more careful," Lou said evenly. "Place went up like a Roman candle. If the gas tanks had blown, lot of people could've been hurt. Maybe he should get a station out of town." He paused. "And more insurance." Then tossed over his shoulder, "Or he could just go back to driving a cab."

Heads nodded earnestly, then turned to snickers as they turned to follow Lou out. Tish's lip curled and she threw Sarina one last withering glance.

"Sand nigger," Tish said. She tossed her head and was gone.

I didn't relish a conversation with Tish. But it was time I paid my respects to the widow. I fortified myself with a large gulp of bad coffee, got in the car and aimed it north through town.

Tisha Miller was the wedge that divided my loyalties the year I left. The butt of farmer's daughter jokes among pubescent boys, Tish Miller ended up being my kid brother's first love. The one we all fall for the hardest. Tish the Dish, who came to grade school in worn clothes smelling of manure and slightly sour milk. The girl who had probably worked harder than any other girl in high school to overcome obvious poverty and a hick family and the snippy jealousy over her naturally stunning looks to become one of the most popular, envied, imitated. The one who'd dumped Henry and left him with a broken heart for my best friend Lou.

Just north of the Union Special plant, custom McMansions were going up on big lots back in a grove of trees. One of Lou's small developments. He'd been his own first customer, building on one of the less choice lots closer to town. I turned left off 47, passing a driving range. At the end of a cul-de-sac, the Tudor-style house afforded some privacy. Rolling fields north of the enclave were still vacant, but the privacy might not last for long.

I pulled into the cobblestone drive. The windows of the house were dark, empty, like the sad, mournful eyes of a dog that missed its master. I made my way up a pebbled walk lined on either side by neatly trimmed knee-high hedges. Shaking off a sudden chill, I pushed the bell next to the massive oak front door and waited. My finger hovered over the bell again when the door swung open silently.

"Darling, you know I—" Tish's face hove into view, eyes rounding, smile fading fast. "Emerson."

"Bad time?"

She flushed, shook her head vigorously. "No. Come in."

I hesitated. "You're expecting someone. I should have called first."

"No, really. I wasn't expecting anyone. I just thought you were someone else, is all. Come in." She opened the door wider, as if to show me she wasn't hiding anything. "Please."

I stepped into a two-story entry, floor covered with gray marble. A sweeping staircase curved upward, framed with a lustrous banister, all in a reddish-brown wood, maybe cherry. A polished brass chandelier hung over the center of the floor. The décor, from moldings to subtle artwork, begged a major-domo in a morning coat to make the picture complete, authentic. It all smelled of money. Tish, in stark contrast, was casually dressed in a powder blue velour sweatsuit that matched the color of her eyes, and white crew socks, no shoes. Her hair was pulled back into a ponytail, taking years off whatever age was listed on her driver's license. Soft pearl polish with a hint of pink on her nails and minimal makeup added to the girlish image. The hoodie was unzipped to the bottom of her sternum, revealing flawless skin the color of maple.

"Come on back," she said. Her voice and my footsteps echoed in the large hall.

She led me through a formal living room large enough for several groupings of heavy furniture upholstered in rich fabrics and leather. The adjacent dining room held a table for twelve. Matching chairs, sideboard and breakfront were all in dark walnut with a finish so luminous their surfaces looked liquid. Crystal in the chandelier over the table and behind the glass doors of the breakfront sparkled in the light from a large bay window.

The rooms were immaculate, tasteful, orderly, elegant. Almost as if professionally staged. Set pieces. Beautiful, but cold. Distant. Impersonal. There wasn't a single thing out of place. No family photographs. No open books lying on a side table. No carelessly thrown coat. No dented cushions marking a favorite chair. No sign that the rooms were actually used, lived in.

Tish pushed through a set of French doors. I followed her into a small conservatory lined with plants and small trees in decorative ceramic pots. She stopped next to a chrome and glass cart stocked with expensive liquor.

"Get you something?" She raised an eyebrow.

"No, thanks."

"Suit yourself." She shrugged, picked up a cut crystal highball already full of what looked like orange juice, and settled onto a chaise.

I found a chair. Parked myself without getting too comfortable. "Beautiful house," I murmured.

"Thanks."

"Say, whatever happened to Jimmy Perkins? Wasn't he the one who said he was going to make it big and buy this town?"

A smile crossed her face. "I don't know. I think he ended up moving downstate, selling RVs or something."

We reminisced, trading stories until the silences between them grew long and uncomfortable.

She took a long sip of her drink. "So, you're back," she said. "To what do we owe the honor?"

"I just wanted to tell you again how sorry I am about Lou."

She shrugged indifferently. "For who? Me? Or you?" My

head tilted. "Sorry. It's been . . . difficult."

"I'm sure it has."

"Lou said you're some kind of writer now. Must be pretty good you can afford to take time off like this."

"I guess. The thing about freelancing is you can set your own hours. Things are a little slow right now."

"After all this time you got curious? Had some time on your hands, thought you'd see how well the yokels are getting on?" She smiled broadly, but there was no mirth in the words.

"What's that supposed to mean?"

She waved it away. "What's that they say—you can't go home again?"

"They're right. I'm just visiting." She looked at me with a hint of mockery. I couldn't read what lay behind those blue eyes. "Look, Tish, I really am sorry about your loss. I always wished the best for you two. Looks like it worked out pretty well. Well, until . . . until all this trouble happened for Lou. You were married, what, twenty years?"

She nodded. "Something like that."

I forged ahead. "As for leaving and not looking back, we all make choices. It had nothing to do with Lou, or the two of you, or even what happened to Henry. It was my choice. I couldn't stay. A lot of people are content with that—grow up, get a job, marry. Settle down in their hometown. Nothing wrong with it. Wasn't for me."

"Tell me something new."

I took in the room, the grounds outside. "Doesn't look like a prison to me. Some reason you couldn't walk away? Start fresh anywhere you wanted?"

She shook her head. Smiled. "No regrets here. I stayed. Could I have done better somewhere else? Who knows? Lou loved me. Gave me what I wanted." She rolled onto her side, drew up her knees, propped herself up on an elbow. Hunched a shoulder up

131

near her ear and let it drop. "Lots of people leave. Everyone knew you were out of here after high school. Especially when you got a free ride to college. No problem there."

"But you've got one. After all this time."

She pursed her lips, looked thoughtful. "Not me. I'm happy to see you. You look good. Glad to have a chance to catch up, even under the circumstances. Lou might have had a problem. Not me."

My brows knitted. "Why would Lou have had a problem?"

She looked at me like I was from another planet. "He was your friend." Said like a question.

"He was done with me. And let's be honest, Tish. You never understood why we were friends in the first place. I wasn't one of your favorite people."

She looked me up and down silently. Took a sip from her glass, still appraising me over the rim. Set it on the floor beneath the chaise.

"Amazing how different two people with the same blood can be," she murmured. "You and Hank . . ." She shook her head.

"What about him?" I asked, confused.

"You were always too good for this town," she said softly. "Better than the rest of us. Hank . . . Hank was down to earth. Could have cared less who you were or where you came from."

My ears burned. "Why'd you dump him then?" I asked, unable to come up with the questions I really wanted to ask.

"He was too nice. Beneath all that bad-boy crap, he was just a sweet kid. No ambition. No killer instinct. I wanted more."

She said it so matter-of-factly it had to be the truth.

"Lou?"

"You didn't see it. You were so busy making plans, dismissing the rest of us, you overlooked your best friend. I knew he had potential. Knew he'd be something in this town. So I stuck with him. I wanted to show people like you."

"I . . . I never thought I was better than you," I stammered. "Or Lou. Just different."

She laughed at my discomfort. "You care? Why? What difference could it make what I think of you? We all want to feel like we're better than someone else." She waved her hand. "Look around. You think I have all this to remind me of where I came from? No, it's to remind me of what I never want to go back to. You feel superior. Admit it. You're thinking how glad you are that you didn't marry some cow and end up working at the plant. Nothing wrong with that."

"So, what *is* your problem?"

"Hypocrisy." She stretched languidly, then leaned forward. "That surprises you?"

The front of her hoodie fell open, revealing cleavage and lack of a bra. There was a subtle transformation in her demeanor, the merest suggestion of an invitation. It hung there for a moment between us like a glistening jewel, so preposterously absurd that before it even registered, it vanished. Offer withdrawn. She shifted back, tucking her knees up demurely.

She smiled. "See what I mean?"

"What?"

"Be honest. You wanted to screw me in high school. All the guys did. I wasn't good enough for you, was I? Not then. Not now."

"I'll chalk that up to the grief talking." I couldn't tell if the anger bubbling up inside was because she'd stung my pride or because there was a grain of truth in what she said.

She stared me down. "You never answered my question. Why are you here?"

I unclenched my hands. "For Meg. She's having a hard time dealing with Lou's death."

"*She's* having a hard time." Her voice was bitter.

"Doesn't seem like something Lou would've done. You don't wonder?"

She looked away, reached down for her glass, drained it slowly. Got up and walked to the cart to pour herself another, starting with a bottle of Grey Goose vodka.

"Who knows how someone gets to that point?" she said as she sat down again.

"He was depressed?"

"Wouldn't you be? Spend twenty years building, investing, and lose it all?"

"You're okay, though?" From the surroundings, I guessed so.

"He did everything he could to save the house. For me. To leave me something. I could kill him for doing this, but he had enough pride left to salvage something."

"For you. No kids?"

She shook her head. "Never happened for us."

Her look didn't invite consolation. I fell silent, trying to put myself in Lou's place, wondering what had gone through his head before he filled it with buckshot.

She interrupted my thoughts. "I never told you," she said softly. "I'm really sorry about what happened to Hank. I always thought I was partly to blame somehow."

I searched her face, wondering what had prompted her. A shared sense of loss, maybe. "Were you?"

Her face hardened. She sat up straight, feet on the floor. "No. Don't be such a dick. I just meant I felt bad I broke his heart. Would have broke it anyway. Your brother was the only boy in town who *was* too good for me." She stood abruptly. "Now, if you'll excuse me, I'm in mourning."

CHAPTER 13

Funny how time stands still. Despite its relentless linear march into the future. I let the car cruise aimlessly while I pondered the strange conversation with Tish. Like trying to decipher a Navaho code talker. All that time gone by, yet all that crap, those juvenile resentments and longings and misplaced feelings, still right there beneath the surface. A dormant virus waiting to form sores and pustules and wreak general havoc. Twenty-five years seemed like a long time to balance a chip on her shoulder.

I recognized only the names of roads. Once familiar farm land now was a nondescript maze of subdivisions, golf courses, strip malls, and midrise office buildings. Middle America. The zenith of mediocrity. A homogeneity that makes one suburb indistinguishable from another. Plunked down in a mall parking lot, Sioux City becomes interchangeable with Salt Lake. Maybe that's why so many people get a global positioning system. The rental didn't have one. Migratory instinct somehow guided me back into the center of town.

The view from the bench in the town square between Coral and Main was pure '60s. Any minute, kids in Little League uniforms would roll up to the bandstand on bikes to wait for rides to a game somewhere. A few would stroll across to the drugstore to get a candy bar or bottle of pop. Coaches and parents would pull up to the curb and mill around their cars exchanging the latest gossip. Most were older sedans. Doug Barrett, Lou's dad, drove a pickup. He got a new one every other year. Guys nearly fought each other to ride in the truck bed. My mom always in a Ford Country Sedan station wagon, passed down every year or two from my dad. The grass was never greener, the sky never more brilliantly blue.

Color had returned to the landscape. I couldn't remember when. A Chicago winter, a Midwestern winter, is all browns and grays. Sky, trees, grass, buildings, snow—it's all some shade of dirt. Intimations that the world is more than a palette of earth-tones can occur as early as March. Like the day Brandt had rung my bell. At some point, though, the grass turns green again. Flowers appear. Trees sprout buds that in another month become leaves. The leaden winter sky gives way to blue.

I admired it all. Mourned how quickly the years and youth had flown. I walked across the street to the pub. Found an empty table—not hard since it wasn't yet lunch hour—and took a seat. Jake strolled over before I'd barely gotten settled and set a large iced tea in front of me. He eased into the opposite chair.

"Thanks," I said, surprised.

He grinned. "Too early to start drinking unless you're Jarvis or one of the other old-timers. They're already so pickled it don't make no difference." He watched me take a big swallow. "I see you didn't take my advice."

Try as I might, I couldn't detect any menace in his voice or demeanor. "I don't know. You didn't say don't do it. Just said I might not like what I find."

"And?"

I stared at the glass of iced tea and watched a bead of condensation roll down the side. It disappeared into the fibers of a napkin. "I'm not sure I'm finding anything."

"Guess it would depend on what you're looking for."

I sighed. "Shit, Jake, I don't have a clue. I wouldn't be here except for Meg. And the fact that things aren't that great at home." That last bit slipped out with no chance to censor it.

"Greener pastures?"

"Maybe. There's a lot to be said for simplifying. And there's always that question of what if. What if I'd stayed?"

He shook his head. "Life's not simple no matter where you go. It might be slower here. No less complicated, though."

"I suppose."

He tilted his head, curious. "Meg still sweet on you?"

I flushed. "What kind of question is that?"

He waited me out.

"Hell, I don't know, Jake. What does it matter? She seems pretty happy. And I'm not available."

"Just wondered. Since you wouldn't be here except for her." He smiled faintly, words echoing mine. "Maybe it's the other way around. You still sweet on her?"

I lifted the glass to my lips like a shield, and took a slow sip. Let the cold liquid dampen the heat suffusing my face. Put the glass down.

"Almost made that mistake once. Of course, you know that."

He nodded. It had been Jake who'd inadvertently prevented me from making it—the "fiasco," as Meg had put it. At the end of a home basketball game senior year, Meg impetuously pulled me under the bleachers where we hid until the gym emptied out. Long after the last sounds of people leaving receded, we prowled the halls of the high school hand-in-hand in the dark, whispering and giggling like little kids. Hearts pounding, skipping from room to room.

We ended up on the stage in the auditorium. There was a couch there. Part of a set. We sat. Talked. Kissed, for the first time. One thing led to another until both of us were half undressed. I cupped her breast, feeling the nipple tauten through the fabric of her bra. She groaned.

"We can't do this," I whispered. "Lou will kill us."

"Shut up," she growled. She pulled my earlobe between her

lips, then put her hand on my cheek and turned my face toward hers and kissed me hard. Her other hand slid down my chest, fingers delving under my waistband until they grasped my hardness, making me gasp.

"We should wait," I whispered. "This isn't right."

"I've waited for this long enough."

With fumbling hands, she undid my belt and I rolled her panties down to her thighs. With the awkwardness of the unpracticed, we pawed at each other in our urgency. She shifted her weight under me, inadvertently giving me an elbow in the ribs. I straightened my arms, but couldn't get enough leverage for a push-up with my pants tangled around my ankles and came down on top of her. She grunted, but didn't stop caressing me, pulling at me. We tried again, she guiding my hardness into her until, slowly, it was engulfed in her warm, wet center.

I kissed her gently, holding myself still, urging her to slow down, wanting to savor the feelings running through me, hoping she felt them, too. But the deeper she pulled me in, the more frantically her hips thrust and gyrated under me, her hands and lips moving from one place to another, touching, clutching, teasing. Forced to match her rhythm, I buried my face in her neck and rode a crest of pleasure until she gave a little cry and I felt her muscles clench around my erection, sending me over the edge into rolling spasms of ecstasy that turned my vision black around the edges. I collapsed against her and felt our chests heave, our hearts beating against the bars imprisoning them, staying that way until our breathing gradually slowed.

Suddenly, a voice out of the darkness said, "I hope you guys used protection." Meg stifled a scream. I jumped a foot, then peered wildly out into the dim auditorium while Meg scrambled back into her clothes. Jake sat four rows back on the aisle, staring at us.

Meg and I didn't talk about it for four days, mortified we'd been caught. I worried every waking moment that Lou would find out and kill me for messing with his kid sister. When we finally did talk it out, both of us tried to act as if it had been no big deal. Laughed it off. Treated it like we'd tried to get away with something, but hadn't, something that wasn't worth trying again. Nothing could have been further from the truth. Not for me.

I studied Jake now. I'd always gotten along with him. Liked him, even—all except his disturbing habit of appearing out of nowhere at inopportune times. Like a ghost. For the most part, though, I had more in common with Jake than Lou. We were both basically loners, both a little awkward and geeky growing up. Probably would have been good friends if not for Lou. But Lou had sucked me into his sphere, held me under his influence—leaving little room for others.

"Good thing you're not looking for love," Jake said.

"No, it's this thing with Lou. It just doesn't seem like something he'd do."

"All the same . . ."

"I know, I know. Tough to argue the fact he's dead."

"I can see where it wouldn't be hard," he said softly. His face took on a contemplative look. "There've been a few times I thought of it. If you ever fired a gun you know it's no big deal to pull the trigger. Easy. No more problems."

I snorted. "Easy when you're killing clay pigeons maybe. Not so easy when it's a living being in your sights."

He clenched his jaw, narrowed his eyes. "You're wrong there, bud. It's too damned easy. You never been in combat. Messes you up, how easy it is."

I hadn't gotten drafted and gone to 'Nam like my brother Robbie. I hadn't joined up like Jake. But I'd been in combat. I didn't tell him about the eleven people I once killed on a farm not thirty minutes away. Or about the sweaty nightmares I still had trying to justify the carnage. *Them, or me. Them, or an innocent woman. Them, or the scores, maybe hundreds, who would have died from the drugs and guns they smuggled.* That didn't matter. It still sullied my soul.

He held my gaze. Convinced he was right, I looked away and sighed. "Meg thinks he got screwed somehow, that he was driven to it."

He nodded. Tension eased in his face. "No doubt. But Lou hung himself out there. He took a lot of risks over the years. Most paid off." He shrugged, hoisted himself out of the chair. "Wrong place, wrong time. He got screwed, but that's life, man. I'd let it go."

"Why are you trying to steer me clear of all this?"

"What's the point? It won't bring him back. Even if someone pushed him to it, what're you gonna do? Lou's the one made the decision to check out." He paused. Had another thought. "You keep stirring the pot, something's gonna fly out you don't want to know about. Let it be."

He watched me try to make up my mind.

"Burger?" he asked.

I nodded and held out the empty glass. "Refill, too."

When someone tells you not to do something it just makes you want to do it that much more. It's human nature. But I was having trouble coming up with any other justification for pursuing Meg's fruitless quest. There could be no winners.

Call me stubborn. I gave my word. Figured it couldn't hurt to talk to Tommy again. Maybe find out what, besides a job foreman, made him nervous.

I came prepared this time, dressed in well-worn jeans, flannel shirt, work boots, windbreaker, even an old hard hat a client once gave me after a ground-breaking ceremony. I didn't bother parking in the lot outside the gate. Just drove on through and around to the back lot near where I'd last seen Tommy working.

Masons laid fieldstone facades on the exterior. Inside, I walked past framers putting up walls. Drywallers covered them. Painters finished them off. I saw plumbers hanging fixtures in restrooms, and electricians wiring lights. All just to provide finished space for retailers. Later, other crews would come in to do the build-out for each tenant.

I found Tommy working with one of the framing crews. He stiffened when he saw me, searching the cavernous space behind me. He turned back to the job, head bowed as if he hoped I hadn't noticed him. I frowned and changed direction, aiming for a small hallway on the other side of the framed wall Tommy worked on. I walked a couple of steps past and looked up toward the ceiling, jotting scribbles on a clipboard as if inspecting something.

"What gives?" I said quietly, risking a quick glance between the studs before craning my neck again at the ceiling.

"Get outta here," he said under his breath.

"What's going on, Tommy?" I murmured.

"You're trouble." He looked up and glanced around the center of the space, refusing to look at me. "Now get the hell out of here before you cost me my job."

I frowned at a bunch of wires dangling from the metal frame of the dropped ceiling. "Why? Who thinks I'm trouble?"

"I don't know. You just are. Now, please go." There was no mistaking the desperation in his voice.

I scrawled my cell phone number on the clipboard. "You've got something to tell me. Something you wanted to say last time I was here. Call me."

I ripped the paper off the clipboard and wadded it up, then walked past him, eyes front. Without breaking stride, I tossed the wadded paper on the floor in a pile of sawdust and wood shavings near the spot where he was working. I scanned the work space. No one paid me the slightest attention. Just in case, I walked out into the sunshine without looking back.

I hadn't been inside more than three minutes altogether, but the encounter had wound me as tight as a Tag Heuer watch. So, when I saw Tommy's supervisor standing next to a panel truck parked at the curb busting some kid's chops, I considered letting loose on the guy. Stood there debating what to do and remembered the panic on Tommy's face. I lowered my head and turned to walk the other way.

"Hey you!"

I pretended not to hear.

"Smart guy!"

I stopped.

"Yeah, you!"

I did a slow turn. Watched as he hitched up his pants, put some swagger in his stroll. He squinted, nodded in self-confirmation, stopped an arm's length away. He rolled a plug of tobacco from inside one cheek to the other and spat. Eyeballed the hardhat on my head then looked me in the eye.

"Nice hat," he said. "Got a site pass? No? Didn't think so." He took a half-step closer, balled the fingers of one hand. "Not as smart as I gave you credit for, are you? Let me spell it out. Get. Your. Ass. Off. The. Property."

"That's it? What, no threat?" My body thrummed with tension, waiting to be sprung.

He went purple, cords of his neck standing out in relief. "Look, asshole, don't make this worse for yourself. You want to make this hard, we can do it your way."

It was tempting. I craved the release. I felt my hands clench and unclench. A golf cart entered my peripheral vision. The supervisor's gaze never left my face. As the cart drew abreast the driver slowed, then swung it to the curb and stopped. The driver leaned over and called out.

"Problem, Gif?"

"Nothing can't be handled," the man in front of me replied, still eyeing me grimly.

The driver of the cart sat up and took the wheel. Reconsidered and stepped out instead. He walked up slowly, gaze taking in, first me, then Gif.

"You got some crews to check on?" He put enough authority in his voice to get Gif's attention.

Gif pulled his eyes off me with a look of distaste. He opened his mouth. Had second thoughts. Shut it.

"I got this, Gif," the man said quietly.

He nodded. "Sure thing, Mr. Jones."

We watched him go. I took in Jones's tailored slacks, loafers, pressed shirt and silk tie under a partially zipped windbreaker. A hard hat was the only nod to his surroundings. He faced me.

"Not a happy man," he said.

"Didn't mean to upset him."

"Unhappy in general," he said. "Could probably use some anger management therapy." He eyed me. "And you are?"

"Old acquaintance of Pete Anderson's."

He smiled wolfishly. "Which tells me nothing."

I shrugged. "I grew up with Pete and some of these other guys. Haven't been back in years. Name's Ward. And you?" I put out a hand.

He looked at it like he wasn't sure what to do. Shook it finally. "Jim Jones. I rep the union on this site."

I flashed him a lopsided grin. "Like I said, I've been away. I was just taking a look around. Guess that seems to be a problem."

"Pete didn't give you a site pass?"

"I didn't want to bother him. He's a busy guy."

He shook his head. "It's a closed site. You don't have business here, you shouldn't be here. Should have gotten a pass."

Michael W. Sherer

"Sorry. Now I know."

He hesitated, then dipped his chin. "Next time. Meanwhile, you best take a hike."

"Sure." I hesitated, tried to look contrite. "So, what's the big deal, anyway?"

He started to wave me off, then relented. "You know—insurance companies, liability. Bad enough a worker gets hurt on the job. We don't need a lawsuit from someone off the street."

"I see what you mean. Got enough problems, huh?"

His brow furrowed.

"I heard you guys went on strike. Hey, I'm all for it. I think these guys should get a fair day's pay for the work they do. Country's losing too damn many jobs." I paused, saw him nod in agreement. "I imagine everyone's just being extra careful now?"

"Yeah, they are." He drew himself up, looking self-important. "It wasn't just about the money, though—the strike. We had some concerns about safety. It's why the tough visitors policy."

"Safety? Like what?"

"Nothing big," he backpedaled. "Little stuff. But it added up. Wages were part of it. We just thought we ought to get an official okay from the village on a few points before we put men back on the job."

I nodded to hide my confusion. "Sure. Makes sense. Hey, I wouldn't want to mess things up. Sorry about the screw-up."

" 'S okay." He tried to look stern again, made his voice sound gruff. "Just make sure you get cleared next time."

"I'll be sure to do that."

He walked with me as far as the cart. I felt his cool gaze on me all the way out to the lot.

CHAPTER 14

Evening tucked the town in under a blanket of twilight the color of blueberries. Stars sparked to life. Without a fleecy cloud cover, the day's heat quickly dissipated, leaving the air cool enough to chill a beer glass.

An afternoon of driving around had raised more questions than it had answered. Change was everywhere. Even the anachronistic view from a park bench downtown. The old bandstand was now a gazebo, though it looked pretty much the same. Construction crews had broken ground on a new administration building east of town to replace the old brick town hall overlooking the square. The high school had moved to a big new campus west of town, and three or four new elementary schools had sprung up around town, plunked down in close proximity to new curved rows of tract houses. There was a new aquatic center, a recreation center and a new library.

It wasn't a little town in the country any longer. More like a giant jigsaw puzzle waiting for developers to fit subdivisions, office parks, retail stores into the holes. Blank spots of farmland. Good earth, where people had once taken pride in growing things. All slowly being transformed, assimilated, covered over by suburbia. Clean streets. Uniform houses. Grass lawns. Progress.

The house I wanted stood at the edge of the golf course on the north side of town, with windows brightly lit. The golf course had been on the outskirts of town when it was built. I must have been in junior high at the time. Now it felt small, squeezed on all sides by housing developments. It seemed like yesterday. Even houses built then were razed to make way for the new. Or more asphalt. Duplexes half my age along Algonquin demolished to widen the road.

I knocked softly on the door, part of me hoping no one would answer. I started to turn, hesitated, changed my mind too late. Rachel swung the door open, bathing me in light. She looked me up and down, face impassive.

"Mom, Uncle Emerson's here!" Her gaze never left my face. Her eyes showed only the barest hint of curiosity, the way she might watch a fly buzz lazily against a screen door.

Elizabeth appeared in the lighted rectangle wiping her hands on a dish towel. "What are you doing here?"

I wondered if my skin had turned green or I'd suddenly sprouted horns. "Is Harry around?"

She shook her head. "He's at a village board meeting. I expect him any minute, though."

I waited. Rachel looked at me, then her mother.

Elizabeth started, as if struck by an idea. "Why don't you come in and wait for him? I'm sure he won't be long."

"Thanks." I stepped inside.

Rachel rolled her eyes. The door closed behind me and she flounced past me, disappearing into the house.

"Come on back," Elizabeth said. "The kids will be heading for bed soon. And I'm not eating 'til Harry gets home."

She led the way to a large, bright kitchen. Harriet sat at a table in a breakfast nook on one side. French doors beyond led out into the darkness. Distant lights silhouetted trees out on the golf course. Harriet gave me a big smile, upper lip covered in milk, a plate with cookie crumbs in front of her.

"Hi, there." I waved. She waved back.

Elizabeth used the bib tied around Harriet's neck to wipe her mouth, then removed it and set it on the table. She cleared Harriet's plate and cup.

"Rachel!" she called, walking the dishes to the sink. "Come get your sister." She turned to me. "Get you something? Soon as I put these in the dishwasher, I'm having a glass of wine."

"Beer, if you've got it. Thanks."

She frowned. "I think so."

I looked around while she opened a bottle of wine, poured a glass and rummaged through the refrigerator for a beer. Rachel silently glided into the room with a glum look and helped Harriet down from her chair. Taking her hand, Rachel gently led her out. Harriet gave me a parting smile. I returned the favor and mouthed the word "thanks" to Rachel. Elizabeth ignored them both.

"Nice house," I said, taking the bottle she handed me.

She sat at the breakfast table. "You've been here before."

I shook my head. "Actually, no." I slid into the chair Harriet had vacated.

"Of course you have," she asserted. "You must have."

"The funeral was the first time I set foot in this town since I left for college."

"But we've seen each other lots over the years."

"I wouldn't exactly call it lots," I said wryly. "Usually at Robbie's. Once or twice at Will's."

She shook her head. "I can't believe you've never been here."

"Never had an invitation."

Her gaze could have withered flowers. "Oh, please. You're here now. And I don't remember inviting you."

That was the thing about Elizabeth. She may have meant well, but it rarely came out that way. "How do you know Harry didn't invite me over?"

"You know what I mean. Fact is, you never should have left in the first place."

I couldn't hide my surprise. "Why?"

"Your family is here."

"Excuse me? Who's here? Not Robbie. Not Will. Henry's dead. So's Mom. Long time, too. What I wonder is why *you* stayed."

Her eyes flashed with anger. "Someone had to. Someone had to take care of Dad. And Henry. I didn't see you stepping up. Or Robbie. Or Will." She waved her arms in emphasis, sloshing wine on her hand that dripped onto the table. She set the glass down hard enough to spill a little more. She roughly wiped her hand on the towel slung over her shoulder, as if annoyed at the imposition.

"Who do you think took care of all of us after Mom died?" she went on. "Who cooked and cleaned and did laundry?" Her face reddened and saliva bubbled at one corner of her mouth.

I looked up at the ceiling. Let loose a breath. "Christ, not this again."

"Not what?" She thrust her chin forward. "Not *what?*"

I met her gaze, shook my head slowly. "Don't be such a martyr. You weren't the only one helping out. We all did, Elizabeth. I can't believe you're singing this same old song after all these years."

"Help?" Her voice turned shrill. She shook a finger in my face. "Help? Did you ever once do a load of laundry?"

I snorted. "Hell, yes. You wouldn't touch any of our socks or underwear, if you recall."

"Well . . . I . . ."

"Shake that finger in my face one more time and I'll break it off."

She looked at her finger. Dropped her hand into her lap and stared at me, jaw clenched.

"I washed all my own clothes," I went on quietly. "Did you ever mow the lawn? Take the garbage out to the dump? Wash the windows? Fix the fence? Paint the barn? At least we helped cook and clean once in a while. I never saw you doing any of those other chores, so don't go giving me this crap about how you took care of the Ward family after Mom died."

"I worked just as hard—harder—than all of you."

"Saint Elizabeth. What, so you could prove that you're better than us?" I swallowed my disgust. "And you stayed because . . . ?"

"I'm not the one who ran out on the family," she said coldly. "I've got more principles than that. Something maybe you never had—a sense of loyalty."

"Don't make me laugh. There was no family left to run out on. Robbie was long gone. Will was gone, too, at college. Who were you staying for, Elizabeth? You think going out to the cemetery once in a while is supposed to make the rest of us feel guilty? Like you're the only one who cared about Mom? Or Henry? The only one who missed them? Jesus, give it a rest."

Bitterness sat like chicory on my tongue. My stomach knotted and my head ached as all the old feelings roiled my psyche like a chuck in a meat grinder.

"You know exactly why I stayed," she said primly. "I was needed here. I bet you haven't even seen him yet, have you?"

I knew who she meant. She wouldn't let it go. A twinge of guilt suffused my face with heat. I pushed it aside. "No, but that's beside the point. He didn't need any of us."

She twisted her face into an ugly sneer. "You don't belong here," she said quietly. "I don't know why you came back."

I raised my hands. "Now you want it both ways? I give up. I never should have left, but I never should have come back."

She crossed her arms. "No, you shouldn't have left. But you did. And now you don't belong. This isn't the place for you anymore."

I shrugged. Let go of the anger. Felt my chest ease. "Never

was. We all have to go out and find our own place in the world. Maybe yours is here. Not mine." I paused. "Maybe you forgot that you didn't belong here once, either. We moved here. We weren't one of the founding families here, like Danny DeHaan's. We were uprooted. Transplanted."

"This place suits me just fine, thank you."

"I like it, too, Elizabeth. Or I did growing up. It just wasn't where I wanted to spend the rest of my life. I wanted to explore. See new things. Find my own way."

She looked down at the table. "Whatever," she mumbled.

"Right. Whatever." Less than ten minutes with her, and it was like I'd never left. I remembered why I had, though. "What's with all of you, anyway? It's like you're all stuck in a time warp. You all think I don't belong here. What about the seventeen, eighteen thousand people who've moved in since I left? They belong here? And I don't?"

"They want to be here." She thrust out her chin again. "They want small-town life. Good schools. Safe neighborhoods."

"It's not a small town anymore, Elizabeth. It's a suburb. Like Schaumburg or Mount Prospect. You can't tell me you're happy about all the growth. Aren't these people messing up everything you stayed for?"

Her eyes narrowed. "No," she snapped. "They move here because they have the same values we do."

"They move here because houses are cheaper here."

"At least they're not stirring things up."

My mouth fell open. "That's what's bugging you? I'm upsetting the apple cart?"

She flushed. "Bad enough your friend splattered his brains all over his wife's wallpaper. You have to come back and ask why? You couldn't leave well enough alone?"

I studied her, wondering why fear lurked behind her anger.

"What am I going to find, Elizabeth? A few rotten apples in the cart?"

"No. That's not what I meant." Flustered, she struggled to gain the upper hand again. "It's just so pointless. All you're doing is making people angry and turning more of them against you, if that's possible."

"I don't care what people think."

"I do. And I have to live here. Why do you always have to spoil things for me?"

"My life's purpose, Elizabeth. That's why I've been gone all this time. Easier to mess up your life."

The sarcasm slid off her Teflon defenses. She gulped down half her wine and sat up straight, as if the liquid courage had hardened in her spinal column.

"I—we've worked very hard to make a difference here," she said, forcing calmness into her voice. "We're respected here. Harry at the bank, of course, and the village board. I have the women's league—I'm president now, you know. And the PTA board. And the church auction. I'm not going to let you ruin all that."

"If you're that important, how could I? I'll be gone soon enough. Like you said, I don't belong here. Ignore me. Do what you've always done—act like I came from another gene pool."

Her mouth set in a grim line. It didn't intimidate me.

"What are you going to do, anyway? Run me out of town?"

"Don't tempt me," she said sharply.

I squelched an impulse to push a little harder, see what it would take to make her boil over. I wondered, instead, what she had in mind. And suddenly realized it made no difference. I shook my head slowly.

"I'm not doing this anymore."

"Doing what?" Her jaw still jutted in a bulldog scowl.

"This." I motioned between us. "I'm done. I stayed away all

these years because of this. I'm not your competition, Elizabeth. You say you've got what you want. I'm glad. I'm no threat to you or your way of life. I never was. I don't want the same things you do. So I'm not going to play this game anymore."

"What are you talking about? What game?"

"I don't know what I ever did to make you think I have it in for you, but everything's a competition with you. If I've got a cold, you've got the flu. If I've got the flu, you've got pneumonia. Bigger, more, better. You always have to be the best."

"Well, you're the one that always—"

I held up a hand and cut her off without a word.

"I never cared," I went on. "I don't know why I let you suck me in."

"Me?" Her nostrils flared. "I'm not the only one. You have no idea what it was like."

"Being the only girl?" The momentary surprise in her eyes said I guessed right. "No, I don't. But I know what it's like to have older brothers. It doesn't make any difference. Robbie was always better at figuring out how things work. Will always got better grades. Someone's always going to be better at something. It never mattered to me. I just wanted to be accepted on my own terms. I couldn't do that here."

She considered me warily. "So, what are you saying? Why are you back?"

"I'm saying I'm not going to take the bait anymore. I'm not going to let you push my buttons, and I'm not going to push yours. We're not kids anymore. If we can't get along, then we don't have to see each other."

"I didn't ask you here." Her eyebrows arched in indignation.

I sighed. Let it go. It would have been like grenade fishing. Too easy, but there's always the danger of blowing a hole in your own boat. I curled my fingers around the beer bottle and watched the tiny bubbles rise to the top.

"I better get going," I said.

Elizabeth looked away and said nothing. I pushed my chair back and stood.

"You don't have to go on my account," she said. "Harry will be home any minute."

"That's okay. I'll stop by the bank tomorrow."

"What did you want to talk to him about, anyway?"

"Business," I said. I knew better than to give her anything she could use as ammunition.

"It's about Lou, isn't it?" Her face looked as if she'd eaten a slug.

"You seem to know everything that goes on here. What do *you* know about Lou?"

Her eyes narrowed. "Lou Barrett was a pig. A rude, arrogant, mean pig. He got what he deserved. I can't believe you were his friend."

"What do you mean 'he got what he deserved'?" A flicker of anger ran through me. Lou and I weren't friends, but once upon a time we had been.

She looked flustered. "I . . . He . . . he brought this all down on himself, Emerson. This was all his doing, no one else's."

"What was?" I waited, but she clamped her jaw. "We all get what we deserve in the end, you know." I pushed away from the table and left her grimly clutching the wine glass in both hands like it was her last friend.

CHAPTER 15

Sleep was elusive. Not just because the bed in the bus was too short. More from vagabond thoughts, restless gypsies that wandered through the carnival funhouse settings in my head. Bouncing from reenactments of old family scenes to replays of recent conversations. Puzzling over past slights and present predicaments.

It might have had something to do with the short phone call to Nell before turning in. The worry and exhaustion in her voice that said more about her mother's condition than any words could. Or the frustration I couldn't keep out of my voice when she had no answers to questions concerning us, our future, even when pressed. The cheery sound of my daughter's excited voice telling me about her adventures. The yawning pit of loss and sadness that opened up inside me at the thought of how much I was missing, how much I missed her.

Maybe it was the confusion that had skewed my sense of place, of self. As if Alzheimer's had bubbled through my head like gas through Swiss cheese, leaving holes of nothingness. *Where am I? Why am I here?*

My eyes snapped open at four-thirty. I closed them, but sleep quit playing hide-and-seek and fled for good. I lay there turning over tendrils of thoughts that had drifted through my dream-scape, looking for ones that would fill the gaps, answer the questions. After half an hour of fruitless searching I gave up, swung my feet over the edge of the bed, and pulled on shorts,

T-shirt, socks and shoes. Topped it off with a light windbreaker and a baseball cap to avoid scaring early risers with a bad case of bedhead.

The faint sound of traffic, the rush of a passing car or rumble of a big rig down-shifting on the way through town, punctuated the quiet. I ran with no purpose, just a hope of emptying my head and exorcising whatever had bedeviled my sleep. I slowly worked my way out of town toward a lightening sky. Chugging steadily if not quickly down Huntley-Dundee Road, I saw houses give way to empty fields not yet earmarked for development. A mile down, they ended abruptly at the edge of more subdivisions spreading out on both sides of the road. I cut through one, sticking to its main street so I wouldn't get caught in its maze. It emptied out onto Kruetzer. I turned west and circled back as the sun came up.

A cruiser sat double-parked next to the motor home when I turned the corner. I pulled up, chest heaving, catching my breath. No flashing lights, and no sign of anyone inside. The motor burbled softly, small puffs of exhaust dissipating quickly even in the chill air. I walked slowly down the block and waited until I was abreast of the cruiser before crossing the street. Coming up on his blind side wouldn't be smart.

"Morning," I called when I finally spied the cop.

He stood in front of the bus, one foot on the bumper, pen poised over a pad on his knee. His head jerked up at the sound of my voice.

He nodded. "This yours?" He aimed the pen at the bus.

"Sure is. Problem?"

He turned back to the pad on his knee, scribbled something and tore off the top sheet. "You might say." He handed me the ticket. "You live here?"

"Visiting." I looked him up and down, discreetly. His craggy face wasn't unhandsome despite being pitted with acne scars.

155

Though beefy from the shoulders down, the weight of the gear on his belt nearly pulled his pants down over narrow hips. A shock of black hair stuck out in places. Graying temples and lines around the eyes suggested he was in his early fifties. He looked vaguely familiar, like a character actor in a film seen too long ago.

"Folks you're staying with should've told you, we've got a parking ordinance here. No parking on the street from two to six." The voice suited him. Deep and resonant, with a slow drawl that reminded me of The Duke.

I grinned ruefully, and shrugged. "Sorry. Didn't know."

He held up the pad. "Figured. This is your second."

"It's kind of big to fit in the drive. I thought it would be okay out here on the street. Now I know."

He hesitated. "Well, here's the thing. It's kind of a double whammy. You have to have a special exemption to park an RV like this in town. Has to be behind the house, on hard pavement."

I stared at him for a minute while it registered. "Guess I have to move it, huh?"

He nodded and walked to the cruiser, pausing with a hand on the door. "That would be the smart thing. Better move that car, too." He jerked a thumb over his shoulder at the rental sedan. "I let it go when it was hitched to the RV. Not this time." He shrugged. "Triple whammy."

A notion to ask Meg to pay the tickets flitted through my head. I pasted some semblance of pleasantry on my face, having to work at it.

"Thanks, officer."

"That would be 'Chief' to you."

"My apologies, Chief . . ." I took a step and squinted at his name tag—R. Tate. Looked again at the vaguely familiar face. "Tate. Randall? Randy?" Another ghost from the past. One of my oldest brother's friends. Never would have pegged him for a cop.

He frowned.

"Emerson Ward. You probably don't remember." I caught a pass from him with my nose in a neighborhood game of touch football when I was eleven. Stung like hell, but hadn't dissuaded me from playing the game.

His expression lightened. "Sure. Robbie's kid brother. Should've guessed. You're the one asking questions about Lou Barrett."

I froze, but didn't hear any animus in the words. "Hope it's no problem."

"Long as you don't harass anyone, no skin off my nose. I get any complaints, that's a different story."

I nodded. "Fair enough." I looked at the ticket pad in his hand. "You on patrol? Or just on your way to work?"

"Patrol." He sighed. "Got a man out 'cause his wife just had a baby. I offered to pull third watch for a few days. Keeps my hand in."

I hesitated, then figured it couldn't hurt. "What's your take on it?"

He looked startled. "Barrett's death? Damn shame, that's what."

"You investigated?"

"Have to." He paused. Tipped his head to look at me, tapping the car roof with his thumb. "Not much we can do except process the scene. Body goes to the morgue up in Woodstock. Everything else goes to the state crime lab in Rockford."

"Anything make you think it wasn't what it looked like?"

He frowned again. "I appreciate what you're trying to do for Barrett's family. Like I said, long as I don't get complaints—and you pay your parking tickets—I'll give you a little leeway. I got enough to do. But unless you got an investigator's license,

157

you watch where you go with your questions."

He looked me up and down to see if the message was sinking in anywhere. "Robbie says you're pretty good at this sort of thing," he went on softly. "Don't look so surprised. I'm always thinking. I hear you're back in town poking around, I'm going to find out why. It's my job." He let that sink in, too.

"Gun Barrett used was a Remington Eight-Seventy Express twelve-gauge. Shell was a Federal Power Shok F-One-Two-Seven with number-four shot. Probably a magnum load. No fingerprints on the gun or the shell but his. Gun was in his hands. Blood spatter supports that. Wife and friends all say he was pretty down about losing out on that shopping mall deal. Suicide's a good bet."

He turned and pulled the car door open. Slid in, closed the door and pulled the gearshift into drive. The window slid down with a hum. He leaned out.

"You a hunter?" he asked. Saw me shake my head.

I grew up learning to shoot—rifles, shotguns, pistols—how to carry them, clean them, respect them. The only thing I ever enjoyed hunting was clay, when we set up the trap on an old wagon out behind the house. Yelled "Pull!" and blasted away.

He went on. "What I'm thinking is, Barrett was a deer hunter. So, why'd he load his deer rifle with birdshot?"

He didn't wait for an answer.

My brother-in-law Harry's guard dog buzzed him to see if he had a few minutes for me. She hung up and gave me a sour look.

"You can go on up," she said. Her tone said she thought it was a misguided idea. Whether she disapproved of me or Harry, I couldn't tell. Me, I decided. The lack of formality, the fact that he hadn't kept me waiting, suggested Harry wasn't eager to let people know our association and wanted to get rid of me quickly. It could be the visit with my sister colored my take.

Harry looked up from his desk when I knocked on the open door. "What can I help you with? Something quick, I hope."

"Sorry. I stopped by last night so I wouldn't bother you at the office."

He waved it away. "Elizabeth told me. Just have a lot on my plate today. What is it?"

I perched on the edge of a chair in front of his desk. "I wanted to know a little more about the mall deal. How the financing works."

He *tsked* and looked at his watch, clearly annoyed. "Could we do this another time? Finance One-Oh-One would just take too long."

I waved my hands. "I don't need the whole course, Harry. Just tell me how the payouts work."

His look turned quizzical. "Payouts? To the architect, contractor, that sort of thing?" I nodded. "Pretty simple," he went on. "The loan agreement stipulates when draws are taken, usually when certain criteria are met. Sometimes the payments are made directly to suppliers. Usually, the bank lets the developer draw against the loan. The developer pays the general contractor, who then pays the subcontractors. But it's all based on things getting done. The architect, for example, doesn't get paid when plans are approved, but when permits are issued. Tighter control that way. Subs like electricians and plumbers don't get paid until the work is inspected. That answer your question?"

I thought for a moment. "Yeah, that helps. By the way, I heard one of Frank's old yards got a contract for lumber and materials."

He nodded. "Milt Seeger."

"That's who bought Frank out? What about Bill Caruthers?"

"Milt does more volume," he said with a slight shrug. "I assume he's got more purchasing leverage. Bill had pretty much retired anyway." He touched a finger to his temple. "Started forgetting things. It was time. Anyway, Milt's a good man."

I pondered that. "One other quick thing," I said. "You never mentioned the strike."

"What about it?"

"Did it start before or after Lou's cash flow problems?"

"I don't remember." He looked at me impatiently. "After, now that I think about it. Work slowed down. The project wasn't hitting its deadlines. I heard there was talk of a strike. When it finally happened, we were already about to foreclose."

"Pete Anderson said it was about money. You ever hear any other complaints?"

He frowned. "Like what?"

I shrugged. "Unsafe conditions? Improper materials?"

He shook his head slowly. "Nothing like that. Why? What did you hear?"

I gave him a puzzled look. "Nothing. Just curious. Fifty cents an hour doesn't seem worth walking off the job for. A grand a year?"

"Not to me and you, perhaps," he said.

I looked out the window. Rubbed my chin and turned my gaze back to him. "I take your point."

"Anything else?" He looked at me expectantly.

I got up. "No, thanks. I'll let you know if I think of something."

He nodded and bent his head to the papers on the desk.

I found a bench with a view of the post office in the park across the street. The sun was warm, but a brisk spring breeze stripped it away. It might make it into the sixties, but wind-chill made it feel like March. I glanced at my watch and folded my arms across my chest to hold in some body heat. It wouldn't be long. The man was like clockwork, if memory served.

Within five minutes a tall, white-haired man with a slight stoop walked into the post office. I took a deep breath, rubbed the tense muscles in my neck, steeled myself. Got off the bench and willed myself across the street. I stopped just inside the door and let my eyes adjust. Spotted him sorting mail on a table in front of the rows of lock boxes.

"Hello, Frank," I said, walking up to him. "I thought I saw you come in here."

He looked up, a smile spreading across his face. "Emerson. The rumors are true."

He put out his hand. His grip was still fiercely strong. Up close, he looked even older than when I'd seen him in the cemetery. But he looked healthy, vibrant. Of course, a good tan could hide a lot of ills.

"Nothing bad, I hope," I said.

"No, just that you were in town."

"Good to see you. You look well. Traveling?"

He rolled his eyes. "Some. Not as easy as it used to be. Don't believe what they say about golden years. Getting old's no fun."

"It looks like you're managing it gracefully."

He flushed, looking angry for a moment, as if uncomfortable taking the compliment.

"Nothing graceful about it, just a pain in the rear when things don't work like they used to," he said, sounding more like the Frank I knew. As if reading my thoughts he put a smile back on his face. "What about you? I hear you're a father now."

I nodded. "A little girl. Just two. She's amazing."

"That's great. Really. About time. So, you around for a while?"

"A while. I'm not sure how long." I sensed his impatience. Not two minutes of conversation and already we were running out of small talk.

"I'm sure I'll see you before you go. Where are you staying?"

"I've got a big RV I brought along so I wouldn't have to impose on anyone."

He couldn't hide his surprise. "Business must be good."

My laugh sounded more like a bark. "I've had it for twenty years. It's practically an antique."

"It must come in handy."

I shifted my weight, licked my lips. Now or never. "It does, but I've got a small problem. Maybe you can help."

His face reflected disappointment, anger, disdain, even a certain dread before he walled it all off with a pleasant mask. "What is it?"

"I'm not supposed to park the RV on the street in town. I wondered if I could park it out at your place. I'll stay out of your way, I promise."

"Is that all?" He waved it off. He'd expected worse. "There's plenty of room."

"You're sure?"

"This isn't complicated, is it? You're just parking the damn thing, right?"

I sighed, willing away the tension that knotted my stomach. "No, it's not complicated. Yes, I'm just parking it. It would help if I could run an extension cord to the house. Or the barn. I'll pay for the utilities."

"Don't be stupid. You need to plug the thing in, well, then, plug it in."

"Right." I shifted my weight again. "You mind if I bring it out this afternoon?"

"Suit yourself." He looked away, started gathering his mail.

"Thanks. I've got a few things to do. Maybe I'll see you this afternoon."

He looked up. "You know where everything is if I'm not around." I nodded, started to turn when he said, "Good to see you, son."

I glanced back, trying to read him. Gave up trying to decide if he meant it, but tipped my head anyway before leaving.

Village Hall was within spitting distance, at least in this wind. I headed there next. Through a reception window in the wall just inside the door I saw a large open office area with four desks. Two were occupied. A woman seated closest to the window looked up when I approached.

"Can I help you?" she said.

"I hope so." I gave her a big smile. "How are you today?"

She stood and rounded the desk. "Not bad. Thanks for asking."

"Enjoying this sunshine?"

"I'd enjoy it more if I was out in my garden." She smiled and winked. "What can I do for you?"

"I'm thinking about making some improvements around the house. I wanted to find out what I need a permit for, how I get one, that sort of thing."

"You came to the right place," she said. She turned to a stack of cubbyholes on the wall next to the opening and pulled out several pieces of paper. She slid the forms across the counter and pointed to the top one.

"So this basically tells you what you need to know," she said. "It tells you about the process and what types of things you need to get a permit for. Then these are application forms for permits, and inspection forms once the work is done."

"Great. Thanks." I turned the wattage up on my smile. "All the building you've got going on in town must keep you busy."

"I'll say."

"Must have a lot of building inspectors to cover all that ground."

"Not hardly enough."

I gave her a worried look. "That won't slow things down, will it?"

"Oh, no," she said hurriedly. "We have enough. They just complain a lot about all the work. We have, what, six or eight now. Right, Connie?" She threw that last over her shoulder. The woman behind her murmured agreement without looking up from her desk.

I pretended relief. "That's good. Say, you know who the inspector is out at that new mall south of town? I thought I recognized him, but I can't for the life of me remember his name."

She nodded sympathetically. "Hang on a second," she said, turning to riffle through some papers on her desk. She held one up. "Bob Kolnik."

"Bob Kolnik," I echoed. "Right. That's it. Thanks."

"You're welcome."

"He wouldn't be in by any chance?"

She rolled her eyes.

I gathered up the forms. "Hey, appreciate all the help. Ladies, have a terrific day."

I like to think it was the smile, but maybe it was just pity that made her stop me.

"You might find him out at the Eagle Inn," she said. "It's getting on toward lunch. He starts early, breaks early for lunch. Drives a blue Taurus."

The Eagle was a big place south of town on Freeman, across from the auto mall. A dozen cars left the lot looking empty. Still early for the lunch crowd. A blue Taurus sat in a spot twenty feet from the door. I rolled past, and wheeled into a space across the lot where I could keep it in my rearview mirror. I climbed out and strolled up to the restaurant's entrance.

Inside, I asked the hostess if I could get a sandwich to go. She took my order. While I waited, I sauntered around the lobby. Poked my head into the dining rooms and the bar to see who was there. Foursomes, one mixed, one all men in suits, occupied a couple of tables in the dining room. Two women sat at a table by the window. A half-dozen men sat in the lounge. Two at the bar, eyes glued to ESPN, slowly shoveling food into their mouths without looking at it. Two more at tables by themselves, and a pair at another table. I noted possibles and wandered back out to the lobby. I got my sandwich and took it back out to the car.

The lot started to fill up quickly. Seemed to turn over at least once in the next hour as more people came and went. The Taurus didn't move. It was after one o'clock when a man approached it, key in hand. One of the fellows who'd been sitting at the bar. Early forties, maybe. About five-ten. Sandy hair, thinning on top. Khakis and a sport shirt. Windbreaker. Too much weight around the middle. He backed into the driver's seat, rear end first. Swung his legs in. I turned over the ignition, eased out of the slot. Waited until he pulled out and followed him out to the highway.

First stop was a house in a newly developed part of the Covington Lakes subdivision. When the Taurus pulled up at the curb, I hung back and did the same nearly a block back. The house was framed, but little else had been done. Kolnik couldn't have much to inspect. Sure enough, twenty minutes later he was back in his car and rolling.

Next, another house in Covington Lakes. After that, a house in a development called Northbridge. And so it went for the rest of the afternoon. More than a dozen houses. Each stop no more than about twenty minutes. Still, it was close to six when Kolnik pulled his car into a drive off one of the side streets near Old Timers Park. Again, I hung back and watched through the windshield as he climbed out, opened the rear door and pulled out a large briefcase and headed up the walk. Looked like home to me. I noted the address, made a U-turn and headed back to my home on wheels.

After stopping at the house to explain to Meg what I was doing, I hitched the rental car up to the RV, fired up the bus and
rumbled slowly out of town. Despite the changed landscape
and the intervening years, I found the way effortlessly. Almost
as if the bus was on autopilot. A few new houses lined Powers
Road. Though civilization encroached on all sides, it still felt
rural here, even this close to town. Frank's place looked
untouched by time. Just fuller, more mature somehow, some of
the trees and shrubbery now full grown.

I'm not sure what I expected. A ramshackle house, maybe, an
overgrown yard, barn in disrepair. The property was large, hard
to maintain. Frank had never been known to part with a nickel
easily. I suppose I had this notion time would turn him into a
recluse with little interest in keeping the place up much beyond
basic functionality. A neat yard and well-tended fields said
otherwise. Paint on the house and barn wasn't spanking new,
but it wasn't chipped or peeling either. No rusted hulks in the
drive. No holes in the roof. No broken, boarded windows. I
should have known Frank had too much pride for that. He'd
grown more willing to ask and pay for help.

I wheeled the bus around behind the barn and parked it out
of sight of the road and anyone coming up the drive. I unhitched
the sedan, stowed the hitch, ran a heavy duty extension cord to
the barn, opened the propane valve, did a walk-around. While I
worked, I caught an occasional glimpse of Frank moving around
in the house. First, through the living room windows, then those
in the kitchen. If he'd noticed my arrival, he didn't acknowledge
it. I had no reason to announce it.

Dusk slowly sapped the light from the sky. I finished my
inspection with a flashlight and climbed back aboard. Rummaged through the little fridge and cupboards for something to
eat. Settled for a cold Goose Island ale, some good English

farmhouse cheddar with crackers and a bowl of ramen noodles with what was left of some fresh, but tired broccoli. I ate slowly and cleaned up. Snapped off the lights up front and took one more look out the windshield at the big old farmhouse before turning in.

The next two days were more of the same. I got up well before dawn. Ran a few miles, showered and dressed. Drove into town and bought a bucket of coffee and bottle of water on the way. Remembered to bring a couple of magazines and an empty plastic jug for emergency relief of boredom and a full bladder. Got to Kolnik's house in time to follow him.

Both days, Kolnik spent the morning at the construction site. I didn't push my luck. I parked instead in a drug store lot across the highway to watch who came and went into the site. Both mornings the blue car exited about eleven-thirty, and I followed it to the restaurant. Ate my lunch in the car while Kolnik ate his inside in front of a big-screen TV in the bar. I went back to Frank's each night to rustle up a light supper. Checked in with Nell and Emily by phone. Watched Frank move past the windows in the house as he fixed his own dinner. Read a little and turned in early. Wondered what had prompted me to pull stake-out duty, why I was in this town where I no longer seemed to belong. Wondered a lot.

By that third day, I'd dog-eared the magazines and trashed the car's interior with empty cups, bottles and junk food wrappers. I hadn't used the plastic jug yet. After I caught myself talking aloud to no one for the umpteenth time, I decided I'd lost my grip on sanity. Until Kolnik varied the routine.

He did three inspections after lunch at the restaurant. On the way to the next job, he surprised me by pulling into the entrance to Diecke Park. I drove on past, keeping my eye on the rearview to see if he was trying to shake me. His car didn't pull back onto the highway. I took the next side street. It led up to the old K–8 school building. Rumor had it even that was going to be developed into condos. I wheeled into the parking lot, climbed out and jogged across the street to the back side of the park. Took a path through the woods up to the lot in the park. Slowed before I broke the cover of the trees. Breathed a sigh of relief when I spotted Kolnik's car off to the left at the far end. Empty.

I strayed off the path, staying close to the tree line. I strolled casually toward the administration building, pausing now and then to scan for signs of Kolnik and pretended to admire the view. I rounded the corner of the building and stopped. Several picnic tables stood at the top of the slope just past the parking lot. A roof sheltered some of them. The line of tables led down toward the baseball diamond on the south end of the park. Kolnik sat at one of them with his back to me. Next to him was a woman with blond hair tied up in a ponytail. Familiar. She turned her head, revealing her profile. Sue Ann Anderson, née Kolnik. Sure, brother and sister. One wide, one thin. I cursed under my breath that I couldn't get close enough to hear them without giving myself away.

It was probably nothing but a friendly visit. I lost interest until I spotted the paper bag sitting on the bench next to Sue Ann. Not a purse. That was under the bench. Not a grocery bag. Too small. More like a sack lunch. Super-sized. They talked for a few more minutes. Then Sue Ann picked up the bag and put it on the table in front of her brother. She said something else, leaned down, picked up her purse, got up from the table and turned to walk back to the lot.

I dropped my gaze and turned away, almost running smack into Jake Reynolds.

"Jesus, Jake!" My hand clutched my chest. "How the *hell* do you do that?"

He grinned. "Do what?" He stood there innocently, hands

shoved in the pockets of his jeans, arms hugged to his sides against the spring chill.

"Lou was right. I never liked that name he called you—Spook. But *chrissakes,* Jake. You scared the shit out of me."

He shrugged. "Sorry." He jerked his head, looking over my shoulder. "Family gathering."

"I noticed."

He lifted an eyebrow. "Same time every week."

My mouth opened. I closed it. Thought about which day it was. A week earlier about this time, Sue Ann had nearly bowled me over on her way out of the Anderson Construction trailer at the site. To pick up her kids, she said.

"How do you know?" I said.

"Once the lunch rush is over, I like to get some air. Gets pretty smoky in there. This is still one of my favorite spots."

I nodded at the shared memories.

"Funny thing," he went on. "She brings him lunch every time."

"He just ate an hour ago."

He glanced over my shoulder again and ducked his head. Grabbed my elbow and pulled me back toward the woods the way I'd come.

"Let's walk," he said.

I fell in step. Behind me, tires crunched the gravel down the drive to the park entrance. When the sound receded, I glanced at him. His grin turned sardonic.

"You don't think there was a sandwich and cookies in that sack, do you?" he said.

"How would I know? What do you think?"

"Like you said. He just ate."

CHAPTER 16

I followed Jake back to the pub and found a spot at the curb out front. I went in and told him I needed a beer. We didn't speak after that. I sat at the bar and nursed the drink. Tried to make sense of what I'd learned and figure out what I didn't know. After a while I gave up and stared at the flickering images on the TV screen hanging over the bar. When my glass was finally empty, Jake brought me another.

Men in work boots and hard hats filed in the front door in groups. Couples in jeans, too. Most off the farm or from jobs in town. Old timers. Simple folks. The noise level steadily increased. Newcomers filled the tables until there was standing room only. The crowd around the bar grew three-deep in spots.

I buttonholed a couple of the construction workers standing behind me. Asked them about the job site, what they did, how they liked working there, whether Anderson was a good company to work for. They answered noncommittally, mostly with shrugs and grunts. After a few questions they moved away. As I turned back to the bar, I caught the eye of the man on the next stool.

"Real friendly fellas," I said.

He looked away uncomfortably. He must have had second thoughts because he turned back. "Look, man, we're in here to forget about work, not talk about it. It's nothin' personal."

"Got it."

He gave me a look that said "whatever" and turned his gaze

to what was on the TV screen. I looked around the room and spotted Tommy through the blue haze of cigarette smoke. I leaned over the bar and got Jake's attention.

"Give me one more and whatever Tommy's drinking," I said, looking over his shoulder.

He craned his neck to see who I meant and nodded. "Sure."

I waded through the crowd with a beer in each hand, gently squeezing through tightly packed bodies, getting jostled plenty. The glasses swung in my hands as if they were on gimbals. I finally inserted myself between two guys standing near Tommy and handed him a beer.

"Thought you looked thirsty," I said, raising my voice over the din.

He glanced to both sides, and took the glass reluctantly. "Hey, thanks."

"Sure. So, what's the deal? You don't call, you don't write." I smiled.

"Been busy," he mumbled, looking at the floor.

"Never guess who I saw today." I didn't wait for him to ask. "Bob Kolnik."

He brought his head up fast, eyes wide.

"You know him, right?"

He nodded. Swallowed hard. Glanced quickly at the guys on either side of me. I sensed their ears perk up, but a few beers had inhibited my sense of caution.

I smacked my forehead lightly with my palm. "Of course you do. He was, what, a class behind you?"

"Same class." He managed a wan smile and stood a little straighter. "Sure, I know Bobby."

"Yeah, I saw him with Sue Ann today."

"I see 'em together all the time," he said quickly. Then casually looked at his watch. "Damn, I forgot I told Wendy I'd pick up some things at the store on the way home."

He drained the beer, handed me the empty glass and wiped his mouth with the back of his hand.

"Thanks," he said. "Gotta go."

He turned and pushed his way through the crowd to the door and left me standing there. The guy on my left stuffed a fist in his mouth to stifle a snicker. I ignored him.

"Hey, wait!" I pushed through the crowd after Tommy, depositing the beer glasses in my hands on a table with a hurried apology to the people sitting there.

Outside, I scanned the sidewalk in both directions. Tommy was at the corner about to cross the street.

"Tommy! Wait up!" I stepped off the curb.

He glanced back and hurried his pace. I two-stepped out of the path of a passing car and trotted after him, intercepting him in the park. I fell in step, breathing hard.

"What the hell is going on, Tommy?"

He kept his eyes straight ahead and walked quickly. "Are you nuts? Talking in there?"

"I just mentioned a guy we both know. Reminiscing. Old home week. What's wrong with that?"

"You really want to mess things up for me?"

"I don't get it. Talk to me, Tommy. I don't know what's going on, but you know something."

"Get the fuck away from me! I don't know anything."

Same as before, whatever it was he didn't know, it had him rattled. The fear in his voice was enough to make me stop and let him walk away. But what or who was he afraid of?

Meg invited me to a May Day picnic at Old Timers Park on Sunday. The weather cooperated, giving us scattered clouds in a blue sky so bright it hurt the eyes, with temperatures in the low sixties. Not too cool to enjoy being outside without a coat, hat and gloves. Buds on trees and other signs of spring suggested we might be able to put the winter clothes away for good. At least until October.

A good turnout filled parking spots for blocks. Color splashed the green grass like the pale ghost of a carnival midway. Cheerful and safe, without the hard edge and seamy undercurrent of the real thing. A brightly hued inflatable castle medieval builders would have found shocking wobbled like gelatin, filled with noisy, energetic little bodies, heads appearing and disappearing over the parapets as they bounced inside. Not far away stood a ringtoss game, the back wall of the booth covered with stuffed plush toys. A white ice cream cart shaded by a large umbrella drew a big crowd of kids. The sun flashed off a silver beer cart that attracted a small crowd of adults. A hot dog stand sat between them, attracting all sizes. Several booths hawked sponsors' services. The bass and beat of some popular song wafted flatly on the breeze from a PA system, no tune discernible over all the background noise. Families dotted the grass everywhere. They spread out on blankets or folding chairs, their picnic baskets spilling over with food and supplies.

A gas golf cart dressed up like a locomotive circled the park on the gravel path towing two cars of young parents with toddlers and babies on their laps. A crowd at the baseball diamond on the far side of the park cheered. Players in the field scrambled after a ball the size of a small melon as runners rounded the bases. Sixteen-inch slow-pitch softball.

It felt innocent. Like Memorial Day or Fourth of July picnics when I was a kid. Before it all changed the year Kennedy and King were shot. The year the streets of Chicago erupted in violence. Even then, Huntley was removed. We watched it on the nightly news, not in the streets. Walter Cronkite's sing-song voice intoned horrors barely comprehensible to an eight-year-old mind. The number of body bags coming home from Vietnam. The bloodied heads of students beaten with nightsticks by

Chicago's finest. The assassinations of men who had just begun to step into greatness.

Robbie remembered even more innocent times: Rockwellian scenes from the suburbs north of Chicago before the family move to Huntley; games of Spud and Kick the Can and Hide-'n-Seek with the neighbor kids in the long summer evenings; sledding in the Forest Preserves; ice skating on frozen ponds on the golf course; three-legged races and swimming races on Fourth of July, after decorating a bike with streamers to ride to the parade.

I remembered some of those things, too, but none of my memories seemed as idyllic as Robbie's. I remember my mother's sadness the day JFK was shot. Twisting wildly to Chubby Checker at a neighborhood get-together. Civil rights marches on television. Girls screaming so loud for The Beatles on *The Ed Sullivan Show* you couldn't hear the songs. News clips of helicopters hovering over the jungles of Vietnam.

Huntley was supposed to be safer than the suburbs. It was, but by the late Sixties, changes were brewing even there. Bad-boy music from The Stones, The Doors, Jimi Hendrix mixed in with sappy stuff from Herb Alpert and Tom Jones. Edgier stuff on television, like *Laugh-In*. A whiff of something every so often from a car window at the drive-in that wasn't tobacco smoke. The rumor that Elden Clegge had run away to Canada to avoid the draft.

These parents thought the same thing ours had then. Move to Huntley. It's safer. From drugs and gangs and AIDS. From date rape and pedophiles and serial killers. For the moment, they were right. Right now it was softball, hot dogs, a Maypole and ice cream cones. Cute babies in prams. Children playing tag. Oldsters content to lounge on lawn chairs and watch, plump arms folded over plumper bellies.

Meg's red hair was a beacon. She shook out a plaid blanket,

let it drift to the ground and bent to straighten a corner. Then she stood with hands on her hips, soaking up sunshine and reflecting it back like phosphorus. Spotted me and waved. Phil noticed and followed her gaze. Nodded slowly and turned back to the business of unpacking a hamper. Unhappy, or maybe just preoccupied. A few yards away Todd squatted nose-to-nose with a yellow lab that was doing its best to lick his face off. Dana was nowhere to be seen. I meandered their way, dodging small children and big dogs.

"Hey, there." Her voice was cheerful, smile high-wattage.

I handed her a container of potato salad I'd carried from the car. Red potatoes, with green onions, blue cheese, a touch of bacon. Not easy to make in the small galley aboard the bus, but well worth it. She accepted it with a murmur of thanks. Passed it to Phil who stared at it for a moment, annoyance on his face while he figured out what to do with it. Meg didn't seem to notice.

"Want some help?" I glanced at the hamper.

His brow smoothed. "Got it. Thanks."

I watched him for a minute more while he organized things to his liking, standing back to look it over.

"What say we go see if they need some big bats over there?" I said. "Or cheerleaders, at least."

He turned his head to see the softball game. Looked at Meg. She smiled again.

"Go ahead," she said. "Todd's perfectly happy. I'll keep an eye on him."

He looked back at me. "You're on."

We walked away in silence. Impatience rippled off him in waves. I sensed him sneaking glances at me.

"What gives?" I said.

He looked at the ground in front of him. Paused before he answered. "She's consumed by this."

175

"Meg?" She seemed almost serene this morning. As if all was right with the world.

"It's eating her up."

"She looks fine."

He shook his head. "This goes way beyond curiosity. It's like she's looking for the key to the universe. I'm not kidding. All she talks about is why we're here. The meaning of life. That there must be something more."

He stopped, turned and looked at me imploringly, like one of the kids in front of the ice cream cart. "She's even talking about chucking it all. Packing up and moving to Belize or someplace. Spend our lives digging wells and building schools for third-world children. It's scary."

"There are worse aspirations."

He brushed it aside with a flicker of annoyance. "I'm all for doing good. Just not ready to take it that far." He started walking slowly again. "The really scary thing? All this philosophy, this talk of doing what's right? It's a cover. She wants revenge. All she wants is to find out who pushed Lou into this. She wants whoever it is dead."

I frowned. It didn't add up. People who lose someone close react either one way or the other. Contemplative and full of purpose. Or bitter and consumed by anger. Not both at once.

"Doesn't sound like Meg."

"It isn't. That's why I'm worried. I think she's losing it." He looked uncomfortable admitting it.

"What do you want me to do?"

"I don't know." He fell silent for a few paces. "Wrap it up, maybe. Stop asking questions. Tell her you've done all you can. Tell her no one's to blame. Sometimes that's just the way it is."

His eyes said he was desperate to believe that.

"She won't let it go at that, will she?" I already knew the answer.

His face slowly melted, eyelids drooping, mouth turning down into a mournful mask. He gave one shake of his head. Looked away too late for me not to see tears glistening in his eyes.

I averted my gaze. Gave him time to pull himself together. We came up behind the crowd standing back from the first base line. Politely made our way through the packed throng closer to the field. Saw a lot of familiar faces there. Scanned those closer to the base line, figuring they were players, looking for someone who appeared in charge. Phil found someone first, motioned me to follow.

The man tore his attention away from the field, gave Phil a quick smile. He looked me up and down, straight-faced. "You want a turn at bat, get in line. I got a lot of kids want to take a whack."

Phil shrugged. "Guess you don't need us."

"Everybody plays; that's the rule," he said. "Hang in there. We'll sub you guys in sometime."

We stepped back to give the players room. The pitcher, batter and other players tossed around competitive catcalls, expressions on their faces half-serious, half-jesting. Hard not to laugh when a tyke barely out of diapers, standing inside his father's stance, laid down a bunt with his father's help. Seeing pitcher, catcher and third baseman all collide trying to field it. Hoots and cheers from the opposing bench as father and son waddled down the base line to first.

I saw Pete over there, talking with a couple of boys I assumed were his. A man in coveralls with stringy hair stood next to them, hands shoved in his pockets. He stared at me with a gap-toothed grin. Recognition beaned me like a hard high inside pitch.

Tish was right.

★ ★ ★ ★ ★

Francis William Ward considered himself a gentleman farmer. He moved his family from a comfortable suburban life on Chicago's North Shore to a big plot of land on the Illinois prairie forty miles away. Almost due west of the former family home. He liked to think he was a self-made man, though he'd probably never done anything in life entirely on his own.

The product of an upper middle-class Beloit family, he was distantly related to Artemas Ward—the Massachusetts Revolutionary War general, not Artemus Ward the nineteenth-century humorist. He served with no particular distinction during the Korean War as a training officer at Great Lakes Naval Station. He broke his leg when his Jeep overturned. Met his future wife in the V.A. hospital there. Finished college after his tour and got a job in the city with a management consulting firm.

Frank parlayed a small inheritance into a sizeable stake with a lucky pick in the stock market—a tip to buy American Express after a scandal pushed its shares down to thirty-five dollars. He sold three years later when the stock hit more than one hundred eighty a share. Found a banker who wouldn't give him a loan but was willing to go in with him as a partner in a business. A lumber yard. Near Crystal Lake. He bought out his partner a year or two later and built the business into a string of yards. Years later, when he'd sold them all, he said it didn't make any difference what business he went into. The point was to generate cash, and then invest it. Stocks. Commercial paper. Real estate.

In the meantime, he couldn't let all that acreage go to waste. It, too, was an investment. One that could earn money. So, he farmed it. Not seriously. He had a business to run and not much spare time. He grew enough crops or raised enough livestock to pay the taxes and make a small profit. We all helped, planting soybeans and corn for a few years. Raising beef cattle for a while. Sheep after that. Growing enough alfalfa to put up hay for the livestock in the winter. Frank paid local farmers to help us with spring planting, fall harvest. Then he leased back some of the acreage, in turn, to those who needed additional pasture for their cattle to graze on.

That first summer, he took me with him to a neighboring farm. For advice, he said. From the farmer, not me. Potholes deep enough to break an axle littered the gravel drive like a minefield. A recent thunderstorm had filled them with muddy water. Most of the paint had peeled from the small square house, wood siding silvered from the weather. Behind it a large barn had faded to the color of dried blood. He drove around the house and pulled up in front of the barn. Then led the way inside, calling out a cheery "Halloo!" as he went.

The cloying August heat and humidity turned the barn into a fetid sauna, the stench of fresh manure a one-two punch to the nose and gut. Dairy cows, about sixty head, stood docilely in their stalls, heads trapped in the stanchions, jaws rhythmically masticating hay, some for the second or third time. Holsteins. Tinny music played from a plastic AM radio on a shelf above one of the stalls. Beneath the music some sort of hum filled the air. A nearby cow swished its tail and a black cloud rose and swirled above its black and white hide, then settled again like a blanket. Flies. Everywhere.

A mangy cat skittered across the cement floor, leaped atop a stanchion and disappeared on the other side. A skinny kid in jeans and a torn, dirty T-shirt, taller and older than me, pushed a coal shovel down the gutter behind one row of stalls. It quickly filled with the viscous green slime. He scooped it up, muscles in his scrawny arms standing out like ropes. He carried it to a manure spreader outside double doors at the far end and heaved it in. On his way back in he peered at us suspiciously, lupine features giving him a hungry, mean look. Eyes feral in their intensity.

I looked away and saw another boy. Robbie's age, maybe. Heavy build. Hair brushed up and back in a pompadour. Like Elvis. Sideburns too sparse to pull it off. He was shirtless, thick torso glistening with sweat as he savagely jabbed a pitchfork into a broken hay bale and pitched pieces into the trough on the other side of the stanchions.

Hay and dried manure covered the barn floor like thatch. I picked my way down the center aisle. A cow lifted its tail and loosed a stream of excrement that fell in globules on the hard floor in splats. Little droplets splashed on my Converse sneakers and bare ankles. Some even on my arms. I froze, horrified, but saw the two boys watching my reaction. I kept going, realizing I was more afraid of their derision.

My father had stopped at the end of the barn, one arm draped over the back end of a cow. On its far side, half-hidden, a man sat on a low stool, hands busy under the cow's belly attaching silver cylinders to its udders. My father's mouth moved, words obscured by the syncopated thumping of the milking machine. The man stood. He wore coveralls, one strap undone. No shirt. Skin the color of the oak dinette in our kitchen from working in the hot sun. Thin and wiry like the smaller boy. Same dirty blond stringy hair. Angular face creased and weathered with age and hard work. He smiled at something my father said, revealing teeth stained brown with decay, coffee and tobacco juice, a front one missing.

He turned suddenly and yelled. "Roy, stop flinging that damn pitchfork around. What the hell I tell you about that? You're gonna put one of them cows' eyes out, dammit."

"Yes, sir." The bigger kid slowed his pace and looked sullen.

"Kenny," the man barked again. "Drop that shovel and come get this milk." He shut off the machine, bent down and deftly pulled the sleeves off the cow's udders.

Kenny shuffled past me, flashing me a look I couldn't decipher. Not resentment. Or anger. More like a sated wolf looks at passing prey. He hoisted the milking machine, tank now full, and lugged it back up the aisle, sleeves flopping like silver tentacles. The man slapped his hands on his thighs and strolled up the aisle, talking with my father. They ignored me. When they drew even, the man called out again.

"Roy, you and Kenny finish up here, then you boys can come on in the house. Get some lemonade afore you work on the chicken coop."

They left me standing there. Kenny came back from the milking room. Roy passed on his dad's message. Kenny shrugged and uncoiled a hose from the wall. Rinsed off the milking equipment, then sluiced the water down the gutters he'd shoveled. Roy finished pitching hay and hung the fork on a nail.

"Fuckin' cows," he mumbled. He kicked straw at the nearest bovine. It merely swished its tail. "Fuckin' cow!" he said, louder this time.

The cow didn't reply. Kenny laughed. Roy rounded on him, face dark with anger.

"You think it's funny? Fuckin' cow. I'll show you funny. I'm gonna fuck this fuckin' cow."

He marched down the barn and picked up the stool his father had just vacated. Stomped back and plunked it down on the floor. Stepped up and unhitched his belt. Shimmied his pants down to his ankles, revealing a rock hard erection. It was enormous compared to the little prepubescent appendage in my briefs. He yanked the cow's tail aside and thrust his hips forward. With a rush like a bath tap being opened, a flood of bright yellow urine soaked him from the waist down, drenching his pants and filling his boots.

"Jesus Christ!" he yelled. "Fuckin' cow fuckin' pissed on me!"

Kenny howled with laughter. I looked from one to the other. Didn't know whether to laugh or run. Finally couldn't help myself. The sight of Roy hopping off the stool with pants around his ankles reeking of steaming urine was too funny. I laughed.

"Jesus, Kenny, you gotta help me," Roy said, desperation creeping into his voice. "You gotta sneak in the house and bring me some dry pants. Shit, if Pa finds out, he'll *whup* me for sure."

Kenny laughed some more. "What'll you give me?"

"I'll give you my foot up your ass if you don't help me, you little shit."

Kenny's face turned hard. "A week's allowance."

Roy squirmed, misery on his face as he pulled up the wet pants to cover himself. "Okay, okay."

Kenny smiled. Roy turned his anger on me.

He waggled a finger in my face. The acrid smell of urine overpowered the barn's other odors. "Not one word, faggot. I hear one word about this, I'll gut you."

I shook my head.

"Come on," Kenny said, motioning to me. Outside, he said, "What's your name?"

It popped out automatically. "Ralph."

He nodded and led the way silently around the house to the front door. A small vestibule was thick with coats on hooks, muddy boots and shoes on the floor. The inner door was open to let any breath of air find its way in. He poked his head through, pulled it back again.

"You wait here," he said. "I'll be back."

He disappeared inside. The grassy scent of sour milk, hay and manure permeated the house, too. I stood still. Picked at the dried flecks of cow dung on my arms. Flicked them on the floor in the direction of the boots. Heard the lazy buzzing of flies. The muffled rumble of men's voices from the back of the house. The steady *chirrup* of a cricket. Closer still, the soft crooning of a little person's voice. I took a tentative step, then another. Poked my head through the doorframe.

I saw the threadbare sagging couch, the chintz-covered recliner with holes worn in the arms, faded gingham curtains in the windows, rag rug on the dusty plank floor. A small plastic black-and-white television sat on a stack of milk crates, balls of foil on the skewed rabbit ears. I saw the hardness, the meanness, the serendipity of farm life long before I saw the little girl on the floor.

She wore a sleeveless cotton shift, smudged with dirt and stained with food, the pattern faded beyond recognition. A Raggedy-Ann doll lay cradled in her arms. She rocked it gently, softly singing in words I couldn't understand. I'd never seen poverty before. Didn't know if these people qualified, and never wanted to find out. The little girl looked up then. Saw what must have been horror on my face before I managed a smile.

A woman bustled into the room, similarly dressed, thick arms bulging out of the dress. "Tisha Miller, I've been looking everywhere for you."

She bent and scooped the girl up, resting her on one hip. Looked over her shoulder at me. "You waitin' on Kenny?"

"Yes, ma'am."

She nodded. Tish's eyes were fixed on me over her mother's shoulder as she was carried out.

I nudged Phil, thrust my chin toward the far side of the diamond. "That Kenny Miller? Over there by Pete?"

"Yep."

"Looks just like his dad."

"The old man died ages ago. Kenny's still working the farm.

Those two next to him? Two of his kids."

The pair next to Kenny weren't kids anymore. Both early twenties, maybe. One Kenny's height, but stockier, swilling beer out of a plastic cup. The other younger, leaner and half a head taller.

"Tish sure came a long way." I watched as one of Pete's boys strode to the plate. Looked about twelve, but big for his age. He stepped into the box, dug his feet into the dirt. Waited, bat cocked on his shoulder, while the ball arced high and curved down toward the plate. Swung with everything he had and popped it hard enough to take one bounce and squirt between the first and second basemen.

"Whatever happened to Roy?"

Phil shrugged. "Got expelled."

"Sure, I remember."

I always got on all right with the Miller boys after our first meeting. Kept my mouth shut and gained their respect, whatever it was worth. Even rode over on my bike every once in a while when things at home got too boring. Tossed around a football or played mumbletypeg if they were done with chores. Watched them if they weren't. Learned how to kill and pluck a chicken, saddle a horse, other things. They never let me help. Never said why, but I got the sense their dad would have backhanded them if they did. Got the feeling he did it often and wondered if it hadn't rattled their brains a little too much. They were both a tad off. The whole family seemed a bit touched in the head, primal, mean.

Roy had been the worst, but Kenny picked on Will mercilessly once school started. Something about my brother just rubbed Kenny the wrong way. The way I heard it, Robbie stepped in one day. Must have been Will's freshman year, when Robbie was a senior. He told Kenny to lay off. Next day Roy came to school with a .38 and waved it in Robbie's face. The last in a bale of straws as far as the school was concerned.

"Then you probably know he ended up doing time at Logan," Phil said. "The place was practically brand new when he got sent up."

"That's right. Burglary? Something like that?"

"I think so." Phil scuffed his toe in the grass. "Anyway, last I heard, he got fifteen years for armed robbery. He's over in Dixon now. Closer to home. Meg told me Tish goes to visit once in a while. At least she used to."

It made me wonder if blood really was thicker than water.

CHAPTER 17

The group around the Brodsky picnic blanket had grown by the time we walked back from the baseball game. Phil's receptionist Diane Rasmussen, Sarina and a woman I didn't know yakked with Meg about food, kids, fashion. The husbands traded guy stories. A passel of kids ranging from Todd's age to midteens milled around, playing tag, wrestling in the grass, asking every few minutes when we were going to eat. Phil waited for a break in the conversation and made introductions.

For a while, at least, the world became a simple place where all that mattered was the sound of children's laughter, friendly voices, the cry of a red-tailed hawk as it soared in a clear sky. The comforting weight of the sun, the scent of new flowers and freshly tilled soil. The feel of green grass beneath us and a warm breeze on our skin. The taste of good food eaten outdoors.

These good people did their best to raise kids with old-fashioned values in a complex and uncaring world. People largely unconcerned with the trappings of material possessions. People just trying to earn a comfortable living and get along with their neighbors. Make the place welcoming, safe, pleasing to newcomers, even while the flood of outsiders changed the very nature of the town.

Their friendships made me a little envious, made me miss Brandt's drop-in visits, our impromptu cocktail hours, and bridge group nights. I wondered if Lou and I could ever have grown into the kind of relationship Brandt and I had shared for twenty years. Looking back, what Lou and I had seemed like a favorite old T-shirt from summer camp—something outgrown a long time ago that now invokes fond but fuzzy memories, faint echoes of what really happened when it had once been worn. It made me wonder if it was time to swallow my pride and call Brandt, tell him how much I needed him around to talk to.

Sarina's husband David was a physician at a hospital in Elgin. Like her, a child of immigrant Pakistanis. Unlike her, born here. From his Midwestern accent with its flat A's to his unrequited love for the Cubs, he was thoroughly American as one can get. Worried about all the usual suburban issues—bad traffic, underfunded schools, uncontrolled growth, gang activity spreading out from the city like cancer.

Jerry Rasmussen, like Diane, was born and bred in Huntley. Now the head groundskeeper for one of the golf clubs in the area. Did some landscaping projects on the side. Said it was a lot like farming, getting things to grow where you wanted, but paid a lot better. An old-timer who'd been there, seen that, but held judgment in reserve until all the facts were in. Saw both sides of every story. Recognized benefits to growth, but mourned the loss of innocence that came with it. Respected tradition, but resigned himself to the fact that life was about change. There's no place on Earth that isn't touched by it somehow.

Phil's friend Nick tried a little too hard. Took himself a tad too seriously. Jumped into every conversation with an experience of his, each a little better, different, more relevant. Nice enough. Just too convinced of his own self-importance. Hiding some insecurities probably. He reminded me of my sister.

Talk jumped from topic to topic, none of it designed to solve the world's problems. Mostly guy stuff—movies, sports, the sad state of the American male. Ty Pennington the new Marlboro Man. Riding the range in a custom bus instead of a palomino. Building houses instead of riding herd and raising barns. Hair gelled into a deliberate mess to evoke the innate slob in all of us. Substituting for the dirty socks we used to leave on the floor like dogs marking our territory. Soul patch a sign of our machismo. Ability to cry on cue for the camera, demonstrating our newfound sensitivity. Our feminine side. The one we're all getting in touch with. A result of sneak peaks at Oprah and Dr. Phil, *Desperate Housewives* and *Cosmo* articles at the checkout stand.

At some unseen signal from Meg, or maybe enough whining from the kids, Phil moved to the hamper and started unpacking food. Jerry manned a second one. They handed out stacks of paper plates, napkins, plastic utensils, buckets of food. It all passed from hand to hand, a Tupperware brigade. Children swooped in from all directions with screaks and squalls like a flock of gulls. Picking off scraps of food while parents fixed plates for them. Gulping food down so quickly that they were half-finished eating and gone before grown-ups had a chance to fix plates for themselves.

The air filled with chatter and laughter and picnic smells—cold barbecued chicken, potato salad, coleslaw. I looked around at the sea of faces, the smiles, excitement, contentment. Saw a husband scoot close to his wife until they were connected at the hip. A mother caress her child's cheek and send her off to play with a smile and encouraging word. A couple share a quick kiss before sitting down to eat. A boy break his cookie in half and offer it to his sister. Saw how easily a touch, a look, a word could convey love as naturally as breathing. And for a moment was filled with such longing for my little family, for Nell and my little girl, that I thought my heart would burst against my ribs.

"Are you all right?" It was Sarina, next to me, in a low voice.

I nodded, blinking hard.

"You miss your daughter."

"You can tell that easy?"

David leaned over in front of her. "She's an eye doctor. You'd be amazed at what she sees." He winked.

Sarina laughed. "My husband, the comedian. I don't know why you put in those long hours, darling. You could do stand-up a few hours a night and make a killing."

"Some people think I'm such a bad doctor I make a killing now."

I smiled, my mood lifting. "Speaking of bad jokes, whatever happened to Eric Jensen?"

"He ended up getting into Northwestern," Meg said.

"Hoping to follow in Ann-Margaret's footsteps," Phil said. "Literally."

Meg feigned a scowl. "He did theater after that. With a theater group in Chicago. I heard he went to L.A. to try to get into movies."

Phil nodded. "He did. Been in a few. None you've heard of, though, I'll bet."

"Like what?" Nick chimed in.

"Really bad B-movies. Like *C.H.U.D.* and *Future Force.*"

"The one with that Kung Fu guy? David Carradine? I saw that. I liked it."

"Last I heard," Jerry said, "he was involved in a hit-and-run."

Sudden concern on the faces of the women. "Really?" Meg said.

Jerry looked somber. "Yeah, he got hit with a divorce and his wife run off with the pool boy."

General laughter. Diane gave him a shove that rolled him back onto the grass.

"Where did you hear that?"

"Tabloids. Honest."

More chuckles. I turned to Sarina.

"Hey, I saw your dad at the store in town. How's the family?" Five kids, if I remembered right. Sarina the oldest. The rest boys. Memories in my head of the five of them crammed into a big Chevy at the grocery store with their mom Safia at the wheel. Thinking she was too young to wear a scarf on her head all the time like my grandmother used to when she went out. Learning that it was tradition, part of her faith. Sarina once telling me she remembered her mother wearing a burkha in Pakistan.

She rocked forward and back. "Good. They're all good."

"Any of them still around?"

"Well, Mom and Dad, of course. They moved into a new place several years ago."

"Big place west of town," David interjected. "Custom-built."

Sarina flushed. Looked down at the blanket. "No one else, really. Saeed works for Dad. He lives in Iowa and manages a bunch of stations there. Rasheed went to New York after business school. I don't even know what he does. Too complicated for me."

"M-and-A," David said. "Mergers and acquisitions. For one of the big investment banks. Hard to remember which, since they've all merged or been acquired, too. A real wheeler-dealer. Bi-i-g money." He rolled his eyes.

"Junior's a lawyer in Chicago." Junior being the third son, named after Sarina's dad. "With Sidley, Austin."

"Big firm," I said.

"He's doing well. Hopes to make partner someday."

Hard not to be impressed. Made me curious about what makes children of immigrants strive so hard to meet their parents' expectations. While so many from white middle-class families squander good educations to go off and "find themselves." Maybe I just felt guilty that I might be one of them. Wondering if what I did made a contribution to society.

"What about Al?" My favorite. Little Ali. Cute as a button. Must have been only six or so when I left for college. Sarina used to bring him to the Barretts' house sometimes when she and Meg got together. Drove Lou nuts. Called him a little turd. Never within earshot of Sarina. Took me a long time to realize he was referring to Al's skin color, not the general pain-in-the-ass behavior of a knee-beater that age.

Sarina looked down again, shifted uncomfortably.

"Al died," she said quietly.

"I'm sorry." Felt foolish even though there was no reason I would have known.

"It's okay." She put a hand on my arm. "It was a long time ago. I don't know why it still gets to me."

" 'Desert Storm,' " David said.

"Iraq? The first one?"

Sarina nodded. "He enlisted as soon as he turned eighteen. Broke my parents' hearts. He was sent over almost as soon as he finished basic training."

"Sarina's dad kind of lost it after Al died," David said. "Wouldn't talk to us. Wouldn't even let us in the house."

Sadness washed over her face for an instant. "He still won't. The only time Mom sees the kids is when he isn't there." She saw my brow furrow. "Dad took it hard. Blamed Bush, Senior, and the government for Ali's death. Said we had no business being over there in the first place despite the invasion of Kuwait."

"Why?"

"Oh, Dad agreed at first. He thought Hussein was a madman who ought to be stopped. But when Ali was killed, he changed. Said that the United States had no business meddling in Arab affairs. He said it was because Americans hate Muslims."

"Your dad? I never thought he took religion seriously one way or the other."

"He didn't. Until Ali died."

"Now he takes it a little too seriously," David said. "That's why he's not so thrilled with us. He thinks we're too Western-ized."

I blinked. "You're Americans."

Sarina shook her head. "It's not that easy. You don't know what it's like. Growing up, I wanted to fit in so bad I did everything I could to be more like kids here. Like Meg."

Meg's ears perked up at the sound of her name. She tried to follow our conversation while engaged in another.

"But you did fit in. I never thought of you as anything but American."

"Maybe. But at home we had one kind of life. Dad was strict, demanding. He and Mom tried to fit in somewhat, too, at first. But he still had the mindset of someone from the old country. That's all he knew. We were American at school and Pakistani at home. It was like trying to straddle two worlds. I never appreci-ated my parents' culture until I met other kids like me in col-lege. I finally began to understand that I wasn't weird."

David nodded. "I didn't have it quite as bad growing up, but I know what Sarina's talking about. I was born here. I grew up with English as my first language. But people still always ask me 'So, where are you *really* from?' "

"You have to understand," Sarina said. "There are a lot of people who don't think of us as Americans. To them, we'll always be seen as foreigners."

"He didn't know any better," Meg blurted.

The group fell silent. Meg looked around the circle of eyes on her and shifted uncomfortably.

"We worked hard to learn your culture," Sarina said quietly. "He could have learned something about ours."

"Who?" I said.

Meg ignored the question. "I won't apologize for him. He's stubborn. And wrong. But I can't change what he believes."

"No one asked him to." Sarina's voice was calm. "But he

should have respected the beliefs of others."

"Who?" I said again.

Sarina and Meg locked eyes, impassive faces masking the undercurrents roiling beneath the surface. Everyone else, it seemed, waited with bated breath for the outcome.

Phil finally broke the silence. "Doug," he said softly.

Meg flinched at the sound of her father's name, but her gaze didn't waver. Diane reached out a hand, concern or maybe fear in her eyes. Changed her mind and pulled it back again, laying it gently in her lap.

I should have known. "What about him?"

David answered this time. "He's a big reason Aazim had a change of heart. Stuff built up over the years. Al's death pushed him over the edge. But Doug started it all."

I should have left it alone. I wasn't being purposely dense, but it irritated me that they seemed to be speaking in code, dancing around something that had happened too long ago to be of any consequence anymore. Sometimes, though, time doesn't heal all wounds. I took another poke at the lid on the can of worms.

"What stuff?"

Without taking her eyes off Meg, Sarina said, "Doug was the one who set my father's gas station on fire."

"It wasn't him," she insisted.

"He was there," Sarina said simply. "I don't blame you, Meg. I never did. And what he did never affected how I felt about you. But you've got to stop denying that he was involved."

"He's my father!" Meg's face screwed up. Couldn't hold it back. With a big sob, the tears let loose. She scrambled to her feet and bolted, stumbling in the grass. Phil rose quickly and followed. Caught up and wrapped an arm around her shoulders. She buried her face in his chest.

Jerry and Diane both looked at me accusingly. Nick looked

clueless, his wife embarrassed. Sarina and David appeared unfazed.

"Sorry," I said.

Sarina waved a hand. "Don't be. It was time we got this out in the open."

"Ancient history. Isn't it?"

"Hard to forget that kind of hate, Emerson."

I couldn't begin to imagine. "I can't pretend to know what it's like for you. I just never thought of you as a 'person of color.' "

She shrugged. "I don't think of myself that way, either. But try to imagine yourself in the middle of Harlem. Or Watts. Get the picture?"

The L.A. riots after the Rodney King beating came to mind. A shiver went through me. After a moment, I thought to ask. "How do you know it was Doug?"

Sarina looked startled. "Lou told me."

I flashed back to spring prom senior year. Remembered what he and Tish had said to Sarina. Feeling small and cold inside at the sound of the words and wishing I'd had the guts to deck him then. But he'd never actually admitted to anything.

"Back then?" I said, confused.

"No. A few years ago." She glanced in Meg's direction to see if she was still out of hearing. "I ran into him in town. You know he never had much to say to me. For some reason he was feeling chatty that day. He told me it was too bad my father wasn't coming in on his shopping mall deal because it was going to make a lot of people very rich. And then he said maybe Dad wouldn't want in on the deal anyway considering how the rest of the investors felt about him. I didn't know what he was talking about. I pressed him on it. He just laughed and said half the investors had been there the night the gas station burned down. Stood and watched. Did nothing until they heard the fire trucks coming. Then they took off."

"He named names?"

She nodded. "His dad. Ron Anderson. Ed Jarvis. Some others."

"He said they set the fire?"

Annoyance crossed her face. "He didn't have to."

I mulled the information. Realized that it didn't take much to believe Doug Barrett capable of a hate crime. Particularly if he was part of a mob. I wondered how Lou had known. Didn't want to consider the possibility that he'd been part of it. Knew deep down, though, that it was likely.

Sarina turned. I looked to see what had caught her attention. Phil was strolling back. Alone.

"Excuse me." Sarina unfolded her legs and stood. Walked purposefully across the grass to her friend. Touched Meg's shoulder gently. Meg looked up. Reached up and put her hand on Sarina's. They leaned in, foreheads pressed together. Phil glanced over his shoulder and saw them that way. Had a smile on his face when he turned back. I looked away, swallowed hard. Turned to David.

"Why'd Al enlist?"

"Kid was red, white and blue. All the way. As patriotic as any old codger down at the VFW hall."

"He didn't have a problem going to Iraq?"

"Because he was Muslim?" He reddened with anger. "You ever serve? No? If you did, think you'd question what religion people are if they're shooting at you? We're not talking The Crusades here."

Jerry rode to my rescue. "These days? After 9/11 a lot of people think so. We're the infidel."

"To fundamentalists. Not to mainstream Muslims." David waved his hand impatiently. "Doesn't matter. Al was just trying to serve his country. It wasn't about religion. Not for him." He

195

paused. Looked thoughtful. "My father-in-law, however, is a different story."

He started to say something else. Stopped when Sarina and Meg strolled back arm-in-arm. Shy smiles on both faces. Made me miss Emily and Nell again. Miss them something fierce.

I rolled into the drive after the picnic feeling tired and drained. In a good way, though. Like the feeling after a day of skiing. Limbs loose and rubbery. Achy, but warm. I parked in front of the barn. Sat in the car for a minute, thinking about what to do with the rest of my Sunday. Took in the view. Sun still high in the west. Hanging over the miniature houses and green fairways of the retirement community off in the distance. Cotton-ball clouds scudding across the endless blue sky. Tips of bright green leaves on tree branches dancing in the breeze in their excitement to burst out of their buds. The old white farmhouse standing on the rise like an outpost guarding against encroaching civilization.

Frank sat on the porch in the sun, holding a newspaper in front of his face. I climbed out of the car. Headed toward the bus parked around the side. Saw Frank push the paper aside at the sound of the car door and peer around it. He mouthed some words. The breeze snatched them away.

"What?" I called.

His mouth moved again. I cupped an ear with my hand. Saw him shake his grizzled head impatiently and get out of the chair. I started toward him. Hadn't gotten more than a dozen paces when an enormous roar behind me split my eardrums. Frank's startled face lit up like a jack-o-lantern in a flash of bright orange light. The ground underfoot trembled and a huge fist smashed into my back, flattening me into the gravel driveway. I rolled over and saw the blue sky filled with a forbidding black rain. Then covered my face with my arms as the rain fell, hard bits and chunks of glass, metal and plastic. And let the roaring in my head wash me away until there was nothing but blackness.

CHAPTER 18

Sirens wailed. Faintly, as though miles away. And muffled by another sound. Much louder. Like waves breaking on shore. No, more constant than that. No ebb and flow. More like a waterfall. A big one. A Niagara of sound. Darkness giving way to blue so deep it was bottomless. But it was up, overhead, not down. Blue so deep it was topless? Infinite? That was better. Faces swam in and out of that sea of blue. Like fish. Fish faces. Unrecognizable. Mouths opening and closing, but no sound coming out.

The sensation of motion, of rising up to meet that infinite blue. Floating in it. Flowing now. Not up, but forward. Like drifting down a river on a raft. Suddenly the blue was gone, replaced by white. Hard, shiny, real. Not infinite or far away. Almost close enough to touch. Too cold, sterile, uninviting to bother. More motion now. No more gliding down the river. Rough and bumpy this time.

More sensations. Someone squeezed my arm. Turned my head to see who. No one there. A wide band of black wrapped around my upper arm instead. Black rubber hoses attached it to a machine on the wall. Felt something cold in my ear. Memories of Robbie giving me a "wet willy." Couldn't turn my head until the sensation was gone. Saw a man in a navy blue shirt, patch on the sleeve, pull his hand away from my head. A silver otoscope with a black plastic tip in his other hand. Cold shifted now to a spot on my chest. Looked down. Stethoscope there pressed against bare skin. Suddenly reminded of stories of alien abductions. Closed my eyes. Drifted into blackness again.

Opened my eyes to bright lights and the medicinal smell of antiseptic. Felt pounding in my head commensurate with the sound of endless tons of water crashing down. Different sounds registered, too. The higher-pitched babble of voices, distant and indistinct. I tipped my head slowly from side to side. Saw bodies in motion. Moving fast and with purpose. All directions. Mostly dressed in white or robin's egg blue. More blue. Others dressed in brighter colors unmoving, adopting postures of resignation. Waiting.

Felt the hum of activity close around me. The jab of something sharp in the crook of one arm. The tap of something hard on ankle and knee. Prodding and poking with fingers. Closed my eyes again, tuned it out. Remembered the picnic, nothing afterward.

Let my thoughts drift like snow to a sunny cold Saturday in January when I was nine. Saw my father bundled up against the cold in insulated rubber boots, a long pea coat, ski gloves, a hunter's cap with ear flaps pulled down. Trudging through a blanket of snow from the barn. Wrestling four-by-eight sheets of quarter-inch plywood up a ladder onto the flat roof over the back porch. I ran up to the bedroom window overlooking the roof. Watched him screw eyebolts into the wood railing that circled the roof, hooks into the plywood. Felt like bursting with curiosity as he pulled long strips of aluminum foil off a roll and tacked them to the plywood with a staple gun. Marveled when he stood the plywood up on edge and hooked it to the railing, nearly blinded by the sunlight that bounced off the foil into the little enclosure. Rubbed my eyes when he started stripping off his coat, hat, gloves, shirt. He stood there in T-shirt, pants and boots, face to the sun. Turned and opened his eyes, saw me. Signaled me through the glass to open the window. I pushed up on the sash.

"Come on out," he said. Saw me sniff the cold arctic air. "What's the matter? Too chicken? Look."

He pointed to a small pile of slush still on the roof. Steam rose from it as it rapidly disappeared. I swung one leg over the sill, then the other. Hopped down onto the tarpaper, feeling the cold quickly seep through my socks. Stepped into the bright light ping-ponging from one silvered wall to another. Immediately felt the warmth. Saw him smile.

"Let's go help your mother pack a picnic," he said.

Thought I heard his voice nearby. Not a memory. Calling me. Opened my eyes again. No one there. Wondered why the blackness didn't go away, why it was so quiet. Even the roaring in my head had receded, as if I'd stepped back from the edge of the waterfall, walked away, leaving it farther and farther behind. A rectangle stood out in the darkness, a lighter shade of black. Not gray, just more defined somehow. Pinpoints of white scattered across the top half. Stars. Twinkling in a night sky outside the window. Couldn't remember when I'd felt this tired, the achy feeling painful now. Closed my eyes once more.

"Feel like shit, don't you?"

I blinked, squinting at the bright sunlight flooding the room. Turned my head. A white-coated bald man with a neatly trimmed gray goatee looked down at me, a clipboard in his hands, edge pressed against his stomach. The smile on his face said he knew exactly how I felt.

"Saw it a lot when I was in Vietnam," he said, putting the clipboard down. He pulled a penlight out of his shirt pocket. Thumbed up one of my eyelids and shined it in my eye. Talked while he examined me. "Most of them got fragged, though. Missing one or more body parts. Even happened to me once. Not in the war, mind you. After. I was a cop before I became a doctor. S.W.A.T. team. I liked the action. What can I say? Got too eager on one job. Went in too early. Concussion grenade, thank God, but sure as hell rang my bell."

He picked up the clipboard again. Jotted down some notes. Looked at me. "You hearing me okay, son?"

I nodded. I could understand the words, but his voice was faint, muffled.

"Ears are still ringing pretty good, I bet. Know your name, son?"

I worked my tongue around in my mouth, tried to wet my lips. "Ward," I said. It came out a croak. "Emerson Ward."

He nodded. "Mine's Thornton. Know what happened to you?"

My head felt as if stuffed with the same cotton that dried out my mouth. Concentrating, trying to remember what happened after the picnic, hurt. Little bits and pieces came back to me. Like black rain.

"Explosion. Big one. Don't know what."

"Good. Well, not so good if that was your RV."

I felt my eyes open wide and round. "The bus?"

He turned down the corners of his mouth, looked sad, like a clown. "Gone. Ka-boom." His face lightened. "Good news is you seem to be not too much the worse for wear. Probably let you go later today."

"Gone? Really gone?" A pang of sorrow knifed through me. Like losing an old friend.

He gave me a stern look. "You're lucky, son. Any closer to the blast radius and you'd be looking at a whole raft of problems. Perforated gut. Ruptured spleen. Pulmonary contusion. Pneumothorax. Concussion. Cranial hemorrhaging. The list goes on."

"Doesn't sound good."

"Wouldn't be if you had any of those things. But you don't.

Know how I know? Paramedic was sharp. Lot of doctors don't even know what to look for. Most have never seen what a high explosives overpressurization wave does to the human body. Pretty unique. First sign? Usually bleeding from the ears, or blown eardrums. If the eardrums are still intact, chances are there's no other overpressure injury. Paramedic checked your ears right away."

"That's it?"

"Nah. We wouldn't make any money unless we ran a bunch of tests. Took some x-rays. Checked for blast lung, a few things like that." He shrugged and smiled. "Near as we can tell, all you suffered were some cuts and bruises from the fall and the flying debris. Worst is that gash on your arm. We stitched it up."

I looked down at the forearm draped over my stomach. Saw the bandage wrapped around it. Suddenly felt the gash burst into flames and winced.

His smile bloomed. Made me think he enjoyed seeing people in pain. What he'd said suddenly dawned on me.

"High explosives?" I repeated.

"That'd be my guess. Low explosive blast—your propane tank, something like that—has a different signature. Blast wind, not a blast wave. Not as much flying debris—what we call ballistics—unless it's a big explosion. More thermal damage. You would have been burned. Badly, depending on how close you were."

He watched me absorb the words, try to put meaning to them.

"Won't know for sure until they finish their investigation," he said. "No sense worrying about it. You're still here. That's what counts."

It was cold comfort.

"I'll check on you later," he said. "If you're not pissing blood by then, you can go home."

"Thanks. I think." It didn't occur to me until after he left that gone with the bus was my home-away-from-home.

He was good to his word. By three that afternoon a nurse gave me discharge papers to sign. I considered my options. Didn't like any of them. Finally screwed up the courage to call Frank for a ride. I dressed in the dirty, ripped clothing I'd arrived in, and was wheeled down to the lobby. The orderly deposited me in an easy chair. Brushed his palms like a Vegas blackjack dealer and left. I felt shrunken and old and not a little sorry for myself.

Twenty minutes later, Frank pulled up out front and honked. Waited for me to shuffle outside and get in. He shifted into gear, checked the mirrors and pulled out, wrist draped over the top of the wheel. Slid a little lower and slouched. Propped himself up on the armrest on the door. Wouldn't look at me. Gave me the silent treatment. Made me feel like I was a kid again, waiting for the other shoe to drop because I'd done something wrong. Like forget to put tools away or leave a bike in the drive. Took me three miles to remind myself I wasn't a kid anymore.

"Thanks for picking me up." I got a grunt in reply and tried again. "Made a pretty big mess, huh?"

"Blew a big damn hole in the barn is what it did." He gripped the wheel tightly in one of his big hands.

"Insurance will pay for it. If it doesn't, I will."

He took a deep breath, blew it out. Glanced at me. Looked out the windshield again.

"You think I give a rat's ass about the barn? Or the bits and pieces of junk all over hell and gone?" He gripped the wheel more tightly to stop his hand from shaking.

I slid against the car door, away from his anger.

"That could have been bits and pieces of you littering the yard. Or me. Why the hell can't you be more careful? Don't you ever think? Use that noggin of yours?"

I stiffened, pressed my lips together. Felt the old defenses go up. Raised the drawbridge, manned the battlements.

"Well?" he pressed. "What the hell is wrong with you?"

I drew a breath. Looked out the side window. Faced front again. "It wasn't anything I did. Or didn't do."

"What do you mean? Damn bus didn't blow itself up." He glanced at me. "What? Someone blew it up?"

"Looks like it."

"Aw, for Christ's sake." He smacked the wheel with his palm. Shook his head slowly. He forced his voice lower, calmer. "What in God's name have you gotten yourself into? Whatever it is, you better not expect me to bail you out. You're a big boy. You can take care of your own problems."

"You're right," I said quietly. "I've been doing it since I was eighteen, in case you hadn't noticed. Haven't asked you for a thing, not a nickel, not a single favor since then. I don't know what's going on. Could have been an accident. I'll just have to wait and see what the investigation turns up. Whatever, I'll take care of it. I'll get the place cleaned up, have the barn repaired. Don't worry. I'll deal with it."

He drove in silence for several minutes. I watched the fence posts whiz by on the other side of the ditch running alongside the road. Saw a herd of cattle in the field beyond, mindlessly working their jaws and swishing their tails. Wished for a moment I was one of them.

"I suppose you need a place to stay," he said quietly.

"I'll get a motel room."

"Don't be stupid. I've got plenty of room."

"Don't trouble yourself."

"What trouble? I live alone in a four-bedroom house. You can even have your old room."

The car hood sucked up the highway's center stripe. I

watched the strips of yellow paint flash past hypnotically, wink-ing and disappearing.

"I'm not even sure I'm staying," I said. "I might just go back home."

"You just got out of the hospital. Driving all the way back to Chicago tonight doesn't sound like a very bright idea to me."

"Wouldn't make sense for me to change now, would it?"

He reddened. "Did you finish what you came here to do?"

"No. Not really."

"No sense in doing something half-assed."

"I'm not even sure what I'm supposed to be doing."

He shook his head. "Can't help you there. At least spend the night. Get some rest. See how you feel in the morning."

"Maybe."

"Christ, you always were stubborn."

"And you always had to be right. What'd you tell me? 'There's the right way, the wrong way, and there's my way'? It always had to be your way."

His mouth opened. He changed his mind and clamped it shut, the muscle at the corner of his jaw flexing.

We turned into the drive, silence in the car as stony as a fal-low field after a spring thaw. As we passed the barn, I craned for a look back. The front half of the bus was a shattered shell. Windows blown out. Roof peeled back like a sardine can. Tat-tered fabric hanging forlornly from bent and twisted metal. Side door dangling from one hinge. Gaping hole ringed with splintered wood in the old barn next to it. Debris scattered in a wide semi-circle on the drive and yard. A miracle that neither the gas tank nor propane tank had ruptured. Or, as Thornton said, I'd have crisped like bacon. Lucky, too, parking the rental in front of the barn, sheltered from the blast.

The car rolled to a stop. Frank got out wordlessly, swung the door shut. Started walking to the house. I climbed out slowly, still sore. Tentatively stretched to see where it hurt most. At the door, Frank turned.

"Are you staying or not?"

I faced him, wiping the grimace off my face. "I'll stay." Cleared my throat so I wouldn't choke on the words. "Thank you."

He held his gaze for a beat then went into the house. I turned and shuffled over to the bus. Circled it warily, giving it a wide berth. Like coming up on a bear in the woods, not knowing if it's sleeping or dead. Skirting the muddy puddles still left from the fire engine that had hosed it down. Thought of the places it had taken me, the things it had seen, the number of times it had been a refuge. The secrets it had held. The fishing trips with Brandt. The weekend jaunts with Nell and Emily. All gone.

I climbed the steps, gingerly touching the blackened door frame to steady myself. The interior was unrecognizable, a jumbled, sodden ruin. Nothing was salvageable. The devastation so thorough it had obliterated any sign of what the remains had once been, what they had once meant. The sense of loss heavy and deep, as empty and black as the hulk around me. And then the sudden realization that it wasn't the loss of the motor home I mourned. It was the passing of the life left behind, the passage of time. The end, not of my youth nor innocence, since I'd left those behind long ago, but of a stage of my life. A part of me. Something I'd outgrown, like my brothers' hand-me-down bike. Time to move on.

I hopped down, turned my back on the bus. Climbed into the rental and drove to the outlet mall down near the toll road. Bought some new clothes to replace what had been destroyed. Stopped at the big supermarket across from Del Webb and picked up a toothbrush, some toiletries and a six-pack of Goose Island ale.

★ ★ ★ ★ ★

Randy Tate came by on his way home. Pulled up in a big Crown Vic. Unmarked, but obviously belonging to the village. A perk of the job. Curse, too, since it had a radio. He climbed out. Stood next to the car and hitched up his uniform trousers. Took off the baseball cap with the cloth shield on the front and chucked it through the open car window. Ran his fingers through his hair. I pushed open the screen door and stepped down off the back porch. Held up the bottle in my hand.

"Beer, Chief?" I said.

He shook his head. Headed for the corner of the house instead of up the flagstone path. "Walk with me," he said.

I shrugged and angled his way. Let him lead us away from the house to the edge of the backyard. He crooked his knee, put one rubber-soled black shoe on the rail fence. Leaned forward and rested his forearms on the top rail. Gazed out over the fields.

"You piss some people off?" he said.

"Heck if I know. What did you hear?"

He looked at me, ignored the question. "I need a statement."

I nodded, told him everything I remembered about the picnic, about driving back to the farm. Heard my voice catch when I told him about changing direction to hear what Frank was saying. He listened carefully. Inspected the toe of his shoe when I was done.

He sighed. "You 'n me have got problems. Hal Jackson—our Fire Chief—says he won't say for certain until they're done investigating. But his first take is one or two sticks of dynamite inside the bus, up front. You lock it?"

"Out here? With Frank in the house close by?"

He shook his head. "It's not the same as when we grew up. People lock their doors now. Anyway, I'll tell Hal. Probably help confirm his theory. Under the bus and it might not have done

207

as much interior blast damage, but more likely would have blown the gas or propane tank. Fireball would have torched the barn."

I raised my eyebrows.

He nodded. "You, too, maybe."

"How'd it go off? I didn't get near the thing."

"Easy enough, Hal says, to wire blasting caps to some kind of trigger—alarm clock or cell phone. Trigger closes a circuit sending a little juice to the blasting caps, which set off the dynamite. Hal's boys found a cell phone in the wreckage. You have yours?"

I nodded. He looked out to the horizon again, watched the sun sinking. Let me think about what he'd said.

"Someone was watching me," I said slowly.

"Seems like. Called the cell phone when it would make a big impression. See your problem?"

"Someone wants me out of the way, and I don't know who."

"Give the man a kewpie doll. Good news is that it seems like they're just warning you off. You're not dead. Yet."

I considered that. Thought of another question. "What's your problem?"

His eyes met mine. "You." He let it hang for a moment. "You know what the most common crime is around here? Burglary. And nine out of ten are thefts from construction sites. We'll ask around. Find out a couple, three, four contractors have had some dynamite stolen recently. Meaning we're not gonna find who it was put that surprise package in your RV. See where I'm going? This is where I tell you to back off. Whatever it is you're poking at, someone's not taking kindly to it. Could get you and a lot of other people hurt. Time to leave it alone."

"I appreciate the concern, Chief. Honest. I'll give it a lot of thought."

"I'm dead serious about this. I haven't got time to babysit you. Unless you can tell me who did this, I can't help you."

"I heard you the first time, Randy." He didn't look convinced. "I'm not happy having a bull's-eye painted on my back. Believe me. Consider me warned."

His eyes flicked across my face. "You take care, then."

He turned and strode back the way we came. I watched him until he rounded the corner of the house. Moments later heard the big engine in the cruiser rumble to life, the crunch of tires on gravel.

The sun dropped closer to the horizon. Rolling plains stretched out to greet it. Closer in, the houses clustered around the golf course in the retirement community. Stark, barren, despite scattered trees and the greening grass. Made me wonder why anyone would want to build houses in the middle of what used to be cornfields. Chicago had magnificent buildings, beautiful parks, trees in the neighborhoods, and the saving grace of Lake Michigan. Night life, music, museums, motion.

How did towns suddenly spring up in the middle of nowhere? What was it that made Tom Huntley, his wife and three kids and a wagonload of belongings plunk down in the middle of the prairie back in 1846? What stroke of luck prompted the Chicago & Galena Railroad to lay tracks out as far as "Huntley's Grove" five years later?

That little towns like Huntley stayed small was no surprise. Living off the land is hard work. The weather is harsh. In the winter, Alberta Clippers sweep across the plains, freezing everything in their path with subzero temperatures and howling winds. Then bury it all under drifts of snow. Summers are often stifling, punctuated by violent thunderstorms and occasional tornadoes. The land is unforgiving. A dry spring, some prolific pest, an unfortunate fungus could ruin crops, sicken livestock, bankrupt families.

There was beauty there on the prairie, too, amidst the hardships and dangers. The simplistic nature of country life. Providing for a family. Helping neighbors. The openness, land and sky stretching to infinity. The power and grandeur of the seasons.

I remembered sitting in this yard as a kid, watching storm fronts move in from the west on summer days. Feeling the air crackle with electricity as the line of black clouds advanced. The wind picking up, stirring up dust devils on the gravel roads. Watching the lightning strikes and counting slowly until the thunder rumbled. Seeing the curtain of rain sweep across the plain, a sprinkle of big fat drops announcing its imminent arrival. Howling in delight with upturned faces when the deluge finally came.

Or the nights camped out in a pup tent, spending more time out of the tent than in. Lying on our backs gazing up at the night sky ablaze with twinkling lights. Counting the shooting stars. Telling ghost stories and bad jokes.

The only way to find that beauty is to slow down. Like my first time in the desert. At first glance, it was all browns and reds and tans. When I stopped and looked, really looked, it came alive. A herd of wild boar moving slowly like sagebrush gently blowing down a dusty arroyo. A coyote trotting across a road, disappearing ghostlike in the scrub. A jackrabbit waiting motionless until it passes to bound off. Tiny purple and yellow flowers blooming on spiked, deadly looking plants. The whirr of a quail's wings. A hummingbird's darting blur of color.

Progress was speeding up life here and paving over the prairie's beauty with malls and roads and houses.

Closer in still, just down the gentle slope of fields, was the wood and concrete colossus of the new mall, surrounded by a pool of black asphalt. Strange that I hadn't noticed it before. Or had I? I frowned, trying to recall. Suddenly remembered the familiar feeling I'd had standing at the back of the construction site and looking out over the fields. These same fields.

I pushed myself away from the fence and made a wide circle

around the house until I was on the opposite side looking east. A few hundred yards east, huge earthmovers sat parked in an empty field, last of the sunlight glinting off their shiny yellow skins. The ground had been scraped bare. Hundreds of little red flags marked streets already being carved out and lots waiting for houses. I'd seen the developer's sign at the entrance advertising "estate homes." Never realized how close it bordered Frank's property.

Frank was getting squeezed pretty good between the mall and the residential estate development. Then again, it probably made his land that much more valuable.

CHAPTER 19

Four bedrooms, seven people. Four of them boys. Meaning the boys bunked together, two to a room. Until Robbie left home. Then Will got his own room. Henry and I bunkmates until I left for college. Then Henry had his own room. Until he was killed.

Frank hadn't touched a thing. The twin beds, set against perpendicular walls, one under the window, were still made up with brown plaid sheets and brown blankets. Hand-sewn quilts neatly folded on the foot of each bed. Nightstand between them with an old lamp in the shape of a rooster on top. Shelf underneath filled with paperback novels—Ian Fleming, Robert Ludlum, Steven King. Poster of Rocky Balboa on one wall, Raquel Welch in *One Million B.C.* on another. Bookshelf filled with an odd assortment, the bottom shelf all old school yearbooks and textbooks. *The American Tradition in Literature, Third Edition. Environment and Man. The National Experience.* Higher shelves were filled with more books, athletic trophies, some Henry's, some mine. Han Solo, Chewbacca and R2-D2 action figures from *Star Wars: Episode IV,* definitely Henry's. Flashlight, pen knife, worn dirty baseball and fielder's glove mine, but likely usurped after I left. On the top shelf, three scale model cars—a 1957 Thunderbird, a 1965 Mustang and a 1968 Stingray.

On top of the oak dresser in the corner was a small stereo system. A stack of vinyl albums lined up on edge next to it. I blew the thin layer of dust off the top, lifted the smoke-colored plastic cover. *Darkness on the Edge of Town* on the turntable. The Boss. Tried to think of what I'd listened to back then. Remembered that my budget in college had been too lean to buy albums.

I rummaged through the drawers. Under the socks in the top left drawer were some loose golf balls and tees, two scorecards, ninety-seven cents in change, a book of matches from a restaurant in Crystal Lake. In the back of the right-hand drawer beneath the underwear was a small wooden box. The lid slid out. Inside, an old Bulova wrist watch with a brown leather band, twelve silver dollars, a brass belt buckle engraved with the initials "H.D.W." and a little blown-glass hash pipe. I sniffed it, smelled charcoal and a faintly sweet scent of marijuana. Like incense. I put it all back. Found only clothes in the other drawers. Wondered why Elizabeth hadn't cleared it all out and donated it to charity.

I sat down at the desk. Above it, a Harley-Davidson wall calendar, May 1979. The desk top neat and uncluttered. Just a desk lamp, clock radio, a framed picture of our mother June. A snapshot of her in sandals, Bermuda shorts, sleeveless blouse, gardening gloves and big floppy straw hat. On her knees in the garden. Trowel in one hand, streak of dirt on her cheek from rubbing her nose with the back of a glove. Face turned to look back up at the camera. Radiant smile, face still full. Not gaunt, the way she looked after the cancer started eating away at her. Three books propped against the clock radio. *The World According to Garp, Beggar Maid, A Bend in the River.*

Strange that a sixteen year-old kid was into writers like John Irving, Alice Munro and V.S. Naipaul. A kid with a Harley-Davidson wall calendar and the nickname "Wild Child." Made me wonder how well I'd known my little brother. Not much better than Robbie had known me. I was twelve when Robbie was drafted. Almost fifteen when he got back from Vietnam.

The following year he came home for Christmas. From college. I drove him up to Woodstock to shop for presents. On the way, he pulled a dime bag from the pocket of his army jacket. The one with his name on it. Rolled a joint, lit it and offered it to me. As coolly as I could muster, I waved him off. Asked him for one of his Camels instead. Got high off the nicotine. These days Robbie is a big executive for an insurance company and doesn't smoke or drink.

I wondered if Hank had thought of me the same way. Mysterious, worldly, mythical. Doubtful. The age difference was only half that between me and Robbie. I'd even deigned to play with Henry when Lou wasn't around and we were both bored to tears. A game of catch. Or spies up in the hay loft, around the barn. Sometimes we'd take a BB gun and plink at soda cans out in the backyard. Usually, he couldn't get the time of day from me. Felt bad about that now. That was nothing new. He was my brother, but most of the time that just meant he was a pain in the ass.

Elizabeth was the one who'd pushed his buttons. Oil and water, those two. I gazed over at the beds. Remembered the time Elizabeth had teased him so mercilessly he'd gone berserk. Got right into her face and started shouting at her to quit. She wouldn't. Tired of both of them, I stepped in. Told Hank to back off, let it go. He was wound too tight. Kept pushing at me. Like it was my fault. I backed him up, down the hall into our room. He was big then, nearly big as me. But still all baby fat. The more he pushed back, the harder it was to contain the anger, the rage I felt. At Mom for leaving us, for dying. At Dad for myriad reasons I hadn't yet figured out. At Elizabeth for being such a bitch. At Henry for letting her get his goat. I pinned him down on the bed. Cocked a fist, ready to punch him in the face. Knew if I did, I'd kill him. Climbed off and started shaking so bad I could barely stand. In that moment, Henry understood. Went quiet, his face pale and fearful. I staggered out, disgusted. With him, with myself.

My cell phone rang, bringing me back to the present. I flipped it open, said hello.

A breathy voice said, "Meet me at my thinking spot. Lunch time."

"Tommy? Is that you?"

No reply. I took the phone away from my ear. Saw the message on the screen, "Call ended."

I sat in the car and kept an eye on the road though the cemetery. Checked my watch every so often while it ticked off an agonizingly slow ten minutes. I was beginning to think I'd made a big mistake when Tommy came in on foot from Mill Street. He glanced over his shoulder every few paces. The car was parked far back on the St. Mary side, a short par three from Henry's grave. Tommy didn't see me. I waited until he was standing at Hank's feet before climbing out. Was across the road before he spotted me. He jerked his head the other way. Like he didn't know me. Shifted his weight from one foot to the other.

I came up next to him, eyes on my mother's headstone. Saw him crane his head every which way out of the corner of my eye.

"Jesus, Tommy. You're making me nervous."

"I'm making *you* nervous? I near turned back three times on the way here."

"What's going on? Why'd you call?"

"Look, I don't want any part of this. But when I heard they blew up your RV, I figured I gotta say something."

"Who's 'they,' Tommy?"

"I don't know. I swear. I just . . ." He scuffed the toe of his boot in the grass. "I thought you should know what's going on at the site, that's all."

I waited him out.

He glanced at me, eyes imploring. "Look, you gotta promise this won't come back to me."

"I don't know what 'this' is."

His eyes took in the little cuts on my face, the bandage on my arm visible under my rolled-up sleeves.

"They near killed you, didn't they?"

I shrugged. "I'll do my best to keep you out of it."

He hesitated, nodded. "It's the mall. I just feel funny about it."

"Funny, how?"

He held his hands out, palms up. Looked from one to the other. They were calloused, dirty. "I been building things a long time. I like the work. Makes me feel good to see a project take shape, know that I'm doing something first-rate. Something that'll last."

He looked at me, shook his head. "I never much liked working on Pete's projects. He always wanted to rush things. Save money, time, anywhere he could. I imagine I could have made a lot more money over the years, but I been a lot happier working for myself. You know? Anyway, thing is, Pete hasn't changed, and I sure as heck haven't."

"Tommy?" I said gently, forcing a lid on my impatience.

He nodded. "Right." He took a breath. "I think Pete's cutting corners on this job. Big time. Not stuff you'd notice right off, but when you add it all up. . . . Stuff like framing load-bearing walls on sixteen-inch centers instead of twelve. Using nails to hang the drywall, not screws. Substandard materials. Well, maybe not substandard, but stuff I wouldn't use. Not if I wanted my name on it. Problem is. I can't prove none of this."

My brow furrowed. "Why not? You know what you're doing."

"It's just too strange. Everyone on that site is keeping his head down and nose clean. I asked about a couple of things—

like the framing—and got told to keep my mouth shut and stop thinking I know more than they do. Made me curious. So I got a look at some of the drawings. Stuff is spec'd that way on the architectural plans. And it's all passing inspection."

"So there shouldn't be a problem, right?"

He looked as uneasy as I felt. "It's just not the right way to build something. Forget pride. Forget the fact I think Pete's a jerk. I'm not even sure it's safe."

My head came up fast, saw the worry etched on his face. "There'd be red flags if it didn't meet code. Wouldn't there? Hell, the bank wouldn't let Pete make draws if it didn't, right?"

He shrugged. "You'd think." He went silent for a moment. Looked at me like I was forgetting something. "Someone *did* blow up your RV."

I gave it some thought. "There seem to be a lot of people who aren't happy I'm back in town."

"Couple sticks of dynamite in your RV? That's a lot of unhappiness." He looked expectant.

"Pete was at the May Day picnic when it happened."

"He's not that dumb." Tommy glanced around furtively, jammed his hands in his pockets. "Look, I gotta get back to work before somebody misses me."

I nodded. "Sure."

He shuffled off, shoulders hunched.

I went for a drive. To clear my head. West, out into the country, away from all the development, all the progress. Didn't take long. Houses gave way to farmland a few hundred yards from the main drag. A half-mile past that, not even the retirement community houses to the south were visible. I meandered out Marengo Road, speed so sedate my grandmother would have been proud. I kept trying to reassure myself that if "they" had wanted me dead, I'd be dead. The bus was a warning. *To do what? A warning from whom?* So much for clearing my head.

On an impulse, I yanked the wheel to the right and turned north onto Seeman. Saw signs of change even out here. A couple of big new houses on lots big enough to stable a horse carved out of someone's farm. Cruised slowly up a long gradual rise. Admired the land gently undulating off to the west, plowed and planted fields not yet beginning to show tufts of green. A couple of farmsteads topped the rise on opposite sides of the road. Buildings on both in good repair, the older barn sporting a fresh coat of traditional red.

The road descended in a wide curve east, straightened and curved north again. I let the car coast down. At the bottom was a large solitary tree off to the left surrounded by brush. Just past it, a railroad crossing. Two sets of tracks. I pulled the car onto the shoulder and let it drift to a stop. Put it in park and got out. Let the memories trickle in.

Electric wires were strung over the nearest set of tracks. Thirty yards northwest, a train signal and small shed stood next to the tracks, a yellow barn in the middle distance behind them. To the southeast, both sets of tracks extended out of sight. The closer set, I knew, ended not much farther away, just before it reached the Kishwaukee River. The tracks were on the old abandoned Elgin & Belvidere Electric Railway line. The right-of-way now belonged to the railway museum up the road in Union. Museum volunteers laid the tracks back in the '60s. Still ran all their old trains on the line, giving rides to visitors.

The other tracks, fifty feet farther, were Union Pacific's. The same line that ran through Huntley. The one they were talking about running passenger service on again. For commuters. Couple of freight trains a day still used the line.

There were no crossing gates. No signal lights. Never had been. Not this far out in the country. Not at a crossing where trains were visible a good half-mile or more in either direction.

Yet this was where Henry had died. Sitting in Pete Anderson's car, drunk. I stood on a rail, bright reflection of a warm spring sun glinting off the cold steel. Wondered why Hank hadn't seen the white Cyclops eye of the behemoth diesel locomotive bearing down on him. Why the engineer hadn't seen the black spot on the tracks, road ahead bathed in white headlights, pavement behind painted red in the dark.

The freight train had been doing only forty-five, according to the engineer's statement. Doesn't much matter when there's thousands of tons of weight behind it. The locomotive caught the side of the SS. Scooped it up and flipped it over onto its roof. Shoved the twisted remains down the tracks another three hundred feet before coming to a grinding, screeching halt. Inside, the twisted, bleeding remains of a bright kid who'd deserved better.

It had been several days before someone thought to call me. Engineer radioed it in. Dispatcher called the state police, who in turn called the county sheriff, and then called a union rep. Engineer was lawyered up within minutes of being escorted into the McHenry County Sheriff's Department. He gave his statement and walked out. They waited until first light to open up the car like scouts opening a can of beans at a jamboree, with saws and pry bars. Henry's body was taken to the morgue in Woodstock. It was late morning before accident investigators for NTSB, the county and the state were satisfied and let a tow truck winch the wreckage onto its flatbed and cart it off.

It would be a week or two before toxicology reports came back. Indicating Hank had a blood alcohol level of point-one-four when he died. But the cops had already called it from a look at all the empty beer cans in the back. To them, the autopsy was just a formality.

It was close to noon that next day before a county deputy went to the house and told Frank what had happened. Elizabeth was there. She called Robbie. And Will. It was Robbie who called me two days later, the day before the funeral, to ask me why the hell no one had heard from me. When I told him I didn't know what he was talking about, he backpedaled pretty quick. Broke the news as gently as he could. Said he thought Elizabeth had called everyone. Apologized profusely. The damage was already done.

A corner of my heart turned to stone. I refused to fly in for the funeral. Made excuses about not having the time or the money. Finals were coming up. My scholarship depended on how I did on them. Later, I gleaned what happened from copies of *The Huntley Farmside*. Mary Barrett sent them to me when she heard I wasn't coming home.

A flock of redwing blackbirds cartwheeled across the sky, spots on their shoulders flashing crimson in the sun. A spring zephyr ruffled the grass and shivered slender tree branches. It carried the scent of freshly plowed earth, a hint of sweet grass, the promise of rebirth. I felt it brush my face, tuft my hair, crumble the hard corner of my heart into dust. Blow it down the tracks like tumbleweed and disperse it into the sky until it disappeared, leaving nothing but emptiness.

The railway museum wasn't far. Another mile north to Hemmingsen. Jog a mile west until Hemmingsen came to the tracks again and turned parallel. Another mile, maybe, after that. The sheer size of the museum, rising up out of empty fields, was always a surprise. The huge barns to house trains, some of them two football-fields long, incongruous out here in the middle of nowhere. Looking more like the train yards in Chicago, Atlanta, some other big city.

The parking lot was practically empty. The place had been open on weekends only since early April. Wouldn't open on weekdays until after Memorial Day, I remembered. The whole place—admissions booth to machine shops—was run by volunteers except for a couple of paid managers. I locked up, ignored the tourist entrance and walked in another way. Unless they'd changed everything, I remembered an office somewhere across from the main row of train sheds. I found it without much trouble.

Danny DeHaan looked up, startled, when I entered. He looked even more surprised when he saw who it was.

"What are you doing here?"

"Well, hello to you, too."

He reddened. "I meant . . . I didn't know . . . I thought . . ." He closed his mouth and blinked a few times. Took a whole new tack. "We're closed, you know."

"Yeah, I know."

"I saw you at the wake," he said quickly. "Sorry I didn't stop and say hello."

"No big deal. I'm surprised you remembered me."

He shrugged. "I didn't know you were back in town."

"A little while now. Just visiting, though."

He nodded and smiled. "That's nice. Catching up with family and friends." The smile faded, as if he'd used up all his energy on the pleasantries.

I jumped right in. "Look, Danny, about the wake. What did you mean when you told Pete he's next?"

He shifted nervously, kept his face blank. "I don't know what you mean?"

My lips pursed. "Come on, Danny. A dozen people heard you. A couple dozen saw you two start to mix it up before Phil pulled you outside."

"I didn't mean anything by it. Honest. I . . . he just pissed me off, that's all."

"It's just that the way it came out sounded like you might know something about Lou's death, you know? Like you might have had something to do with it. And maybe Pete's next."

He sat back in his chair, blinked. Put his hands out as if to hold me back. "You've got me all wrong. Swear to God. Look, Emerson, I know you and Lou were friends. Nothing against him—or you—but I don't like what's happening to the area. The growth, it's inevitable, right? I mean, we're part of the 'northwest corridor' now. We're next to a major interstate. I get all that."

He took a breath, dived right back in as if afraid I might interject and try to dissuade him. "You haven't been here. You haven't seen what's been going on. Looks different, doesn't it? You might think it's less noticeable when it happens little by little, when you live with it every day. It's not. It's more like death from a thousand cuts. It plain hurts to see it."

"How are you going to stop it?"

"I'm not. I know that. But I can slow it down, maybe. Add a little sanity to the planning process. So it's not so haphazard, so slapdash. Like what happened in Algonquin. You know we didn't even have a village planner until, I don't know, five, six years ago? Village had a planning committee. Guess who was on it? Realtors, developers, couple of bankers."

"Sounds like a conflict of interest."

He shook his head in disgust. "Conflict? Why do you think the village finally hired a planner? We finally got the village to set up a preservation commission. You know how many historic houses we lost because there was no review process before the town used to issue demolition permits? Heck, Thomas Huntley's house—the one on Woodstock and Third? That was recognized by the county historical society four years ago. The village just gave it landmark status this year. Wouldn't have happened at all if we hadn't pushed preservation so hard.

"The bandstand in town? You know it's new, right? Well, relatively. That was plaqued by the historical society back in nineteen-ninety-two. The village decides it's beyond repair, tears it down. Built the new one. Historical society took back the plaque. At the time, that was the only recognized historical site in town. We could have restored it. 'Too much trouble,' they said. 'Knock it down. Build a new one.' It's stupid."

He fell into a moody silence. I considered him, wondering how strong his resolve was. Thought of the lone student in Tianenmen Square who had brought a column of tanks to a halt.

"What about Lou?" I said. "You and him have a problem?"

He looked down, bald pate shiny with perspiration. Rubbed his palms on his thighs. "Like I said, I know you were friends."

I waved it aside. "Once, maybe. I never saw him again after high school, Danny."

He hesitated, looked me in the eye. Straightened his shoulders and went on. "Yeah, I had a problem with Lou. It was all about the money for Lou. That and the power trip. Lou would do just about anything to push a deal through."

"Like what?"

"Do projects on the cheap. Push for zoning variances. Fudge the impact studies."

"How could he do that?"

Danny shrugged. "I don't know. All I know is that when Lou wanted to get a project off the ground, one way or another it got done."

"So what happened with the mall project? How'd he get squeezed out?"

He looked thoughtful. "You know what our biggest problem is? Aside from the fact there are too many people? Transportation. We don't have the infrastructure to handle all the traffic. You tried getting through town on 47 recently? It's a parking lot. Me? I don't mind. I hope they all get sick of it and go somewhere else.

"Lou took a chance. Saw that the state wouldn't put money

into widening the road or building a westbound exchange on the toll road unless there's business in town to support it. The village can't pay for new arterial streets without a bigger tax base. Meaning more retail business. So he put the mall deal together. Win–win, for everyone except those of us who'd rather see progress go somewhere else."

He gazed out a window, sighed. "My guess? The village board finally got smart a while back. We had to push them, but they raised the transitional fees substantially." He saw my blank look. "Fees for impact studies, permits, all the upfront stuff. They sort of substitute for taxes while a development is being built. The board basically raised the ante, the entry cost for developers. To raise additional funds and to discourage low-cost developments. For a shopping mall? Fees had to be pretty steep. I heard Lou was leveraged to the hilt."

That much I already knew. It didn't explain why Lou got pushed out. Then again, maybe it was like Harry said—bad timing.

"Look," Danny said, "I'm sorry Lou took it hard enough to kill himself. But you ask me, I think he got what he deserved. What I said to Pete? All I meant was that if he doesn't watch how he does business, same thing'll happen to him."

"Why? What's he doing?"

His face and scalp pinked up again. "I've already said more than I should." A thought changed his demeanor. "Why're you so interested in all this, anyway? After all these years what do you care?"

"Maybe it's none of my business. And frankly, I'm tired of the whole mess. It's like being back in high school again. I'm just trying to find out if Lou got a fair shake."

"Not like he deserved one. Pete, either."

"So you said."

He shook his head slowly. "All I can tell you is what I hear.

It's been going around for years—Pete and Lou built cheap and charged too much."

"Free-market capitalism at its best," I said lightly. "Or worst, depending on your point of view."

He wasn't buying. "Not when you're taking the kind of shortcuts I've heard about."

"What kind is that?"

"Safety issues. Things that if they aren't code violations ought to be."

"Any problems? Complaints? People dying because of whatever?"

He folded his arms across his chest and leaned back in the office chair. "Only a matter of time. Anyway, just because no one's heard complaints doesn't mean there aren't any. I imagine they'd both be pretty eager to keep people quiet. Probably go out of their way to make things right for the one or two who do complain."

I rubbed my chin. Took a deep breath and blew it out.

"Thanks." I turned for the door, stopped when I got there. Tapped my foot a couple of times before making up my mind to ask. "You ever hang out with Henry back in high school?"

Danny drew back in surprise, then furrowed his brow. "Your brother? Not really."

"You were in the same class, right?"

His head bobbed. "He ran with a different crowd. I was one of the geeks. Still am, I guess." He flushed with embarrassment. "Why?"

I shrugged. "No reason. Just been thinking about him lately. Wondering what he might be like now, where he might have ended up."

He nodded again. "Hey, you're welcome to walk around, look at the trains. Long as you're here."

With a short wave I ducked out. Stood on the steps a moment and decided to take him up on his offer.

CHAPTER 20

The silence was worse than anything Nell could have said, filled with unspoken recriminations as loud as a roomful of gossip columnists. Her disappointment was palpable, and more than I could bear.

"It's not that big a deal, really." I said. The words didn't convince even me.

"Goodness, Emerson, someone tries to kill you, and you want me to just accept it?"

What I wanted was to hear her yell and scream, use an expletive or two, tell me "I told you so." What was the point of feeling guilty otherwise?

"No one tried to kill me." I put more reassurance in my voice this time. "Someone just wanted to scare me off."

"Off of what? What are you doing there?"

"Just trying to get some answers, that's all."

"Answers to what? I don't understand. Your friend is dead, Emerson. No 'answer' will bring him back. People die. Sometimes for no reason. You just have to accept that and move on."

"It's hard to explain."

"Try." It was a command. In a softer voice, she said, "I really want to understand. I'm trying."

"Lou was never a quitter, Nell. He was lazy sometimes. Took shortcuts. Looked for the easy way out. But when his back was up against it, I never saw him quit. Something's going on here that doesn't feel right. I think Lou was pushed to the breaking point. And if that's true, then he deserves a little justice."

"Why you? This isn't some frontier town we're talking about, Emerson. And you're not 'The Lone Ranger.' If you have suspicions, for goodness' sake, take them to the police and let them handle it. If you keep stirring things up, next time they'll do more than wreck your motor home."

Her anger came through the measured words.

"I told you, whoever it was just meant to scare me."

"Well? Are you scared? You should be. *I* am. I'm terrified."

There was a tremor in her voice. Not anger this time.

"Nell, I'll be careful. I promise."

"Why do you keep doing this? Why do you have to keep playing the hero?"

"I'm not. . . . That's not why . . . I . . ." I took a breath. Tried to ease the tension in my shoulders. Started over. "I'm not trying to be a hero. I'm just trying to help a friend."

"You don't understand, do you?"

There were tears streaming down her face I knew, even if I couldn't see them over the phone.

"I think I do," I said softly.

"But you won't stop, will you?"

"I can't, Nell. I don't have a choice."

"There's always a choice, Emerson. Walk away. It's as simple as that. Your pride, your silly chivalric code or whatever it is, none of it matters. Just walk away. This is your life we're talking about. If you won't think of yourself, at least think of Emily. Don't leave her without a father."

"She doesn't have one now."

I regretted the words as soon as they were out of my mouth. From her silence I knew the tears had stopped.

"That's not fair," she said quietly.

I sighed. Couldn't summon enough sincerity for an apology.

"How's your mom doing?"

It was a moment before she relented. "She has her good days and bad days. Today wasn't so bad. No nausea to speak of, and she was strong enough to play a bit with Emily. We just take it day by day."

"Please give her my best, will you?"

"Of course."

Silence again. This time I broke it.

"I'll think about what you said. I promise. I don't want you to worry. You have enough on your plate."

"But I do worry, Emerson. I care for you. I care about what happens to you."

"I know that. I care for you, too. I want us to grow old together."

"Then you better watch out for yourself a little better."

She was deadly serious, but there was a lightness in her voice that said she didn't want to fight about it anymore. Not now. But she wasn't done with me yet.

"I miss you," I said, voice husky.

She hesitated a beat. "I miss you, too."

"How's our little girl?" I forced bright and cheery this time.

"She's fine. And into everything, the little imp."

She related Emily's latest adventures, and for the next few minutes, we steered the conversation toward the superficial, keeping it light.

"When are you coming home?" I said after we'd run out of chit-chat.

"Goodness, I don't know, Emerson. Let's just get through this first round of chemo and see, all right?"

Another month, at least. "I'm sorry to sound so selfish. Bad-hair day, I guess."

"I know this is less than ideal. For all of us. But I need you to be patient. Please." She paused. "I do miss you, Emerson. Emily does, too."

"Give her a kiss for me."

"I will."

I hung up discontented. Like I'd eaten salad instead of steak. That happened a lot lately. With Nell, it was the lack of any sort of resolution. A knock-down drag-out fight would be preferable. Instead, we danced around the issues because circumstances held us in limbo. Even if we worked out our problems, she was still thousands of miles away.

I headed for the kitchen to look for something more satisfying, a bone to gnaw on. Found Frank instead, at the table, glass of Scotch in his hand, *Wall Street Journal* spread out under the hanging light. I opened the fridge, pulled out a beer.

"Just got off the phone with Nell," I said.

"That your girlfriend?" His eyes didn't leave the paper.

"Jesus, Frank, she's the mother of my daughter. Don't you pay attention to anything?"

He looked like he'd been slapped. "What the hell's wrong with you?"

"Aw, forget it."

His face colored, red creeping from the neck up. He modulated his voice. "You haven't exactly been free with details of your life for a while now. Can't expect me to know everything. You've been gone a long time."

"Well, I'm here now. You've been avoiding me like the plague ever since I got back."

He raised his hands as if in surrender, glass swinging in his fingers like it was on gimbals. "I don't know what your problem is, but I don't have one. I'm not trying to stay out of your way. I'm just living my life like I always have. You're an adult. I expect you to do the same."

"What's that supposed to mean?"

He swirled the ice in the glass, took a swallow. Spoke quietly.

"You don't live here anymore, son. You're not home from school on vacation. You're all grown up. You don't need a father."

I stared at him. "You're kidding, right? You never were a father. Not in any real sense. Hell, you were never around long enough to be a father."

"Because I worked my tail off for you kids? Because I had a business to run that helped clothe and feed you and keep a roof over your head? What's this really about? I didn't hug you enough when you were little? Didn't pat you on the head often enough? Tell you what a good boy you were?"

"Would it have killed you? A little encouragement now and then? Ever hear of the carrot and the stick? Where was the fucking carrot, Frank?"

His face purpled, veins in his temples standing out. He managed to keep his voice even. "The carrot was a nice home, good food on the table, summer weekends playing golf at the club instead of working the fields, a housekeeper so you wouldn't have to do chores."

I shook my head, mouth set in a grim line. "I never asked for any of that. I never asked for a dime from you. Got a scholarship. Worked my way through school. Never once asked you for help. And I still didn't measure up, did I? I still didn't meet your expectations. Why? Because I didn't want to get into the business? Hell, you never even let me get a summer job there."

He watched me silently, his color receding. "The only expectations I had were for you to make your own way in the world and find a way to be happy. That's all. And you did that. This grudge you've been carrying around all this time, it's stupid. You never had to meet my expectations. Only your own. You want to be mad at me, pick another reason."

I took a long pull off the beer bottle. Wiped my mouth with the back of my hand.

"You want another reason? It was always about money with

231

you. Always about how much this cost, or that. About how much you had to earn to pay for everything. I never knew anyone as tight with a nickel as you, Frank. And you never let us forget it. Like you resented us because we weren't income producers."

"Don't be an ass."

"Why? Am I wrong?"

"I never resented you."

"You weren't very proud of us, either. You never had a nice word to say about Robbie until he made vice president. Never did have anything nice to say about what Will chose to do with his life. I stopped listening. I knew there wasn't a damn thing I could do that would please you, no matter how much money I made. Lord knows, I tried for a while."

"That's a lot of hooey, and you know it."

"Really? You held money over our heads like a sledgehammer. Like you could buy our love."

He regarded me coolly, said nothing. It was like banging my head against the wall. I took a breath, let my pulse settle some, wondered how long I'd been balancing the chip on *my* shoulder.

"So what's the deal with the estate homes going up out back?" I said, switching gears.

His mouth turned down. "The *deal* is I sold the land to a guy who offered me way more than it was worth. What he does with it is his business."

"You hate being crowded. You never liked having a neighbor half a mile down the road. Now you're going to have a whole neighborhood right next door?"

"I won't be here forever. I don't need this much house, this much land at my age."

"What are you talking about?"

"I can't take care of this place by myself anymore. Don't want to, either."

"Where would you go?"

He shrugged. "I don't know yet. Maybe across the highway."

I laughed. "You? Over there?" I mulled the thought. "It might not work out so bad. When all your neighbors run away screaming you'll have the golf course to yourself. Oh, but wait. You hate golf."

He looked peeved. "Don't be stupid. I'm not ready yet, but there will come a time when it would be foolish for me to stay out here by myself. It makes a lot more sense to get a small place over there—a condo, maybe—where if something happens there are people around."

"Right. You being a people person and all." I smiled, hiding my ambivalence. Hard to imagine him considering his own mortality. "See, the thing is," I went on, "I sort of wonder why you're still here."

He tipped his head, curious. Didn't volunteer an answer. I shrugged.

"I mean, you've got the money to go wherever you want. No family here to hold you back. Unless you count Elizabeth, of course. Never seemed to me like you had that many close friends here. But I suppose that could've changed over the years. I guess I'm surprised you stayed. The way you talked about people in general, the way you looked down on people in this town, I always figured you'd go someplace more remote. Wyoming, or Montana. Get a big spread where the nearest neighbor is miles away. Trout stream running through it. Too cold, maybe. You could buy your own island in the Caribbean. I think that's what I'd do."

He watched me, faint amusement slanting his mouth.

"Then I got to thinking about what you're sitting on," I said. "Big chunk of land in a town that's busting at the seams. Guy that's building those houses out back must have paid a pretty penny for the land. I can't imagine you letting go of it unless it was a hell of a chunk of change he was offering. I look out the living room window, and just down the rise a ways is that big new shopping mall Pete Anderson's company is putting up. Don't know where that property line is, but it must just about butt up against yours."

His eyes narrowed. "What's your point?"

"Just that I see how the land here must be getting more valuable all the time. I can understand why you would have wanted to get into the syndicate that put up the original money for the mall. Makes your property even more valuable."

"I suppose."

"What I find really interesting is who got the materials contract."

His eyes didn't even flicker.

"Milt Seeger," I prodded. "The fellow who bought out your business."

"You lost me. I still don't get your point."

"Oh, please, Frank. Give me a break. You know how it looks. You stand to make a lot of money on this land. You stood to make a lot on the mall. Maybe even more if Milt expressed his gratitude the right way."

His jaw worked. "Don't be stupid. Of course the farm is valuable. Of course, the mall makes it more valuable. As for that other, I ought to slap you silly. I sold the business a long time ago. I'm out of it. How Milt Seeger runs it is none of my concern." He held up a hand. "Before you say another word, let me tell you you're dangerously close to crossing the line with me. RV or no RV, family or not, you're a guest in *my* house. If you want to keep on insulting me, you can just pack up your bags. I'm not going to sit here and listen to your insinuations.

"I lost a lot of money on that mall. I went in on it because I saw—what's his name, Barrett?—do a lot of developments around town and figured he must know what he's doing. And because several people I respect were so gung-ho about this being good for the town and how we couldn't lose. Well, we all lost. Most of us, anyway. I think your friend—Lou, was it?—ended up being a pretty dim bulb."

"If you're so innocent in all this, then who's the dim bulb? You got taken for how much?"

"Enough to make me very unhappy with your old pal Barrett."

"Enough to try to push him out of the deal, maybe?" I shot back.

"Now you're being stupid again."

"Enlighten me if I'm so dumb."

He shook his head disdainfully. "Think about it. No? Still don't see it? What pushed him out was the same thing that screwed us all over. He bit off more than he could chew, and our pockets weren't deep enough to save him. It would have been like throwing good money after bad, anyway. The strike killed the deal."

"That was convenient, wasn't it?"

"Not for me, it wasn't. You go lose a couple million. Tell me how it feels. I don't know what you're doing here anyway trying to figure out what happened to that jerk. Pretty simple if you ask me."

I gritted my teeth. "He was my friend."

"Oh, for Christ's sake. Lou Barrett was never your friend. Not even when you were eight, nine, whatever. The minute I laid eyes on that kid I knew he was bad news. Nothing but trouble."

"That's not true."

"Really? Name one thing he ever did for you."

My hesitation should have told me something, but I dredged the silt of memory even harder.

"He fixed my bike once." It came out lamely. "He always had my back. Never let anyone at school pick on me."

"More like you had his back," he scoffed. "How many times did you save that kid's ass, Emerson?" My eyes widened. "What? You think I don't know about even half the times you covered for him?"

He paused, watching it sink in. Went on softly. "You're too old to be mooning around over what happened when you were ten."

"I'm not 'mooning around.' "

"Whatever you say." His eyes mocked me. "You come back after twenty years—"

"Twenty-five."

He shrugged. "—and you step in your past like it was a fresh cow pie. This is my present. This is where I live, son. I'm happy with my life the way it is. You come in here and muck around like you know what's going on, like you know these people. But you don't have a damn clue. You didn't then. You sure as hell don't now."

He appraised me. "You've got a girl—you love her, right?—and a daughter. So, what the hell are you doing here rooting around through dusty old yearbooks?"

I didn't have an answer. He watched me for a moment, then lifted a corner of the paper and pushed his nose up close to focus on the print. He scanned the page up and down.

"You made your choice a long time ago," he said, eyes still on the paper. "It was the right choice for you. I have no problem with that. Somebody else seems to think this isn't the place for you, either. You might want to start paying attention."

He glanced at me over the top of the paper. Calmly went back to reading. I watched him raise the glass to his lips, hesitate while he read a line, the mannerisms as familiar to me as the contents of my kitchen drawers. The line of his jaw, the little cleft in his chin, the whiskery cheeks that had felt like sandpaper when I bussed him goodnight as a kid—all the same. Just features on a face. No longer capable of instilling me with fear. Or love. Or even respect.

Still, I wondered if he'd pitched his tent with those who wanted to see me gone. And why a chat with him, even after all these years, roiled my insides like lava in a volcano.

CHAPTER 21

Twenty minutes later I walked into the tavern downtown for my second beer. The place was nearly empty. Jake stood behind the bar, towel in one hand, eyes raised to a TV screen. He held a pilsner glass by its heavy bottom in his other hand. Slowly twisted it dry against the towel. He glanced over at the sound of the door. Nodded and turned back to the TV.

I claimed a stool at the bar. An older couple talked quietly at a table by the door. Raucous laughter erupted behind me. I swung my head around and saw four men at a table in the back. Noted eight or ten beer glasses on the table, most empty. I caught the eye of one facing me and scowled. He looked away. Leaned across the table and said something to the man opposite. Looked my way again and lifted his chin. The fellow with his back to me turned around. Pete.

"Well, look what the cat dragged in," he said loudly. "Thought I smelled something funny."

The other two stopped talking, craned to see. Laughed. I sensed Jake coming up behind me, turned to give him my order.

"Hey, Jake," I said quietly.

He nodded, set a bar napkin in front of me.

"Give me a bottle of the most exotic thing you've got."

He turned and stooped, pulled a Heineken from a cooler. Uncapped it and set it down on the napkin. I frowned at it.

"Stare at it all you like," he said. "It's not going to change into something else. Glass?"

238

I shook my head as I picked it up. Tipped it back and let a third of it gurgle down my throat, cold bitterness filling my mouth.

"Rough day?" Jake picked up another wet glass from the drain board. Twisted it in the towel.

"Not so bad. Just thirsty, I guess."

"You're looking pretty good, considering." The explosion was still big news. He waited a beat, then moved a few feet away. Leaned back against a cooler, looked up at the TV. Dried another glass.

I nursed the rest of my beer. Hunched over the bar and ignored the lewd jokes and loud guffaws behind me. Mindlessly watched a TV screen on the opposite wall. Baseball. Like watching grass grow. Hard to believe some guys get paid ten, twenty thousand an hour to stand in a big field doing just that. In football, at least we got to rip it up. An inning or two later, the scrape of chairs and rustle of windbreakers.

"Time to go." Pete's voice. "Just stinks too bad in here." He sidled up next to me and leaned over the bar. "Jake, you oughta air this place out. Maybe be more careful who you let in."

He turned, beer-breath sucking the oxygen from the space between us. His eyes stumbled all over me, struggled to focus. Landed on the tip of my nose.

"Pretty stupid you can't take a hint," he said.

I gave him a friendly smile. "Guess so."

His brows knitted and he tried again. "I mean it. I was you I'd take my act somewhere else. Looks like you *bombed* in this town."

He half-turned and waited for the delayed laughter from his cronies.

I sighed. "Give it a rest, Pete. We're not in high school anymore."

He grunted. "You're right about that. You might've thought

you were hot shit back then. But you ain't big dog around here anymore."

"I never thought I was."

"Sure you did. Just remember who made you look good. It wasn't for me, you'd never've amounted to shit."

"Whatever you say, Pete."

"Fuck you. It's true."

I remembered it differently. Ever since the day Randy Tate had bloodied my nose with a football I'd made a point of getting my hands in the way instead. Never very quick or clever, I'd just put my hands in front of the ball, wherever it was. High, low, didn't matter where Pete threw it. I got my hands on it and hung on for dear life.

I remembered something else.

Two of them leaned against the trunk of the car. A third stood facing them, slouching casually, drink cup in one hand. He raised it, sucked on the straw sticking above the rim. Grinned at his friends.

"Do you believe that shit in the ninth?" he said.

All three wore baseball caps. Black and gold. Harvard colors. High School, not University, in the town up the road. Harvard billed itself as the "Milk Center of the World." Had a "Milk Day" every year. Parade and everything. Even got President Ford's daughter, Susan, to show a couple of years before. Put up a fiberglass cow in the center of town when I was ten. Called it "Hamilda." Go figure.

"Man, that was sweet," said another. "Pitchers couldn't throw worth shit."

I gritted my teeth. Lou had parked his dad's truck next to them, in the end slot at the drive-in. Hauled me out of the passenger seat, put the tailgate down and made me sit in the truck bed while he went to get us burgers. Just in case I got the whirlies and felt like puking.

Earlier that day, our last game of the season, we'd blown a chance at a conference playoff berth. Afterward, a few of us went to Bud Jurgensen's house to drown our sorrows. Someone made a beer run. Up to Walworth most likely. Across the state line where we could legally drink at eighteen. Five of us killed a case before sunset.

Remnants of daylight silhouetted buildings and trees across the highway in a faint orange glow. Here in the lot, floodlights cast sharp shadows across the gloating faces of the tormentors next to me. Listening to the enemy denigrate our troops turned my vinegar mood mean.

"Yeah," the first one chortled, "nothing like walking three in a row to load the bases."

"Then that bozo outfielder just handed Donny the grand salami on a platter," said the third. "How awesome was that?

"That 'bozo,' " I said, sliding unsteadily off the tailgate onto my feet, "out-hit and out-played everyone on your team."

Three heads turned in unison. They jiggled out of frame and snapped back like a horizontal hold in need of adjustment on an old picture-tube TV. Fact was, Bud had pitched a shutout for seven innings, and we'd been up nine-nothing. Then he gave up three runs in the eighth before good defense had ended the inning. Coach had pulled him in the ninth, his arm mostly Jell-O. Jim Nichols gave up two runs before the first out. Jerry Sweet gave up another run, got the next batter to fly out, then walked three in a row. Lou was the bozo who had put a glove on a fly ball back at the fence, but hadn't been able to hang on.

"Guy couldn't hit his way out of a wet paper sack," said the one standing.

I enunciated my words clearly. "My sister could hit better than your team." An exaggeration. My sister couldn't, but Lou's could.

They cackled before one replied, "Whatever you say, buddy."

"Fuck you." Brilliant response. "It's true."

The one standing took a step toward me, smile disappearing. The two on the trunk tensed, but stayed put for the time being.

"Fuck me?" he said. "Fuck us? What? You interested in some of this?" He grabbed his crotch and thrust his hips forward. "Huh, faggot?"

I lowered my head and stumbled toward him. He got his hands up before I could drive a shoulder into his midriff. Back-pedaled a few steps until my momentum slowed. Regained his balance and found some footing. Then shoved me back, throwing me off. I saw the other two push off the trunk lid onto their feet, watching us warily. Smiling, though, at my opponent's quick recovery.

I moved in again, threw a punch. He turned and hunched a shoulder so it glanced harmlessly off. Stepped inside my swing and popped me in the mouth. I staggered back a few steps, hands going to the site of the pain, feeling the warm, wet blood trickling from a cut lip.

"Oo uggin' lit 'y lip," I said, more surprised than hurt. That would come later.

"I'll split more than your fucking lip, asshole."

He took a menacing step forward, compatriots lining up behind him. I stood flatfooted, as bewildered by the punch as the beer buzz that lingered. They were about to beat the crap out of me, but my feet felt planted in cement. I hunched my shoulders, waited for the rain of blows. Saw a dark silhouette slide up behind the pair in the rear. Suddenly the one on the right crumpled soundlessly to the ground, hands cupping his crotch. The other one turned to see his friend go down. Got cold-cocked with a right cross. The flying fist still held a sack of burgers. Lou's grinning face appeared in the light.

An involuntary giggle bubbled from my bloodied mouth. My

opponent hesitated, confused. Turned to see what had set me off. I had the sense to charge him again while he was distracted, still snorting with laughter. Knocked him off balance. He stumbled back, fell over one of his buddies. Lou strode up, gripped my upper arm in a big hand and hustled me over to the truck. Grabbed my belt with his other hand and tossed me into the truck bed. Slammed the tailgate. I heard a door close, the motor roar to life. After that I barely held on. The truck flew into reverse, jerked to a stop. Peeled out of the lot, tires squealing. Zig-zagged through town, tossing me from one side to the other.

The ride smoothed out. I lay on my back, gazed at the stars overhead. Nursed the fattening lip with my tongue. Eventually, the truck slowed and bumped to a stop. I sat up and looked around. No lights visible, so we were out of town. A quarter moon brightened the sky enough to make out shapes on the landscape. A soft yellow glow spilled back from the headlights.

Lou came around the back of the truck and crooked his finger. "Get out here."

I scooted my butt toward the tailgate. "Where are we?"

"Doesn't matter," he said. "Get out here."

"Jeez, I'm coming. Gimme a break." I jumped down and faced him.

"What was all that about back there?" he asked.

"Hey, I was just defending you."

"Me? What are you talking about?"

"Guys were bad-mouthing the team."

"So what? What do you expect? They're from Harvard."

"They called you a bozo," I mumbled, ears burning.

He stared at me a long moment, eyes glinting like new quarters in the moonlight. He hauled off and slugged me in the gut, doubling me over. Put his hands on my shoulders and gave me a shove, planting my tailbone on the grassy shoulder with a thud. My shoulders and chest wracked trying to suck in a breath. When I finally looked up, Lou sat on the tailgate, legs dangling over the edge, shoulders hunched, watching me without expression.

"What'd you do that for?" I asked. My head throbbed, my lip stung, my ass hurt, and I vacillated on how much I wanted to throw up.

"You're a dipstick, you know that?"

"What's your problem?"

"You don't even like baseball. You're not the one who dropped that fly ball. That was me. And I got over it about two hours ago. So what makes you think you have to defend me? Who the fuck put you in charge?"

I recoiled from the heat of his anger. Somehow it hurt more than all the other injuries. "Jeez, nobody, Lou. I was just trying to stand up for you."

"You being such a big shot and all."

"I never said that. Why are you so pissed? What did I do?" The words came out in a whine. I tried to scowl, hoping I hadn't looked as petulant as I sounded.

He waved in disgust and looked away. "Nothing."

"No, really, I want to know."

He turned back, considered me. Hard to see what was on his face let alone on his mind.

"It's no big deal," he said quietly. "I'm just tired of bailing your sorry ass out all the time."

"Bailing *me* out?" My sodden brain recalled the many times I'd helped him write papers and study for tests. The times he'd pull some stunt and leave me holding the bag. "Well, I guess you won't have to worry about that anymore."

"Yeah, *you* made sure of that. Didn't you?"

I blinked. Heard the cry of a whippoorwill in the darkness. Felt the warm cleansing breath of a gentle breeze wash over me.

Tasted clover and dandelion in the air, the scent of summer coming after the season's first really warm day. Suddenly, I saw Lou as clearly as if he'd been bathed in the beam of a searchlight.

"You're jealous," I said.

His head snapped back. "Of you? Don't make me laugh."

"That's it. You're jealous. You're pissed that I'm going to Colorado."

"You're wrong." His voice went quiet again. "You're smart. You could have gotten into one of those snooty Ivy League schools if you wanted. I never thought we'd end up going to the same college. How dumb do you think I am? You want to know what ticks me off? The fact that you got a free ride, that's what. For playing football. What a joke."

"Hey, it's not a free ride. Only a partial scholarship."

"It's still a joke."

"You're just mad you didn't get any offers."

He looked down, crossed his ankles and swung his legs back and forth, but said nothing. Finally, he hopped off the tailgate and came my way. I kept a wary eye on him. He stopped next to me and extended an arm. I looked up at him. Took his hand and let him haul me onto my feet. We stood toe-to-toe, noses only inches apart.

"You still hit like a girl," he said.

He turned on his heel and got back in the truck.

Doesn't matter to a drunk if you agree or disagree with him. In his inebriated mind, you're either patronizing him or trying to prove you're better than him. Pretty much one and the same.

The light in Pete's eye said his mood verged on violence. Didn't know whether to punch me right there or invite me outside. I didn't want to give him the chance. I slumped a little lower, tried not to tense.

"It's not worth it, Pete," I said in a low voice.

His brow furrowed, forcing his eyes to cross. "What? Whadya mean?" He pulled his head back a little and struggled to focus.

"*I'm* not worth it."

He still looked confused.

"Look," I explained, "at best you wake up with sore knuckles, maybe even a broken hand. At worst, 'cause you've had a couple and I'm still sober, I get in a couple licks and bust you up some."

He hesitated, weighing the idea. Seemed to be tracking me okay.

"How 'bout this," I went on. "You lean in close like you're going to give me some advice. Keep your voice low and say a few threats. Then tell your buddies I just about pissed my pants. I'll back you up. Jake, too."

Pete glanced from me to Jake and back, suspicion changing to disbelief, then acceptance. He gave a short nod. Swayed a little and leaned in, one hand on the bar to steady him.

"You fuckin' come near my construction site again, or mess with me or my family, I'll fuckin' tear you a new asshole. Got it?"

I cowered, slouched some more. Stared down at the floor between my knees. Stayed that way while he pushed away from the bar, cuffed the back of my head and strutted away. Heard the guffaws when he told his buddies. Didn't move until after I heard the door close on their laughter.

Jake stepped in front of me and pointed at my glass. "Ready?"

I started to nod, but changed my mind. "Make it a club soda on ice. Squeeze of lime if you have it."

"Sure." He filled a glass and traded it for the empty in front of me. "Thanks, by the way."

"For what?"

"For not letting Pete mess up my bar."

I shrugged. "Self-preservation. Lou always said I was no good in a fight."

He shook his head. "You still haven't let that go?"

I looked up. "What?"

"This business with Lou." He searched my face. "Not even after what's happened?"

"I can't."

"Why not? Man, I thought you'd have given up by now."

"I don't know. It's just . . ."

He lifted an eyebrow.

"It's Meg," I said. "I feel like I owe her."

His forehead crinkled. "Meg? I thought this was about Lou. I mean I know you're trying to give her some closure and all, but what do you owe Meg?"

I shifted on the stool. Couldn't find a comfortable position. Looked around to see who might be within earshot. "You know." I sighed. "She's holding the accident over my head."

Confusion, then surprise played over his face. "Out at your place? When we were kids?"

I nodded, swallowed hard.

"You're kidding. Man, that wasn't your fault. Why is she . . . ?" He peered at me closely. "She doesn't know. After all this time?"

"I never told her. I'm guessing you didn't. Lou sure as hell wouldn't have."

"Sweets? Bud?"

I shook my head. "They never really saw what happened. I think Lou put the fear of God into them anyway."

"Well, tell her." Like it was the simplest idea in the world.

I studied him and wondered if living in Huntley all his life made it easier for him to see things in black and white. I wondered, too, why I'd let Meg use this on me. It held no power anymore. Not with Lou dead. Just another example of who'd been the bailor and who the bailee.

"Maybe," I said.

CHAPTER 22

I walked out of the bar an hour later. No wiser, but no drunker, either. In the old days, four of us could finish off a fifth of Scotch in an evening playing bridge. These days I rarely touched the stuff. I drank an occasional beer with dinner. When I did drink, I limited myself to two. Any more and I woke up the next day with a head full of cotton, a mouth as dry as the Sahara, and a stomach convinced the rest of me was somewhere at sea in a gale.

Jake hadn't managed to make me feel any more useful, and I was beginning to come around to the commonly held view in town. I didn't belong. The one person I knew who could ground me, help me figure out where I fit in, had left. I wasn't sure when she was coming back. Or if. I didn't want to consider that.

Dusk bruised the sky a dark purple, and streetlights popped on around the park. I tried to make up my mind whether to call it a night and head back to Frank's when Pete came out of the restaurant down the block. I backed into the doorway ready to retreat into the bar. He headed in the opposite direction without seeing me.

Food may have sobered him some. Gait steady, he stepped off the curb and cut across the intersection. Halfway down the block, he fished keys out of his pocket, aimed them at a red Corvette and unlocked it with a chirp. On an impulse, I jogged around the corner, slid into the rental, and got it started. Pulled up to the corner just in time to see the Corvette wheel around in a U-turn, hang a left after a rolling stop and head east on Main. I nosed the car around the corner and followed slowly.

Pete's lead quickly increased. I had to push the rental almost fifteen over the limit to stay with him. The Corvette hugged the curve of Huntley-Dundee Road on the way out of town, its taillights dwindling as it leapt ahead. When it pulled away a good half-mile, I punched the rental up over seventy to maintain the gap. Four or five miles down the road, he slowed as countryside gave way to development heading into West Dundee. I closed the gap, but hung back several blocks and let some of the light traffic fill the space between us.

More subdivisions flowed by the windows. The huge Spring Hill Mall loomed up ahead on the right, a giant starfish with big-box department store arms that filled the windshield one by one on the way past. Lou's common sense came into question, if not his sanity. It seemed pretty obvious now why building a big retail mall a dozen miles away from this behemoth had been financial suicide. So what had convinced Lou to try? And why had Pete stepped in to save the deal? Why not just bail? It didn't make any sense.

I wondered if maybe Pete planned to check on the competition, but the sports car turned south on 31. I followed moments later. Watched the lights of the mall slowly recede in the rearview. Thought of Nell as Pete led me deeper into the urban density of Elgin. Thought about how both of us, after years of estrangement from our families, had ended up back in our childhood homes. I wondered if she felt some of the same mixed emotions I did. I wondered, too, whether we had taken these journeys not out of a sense of obligation to our past, but to escape something in our own present.

I missed seeing her soaps and lotions on the bathroom counter, her nightshirt and a few changes of clothing hanging in the closet, her fuzzy slippers on the floor next to her side of the bed. I missed the scent of her on the sheets. The look on her face each time she saw Emily wake from a nap. Her little sigh when she settled into an easy chair after tucking Emily in that spoke of her contentment. I wished I knew her thoughts.

As often as I beat myself up for that single lapse of fidelity a few years before, I wasn't wholly to blame for whatever wasn't right between us. I'd never loved anyone the way I loved Nell. The depth of it, the intensity, almost frightened me at times. The sight of her, even from across a crowded room, still took my breath away, left me weak-kneed. I wasn't perfect. It had taken time to change habits of a lifetime lived alone. Time to make room for her in my routine. Time for me to adapt to the strain of joint parenthood from separate homes. Both fiercely independent, I still couldn't help thinking how much easier it would have been if she'd just moved in when Emily was born, if she'd married me when I'd first asked her.

She couldn't mistake my commitment, though. Even if she knew about Audra, she had to know it wouldn't happen again. Her reticence had something to do with more than just my faults and foibles. More than her mother's illness. The gossamer curtain that hung between us, transparent and weightless, felt impenetrable. As much her making as mine. I searched for the thread that might unravel it. Like everything else she did, she'd woven it beautifully and too tightly.

Elgin's downtown skyline slid by on the left, across the Fox River. The Corvette ahead passed it by. A quarter mile farther south it turned left. The street did a quick S-curve toward the river. As Pete crossed the bridge ahead of me I suddenly realized where he was headed. Glittering like a Vegas show girl on the far bank floated Elgin's riverboat casino.

I slowed on the bridge, admired the lights reflected on the water. Hung back when the Corvette turned the corner up ahead, left toward the casino. On the right was a mall entrance. I went straight through the intersection. Half a block up I wheeled into a side entrance of a mall parking lot. Backtracked to the main entrance, catching a glimpse on the way of the Corvette's taillights disappearing into the parking garage across the street from the casino.

I cruised the parking garage slowly, one floor at a time until I spotted the Corvette. Found an empty slot farther on that he'd have to pass to get out. I parked and locked up, meandered slowly across the covered walkway over the street and through the pavilion. Inside the casino, I kept a wary eye out for him, hoping to spot him before he spotted me.

Though a real riverboat, the casino no longer plied the waters of the Fox River. Illinois slid a little further down the slippery slope toward legalized gambling back in 1990. Addicted to the revenue generated by lottery sales and horse-racing tracks, the state figured a little more money from "gaming" couldn't hurt. So it passed quaint legislation that allowed only riverboat casinos to operate in the state. Thereby preventing big gaming interests from lining the shore of Lake Michigan from Hammond to Waukegan with casinos.

When they first opened, casinos ran games only when the riverboats actually sailed. Boats took guests on two-hour gaming cruises, docked and picked up new loads. The practice had been short-lived. Lawmakers saw the benefit of letting riverboats operate dockside twenty-four/seven.

Slots took up almost the entire first deck of the casino. Most of them, surprisingly, the nickel variety. The place was hopping for a Tuesday night, filled with elderly couples. Women in stretch pants and athletic shoes, men in windbreakers or sweaters and slacks cinched up too high. Spending their Social Security checks five cents at a time. The flashing lights, bells and buzzers a wet dream for a person with attention-deficit disorder. Yet without the sensory overload of a Las Vegas casino. Something was missing, besides scale.

I stood and watched players at a bank of machines. Video poker and slots. No arm on the bandit. A neat trick. The machines had the requisite bells, but lacked jingle and clank. When a machine's buzzer went off, I saw why. Jackpots paid off in credits on the machine, not coins in the metal hopper. Players got a printed receipt when they wanted to cash out.

Gaming tables were on the upper deck. I figured Pete for blackjack or poker. Poker in Illinois casinos is either an odd three-card version or five-card "Caribbean Stud," so I bet on finding him at a blackjack table. I mingled with knots of guests as they moved slowly down the floor, slouching some so my height wasn't so obvious. Pete was in the last seat at a twenty-five-dollar blackjack table, his back to me. I stopped, circled around the other way until I stood across the pit and a little behind him. An empty stool sat in front of a slot machine just off the main aisle. From there, a little lean to the left provided a clear view of his table.

I fished in my pocket for quarters. Realized the machine took tokens instead. I pulled out some bills and fed a couple into the currency validator. The screen blinked and issued me credits. A cocktail waitress came up the aisle holding a tray with a few empty glasses. I waved her over, ordered a soda, then idly pushed a button and watched Pete across the pit push a wager into play. Players occupied all the seats at the table except one, but the hands were dealt briskly. The small stack of chips at Pete's elbow dwindled and disappeared. He straightened a leg, dug deep in his trousers and pulled out a roll of bills. Peeled off several and pushed them toward the dealer. Got a bigger stack of chips in return.

The waitress returned ten minutes later, my soda the only drink left on her tray. I handed her a twenty. She started making change, boredom tattooed on her face from thousands of repetitive, empty transactions like this every week.

"Keep it," I said. She looked up sharply. I nodded. Put another twenty on her tray. "Maybe you can help me."

Her eyes narrowed in suspicion. I went on before it had a chance to form and harden.

"There's a guy at the end seat of a table behind you," I said. "No, don't turn around yet. Table sitting catty-corner across the pit, the direction I'm facing. Big guy. Wearing a blue windbreaker."

She looked at me a moment longer. Casually turned. Swiveled her head back to face me. "What about him?"

"Have you seen him in here before?"

She transferred her weight to one leg. Brushed a strand of hair out of her face and let her hand rest on her hip. "You have any idea how many people I serve a night?"

"I could take a guess. I figure if he's a regular you might notice." I put another twenty on her tray. "Need another look?"

She shook her head. "I've seen him before."

"He come in often?"

She shrugged. "Often enough. Two, three times a week maybe. Sometimes less. Like I won't see him around for a week or two."

"He always gamble that way? Peel bills off that roll until it's gone?"

"I wouldn't know. I don't have a lot of time to stand around watching how people lose their money."

"Point taken. Ever wait on him?"

She peered at me. "You a cop?"

"Nah, just an old friend who's worried about him. His wife asked me to see where he's spending his evenings and maybe try to talk some sense into him." I gave her a moment to consider it. "So?"

"Sure."

"He drink a lot?"

"Not so much that you'd notice." She shifted her weight, glanced away.

"How about his general demeanor?" She looked puzzled. "His attitude," I said. "Does he seem like a winner or a loser?"

She shrugged. "He has his good days." She chewed her lower lip, looked over my shoulder. "Overall? It's hard to say."

I smiled. "Odds are in favor of the house, right?"

Her head swiveled again to take in the room. "The ones you see in here night after night are losers hoping lightning will strike. The ones who don't mind dropping money just for the fun of it are in the club area. You figure it out." She waited a beat. "I have to get back to work."

"Sure. Thanks."

I watched Pete for another hour, and lost a hundred in the process. His style of play never varied from what I could see. He ordered a couple more beers, but the alcohol didn't make him bet more aggressively. The stack of chips in front of him grew for a while, then dwindled. Grew again, shrank and disappeared like before. He pulled money out of his pocket two more times. From the stacks of chips he got in return, I guessed five hundred each time.

When he waved a cocktail waitress over to the table a little before ten-thirty, I decided to pack it in. I took a receipt for the remaining credit on my machine over to a cashier's cage. Got a whopping seven bucks back. Turned to go, but thought of a question instead.

"Excuse me, do you extend credit to players?"

The woman, a brassy bottle-blonde in her late fifties, shook her head. "No, sir. You're welcome to take a cash advance on a credit card, if you wish."

I smiled, leaned in closer. "What I meant was, does the casino extend credit for its 'special' guests?" I gave her a conspiratorial wink. Her expression didn't change.

"No, sir." She spoke politely, but firmly. "We don't extend credit to anyone. It's against Gaming Board rules. We accept cash, cashier's checks, credit card advances, money orders, travelers' checks, or wire transfer service checks." She ticked them off in rote monotone.

"I didn't know that. Thanks."

"Did you want to go ahead with another transaction?" Her eyebrows arched.

"No. Thanks. I'm done for the evening."

"Have a nice night, sir."

A nice night, indeed. I doubted, at this point, there was much that could salvage it. I made my way back to the car, got in and settled down for a long wait. I flipped on the dome light, scoured the interior for a magazine, a paper, anything. Checked the glove compartment. The car was as empty as a pocket on wash day. I leaned back, slid down in the seat, put my head on the headrest. Closed my eyes for a minute. Thought of Meg this time. Thought of how Jake was probably right. It was time she knew.

I opened my eyes later and pushed the stem on my watch. The face lit up with a soft blue-green glow. After midnight. I shook myself. Sat up and looked out the windshield. Breathed a sigh of relief to see the Corvette still there. I switched the radio on and scanned the dial for a station that would keep me awake. Settled on BBC News on one of the Northern Illinois University FM stations.

Ten minutes later, Pete approached the Corvette and leaned against the door while he fished in his pocket and fumbled a key into the lock. He slid behind the wheel. I slumped over in the seat when the 'Vette's engine roared to life and the headlights blinked on. Heard him pull out and pass me by. I sat up and twisted the key in the ignition, pulled out behind him.

He took the Northwest Tollway home. Let the Corvette have its head after the toll booth in Elgin, putting some distance between us. I followed at a more sedate seventy-five. Afraid I might lose him, I pushed it the last mile. Even so, I barely made out his taillights heading north on 47 when I got to the top of the exit ramp. I gunned it, closing the gap on the way into town. He caught a red light at Main Street. I pulled within a few blocks before it changed.

It occurred to me that I didn't know where Pete lived, so I don't know why it surprised me when he turned past the driving range on Algonquin. I gave him plenty of room, watching the Corvette ease up a few blocks and turn onto a side street. I drove on past and saw him pull into a familiar drive. I followed the street as it curved and wheeled into a driveway to turn around. Killed the headlights and slowly rolled back down the street until I had a clear view of the Corvette parked halfway up the drive. A fixture on the side of the garage cast a circle of yellow light on its nose.

Pete sat in the dark car, his profile unmoving. Like he was waiting. Or making up his mind. His head tipped forward, then straightened. He raised an arm. Waited. An upstairs light popped on in the house. Pete leaned forward, craned his neck to look up through the windshield, his features revealed in the light from the window. A cell phone pressed to his ear. He talked some, then listened. Spoke a few words, listened some more. Pulled the phone away from his ear and shook his head. The upstairs light went out.

Pete stayed there for a few minutes. Finally started up the 'Vette, backed out and rumbled back the way he'd come. I leaned all the way over in the seat as his headlights swept over my car. The interior lit up brightly and went dark. I waited until the grumble of the 'Vette's engine faded as it pulled away from the stoplight back at the highway.

This time he led the way to one of the subdivisions east of town. We wound through a maze of streets until he pulled up in front of a split-level, parked and got out. I eased over to the curb a block back, watched as he walked up the drive through a jumble of bikes and toys. He kicked a tricycle onto the lawn and disappeared around the side of the garage. Moments later, a light came on in a ground floor room. Kitchen, maybe. The rest of the house remained dark. Five minutes later the light went out. I waited a few more minutes, but it looked like this was home, and he'd packed it in for the night.

A yawn threatened to unhinge my jaw. I stretched. Started the car, and let it roll slowly past the house Pete had entered, taking down the number. Wondering on the slow drive back to Frank's why Pete had called on Tish Barrett in the middle of the night.

CHAPTER 23

The massive, long-nosed Peterbilt big rig maneuvered slowly into position, a battleship changing course. A tow truck with a twenty-six-foot hydraulic rollback flatbed on the back, it looked malformed, disfigured, its parts disproportionate. No telling where the insurance company had found it. Obviously experienced, the driver jockeyed it like a sports car until it lined up with the shattered remains of the RV squatting forlornly next to the barn.

The chrome flaps atop the vertical exhaust pipes quivered skyward as the huge Cummins diesel engine revved. The truck rumbled slowly in reverse. With a squeal and hiss of brakes it lurched to a stop. The engine settled into a steady deep-throated burble. The driver jumped down from the cab. Fiddled with some levers that raised the front of the flatbed. Let some cable unwind off a winch with another lever. He armed himself with chains, got down under the front of the RV and hooked it up.

I stood on the gravel drive under a sky the color of slate watching. Shivering. The month of May exhibiting the worst of its bipolar disorder. Warm, seductive one day, cold, unforgiving the next. It felt like March. The screen door banged. Frank appeared at my side a moment later.

"Reminds me of the time you had that Howard Rotavator brought in to till Mom's vegetable garden," I said, glancing at him. Saw his raised eyebrow. "You don't remember?"

Hard to believe he didn't, but maybe it had made a bigger

impression on me. It was the biggest tractor I'd ever seen, with the largest rototiller the Howard Rotavator Company made. Brought in on a low-slung forty-foot flatbed.

"George Rhys-Davies offered us a Rotavator on several occasions," Frank said.

"The big one," I said. "Took the driver nearly an hour to get the rig in the driveway and unload. Then only two minutes to dig up the garden. Two passes and he was done. Maybe you weren't there."

He nodded. "Your mother was none too happy. I remember. It dug so deep, she sank up to her ankles in loose soil. It took her half a day to rake it level."

The engine's pitch changed, growling steadily now. The steel cable tautened, thrummed. The RV jerked, inched forward, nosing up the incline of the raised flatbed. A carcass now. A thing. Dead, useless. It had a soul once. A history, at least. It had heard and kept secrets, provided shelter and even solace. Been friend and frustration.

"You going to replace it?" Frank said.

"No. I don't think so." I turned away, feeling foolish. Surprised that it hurt so much to say goodbye.

The driver lowered the flatbed, chocked the RV's wheels, chained it to eyebolts on the flatbed. He disappeared behind the Peterbilt, his head reappearing a moment later in the windshield of the tall cab. Shortly, he crunched across the gravel drive jotting on a clipboard. Handed it to me.

"Sign here." He stabbed the paper with a finger.

The pen hovered, hesitated. I pushed down hard and scrawled my name. "That's it?"

He nodded. "That's it. Have a nice day."

He climbed in the truck, swung the rig out to the right, and arced in a wide circle back to the left. We backed up close to the house to give him room. Watched him complete the circle and head out to the road. The motor home rocked gently on the flatbed as it turned out of sight. A part of me left with it.

Pete pulled out of the construction site a few minutes after five. Unless he went somewhere while the RV was being towed, he'd stayed on-site all day. He drove straight home. I circled the block and parked up the street. I worried about drawing attention. Didn't have to, apparently. Seemed people hadn't taken the trouble to get to know each other here. No one seemed to mind a stranger sitting in a car. I had a couple of magazines with me this time and an old paperback mystery I found on a bookshelf at the farm.

An hour and a half later, a car pulled out of the Anderson's drive. Not the Corvette this time. An SUV, a big one. I saw Pete and Sue Ann, but tinted windows obscured any passengers. I followed them out of the subdivision up to one of the two new elementary schools on Reed Road. Watched them park and walk across the lot, Pete's stride slow and reticent, telling Sue Ann without words that he didn't want to be there.

I waited until they were well inside the building. Got out and started toward the school. Changed course midway and intercepted a couple heading the same way.

"Excuse me, what meeting are you going to?" Their expressions begged further explanation. I shrugged, had no problem looking embarrassed. "My wife told me to meet her at school, just not which one, which kid."

They nodded knowingly. "It's the PTA spring fling," the woman said.

"Oh, right," I said. "Wrong place, though. I'm supposed to be at a sports presentation. Trophy night. She must have meant the middle school. What time does this go to?"

They looked at each other. "Eight-thirty, nine, maybe," she said. "I don't think there was a set time."

"Thanks."

I left them there, went back to my car. Drove into town for something to eat. Settled on the Dairy Mart. An hour later I drove back to the school and parked where I had a clear view of the exit. About twenty minutes after that, I spotted the SUV leaving. It led me straight back to the Anderson house. I parked a few blocks away this time and walked the neighborhood, worried I might stray too far and miss Pete if he left, worried someone might call the cops if I hung around too long.

I paced the streets for a long time, trying to stroll, look casual. I hunched my shoulders against a raw wind blowing out of the west, watchful for faces at windows and cars slowing down for a second look. Circling, I tried not to cover territory the same way twice. Would have been easier with a dog. Or Emily and her stroller. It was too cold for that. A shudder went through me, shock that I actually considered using my daughter as a decoy on a stakeout. And then a rueful laugh. No wonder Nell had her doubts.

I missed them both. Wondered for the thousandth time why I wasn't with them. Or they with me. Why I was rooting around in other people's lives like a pig sniffing out a truffle. When I couldn't even manage to sort out my own life. Frank was right. I'd stepped in it good. Pretty dumb to wonder why I didn't smell so sweet. That was the problem with stepping into the past. Let a cow pie alone long enough and it'll crust up. Step in it, though, and it'll still be soft and messy inside. Let it alone long enough to dry out completely, you're still stepping in shit.

Pete's car was still in the drive on my next pass. I checked my watch, blew on my hands to warm them. After ten-thirty. Kids, the younger ones anyway, had probably been in bed a while. I figured Pete was in for the night and went home. At least what used to be home a long time ago.

★ ★ ★ ★ ★

Thursday night was a repeat of Tuesday. Pete stopped in the bar for a couple of beers, had dinner down the street and ended up at the blackjack tables in Elgin. He didn't stay out quite as late. Accompanied most of the evening by a striking brunette packaged in a way that made her seem artificial. Like one of those new fake Christmas trees that look almost real until you get up close. I got snapshots of the two of them with the camera on my cell phone. Pete didn't stay long after she left.

On the way home, he drove past Tish Barrett's again. He slowed, but didn't stop this time. He inched his car past her corner like he was trying to make up his mind. Then he sped up. I made a quick turn into the driving range. Killed the lights and engine. He did a sloppy three-point turn in the next driveway down and bounced across the grass shoulder. Accelerated up the street and barreled past me through a yellow light at the highway.

I made a point of getting up before dawn on Friday. Went for a run to loosen muscles and joints grown stiff from sitting in the car. I showered, dressed and packed a lunch as the sun rose, light and warmth streaming through the kitchen windows. On a whim, I stepped into the den. The small room held little save an old spinet piano; chintz loveseat, the pattern so faded that it was unrecognizable; and a brass floor lamp, finish dulled to a muddy brown. Built-in cupboards and bookshelves covered one wall. A shaft of sunlight slanted through the window, brightly illuminating a column of books, spines faded from long exposure. Dust motes lazily drifted toward the ceiling, sparkling as they turned in the light.

The room smelled musty, felt familiar, brought back old memories. An encyclopedia set, decades out of date, took up three feet of shelving—our homework research resource, long before the Internet. A six-inch-thick dictionary sat open on the counter atop the cupboards, the only time we were excused from the dinner table in the middle of a meal to use it. Other books from childhood, the authors' names as familiar as old friends—A.A. Milne, Jack London, Victor Appleton II, Carolyn Keene, Franklin Dixon, Madeleine L'Engle, Sterling North. I pulled down a birding guide, took a pair of binoculars from the cupboard. Closed the door softly.

After following Pete to the site, I found a spot on Powers Road with a good view of the whole mall. I got out of the car and walked around. Breathed in the scent of summer as the sun quickly took away the morning chill. Listened to the familiar songs of birds I remembered from summers on the farm. Used the glasses to find one of the songsters perched on a fence or in a tree. Swung them around every so often to check on comings and goings at the site.

Long after lunch time, I recognized the big SUV pulling out of the construction site and steadied the binoculars on the roof of the car. Sue Ann sat behind the wheel. A thought bubbled up, took form. I yanked open the car door, threw the glasses across the seat and climbed in. Turned the key and spun the car around. Gunned it down the road to the highway, checking for cross traffic, slowing just enough to make the turn. I hoped she headed the same place I did.

There was no sight of the SUV in the rearview as the road curved into town. Either I had a big lead or I'd misjudged and had lost her altogether. No time to wonder. Already committed, I turned into Diecke Park and sped up the hill. Wheeled into the gravel on the left this time. Nosed into a spot halfway down toward the baseball diamond. Grabbed a baseball cap and the sack lunch from the backseat and jumped out. Ran up to the covered picnic pavilion, slid into a seat and pulled the cap down low over my eyes. I reached into the sack for a sandwich, caught my breath and took a bite.

Minutes later, Sue Ann hurried up the walk and took a seat at one of the picnic tables out in the sunshine. Same one as before. Force of habit. I kept my head down, saw her fidget, anxiously glance the way she'd come. It was another five minutes before Bob slouched up the walk, hands in his pockets, eyes downcast. He slid onto the seat next to her, scowling. She spoke to him, her expression stern, reprimanding him for being late. He responded angrily. No love lost between them.

I took my cell phone out of my pocket and pretended to dial while snapping a photo of the two of them. Snippets of their conversation drifted my way before being snatched away by a gentle breeze. She: ". . . can't go on . . . no more . . ." He: ". . . you promised . . . I'm in too . . . why can't you . . ."

Sue Ann shook her head. A storm brewed on her brother's face. He snatched up the paper bag she'd left on the table and looked inside. I snapped more photos, watched his face widen in surprise. The storm broke. He reached into the sack, snatched out a fistful of money. Stood and shook it in Sue Ann's face.

"What's this?" His voice loud this time.

She tugged on his sleeve and mouthed some words.

"It's not enough!" he said.

She shushed him, grabbed his hand in hers and pulled it down under the table, forcing him to sit. She started to look around. I quickly turned away, hunched over my sandwich, phone pressed to my ear. When I dared look again, there was no sign of the money or the sack. They bent low, heads nearly touching, Sue Ann talking earnestly, Bob clearly unhappy. I strained to hear, but they kept their voices lower than before.

I didn't wait for more. I gathered up my lunch, slipped the phone in my pocket. Slid off the picnic bench keeping my back turned, and casually strolled down to the car. Drove back to my perch up on Powers Road. Finished my sandwich and washed it down with a bottle of water. Spent the afternoon thinking. Tried to make the pieces fit.

I pulled up to the curb in front of Meg's house. Her SUV was parked in the drive in back, tailgate wide open. I got out and walked across the lawn around the corner of the house. Watched Meg come out the back door in shorts and a tank top, unruly red hair lashed in a thick braid. She reached into the SUV. Stretched onto tiptoes, putting definition into the shapely, freckled legs and arms. She wrestled two bags of groceries into her arms, started to lose one as she turned.

"Need some help?" I took two long strides and put a hand on the bag before it fell. Startled, she almost lost the other. I put a free hand on her arm to steady her. Felt the warmth of her skin under my fingers. Looked into ocean-deep green eyes just inches away. Let my hand drop and took a step back.

"Jeez, you scared me," she said. "Thanks."

I took the bag from her. "Sorry. This all?" I turned to look inside the SUV.

She nodded and shut the tailgate then turned toward the house. "What's up?"

"We need to talk."

She paused, nodded again. "Come on in. You can help me put these away."

I followed her in, put the bag down and unloaded the contents onto the counter. Meg put them where they belonged with efficiency.

She turned to look at me. "What's going on?"

I shrugged, felt my face flush. "It's no big thing. I just wanted to let you know that I think I've gone as far as I can looking into this business with Lou."

She held my gaze. "As far as you can, or as far as you want to?"

"Both, maybe."

"Look, I can understand you're probably shaken up by the explosion and all, but—"

"It's not that. I'm not sure that has anything to do with Lou's death." I paused, switched gears. "How well did you know your brother?"

She started. "Pretty darn well. Why?"

"Trouble is, I don't think you knew him at all. I don't think anyone knew him very well."

"How can you say that? I grew up with him. So did you. I've lived in the same town with him all my life."

"What kind of toothpaste did he use? What brand of socks did he like? What side of the bed did he sleep on? Did he wear boxers or briefs?" She reeled under the onslaught of questions. "You don't know, do you?" I went on. "There're a zillion other things you don't know about him, either. Problem is, the more I dig into this, the more things I find that I'm pretty sure you're not going to like."

"Like what? You think I can't take it? After all the things Lou's done that I *do* know of? My God, Emerson, he killed himself. Could I feel more shame than that?"

I sighed. "Look, I don't know anything for sure. But it doesn't look pretty. You don't need this. Your folks don't need this. Your family doesn't need this."

Her eyes glistened. She made no sound, wouldn't let the tears go. "I need to know what happened to him. Don't you understand?"

"No matter how ugly?"

She nodded.

"I'm just not sure I want to go there, Meg."

"You owe me. You owe Lou."

"No, I don't."

She heard the hardness in my voice, made one last desperate

plea. "Good God, he saved your life. The least you could do is help find out what happened to make him do this."

"He didn't save my life that day, Meg."

She froze, uncertain now. "What do you mean? I was there."

I took a deep breath.

A pale yellow sun hung high in a cornflower blue sky. I felt the weight of it through the thin cotton T-shirt, felt its heat turning the back of my neck and tops of my ears the color of rust on an old pump handle. Fingers of a hot breeze stroked my skin, riffled the fabric of my shirt. The thunderous roar of the tractor drowned out the summer sounds of crickets and birds.

I leaned in close and shouted over the din. "Ease up a little, will you?"

Lou glanced at me, a demonic grin on his freckled face. He hunched over the big steering wheel, perched on the edge of the metal seat, legs stretched to reach the pedals. He swung the wheel back and forth, keeping the tractor straight as it bounced along the rutted path. I leaned on the fender, one hand clutching it by the edge, the other braced against the instrument panel. Meg leaned on the opposite fender, feet braced against the base of Lou's seat, white-knuckled little hands gripping the back of it.

"We're barely moving," he shouted back.

"We're going plenty fast." I looked across at Meg. "You okay?"

She nodded, managing a grin.

I turned and looked the way we'd come. Behind the tractor trailed a twenty-foot length of heavy chain with a hook on the end. It was looped through a twelve-foot section of chain-link fence and hooked back on itself. The length of fencing kicked up little clouds of dust as it dragged through the grass. They hovered and were whisked away in whorls and eddies by the breeze. Hoots of laughter sounded faintly over the tractor's growl. Jake, Bud, Sweets and Jimmy were back there "pasture surfing." A game Robbie invented.

Simple, really. Just run alongside the piece of fence and jump on. Go for a ride. Only it wasn't that simple. The chain link chattered over the rough ground, jerking this way and that, hitting a rock every so often. It could be as challenging as the real thing, though none of us had ever been near the ocean, let alone a half-pipe.

Jake and Bud rode solidly, arms out for balance, swaying with the bumps. Sweets ran alongside shouting encouragement to Jimmy, who backpedaled, arms windmilling as he tried to regain his footing.

The best place for pasture surfing wasn't in a pasture, but in a marshy grove down the slope, south of the house. Unless we had a really wet spring, most of the grove dried up in the summer except for twin ponds shallow enough in spots that brush and trees still grew out of them. That left a maze of dry grassy waterways through the grove as well as tracks on high ground cut from years of use.

The tractor slewed, throwing me off balance. I held on, jerked my head around. Fear showed through the bravado on Meg's face. Lou grinned even wider.

"Watch it," I shouted over the engine. "You're going to get us in big trouble."

"Why?" he yelled back. "Your dad does this with you guys, doesn't he?"

I hesitated. "Yeah, once in a while. But he doesn't drive this fast."

"So?"

"So, he'd kill us if he knew we were going this fast. Ease up."
He smiled, kept his foot on the gas.

"I mean it, Lou. Slow down. I'm not even supposed to let you drive, you know."

"I know how to drive."

"Nobody said you didn't. But my dad'll kill me if he finds out. Ease up, will you?"

Disgruntled, he backed it down a hundred rpm or so. I glanced at Meg. She put on her brave face and gave me a little smile. I turned to watch the guys. Got mesmerized by their antics, lulled by the hot sun, the drone of the engine, the bump and sway of the tractor. My mind took a stroll. I wondered what Mom planned for dinner. Reminded myself I'd have to fill the tractor with gas when we were done. Hoped Robbie would give me a ride into town later to refill the five-gallon gas cans.

The tractor hit a big bump and jerked to the right, bending me back over the big knobby tire. My toes reflexively hooked under the seat before I flipped all the way over, and I strained to pull myself up, stomach muscles burning.

"Lou! Slow down!"

"I'm trying!"

He stepped on the brake, but the tractor roared on. The hand accelerator was set. I reached for it, still fighting to regain my balance.

"The lever! Push the lever up, Lou!"

Meg had been thrown into Lou. He tried to push her off with one hand, keeping his other hand on the wheel.

"Straighten the wheel! Cripes, Lou, do something!"

"I'm trying!"

He got both hands on the wheel, swung it the other way. With a grunt, I pulled myself up far enough to yank the lever on the instrument panel just as the tractor lumbered over the bank of one of the ponds. It tipped violently to the right and came to a dead stop. Lou's forehead bounced off the top of the steering wheel. Tossed like a rag doll, arms akimbo, Meg flew over the fender into the water. The splash was small and sounded funny, like there wasn't enough water in it.

"Oh, shit! Oh, shit!" A nameless dread filled me. I felt like throwing up. Lou looked at me, dazed. "You okay?" I asked. "I think so."

I hopped down. Ran around the back of the tractor. The right front wheel had sunk into the muddy water. Meg lay face down on a boggy islet of grass ten feet from shore, a large rock poking above the water next to her head. I stumbled down the bank. Splashed toward her, cool water snaking up my legs. The guys ran to the edge of the bank and stopped, shouting instructions all at once. I stooped, hooked my hands under Meg's armpits. Flipped her over and dragged her toward shore. Behind me, Sweets, Jimmy and Bud stood helpless on the bank, yelling and waving their arms. Jake waded fast through the knee-deep water toward me.

"Jake! Shit, Jakey, she's not breathing! What are we gonna do?" I blinked back tears.

He didn't answer, his eyes drawn to something in the water behind me. Red streamers, spread and faded to pink a few feet away, ribbons of blood attached to Meg's hair. Jake grabbed one of her arms and pulled. I choked back the fear, followed his lead. We dragged her up onto solid ground. A determined look on Jake's face gave me sudden confidence. Calm settled over me. He knelt next to her head.

"I saw the fire department do this," he said. "CPR. Get over here next to me. Quick. Put your hands on her chest and push. Like this."

He showed me. I put my hands in the same spot and pushed. One, two, three . . . Jake leaned over her face, now a pale gray. He pinched her nose shut and put his mouth on hers, blew once, twice, then pulled away.

"Stop," he said. He tilted his head and put his ear to her mouth. Straightened up and put two fingers on her neck. He shook his head. "Do it again. Fast and hard. Don't worry, you won't hurt her."

He bent and put his mouth on hers again. I leaned over and pushed on her chest. Hard and fast, faster than my racing pulse. Sweat broke out on my forehead, dripped into my eyes. I shut them tight against the salty sting. Felt eyes on us as the guys gathered in close. Heard the rushing wind of their frightened breathing, the thudding of my heart against my ribs. Heard flies buzzing lazily in the tall grass at the top of the bank. Heard the whistle of a bobwhite quail in the brush, the warble of a meadowlark in a tree overhead. Nothing from Meg.

I said a prayer then. I felt foolish telling God I'd do anything if He let Meg live knowing that I'd forget in a day, or a week. Go back to doing all the things they told us not to in Sunday school. My cheeks flushed at how it must look. To God. To Lou and Jake and the boys. I prayed anyway, muttering under my breath, "Don't die, don't die."

I looked at the circle of faces above us, all reflecting the anguish I felt. All except Lou's. He still sat on the tractor, twisted round in the seat, watching with a blank look on his face. As if he didn't understand what was happening. As if he didn't even see us.

Meg's thin body shuddered under my hands. I pulled away, startled. Jake did the same. She coughed once. Spit up water. Coughed again, her body seized in a paroxysm this time as she rid her lungs of pond water. Color came back to her face. The fit subsided. Her eyelids fluttered open and she started crying. Jimmy, Sweets and Bud cheered. Lou jumped off the back of the tractor. Rushed over and muscled me aside.

Filled with a sudden urge to be alone, I left them there and walked to the water's edge. I knelt down and scooped some up, careful not to stir up too much algae and muck with it. Tried to keep it from spilling out of hands that wouldn't stop trembling. I splashed my face. Did it again. Felt cool rivulets run down my chest, making my T-shirt stick to my skin. My head cleared as if a fast-moving front pushed through, summer sun suddenly shining on the enormity of what had just happened. I turned toward the babble of voices.

"Jake! Lou! Get over here, quick!"

Their heads jerked. The look on my face must have convinced them not to ask. Wordlessly, they got to their feet and hurried over. The others watched them go, curious. I pulled Lou and Jake into a crouch, turned to Jake first. Kept my voice low.

"Jakey, I owe you big time, buddy. That was amazing! You saved her life, man."

He seemed to fill his T-shirt for the first time. I turned to Lou. A goose egg had risen on his forehead, started purpling. He looked at the ground, then raised his eyes defiantly.

"You're mad at me," he said.

"Damn straight." I nodded. "But we've got a big problem if this gets out. Does she know what happened?"

He looked confused. "I don't know. I suppose so."

"Jake?"

Jake shrugged. "Probably. No reason she shouldn't. Bump on the head doesn't look *that* bad."

"Then we have to convince her otherwise."

"What for?" Lou's eyes narrowed.

"Cripes, Lou, think about it. She nearly *died* 'cause you were going too fast."

"Was not."

"Oh, shut up," Jake said, startling us both. "He's right. Listen up." He looked at me expectantly.

I explained it patiently. "Look, your dad would kill you if he found out what happened. And my dad would kill me if he knew I let you drive. If he thinks I was driving, he'll just be good and pissed. If neither one of our dads finds out, so much the better, but just in case, we gotta have a story. You know little kids. They can't keep a secret."

"Meg's not a little kid," Lou said. "Anyway, she'll never tell."

"Maybe not, but if she does, you want her telling the truth?"
He hesitated, shook his head.

"Okay, then. So, here's what happened. I was driving—"

"But you weren't," he protested. "How's she gonna believe that?"

"I told you to slow down. She'll remember that. You wouldn't, so we'll say I told you that you couldn't drive anymore. Okay? So I was driving, hit a bump and lost control. Meg got thrown off and hit her head. But she didn't almost drown or anything."

"Then who did?" Lou said.

"Nobody." My brow furrowed.

He shook his head slowly. "She's not that dumb. You know how scared you guys looked?"

I blinked. "Us?"

"She saw you. She has to know it was something serious. If it wasn't about her, then who?"

"You're kidding."

"Uh-uh. Not if you want this to work."

"Fine." I felt heat rise up my face again. "You and Jake, then. Tell her I got thrown, too. You pulled me out of the pond. Did CPR on me. Saved my life. That do it for you?"

Lou nodded. "Might work."

"Better go tell her then. Send the guys over here. I'll clue them in."

Lou got to his feet, clapped me on the shoulder. "It'll work. You'll see." He turned on his heel.

"Hey!" I stopped him. "We keep this to ourselves. Anybody asks what happened, we were fooling around down here and Meg tripped and fell."

He nodded. "Got it."

"Swear."

He rolled his eyes. "Okay. I swear."

Jake threw me a look and followed him without a word.

Meg slumped silently onto a stool at the counter. I found a glass in a cupboard, went to the sink and filled it with cold water and handed it to her. She looked at me, eyes sluggishly focusing on the glass. She took it and sipped slowly.

"You okay?"

She looked up, started to tip her head. "Yes, it's . . . all this time . . . I just have to figure out which memories are real." Paused. "Why?"

I fumbled for an explanation. "There just never seemed to be a good time. After a while, it felt like it was better left alone. Then I left. I mean, when was I supposed to tell you?"

"No, I mean why did you do it? Why take the blame? Lou was driving."

I had no ready answer. Maybe no answer at all. After all these years, I was still protecting her from the truth. We both turned at the sound of the back door opening. Phil walked in, momentary surprise on his face fading quickly, replaced with a somber mask. The room went silent, quiet enough to hear the wall clock tick.

"Honey?" Meg said in a small voice. "What's wrong?"

He paused. Scratched his head, puzzled. "It's Danny De-Haan. Out at the train museum? He's dead."

CHAPTER 24

"When?" I said.

Phil looked at me. "Last night some time."

Meg went white.

Phil put an arm around her shoulders. Bent down, concern on his face. "You all right, honey?"

She nodded, took another sip of water. "It's just . . . so sudden."

"Any idea what happened?" I said.

He gave his head a slow shake. "Some sort of accident out at the museum, I guess. I just heard."

"Who found him?" Meg looked as if she didn't want to know the answer.

"Some of the volunteers, from what I can tell. Whoever was opening up for the day, I guess. Apparently, it's a real zoo out there. Or at least it was this morning. It may have calmed down by now."

"How'd you hear?" Meg, more curious now.

He gave her shoulders an affectionate squeeze. Walked to the fridge and pulled out a pitcher of juice.

"I finished up at the office a little early. Decided to gas up the car. Ernie Savitch—" He turned to me. "—he's one of our patrolmen. Ernie's there at the station gassing up. Says he's already had his most exciting day all year."

Meg put a hand to her mouth. "What a horrible thing to say."

Phil shrugged. "Not every day you find a dead body. Not one crushed by a train, anyway. Not his place to tell me, either, but he knows Danny was a friend. Thought I should hear it from him, not through the grapevine."

Meg's face reflected the revulsion in the pit of my stomach.

"Is that what happened? He was run over by a train?" I asked.

"Sort of. From what Ernie told me, it sounded like he was caught between cars. Couldn't make out exactly how that happened, but I suppose that's what they're still trying to figure out."

"What a shame. Danny was an okay guy."

"A little . . . eccentric," Phil said, "but yeah, he was a nice guy."

"I don't suppose the funeral's been set yet," Meg said.

"Body's just been sent up to Charmaine's office, honey." He glanced at me again. "Charmaine Harris. County coroner up in Woodstock." He must have mistaken my uneasiness for confusion. "She gets all accidental deaths. You probably know that. She's good. I like her."

"You've worked with her?" Now I was puzzled.

"Met her a few times. Sent her dental records once to match to a burn victim. House fire. Nasty one."

"What was Danny doing out at the museum at night?"

Phil shrugged. "He practically lived there. Loved those trains."

"Seems he would have known better than to do something he shouldn't without help."

He sighed. "No telling what he was doing. Accidents happen."

"I guess they do."

The silence grew awkward. I tried to fill it. "I better get moving." I turned to Meg. "You going to be all right?"

She nodded, traded a look with Phil that said she would explain later. To me, "What are you going to do?"

"I don't know. I have to think about it."

It was the truth, or as close to it as I was going to get.

"Daddy!" My little girl's squeal of delight sent pangs of sadness and regret through me, and put a smile on my face at the same time. "I got a big girl bed!"

"You got a big girl bed?"

"A big girl bed. All for me. Here's Mommy."

"Okay. Love you." She'd already gone.

"Hi." Nell's voice.

"Hi. How are you? You sound tired."

"I am. This isn't easy."

"I'm sorry."

"Not your fault." She sighed. Then in a brighter voice, "Anyway, Mom's doing better. She's eating again. She seems to have some of the old fight back. She's not so depressed."

"That must be a relief. I'm glad." I paused, went on when she didn't respond. "So, Emily has a new bed?"

"Oh, yes. She's quite excited, as you may have gathered. She's really outgrowing her crib, and what we had set up here was sort of makeshift anyway. I found a small bed frame the same size as a crib mattress at a yard sale. It's just perfect for her. There's a rail to keep her from rolling off, but you can take it off when she's ready. She just loves it."

Nell hadn't been that enthused in weeks. It set off an alarm bell somewhere.

"Sounds like you're settling in nicely."

"We're doing all right," she said, her tone cautious.

I tried to pick my way through the minefield. "So, if your mom continues to do better, have you thought of what your plans might be?"

For a moment I thought we'd been disconnected. She gave a small sigh.

"Yes, actually, I have. I don't know how much time she has. It could be a few weeks or a few years. For the time being, I'm going to stay here. I'm going to be with her for whatever time she has left. Or as long as she wants me here."

It took a long time to find my voice. "And us?"

"I can't answer that, Emerson."

"What does that mean?"

"It means that I don't know what happens to us. I haven't really had time to think about that. This just seemed to be more important right now."

I had a million questions. None of them seemed right. One just popped out. "What do you want me to do, Nell? What do you want?"

After a moment's silence, she spoke in a quiet voice. "I want you to be my hero. *My* hero. I want you to read bedtime stories to our daughter and help me plant flowers. I want you to come to my rescue when I have a flat tire and hold me in the middle of the night when I have a bad dream. I want you to be happy taking out the garbage and fixing a leaky toilet.

"I want to be normal, Emerson. I don't want to be afraid anymore. I don't want to wonder if you'll grow tired of me. Of us. Our family. I don't want to wonder if some woman from your past will turn your head. Or if some favor you do for a friend will get you killed. Goodness, what do you think I want? I want you."

I squeezed my eyes shut tight, choked out the words. "Don't you know you have me?" There was no reply. I swallowed hard, swiped the back of my hand across one cheek. "You're really moving?"

"For now. If Mom gets well enough that she doesn't need me, I may come back."

"You've thought this through."

"Yes, Emerson, I have."

"I thought we were in this together."

"We are. Weren't you the one who said I should go? Sometimes we have to make choices. This isn't a choice I wanted to make, but for now it's the only choice for me. I need to be with my mother. She needs me to be with her."

"I need you, too."

"In a different way, yes. I need you as well. I need you to be there for me if we're going to survive this, if we're going to make this work."

"And give up who I am?"

"No, just rethink it. I don't know. Re-channel it somehow. So you're safe. Let's not talk about this now, please?"

If not now, when? I bit back the words. "All right. Can I say goodbye to Emily?"

"Of course. I'll get her."

I heard my daughter's voice again, gave her a goodbye kiss, closed the cell phone, dropped it in a cup holder. Sat for a minute. Watched the blossoms on a black cherry tree dance in the light breeze. Stayed there until my head emptied. Then drove over to Alison Court where the P.D. had temporary quarters until the new administration building was finished. Almost ran into Randy Tate coming out the door just as I headed in. He didn't stop. I turned and fell in step.

"I heard about Danny."

"Whole town has."

"How'd it happen?"

"If I knew, for darn sure I wouldn't tell you. So happens I don't. Not yet."

"Preliminary thoughts?"

He stopped to look at me. "I thought we had an understanding."

I nodded. "I went out to talk to Danny earlier this week. I heard he wasn't happy with all the growth here. Figured he might have some thoughts about Lou. He did. A few thoughts about Pete Anderson, too. Didn't share much, though. He knew a lot more than he was telling. Now he's dead."

"What sort of thoughts?"

"Pete and Lou had a reputation for building on the cheap, apparently."

He grunted softly. "Accidents happen."

"Like what happened to my RV?"

His eyes roamed my face. "Doesn't look like it. But I'll keep it in mind. Part of my job."

"You'll let me know?"

He started walking again. Spoke over his shoulder. " 'Bout time you let it rest."

I called Brandt, asked him what he was doing. He said the usual, told me the Alfa was fixed. Finally. I suggested he go pick it up, take it for a drive. Out to the country. Huntley, maybe. He said a Sunday drive sounded like just the ticket. I said he might want to pack an overnight bag. Just in case.

He showed up after lunch the next day. Temperature had already climbed into the eighties, prompting me to make a pitcher of iced tea. I poured a glass and took the Sunday *Tribune* onto the porch. Frank was happily reading a stack of old *Wall Street Journal*s in a deck chair out in the sun. I pushed open the screen door when I heard the Alfa come up the drive, ambled out onto the gravel. Frank bent a corner of the paper for a look, went back to reading. Brandt got out, grinning like a kid at Christmas. Pulled me into a bear-hug.

"I've missed you, you old goat-roper."

"Missed you, too. Just made some iced tea. Come on in. I'll show you where you're bunking." I leaned into the car and grabbed his bag off the passenger seat.

I led him over to Frank's chair on the way to the house. He

pushed the paper aside and looked up at me, squinting in the bright light. Blinked behind bifocals.

"Frank, this is my friend Brandt Williams. He lives up the street from me in Chicago."

He swung his legs over the edge of the deck chair and stood while I talked. Still had manners, just hated to use them. I turned to finish the introductions.

"Brandt, this is my father, Frank Ward."

For an instant, Brandt looked like he'd been poleaxed, but he recovered nicely. He stuck out a hand. "Pleased to meet you, Mr. Ward."

"Brandt, is it? Call me Frank. Nice to meet you, too. Make yourself at home."

"Thank you. I will."

Pleasantries over, Frank eased back into his chair. I turned for the house. Brandt followed. Halfway there he leaned in and spoke in a low voice.

"I thought you said you father was dead."

"I did."

He straightened. Said nothing until we were on the porch. "No, I mean dead. Deader 'n two-day-old road kill."

"I did." I led him into the kitchen. Poured him a glass of iced tea. "Long story, friend. Let's just say we weren't that close for a lot of years. It seemed easier."

His eyebrows went up. "Than what?"

"Than trying to explain at holidays and all that crap." He wasn't buying. "Look, I left here when I was eighteen. Never looked back. He was dead to me most of that time."

"What changed?" He eased into a chair at the kitchen table.

I shrugged. "Nothing." He waited. "The bus blew up. I needed a place to stay."

He gave a low whistle. "What? Oil leak? Throw a rod?"

I shook my head. "Dynamite."

He got that odd look on his face, a combination of fear and excitement, like a kid on a rollercoaster climbing the crest of that first drop. A kind of thirst that's hard to shake without going for the full ride.

It took a while to tell it. My mouth felt parched when I was done, my iced tea glass empty and warm. Brandt rubbed the gray stubble on his chin, stared into space.

"You hungry?" I said.

He looked at me, looked at his watch. "I could eat."

I showed him up to Will's old room. Neat as a pin. Little in the way of mementos to suggest it had been a boy's room. A few sociology and psychology textbooks in the bookcase. A boomerang from a student ambassador trip to Australia one summer. Framed certificate on the wall for Speech Club. Next to it hung a framed photo of a group of kids on the Capitol steps in D.C. surrounding Adlai Stevenson, III, U.S. Senator from Illinois. Will's somber face just over his right shoulder. Frank was probably still chapped that it wasn't Chuck Percy. Or anyone else, for that matter, as long as it was a Republican.

I told Brandt I had to go into town to pick up a few things. Gave him the option of staying and freshening up or coming along. Five minutes later we were on our way out the door. Frank was in the kitchen pouring himself a whiskey on ice. I let him know where we were going, said I'd cook dinner for us all when we got back. He nodded.

The lightness and quickness of my car felt good after weeks of the sluggish, mushy ride of the rental. The burble of the exhaust announced the little car's eagerness to be driven, not just steered. We cranked down the windows, let the summery air ruffle our hair.

"Purrs like a cat full of cream," Brandt said, patting the dash.

At the grocery store I picked up a big halibut filet, a six-pack of pale ale and a few odds and ends. I took a long route back, driving slowly, scouting for asparagus growing in the ditches. Stopped to hop out every so often and pick several stalks. Had close to two pounds by the time we got back.

Frank had showered and changed. His short hair was damp, parted and neatly combed, face scrubbed and shaved. He'd exchanged shorts and an old chemise Lacoste for slacks and a dress shirt open at the collar, tan skin dark against the white cotton. As hard as he'd been on his family, he'd always been charming to company. I watched him turn it on, drawing Brandt out while I started in on dinner. I could hear him warming to the subject when he learned what Brandt does for a living. Nothing like talking business to stir the cockles of his heart.

I uncapped beers for Brandt and me. Downed half of mine quickly to soothe a still-parched throat. Started on a second one before the halibut had finished marinating a full twenty minutes. Should have known better on an empty stomach. Should have paced myself. The more they talked, the more they bonded. The more they bonded, the closer I felt the presence of an ugly green monster. I tried to ignore it, push it aside while I worked.

I put the halibut on the gas grill outside. I tossed a Caesar salad, threw the asparagus in a big steamer insert and set it inside a stock pot of boiling water. Drank more beer. Listened to more tall tales, Bunyanesque stories of financial derring-do and Wall Street wizardry. Realized I was still pissed at my best friend for losing most of my retirement fund, still angry at Frank for who knows what. Or maybe that was the beer talking.

At some point during dinner around the kitchen table Brandt turned the tables and got Frank talking about himself. Asked him questions about life in Huntley, the family, my childhood. To my surprise, Frank remembered some of the good times, some of the times I'd forgotten. Flinging us down the slope out back on a snow coaster when we were still small enough to fit on it. Teaching us to ski up at Majestic Hills, the man-made ski slopes south of Lake Geneva. Winter picnics on the porch roof. Summer picnics out in the middle of nowhere on Sunday drives to see a Frank Lloyd Wright house somewhere, or the Kettle Morraine, or the hills above the Mississippi in Galena. The good memories just made me wonder all the more why Frank had changed as we'd grown older, why he'd soured like wine left open too long. That *was* the beer talking, I knew, but I let it.

Frank sighed, settled back in his chair. "Those were the days. Right, Emerson? One minute you were all kids. Next thing I knew, Robbie was in the Army." He watched a film clip of memory. Sighed again. "Things just weren't the same after Hank died."

Brandt glanced at me, the question in his eyes.

"Henry," I told him. "The youngest. Died in a car accident."

"You never told me."

"Don't like to think about it." To Frank, "You know, things were never the same after Mom died."

He picked up the tumbler of Scotch and sipped. Stared at me for a long minute over the rim. "What's eating you?"

I stared back at that familiar face, a Dorian Gray image of my own. The years melted away and the dam holding back all the repressed feelings, the unspoken thoughts, broke.

"What's eating me? Christ, Frank, Mom died and you basically checked out. The kids needed you. Hank, Elizabeth . . . you weren't there."

"Balderdash. Of course I was there. I was always there for you kids."

"You are so full of shit. You were about as remote as the Himalayas. And about as cold. I bet you didn't even know Henry cried himself to sleep every night for a year after Mom died. No, not you. Why? Because, God forbid any of us shed a tear in front of you. He was so scared of you, he didn't dare let you know how much he missed her, how much he needed something from you. Anything. A hug. A kind word. Hell, we all were afraid of you."

"Did you ever stop to think about what I needed?"

"I don't give a shit. Jesus, Frank, we're your kids. You were supposed to be there for us. Take care of us."

"So this is about you."

"No. Well, yes, but not just me. All of us. I can't remember one time you said you were proud of me, of any of us. Not one time you said you loved us."

"Oh, for Christ's sake, you're back on that again? All that sentimental crap? Did I ever beat you? Abuse you?"

I frowned. "No."

"So, what's your problem?"

"That's your idea of being a good parent? You didn't beat us?" I had one vivid memory of him taking a belt to Robbie's bare butt, another when he grabbed Robbie by the front of his shirt and tossed him into a wall.

"You make me out to be this ogre, so tell me what I did that was so bad."

"Where do I start?" I said. "How about this? How about the fact that you cheated on Mom? How about your affair with Harry's mother? You think we didn't know about that?"

The color drained from his face, leaving him looking older, more vulnerable. He picked up a folded section of newspaper. Leaned over and whacked me on the side of the head with it.

"You watch your mouth."

I sat back in surprise. Saw Brandt jump, too. Nearly laughed. He'd used that technique on us at the dinner table when we were kids. To teach us manners. Whack us upside the head with a rolled-up linen napkin when we misbehaved. Get up from the table to fetch the paper and whack us with that for more serious infractions.

"Or what, Frank?" I said. "You'll get out the belt?" I plunged on, slashing and jabbing as I went. "It was so obvious, how you flirted with her at dinner parties. God, it made me sick. And you think Mom didn't know? You don't think she figured it out? Why she never left you, I'll never know. Say, here's another one. How about the fact that you killed Mom? You killed her with your neglect and your slights. And your screwing around. Hell, for all I know, you had more than one mistress on the side."

His hand tensed, poised for a moment to hurl the heavy tumbler at me. The words kept tripping out of my mouth.

"It's one thing to deprive your kids of love and affection. Like you said, we grow up, get over it, make peace with it somehow. Chalk it up to how you were raised. All that macho bullshit about how men aren't supposed to show their feelings. But to do that to your own wife? Christ, Frank, she loved you. She would have done anything for you. And you just let her die."

He sat there and trembled. Then he spoke, so softly I strained to make out the words.

"You don't know what the hell you're talking about. I'm not the one who held back all those years."

"Held back? What do you mean?"

His eyes burned into me while he made up his mind what to tell me. "You think your mother just got sick one day and died? She was sick for a long time. She never said anything. Never let on. You think I didn't know? Of course I did. I begged her to see a doctor, find out what was wrong. She would just smile and tell me not to worry so much.

"Why do you think I had the affair with Rose Hammond? It was stupid. I admit it. I was weak. I had needs. Your mother couldn't . . . the cancer . . . it was too painful. We didn't even know it was cancer. She refused to get help. It's no excuse, I know. But there it is. And frankly, it's none of your damn business. But you're so hell-bent on learning the truth, there it is."

287

He hung his head. I burned with shame and anger and remorse. I'd never seen him like this. Old and empty. Unsure of himself. Used up.

He slowly raised his head until his eyes met mine. "When your mother died, I died with her. I was devastated. Maybe you needed to see me fall apart to prove that I loved her. But I couldn't. I had you kids to think of. I had to keep going."

I said nothing, the whirling thoughts in my head too disjointed to vocalize.

"I made mistakes," he went on. "It's not easy to admit, but I did. I just didn't cry over them, son. I moved on. I lived life the best way I could. The best I knew how."

I wanted to let go of the anger. Wrap it in heavy chains, weight it with an anchor and deep-six it in a bottomless trench where it would never again see light of day. But it still gripped me by the throat.

"What about Henry?"

He started, pain flashing across his face. Then he straightened, the Frank I knew reanimating the old man in front of me.

"What? Now you're going to blame me for Hank's death?"

"Damn right, I am. Where the hell were you? If the rest of us broke curfew by a minute we were grounded for a week. You let Henry run wild after Mom died. Where the hell were you when he got killed?"

I never once saw Frank cry when I was growing up. Not even at my mother's funeral. Now his pale blue eyes misted. In spite of myself, the anger started to loosen its hold. I yanked on its tether, kept it reined in tight. He blinked a few times. Wouldn't look away. Wanted me to see his pain, something I'd never considered possible from him.

"Where the hell were you when we buried him?" he said quietly. He watched me redden with shame. Didn't wait for an answer I couldn't give. "This really is none of your business.

And it's water so far under the bridge that it's probably reached the ocean by now. I did my job. I taught you right from wrong. Gave you a sense of values. Made you appreciate the value of hard work. And you seem to have done pretty well for yourself. But maybe you're right. Maybe I wasn't as good a father as I could have been. Get over it and move on, I always say. But maybe you need this in some way. I never could figure out what makes you tick. Never had a problem with Robbie or Will. Not even Elizabeth, though she's always been a pill. You were different. There was a wall between us. I don't know who put it up, you or me, but it was there. I never had the time or the energy to try to knock it down."

His eyes were drawn to my fingertips softly drumming on the tabletop. A smile flitted across his face so fast I almost wasn't sure I'd seen it. He leaned forward, putting his elbows on the table.

"Did you ever wonder why I never remarried?" He took in my surprise. "Think about it. I was about the same age you are now when your mother died. I'm not a bad-looking guy. At least I wasn't back then. I had a successful business. I could have found a pretty good catch."

"I . . . I never thought about it, I guess."

He nodded. "You thought about how *you* felt when she died. You never thought about how *I* felt." He held up a hand. "I'm not blaming you. I didn't expect you to. You were kids. Even Robbie, and he was a soldier then. Remember?

"The reason I never got married again is because your mother was the only one for me. The only woman I ever truly loved. Can you understand that? Can you try to imagine, for one moment, what it's like to lose someone like that?"

My thoughts twitched and jerked, fish on hooks, leaping from loss to loss. My mother, my brother. Jessica and Cat. Now Nell and little Emily, not gone, but far away. He had no idea how well I understood. I'd just never thought him capable of feeling. Anything. I swallowed, nodded.

"Hank was so like your mother." He gazed at a memory only he could see. "Maybe you think I'm nuts, but he was. I didn't have the heart to cage him up like I did your mother."

The corners of my mouth turned down. "What are you talking about?"

"She hated it here."

"She seemed happy to me."

He shook his head. "She never complained. Either she was too polite or she really was crazy for me. But she wasn't cut out for country life. She was a society girl. I took her away from all that. But that was your mother. Always making the best of things. Henry had the same free spirit."

His smile faded. "I was supposed to pick him up at work that night. He called, said he had a ride from someone else. I didn't give it a second thought." He paused, considered me. "You thought he was out of control, but he always kept his word to me. If he said he was going to be home at midnight, he was home two minutes till."

He raised his eyebrows, knew he was right. I didn't challenge him. Midnight to the rest of us had meant sometime before two. But then my mind had already latched onto another thought.

"No one ever came forward," I said. He frowned. "The police never found anyone who said they offered him a ride. How did he get the beer? Or get to Pete's to take his car, for that matter?"

He rolled his eyes. "Think about it. Would you admit it if it was you that bought him beer? Knowing the trouble you'd be in?"

"Didn't you always say it's better to tell the truth, no matter how much it hurts?"

"You're not that dumb. Or naive." His eyes narrowed. "Are you?"

I shrugged it off, too late to think he hadn't seen the barb hit home.

He sipped his drink. "It doesn't matter. It was stupid. Senseless. And nobody's fault but Henry's. Time to let it go."

I stared at him. "How can you do that? Act like they never existed."

"Ah, now you're being stupid again. I miss them. Of course I miss them. I just don't think about them every waking moment. Do you?"

I slouched in my chair, examined the bottle cradled in my hands. "No."

"I didn't think so. I'm too old to live in the past."

"You're not *that* old."

"Old enough. Enough to know that I don't want to waste what time I have left thinking about what might have been. Do I miss your mother and your brother? Hell, yes. But they're not here anymore. And if they were, they'd be the first to tell you to get on with your life."

CHAPTER 25

The sky was awash with stars, thick as clotted cream or spatters of white paint on a jet black proscenium. Easy to forget, in the city, how beautiful the night sky really is.

I traced familiar constellations with a finger—Ursa Major and Minor, Orion, Gemini. Stellar connect-the-dots. A meteorite flashed by, an arc of light so brief only its echo made an imprint on my retinas. Picked out the steady movement of a satellite on a straight line through the background of stars. Felt Brandt ease into the chair next to mine. Heard his intake of breath.

"Some view," he murmured. A moment later, "Brought you some coffee, partner."

I turned and saw the mug in his hand. Took it and sipped gratefully, gathering my thoughts.

"Sorry about that," I said finally, leaning back and looking at the sky. "In there."

My anger with Frank had blinded me to Brandt's presence, until I'd turned away, finally, and saw him sitting silently, looking at the floor as if pretending he didn't hear.

"No need to apologize. Had some arguments around our family dinner table that make that look like a sewing circle."

He let it sink in, broke the silence a minute or two later, still trying to reach me. "So, what's going on?"

I leaned forward, straddled the chair, resting my elbows on my knees. "That? Jealousy, pure and simple."

"You're jealous? Of me?"

I shrugged. "He likes you. Likes what you do, who you are. You measure up. None of us ever did. It's no big deal. It just pushed some old buttons, that's all."

"Sounded like a big deal."

"I guess there were a few things I wanted to get off my chest. Doesn't change anything. Doesn't change who he is."

"Maybe changes how you see him, though."

I gave it some thought. Nodded. "Not that it makes things any better, but yes, it does."

"He's right, you know. I wouldn't know about all of it. But about moving on."

I had moved on. I'd spent most of my life moving on. But maybe you don't get over something—someone as big as my mother and my brother had been—all at once. They'd both been larger than life to me. She the quiet rock, always there with a kind word, a way to fix whatever the problem was. He the wild child, the Brainiac Type A too bored with small-town life to sit still. I'd said goodbye a thousand times. A piece of me, a small child inside, hadn't let go. I knew it was time.

"We can pick our friends," he said. "Can't pick our family."

"I know. I made peace with it long ago, accepted the fact that he is who he is. That he's not going to change. I guess I just never forgave him. That might still take me a while."

"I'm sorry as sittin' on my spurs about the both of them— your mom and your brother. Even sorrier you couldn't tell me before now."

"It's okay. I should have. You deserve that."

We sat in comfortable silence. Watched the celestial sphere slowly rotate over our heads. Listened to crickets chirp, the song of a whippoorwill, screech of a barn owl. In the distance, like surf breaking on shore, the whoosh of cars on the interstate.

"I'm tired," I said.

"Thinkin' about turnin' in?"

"No." I stifled a yawn—power of suggestion. "I'm tired of trying to relive the past. Trying to find some parallel universe, some alternate truth. I'm tired of trying to answer unanswerable questions. Like I'm some oracle."

No response. No surprise there.

"I miss Nell. And Emily. I miss my house, my bed. I miss you, friend. I miss our bridge games, our Sunday Bloody Marys."

He let me get it out my own way.

"I'm thinking of quitting."

"Not working out the way you thought?"

"No, trouble is it's working out exactly the way I thought. I still don't have any real answers, but the deeper I dig, the uglier things get. It's like high school only ten times worse. I'm not doing anybody any good here."

"Talk to me."

I told him everything I knew. Everything I'd learned about the mall deal gone south, about Pete somehow finding a way to save it after the strike forced Lou into bankruptcy. About a new investor or maybe a syndicate coming in, a new bank buying out the note from Harry. I told him about the materials contract with the lumber yard Frank used to own, my suspicions that Pete may have cut deals with other subcontractors. Tommy's concerns about corners being cut. The rumors I'd heard about Pete and Lou building on the cheap. Pete's gambling problem. And my suspicions that Pete had as much trouble keeping his dick in his pants as he did money.

I told him about the couple of times I'd seen Sue Ann and Bob Kolnik meet in the park, the fact that more went on there than just a family picnic. I told him about Danny DeHaan, about his scuffle with Pete at Lou's wake and what he'd said, about my conversation with him out at the train museum, and oh, by the way, wasn't it an interesting coincidence that Danny died. He listened the way he always does. Intently. Sympathetically. Without comment or judgment.

The more I talked, the more Pete seemed like a lodestone, all the coincidences turning his direction like compass needles. Even then it still made no sense.

"I hate to be repetitive," Brandt said when I finished, "but what's eating you?"

"Funny." I gave it some thought. "Okay, let's suppose Pete's a crook. Let's say he's using inferior materials and cutting corners to skim some money off the top of the mall project."

"It'd make sense, especially if the owner of the lumber yard—Seeger?—is in on it, getting a kickback."

"Right, it would. Though I still wonder if Frank fits into that equation somehow." I caught his look. "Okay, I never knew him to do anything crooked in his life. Doesn't cross him off the list yet."

"He's still your old man, Em," he said softly. "Think he could blow up the bus? Nearly kill you?"

I couldn't answer that. I realized there was a lot about Frank I didn't know. I let it go and turned my thoughts back to the issue at hand.

"So, the scam works because Pete has the building inspector—who just happens to be his brother-in-law—in his pocket."

I tried to work it out in my head. Still couldn't get it all to fall in place. "Meg thinks Lou got screwed. I think he was in on it."

Brandt waited. I looked for a way to explain it.

"He was my best friend way back when. He was everything I wasn't. Strong. Brave. Funny. Charming. It took me a long time to figure out most of that wasn't real. Stage set. A part that he played. I probably knew him better than anyone, and I didn't know him at all. Not really. But I saw stuff that no one else did.

Not even Meg. The racism he got from his dad. How he never failed to cut a corner if he could. The things he did to make himself look better. The petty jealousy. I overlooked it all. I made him my hero. Now I can't think of one reason why."

"Does it matter?" He tried a different tack. "Old saying: a friend is someone who knows all about you and likes you anyway."

I nodded. Wondered now if friendship with Lou had ever been a two-way street.

"Seems to me Lou finally found himself in the wrong place at the wrong time. Couldn't find a way to cover his ass."

"So, tell Meg that, and let it be."

Good advice. I couldn't figure out why I didn't take it. Why I didn't jump at the chance to run back to my life, to my sweetheart and child. Why I still felt unsettled. Like I was walking out on a movie in the third act. Maybe it was because I'd already run away from home once. Maybe I felt guilty about running away again. Or maybe I was supposed to have come home again at this point in my life, to have come back for some reason. Something nipped at the edges of my consciousness. A no-see-um nagging at me, buzzing around the inside of my head.

"Unless . . ."

He cocked his head. I picked my way through it slowly and told him about the couple of times I visited the site: the pugnacity of the union reps, Tommy's fearfulness, the comment Jim Jones made that sent me to the village hall to look up the building inspector on the project—Bob Kolnik.

Brandt had no trouble following. "You're thinking maybe Pete encouraged the union to strike? Knowing the delay would stretch Lou too thin."

I nodded. "What I can't figure out is why Pete would try to push Lou out of the deal. If they've been doing this all along, why go it alone now?"

"Greed," he said simply. "Stakes are bigger."

"Why take the risk? How did Pete know he could salvage the deal after the strike? He faced the same problem. Didn't he? Project goes south, he's got subs who haven't been paid. Suppliers, too. Seems to me the strike could have pushed him into bankruptcy just as easily."

"Unless he already had a deal lined up. Maybe he had investors, a bank, all ready to go."

"Why not just buy Lou out then?"

"Maybe he got tired of having a partner."

I picked up the thought, finished it. "A rival, you mean. A buyout wouldn't have worked. He wanted Lou out of the picture completely. Ruined financially so he couldn't compete. Who knew Lou would take it so hard?"

We contemplated possible answers. Out there in the dark, hundreds of other dramas played out at the same moment. Families left wondering the same thing. Why? Why someone close, loved or hated, was taken from them. Why they're left with so many unresolved questions. Under that canopy of stars, it all seemed so insignificant. The losses. The questions. But they weren't. Not to those who mattered.

"You know much about commercial real estate?" I asked him. "A project this size, there are a lot of people involved."

"Sure."

"Seems like Pete would have to have a lot of people in on it to pull this off. Think about it, Brandt. Say he's got Sue Ann's brother to sign off on all the inspection reports. What about the plans? Tommy seems to think there's two sets. The original, which all the bids were based on. And the set the crews are working from. Somebody had to draw them up. Then there're materials contracts, like the one Seeger got. And subs. Who knows if any of them are in on it?"

He frowned. "Where you going with this?"

"I don't know. It just seems like a lot of people to pay off. Too many to keep quiet." My mind took a walk and came back. "Harry said Pete's draws depend on stages of completion. Get the concrete poured and inspected, you get a draw. Put in plumbing or wiring and pass inspection, get a draw."

"That sounds about right."

"The bank's not going to rely just on the building inspector, is it? Doesn't the bank have its own consultants or specialists or something? Folks who check on the progress being made?"

"Banks usually hire outside professionals to visit the job site, review the inspection reports, check the invoices."

"How's Pete getting around them? Good God, Brandt, how many people do you think he's got in his pocket? How can he afford that? Doesn't seem like it would be worth it."

His eyes gleamed in the dim light thrown from a window behind us. "Damn good questions, Em. Maybe I can help find out. Harry, he's your brother-in-law? Call him. Ask him which bank bought the note."

I lifted my wrist, turned the watch to the light. Not too late. Pulled the cell phone out of my pocket and dialed Elizabeth's number. Hoped Harry picked up, not her, and felt a wave of relief when I heard his voice. I could take only so much family in one night. Said I was sorry to disturb him so late, and asked him the question. Felt my mouth drop open when he gave me the answer.

"What?" Brandt said when I tucked the phone away.

I told him the name of the bank.

He swore softly. "Durned if that ain't enough to make a rabbit spit in a pit bull's face. That would be the bank George Saunders worked at, now, wouldn't it? Ain't that a co-inky-dink."

"I don't think I believe in coincidence anymore. Do you?"

He smiled, shook his head.

"Question is," I went on, "where did George fit in? In on it? Or did he get in the way?"

He rubbed his hands together. "Much as I hate to admit it, my money says he's in on it."

"Not any more he's not." I paused. "What changed your mind?"

He gave his head a shake. "Too much about him changed. He wasn't the George Saunders I knew anymore."

"So, why's he dead?"

"Sounds like we got work to do, partner."

"We?" His face fell. I couldn't hide a smile. "Yes, we do."

Next morning Brandt and I split up. Divide and conquer. Not *divide et impera,* which the British used so successfully to subjugate an entire subcontinent among other territories. The other kind. Break a problem down into smaller subproblems. Find the answers and add them all up again, see what results.

Brandt took the rental car. Said he was going to do some networking, find out what he could from his banking buddies about how the financing for the mall was structured. I figured he could do most of that on the phone, but he told me he also wanted to drive down to Elgin, talk to someone there. He acted very mysterious about it. I shrugged it off. Told him to help out whichever way he saw fit.

I drove to the library and spent some time checking e-mail, for the first time since I'd left the city. The laptop computer had perished along with the RV. Four thousand seven hundred sixty-two messages in the bulk mailbox. Nearly a hundred that made it through the spam filter. Most digests of messages posted to forums I scanned from time to time. Writers' groups, that sort of thing. And sales pitches from the few companies whose mailing lists I'd actually put my name on. Half a dozen queries from editors and clients about potential jobs. I responded to those, accepting a couple of assignments with deadlines far enough out that I didn't have to think about them for a while. Deleted all the rest.

Brandt and I had little to go on. A bunch of suspicions based on behavior I found odd. And old prejudices. My history in this place, a past I couldn't seem to escape, colored my judgment. Time to just acknowledge and accept it and move on. We needed more, though, to satisfy both our now mutual curiosity and my self-imposed obligation to Meg. We needed proof, a way in. I had one lever. We talked about the risk of using it now, the risk of sending everyone scurrying for cover, leaving us with nothing. Decided it was worth it.

Still, I left the library feeling nervous. Cold drops of sweat traced salty rivulets down my sides. My hand had a slight tremor as I reached for the car door. I took a deep breath. Got in and drove through town out to the Eagle. Took one turn through the lot, spotted the blue Taurus in its usual slot. I parked and waited, not long.

Kolnik stepped out the front door of the restaurant, dressed in slacks and a short sleeve sport shirt voluminous enough to cover his large gut. He paused to peel the wrapping off a toothpick and poke at some food stuck between his front teeth. His hand fell away, toothpick still clamped in his teeth. Started ambling toward his car again. I strolled along the sidewalk, slowing my gait to intercept him at the car. He paid me no attention and fished car keys out of his pocket. The locks popped audibly. He pulled the door open and started to swing a leg in. When he turned I stepped off the sidewalk and quickly slipped between the cars. I yanked open the passenger door and eased inside at the same time he did. He jerked back in surprise.

"Who the fuck are you?"

I gave him a big smile. "You don't remember me, Bob? Emerson Ward. Knew your sister back in high school. Played football with Pete Anderson."

His face went kabuki white. He turned for the door. My fingers found the auto lock, pressed it.

He turned back slowly. "What do you want?"

"Just talk, Bob. Saw you and thought I'd say hello."

"You said it. Now get out."

"Is that any way to treat an old acquaintance? I'm hurt. Thought we might talk about old times, look through some photos."

He regained some composure, started to look annoyed. I pulled my cell phone out, flipped it open. Held it out so he could see a shot of him waving a fistful of money in Sue Ann's face.

He swallowed hard. "So?"

I showed him another. And another.

"Shit," he whispered.

Pete would have told me to screw myself, call his lawyer. Bob didn't. I guessed it had been eating at him. But he'd wanted the money more than he wanted a clear conscience. Now that he'd been caught, I had a feeling he'd bare his soul.

"How much was it, Bob? About a grand a week?"

He licked his lips, tried to talk. Nothing came out. He nodded.

"And what? They came up short last week?"

He nodded again, miserable now. "You know everything?"

"Enough."

He broke into sobs that shook his belly and convulsed his shoulders. Big wet tears rolled off his cheeks, leaving spreading dark spots on the front of his shirt. I leaned back against the door, waited him out, a mix of disgust and pity leaving a sour taste in my mouth. He got himself under control, wiped his face on his sleeve.

He stared out the windshield, sniffling. "What do you want?" This time with no bravado in the voice.

"How long has Pete been paying you to look the other way?"

He sighed. "Christ, it was so long ago I almost can't even remember how it started. A long time. Something came up on one of his houses. Something small. Like it wasn't even a big deal. Outside staircase, that's what it was. From a deck down to the backyard. Steps weren't the proper depth. He bitched and moaned about having to do it over. Said it'd cost him a day's pay at least. He pulled a couple of twenties out of his pocket and told me to forget it. What's the harm?"

He sighed, fell silent, big arms draped over the steering wheel, staring out at the memory.

"I should've known better," he said. "Couple more times and I was already in too deep. He knew he could cut corners, tell me not to write it up. Knew that if I didn't he could turn me in, make all kinds of trouble for me. Instead, he upped the ante. Paid more, but asked more." He shook his head. "Scared me some of the things he did."

"Cheap materials?"

"Cheap materials, shoddy workmanship, shortcuts . . ."

"What about Lou Barrett?"

His head came up, surprise then wariness in his eyes. "What about him?"

"Did he know?"

He hesitated. "I don't know. Hard to believe he didn't. But he never approached me. He didn't spend a lot of time out on the sites. Too busy selling or working the next development."

"So, Pete moved on to bigger and better things. Tell me how it works."

"The mall? Jeez, I don't know. The same?"

"Who else is in on it? Has to be a lot of people. Can't tell me you're the only one looking at plans. And who did the second set?"

He looked at me helplessly. "I don't know what to tell you. I've only seen one set of plans. It meets code. I wouldn't say Pete's building's the Taj Mahal, but the plans are to code. It's not the way I'd recommend building it, but . . ." He shrugged.

"You're telling me he's not skimming? Not cutting corners?" I wondered if Tommy had been wrong.

He squirmed in his seat, turned red. "I don't know. Honest to God. He pays me to look the other way, I do it. The plans are to code. He says he's building it to plan, I sign the inspection reports."

"Oh, come on, Bob. You can do better than that."

"Is he cutting corners? Hell, yes. Does that mean he's skimming? I suppose so. I wouldn't know. I've never seen the books."

"And you don't know if anyone else is helping him?"

"No. I told you."

"What about the union? The boss—Jones?"

He shrugged. "Maybe. I guess it would make sense. Look, I do what Pete tells me, and I don't ask questions. Started out, he was giving me a couple of bills a week. I told him I was risking my job, everything. He bumped me up to five hundred, then to a grand. When the bag was short the other day, I lost it. I told Sue Ann it's not enough. I told her I can't do this."

"She know what it's for?"

He nodded, even more miserable now. "Hell, I've got two kids at home. Figured I'd never be able to send them to college on what I make. That's why I took the money. I figured it couldn't hurt and it was for a good cause. Sue Ann's got *five*. Oldest going off to college soon. She thought giving Pete kids would make him more loyal, keep him at home. She finally realized he wasn't ever going to change. When she figured out Pete was slipping me money on the side, she confronted him.

Told him that if he was going to screw up their lives, least he could do was let her help hide what he was doing. She's been putting money aside for the kids ever since.

"And now here you come and show me a photo, show me what I've sunk to. I've been afraid this day would come for years. Always looking over my shoulder. Wondering. Didn't expect it would be someone like you, though. Always thought it would be Randy Tate. The Sheriff and some suit from the county, maybe."

He fell silent once more. Stared moodily out the windshield. I weighed what he'd told me. Knew he was holding something back, to maintain some small sense of pride or empowerment if nothing else. Wondered how important it was.

"Who's backing Pete?"

He faced me, frowned. "I don't know."

"Gotta be someone, Bob."

He shook his head, raised his eyebrow. "I don't know. Honest. Not anyone in town, if you ask me. Too many people got burned first time around."

"And they're all pissed at Lou. Wonder what they'd do if they knew Pete was the one who made the original deal go sour."

His eyes widened. "Why would he do that?"

"Why would you jeopardize people's lives by approving buildings that aren't safe?"

His head drooped, shame painting his face with despair. He opened his mouth, closed it. Tried again, but couldn't bring himself to look at me.

"What are you gonna do?"

I contemplated. "I'm not sure yet. I could let Pete know somehow. He'd probably have you killed. Maybe do it himself. Or I could call the cops. Thing is, Pete's been doing this so long, he must be pretty good at covering his tracks. If what you say is true, could be the most he gets is a slap on the wrist. I don't think I could let him get away with that."

"Shit," he whispered. "You're going to try to bring the whole thing down?" He moaned softly. "I'll be ruined."

"What did you expect?"

"What should I do?" His lower lip quivered.

I wondered how much of a liability he was now. I didn't think he'd risk saying anything to Pete. But if Pete saw him like this, Pete would know something was wrong. Brandt and I needed time to figure this thing out, find a way to go at him.

"You have any vacation time coming?" I asked.

"Sure." His ears perked up, face reflecting momentary hope before turning wary again.

"If I were you, I'd take it. Get away. Think about things. You don't have a lot of choices here, Bob. Pete finds out, you're dead. Stay, and you go down with Pete. You could run, but you'd be running the rest of your life. I think I'd try to get out in front of this thing. Take your family and get out of town. Find a nice place to stay with a pool for the kids. Wait a week. Give me some time. Then call the county State's Attorney. McHenry or Kane. Whichever county has jurisdiction. Tell him you want to make a deal. See what happens."

"I'll go to jail." He looked close to tears again.

"Probably, since you don't seem to have much to trade. But if you cop to your part in all this and cooperate, you might get a lot less time than if they have to hunt you down."

"Christ, what a mess."

I studied him. "Why'd Pete short you last week?"

He frowned. "Sue Ann didn't say. Just that money was tight, and I couldn't count on getting the usual anymore."

"Everything okay at the site? Anybody unhappy? Any talk from subs about not getting paid?"

His eyes widened again. "Come to think of it, yeah. I heard a couple of contractors grumble about some late invoices. One of 'em asked me if I was holding up any reports. Not likely with Pete riding my ass."

I hesitated, figured I'd gotten all I could. I opened the door, started to get out. Turned to make a point.

"Breathe a word of this to your sister, to anyone, and I'll hunt you down myself."

CHAPTER 26

Brandt finally showed up a little after seven, tired but pleased with himself. His Cheshire Cat grin said he had a lot to tell me, but he kept me in suspense while he washed up and changed out of his suit and tie. I got us both beers and we took them out to the deck. The sun's glow still felt hot on my face, but the air had cooled some.

"So, how was your day, dear?" I flashed him a grin.

He took a long swallow, wiped his mouth with the back of his hand. "Productive. How 'bout yours?"

"Not bad." I briefly rehashed what Kolnik had told me.

He grunted. "It fits what I learned about Anderson. He's bad news. The boy's none too bright, either, from what I can tell. All hat and no cattle."

I gave him time to explain.

"I paid a visit to a friend of mine down at the casino in Elgin," he said. "Guy Franklin. Works for the hotel company that manages it. Franklin did some digging for me. Took me to meet some of the crew. We spent some time with one of the pit bosses—Manny Campos. Seems the previous management considered Pete a nice source of income. Not a whale by any means. Flipper, maybe, according to Manny. Anyway, IGB—the gaming board—prohibits casinos from extending credit to guests."

"So I learned." I told him about my inquiry at the cashier's cage.

He nodded. "Someone, though, made introductions, and helped Pete get a line of credit at a local bank. I pulled some strings. Found out he's into the bank for some real money."

"How real?"

"Close to a quarter-million. Couple hundred thousand, anyway."

"Unsecured? Is that even possible?"

He shrugged. "That's pocket change to some folks."

I felt my eyebrows lift. "You serious? Pete? I don't know. Sounds like a lot of money to me."

He waved a hand. "Here's the thing. Everything else Anderson owns is leveraged to the hilt. He's got a second mortgage on the house. Cashed out all the equity in the company. Just this last week, he tried to tap this unsecured line of credit for another fifty grand. The bank told him no. I've got a call in to the loan officer. I'll see if I can find out more."

"What else?"

"Manny says he has a predilection for ladies with certain talents." He flushed. "Expensive ones."

"Ladies? Or talents?"

"Both."

"Manny knows this?" I thought of the brunette who'd sat next to Pete for an evening.

He swallowed. "Pit bosses—the good ones—know what's going on. They've got sharp eyes. Hear things. Manny says Anderson shows up at the tables with a woman sometimes. A couple different ones, but always one or the other. Says he knows them from the strip clubs in town. Knows they moonlight as escorts, has heard of other services they might provide under the right circumstances, if you know what I mean."

I did. Not firsthand, but I did. It made me wonder why a guy with a wife as attractive as Sue Ann would fork over hard-earned money and risk it all for a few kinks. Then again, maybe I wasn't one to be tossing rocks. I'd had my head turned once. I rationalized it by telling myself that I hadn't been sure of my standing with Nell at the time, that we didn't owe each other anything. But I'd known better. In my heart, I'd known she was the girl for me, no matter how big a bump we'd hit in our relationship. The fact that I'd done it to help ease the suffering of someone in pain didn't make me more altruistic. Or change the fact that I'd strayed.

A shard of anger coursed through my veins, hot and feral and familiar. Nell's leaving felt like punishment. A feeling that stemmed from my guilt, not her choice. Circumstances had demanded she leave. I couldn't help feeling, though, that she'd used her mother's illness as a welcome excuse, that she'd convinced herself she couldn't completely trust me again. A sudden feeling that she was never coming back filled me with dread, a ballooning sense of helplessness. With nothing to do but wait, and hope.

"You okay?" Brandt asked.

I swallowed hard, squelched it all, pushed it back down deep. Nodded.

"So, I was right about Pete. Don't tell me that's all you did today."

He winced, mock hurt on his face. "Course not. I found out more about the financial deal on the mall. It's Saunders's account. Or was. He was the senior loan officer on the project. Odd thing is no one else at the bank knows much about it. Loan was approved in committee. It must have passed muster. But his assistant says he handled the account personally, so she's not familiar with the particulars. Said she'd pull the file for me if I got approval from another loan officer."

"Which you did?"

"Not yet. See, here's the thing. Most banks, by nature, are conservative. Especially since that subprime mortgage mess.

Not only do they have to follow a whole passel of laws, they're also in the business to make money. They try to exercise caution when it comes to lending money. The four C's, you know. Capital, collateral, cash flow, conditions. Often, though, it comes down to gut instinct. The fifth C—character. The relationship between a banker and client. But no matter how small a risk, banks usually have systems in place. Procedures if people on the account change—bank or client side."

"And the bank isn't following procedure?"

"The bank should be all shook up over a deal this big. Loan package has to be pretty sizable. Someone should have picked up the slack after George got himself killed. His assistant acted way too calm, seemed way too uninformed. Like this deal is off the bank's radar. I thought we might try to work around the edges first. Otherwise, we might put the bank into a panic the size of a blue norther. There'd be an investigation and we'd get nowhere."

"So? We're still nowhere."

"Not really. I did find out that Anderson Construction hasn't taken a draw since George died."

"You think Saunders must have been in on it?"

"Why else?"

"What difference would it make? If Pete has people like Kolnik signing off on inspections, why not just keep submitting reports and acting like everything's normal?"

He shook his head. "My guess is he can't take the chance. Looks like George was a lone wolf on this one. Maybe even dummied up the reports to make it look like he'd put together the usual team to review the construction."

"Like a ghost team?"

"Sure. Chicago's famous for it. Dead voters, ghost employees . . . why not?"

I gave it some thought. "So, Pete can't ask for a draw because there's no one to write up the phony reports for the bank."

Brandt got up, walked to the edge of the deck and stood motionless, taking in the view. A moment later he faced me. "Pete's got two choices," he said. "Either he prays the bank doesn't find out, and plays it straight from now on."

"Meaning he's skimmed all he's going to."

"Right. Not likely, though. Whoever takes over the loan will want to talk to the team. If there is no team . . ." He watched it sink in. "Or, the other option is he buys off the new loan officer."

"And if he can't?" I said.

"Trouble in River City, partner."

"We could take all this to the bank," I ventured. "Dump it in the bank's lap. See what happens."

He shrugged. "We could."

"But we don't *know* anything."

"Nope. Just guessin'."

If we'd guessed right, we'd stumbled on a Chicago tradition—"the city that works" thrives on kickback deals. Without a paper trail, we had nothing. Blow the whistle now and everyone might scatter like autumn leaves. Or Pete would say a *mea culpa*, and point the finger at everyone else. Kolnik, for approving the work. Suppliers for providing substandard materials. A dead banker for stealing the money. If anything, maybe Pete would get a slap on the wrist, pay a fine. Unless we had more than guesses.

I heard tires crackle up the gravel drive and stop. A moment later came the slap of the screen door. Silhouetted against fleecy clouds turned pink by a sinking sun, a red-tailed hawk drifted in lazy circles over the fields. A hinge creaked behind us. I craned my neck, saw Frank poke his head out the door.

"Have you boys eaten?"

" 'Boys,' Frank?" Once a father, I guess, always a father. "No,

Michael W. Sherer

we haven't gotten that far."

"Interested in pizza? From Red's?"

"You drove halfway across the county for pizza?"

"Best there is." He looked at Brandt. "You like pizza?"

Brandt looked at me questioningly. Looked at Frank. "Who doesn't?"

"About ten, fifteen minutes, then." Frank disappeared inside the house.

Kitchen sounds floated out through the screen door—a pot banging on the stove, oven door closing, water running in the sink—followed shortly by the tantalizing smell of cooking food. I thought of my mother standing in front of that sink, washing celery, slicing onions. Pizza had been an occasional Sunday night tradition. A "night off" for Mom. Frank went to get pizza while she sautéed olives, onions and celery—a concoction known as "olive bowl." The same pizza every time—sausage and onion. Thin crust. Four extra large if everybody was home. Always from Red's, even though it was forty-five minutes to an hour round-trip. Par-baked there, finished off in our oven so they'd come out hot.

Caesar salad relieved Mom of KP duty about one Sunday a month, too. Frank was in charge of Caesar salad. Every other meal—probably three hundred fifty a year—made lovingly from scratch by my mother. She'd been a fabulous cook. What I knew about food and cooking I learned from watching her. It seemed such a long time ago, the memories faded like sepia-toned photos.

"He really went out and got us pizza?" Brandt asked.

I raised my hands. "I guess. It's not even Sunday."

He gave me a curious look, but didn't ask.

Twenty minutes later we sat at the kitchen table with fresh beers and hot pizza in front of us. Chicago might be known for its deep dish pizza, but to me nothing can compare to good thin

312

crust pizza. One bite reminded me that I'd never had any better anywhere. Brandt chewed, smiled contentedly, finished off two pieces before uttering a word.

"Frank, this is terrific," he said. "Thanks."

"My pleasure," he replied.

"Say, Emerson and I were talking about the new mall."

Frank looked at him politely. Waited for him to make a point. Out of Frank's sight I waved my hands and pulled a finger across my throat.

Brandt ignored me. "You were part of the original syndicate that put up seed money?"

Frank nodded.

"What do you think of this Anderson fella?"

"I think he's a crook." He glanced at me pointedly.

"Why do you say that?"

Frank helped himself to another piece of pizza. "I'll give you two reasons. First, his old man was a crook. One of the cheapest s.o.b.'s I ever met. The apple doesn't fall far from the tree. Second, when Pete first started building houses he used to come to my lumber yard for materials. But only when he'd overextended his credit with Bill Caruthers here in town. Tried to pull the same crap on me. I told every one of my managers he was on a cash-and-carry basis only."

He looked at me while he talked some more. "When he threw in with Emerson's buddy Lou, it gave him more buying clout, better credit. He still bought cheap. I saw some of the stuff he hauled out of the yards. He'd scour places for scrap lumber. Some of it never should have been used to build a house. Outbuildings, maybe. Sheds and such."

I sighed. "If he's such a crook, why'd you invest?"

"I told you. It seemed like he and Lou were making money. I figured I might as well make some money, too. A lot of people thought the same."

"So, it didn't work out. Stop blaming me. You didn't have to throw in with Lou just because he and I were friends once."

He blinked, feigning innocence. "Who said anything about you? I never said I blamed you."

Brandt came to the rescue. "It's hard to be on the losing end of an investment, that's for sure. What we're trying to figure out is how Anderson managed to pull this project out of the crapper." He had Frank's attention again.

"He was the general contractor on the job," Frank said. "Seems to me even new investors would stick with him. It wouldn't make sense to start from scratch."

"We're thinking he put his former partner out of business," Brandt said. He waited while Frank took a bite of pizza and chewed. "Like as not, you won't ever get your investment back. But maybe Anderson shouldn't be profiting at your expense."

Frank eyed him warily. "What's your point?"

Brandt shrugged. "To be plain, sir, I agree with your assessment. Anderson's crooked as a dog's leg and wolverine mean. I don't think he should be in business."

"You have something in mind?"

"We're not sure yet. But it would help to know why Anderson saved the project, what incentive he had. You mind sharing what you know?"

Frank took off his glasses, cleaned them with a napkin. Put them on and pushed them against the bridge of his nose with a finger. "I don't suppose it would hurt any after the fact."

"What can you tell us about the original deal?"

"What do you want to know?"

Brandt rattled off a list. Frank nodded and excused himself. He came back a few minutes later with a thick file folder. He pushed his plate aside and set the file down. Opened it and riffled through documents. Pulled some out and handed them to Brandt. I helped myself to more pizza and olive bowl and watched them pore over papers. I finished eating and got another round of beer from the fridge. I set them down on the table.

"What are we looking for?" I asked.

Brandt glanced at Frank. "Is this pretty much what the actual first-round construction financing looked like?"

I twisted my head to read the upside-down prospectus in front of him.

"I think so," Frank said. "One way to find out. I'll call Harry."

He pushed away from the table, walked over to the wall phone. A beige rotary model that had hung there since our family moved in, the handset now darkened with use. He dialed the number from memory. Walked around the corner into the hall when it connected, stretching the coiled cord taut. His voice was muted, tense. The one-sided conversation a series of staccato remarks separated by silence. A change in inflection midway through suggested someone else had gotten on the line. He walked back in, hung up.

"Budget for the first phase of construction was fifty million," he said as he sat down. "The bank put up twenty-five million. The investors, me included, put up the other twenty-five."

Brandt nodded. "Good. I'll check with the Chicago bank in the morning, see what the new loan package is."

"You think Pete went after more money?" I said.

"It makes sense. Sweeten the deal for everyone, especially if Saunders was in on it."

"What about the new investors? Do we know anything about the group that bought it?"

Brandt's gray head wagged. "Not much. They're being cautious, whoever it is. I traced ownership to a couple of shell companies. Incorporated offshore, of course. I've got people doing some digging for me. Should know in a day or two."

"Could be they're in the dark the same as we were," Frank said.

"We're still in the dark," I said. They looked at me. "Well, we are. We're guessing."

"We're close, partner," Brandt said, "thanks to you. You stirred things up, looks like."

I thought about that. Thought about how many people from the old days looked at me like I was a cancer, a foreign invader programmed to move in and alter the genetic makeup of their lives, suck the life out of their world. Not too many were happy I was back asking questions. They didn't see that the disease came from within, and only was hastened by environmental factors. Growth and all its attendant problems could be managed. The lure of a fast buck, though, had turned some rotten, slowly eating away at them, at the town.

Something else had stirred the pot. It looked like George, Lou, and maybe even Danny were dead as a result. I didn't think I'd stirred so much as poked at what floated to the surface.

"He never could leave well enough alone," Frank said to Brandt.

My head jerked around. Supposed to be a *knee*-jerk, I thought. Supposed to be *he's a jerk*. I took a breath. The words came out anyway, but with far less animus than I felt.

"What the hell's that supposed to mean?"

Frank shrugged. "You always were a sucker for a sad story. A soft touch." He turned to Brandt. "He used to bring home stray animals. Birds with broken wings. A baby rabbit with a broken leg once. Mangy dogs. Cats."

To me again. "You remember the old man that used to sit outside the VFW? Jim Hartigan? You would have given him your life savings if I hadn't told you he wasn't homeless."

"A good deed once in a while is good for the soul," I said softly. "You ought to try it."

I turned to Brandt when a thought bubbled up to the surface. "Pete's not taking draws. He shorted Kolnik last week, and Kolnik says he's hearing grumbling at the site about late payments." Brandt paid attention. "Pete has to be getting a little desperate, don't you think?"

I saw the wheels in his head start to turn.

Tuesday dawned hazy and warm. A " 'tween" day, sultry enough to be summer, but with an unsettled feeling typical of spring. As if things could change at any moment. I spent most of it working outside in jeans and T-shirt. Raking the drive and picking up debris from the bus. Mowing grass, trimming bushes, much as I did as a kid on summer weekends. Trying not to think too much. About Pete and Lou. Nell and Elizabeth. About Frank and June, and my brother Hank. About the reasons I came back after all these years. I threw myself into the labor, pushing myself, warm sun on my back making it easy to break a sweat.

Brandt sat contentedly on the porch with a book. *Disney War* as exciting to him as a good mystery is to me. He made occasional forays out into the sunshine to stretch his legs, check on my progress, bring me water. He didn't say much, but I sensed he was as antsy as I. We all wait in our own way.

The day dragged, the only thing good about it the phone call Brandt took after dinner. Curiously one-sided, it widened his eyes, made him whistle.

"What was that all about?" I asked when he clicked off.

"The skinny on the new construction loan." He paused for effect. "*Thirty* million. With another thirty coming from investors. For just the first phase."

I chewed on it a minute. "You think the project getting shut down for a while forced them to change the budget?"

Brandt shook his head. "Not that much."

"So, either the scope of the project changed or there's ten

million going into somebody's pocket."

"See, that's the thing. Even if the project changed on paper to justify a bigger loan, Anderson's still cutting corners, right? Building it the way he has been all along?"

"And this is just Phase One. Who knows how much they would have gotten out of the next round of construction if George hadn't been killed?"

Something to sleep on.

A Huntley P.D. cruiser pulled into the drive before the first cup of coffee next morning. Its tires threw muddy water onto the grass from puddles left by thunderstorms. Big boomers that had wakened me before dawn. A black sedan followed in the cruiser's wake. I watched through the kitchen window as the cars came to a gentle stop. Randy Tate sat behind the wheel of the cruiser. Profiles of two men stood out in the other car. Tate leaned over the wheel, peered at the house through the windshield. The passenger door of the big sedan opened, then the driver's. The two men climbed out, stood a moment, looking around. Both wore sunglasses despite the heavy overcast.

The man on the passenger side stood barely a head taller than the car, but nothing about him suggested he was small. Smartly dressed in dark gray slacks and navy blazer, not even his neatly combed hair ruffled in the gusts of wind rippling the puddles in the drive. He turned casually, eyes slowly panning the property. An air of self-assurance just short of arrogance on his square-jawed face.

The driver swung his door shut, stepped away from the car. He shoved his hands in his pockets and hunched his shoulders against the raw wind. His tie escaped from between the lapels of a gray suit coat, fluttered like a pennant on a mast under his long thin face. Droopy eyes framing a Cyrano-sized nose and long earlobes gave him the sad look of a basset hound. Short tufts of hair danced on top of a head that was nearly bald.

Footsteps sounded behind me, and Brandt appeared at my elbow. He reached for the coffee pot on the counter.

"Company," I said.

He followed my gaze. "Looks official. Anything you want to share?"

I glanced at him. "Don't look at me. It wasn't anything *I* did."

Shorty started toward the house as if on some unseen signal. Sad Sack followed. Randy scrambled out of the cruiser, said something that made the pair pause and turn. They waited while he caught up and led them the rest of the way to the back porch.

I turned to Brandt and shrugged. "Might as well see who they are, what they want."

Frank was already on the porch, standing at the screen door when Randy came up the steps. The other two waited on the drive. I hung back in the shadows of the entryway, Brandt at my shoulder.

"Morning, Randall," Frank said.

In a whisper, I told Brandt who Randy was.

"Morning, Frank." Randy stood with one foot on the top step, hands on his hips. "Sorry to bother you so early."

"Must be important," Frank said.

Randy rolled his eyes. The house call not his idea, apparently. "You have a guest here, name of Brandt Williams?" He jerked a thumb over his shoulder. "These gentlemen would like a word, if he's here."

Frank's grizzled chin ticked up a notch. "And who might you be?"

Shorty stepped forward and answered. "F.B.I., sir. I'm Special Agent Duran." Without looking, he indicated his compatriot with an upturned palm. "This is Special Agent Lipscomb."

I nudged Brandt with an elbow. He looked like he'd been blinded by the flash of a *paparazzo*'s camera.

"And your business with my houseguest, Mr. Duran?"

I couldn't help a wry smile at how Frank had adopted Brandt. Felt the tiniest remnants of jealousy from a few nights before.

Shorty pulled off his sunglasses and squinted to get a better look through the screen. "We'd just like to talk with him, sir. He may have information relevant to a case we're working on."

Frank shifted his gaze. "Is that your understanding, Randall? They're just here to talk?"

Randy glanced over his shoulder, shrugged. "Yes, sir. They gave me no reason to think otherwise."

Frank addressed Duran again. "I'll have to check with my guest. If you don't mind waiting. He might still be asleep. In which case, you might want to come back later."

I'd always thought of my father as an ornery, stubborn, stern, forbidding man. But grudgingly, I felt proud of him for standing up for someone he barely knew. He was being pissy on principle, not because Brandt was my friend. I still had to admire him.

Brandt brushed past me. "It's okay, Frank. You can let 'em in. If you don't mind, that is."

Frank wrinkled his nose. Pushed the door open and held it. Randy sidestepped to let the two Fibbies pass. I led them all to the kitchen, figuring that's about as far inside the house as Frank could stand them. I set clean mugs on the table and brewed another pot of coffee. Duran paid Frank a compliment on the farm and sat at the table opposite Brandt. Lipscomb commented on the change in the weather and took a seat to Brandt's right. Frank slid into the empty chair across from Lipscomb.

After that, silence fell over the room like a scratchy blanket. The room grew warm and close in the stillness. Once I poured coffee the room grew so quiet that a muted cough from Randy sounded like a gunshot. Duran stared at me, then at Frank. Frank ignored him. I smiled politely. Duran cleared his throat, leaned toward Frank.

"If you don't mind, Mr. Ward, we'd like to speak to Mr. Williams in private." He threw me a look that said "you, too."

Frank's eyes widened. His gaze shifted from Duran to Brandt. Dumb like a fox, old Frank. "This *is* private. My home, my private property. Into which I've kindly invited you. Do you have a problem with that?"

Duran swiveled on his chair, looked to Randy for help. "Chief Tate, would you explain to Mr. Ward the gravity of our situation?"

Randy scratched his head. "Problem is, sir, he's got a point. I mean, we could take Mr. Williams here down to the P.D. if you want. But he could refuse, since none of us seems to have shown up with a warrant. Seems like this is as comfortable a place as any." He tipped his head at Frank and me. "I don't know what you're after, but these two aren't going to be any problem."

Duran mulled it over. He didn't look happy. Glanced at Lipscomb, who nodded. "All right, then. Just so you know, I'm Assistant Special Agent in Charge, FBI resident agency in Lisle. Lipscomb here is my counterpart in the Rockford resident agency. Both our agencies are part of the Chicago Field Division office."

Brandt lifted an eyebrow. "Interoffice cooperation?"

Lipscomb nodded. "Something like that," he said, the timbre of his voice surprisingly deep. "Huntley straddles two counties. Half's in Special Agent Duran's territory, half's in mine."

"I live in Chicago, gentlemen," Brandt said. "Would have saved you a lot of trouble if someone there had just picked up a phone. How'd you track me down, anyway?"

"We checked with your office, sir," Duran said. "You left

word that you'd be out of town."

Brandt nodded as if that was explanation enough. "What's so important you have to come all this way and roust the locals to find me?"

Duran swiveled his head, still uncomfortable with our presence.

Lipscomb noticed, jumped in before he had a chance to protest again. "Mr. Williams, two days ago a man named Stan Whitaker executed a computer search of banking records, intended, we think, to reveal the names of investors in a real estate investment trust. Are you acquainted with this man?"

"Of course," Brandt said, without hesitation. "He's an old friend."

Lipscomb acknowledged him, went on. Pulled a small notebook and pen from an inside pocket as he spoke. "Shortly before he conducted that search, Whitaker received a call from your cell phone. Did you instigate that search?"

"Sure," Brandt said easily.

Silence hung over the table like a nosy aunt. As if they expected him to say more.

"Would you tell us why, please?" Duran this time, a polite smile squeezed out as hard as the last toothpaste in the tube.

Brandt's eyebrows rose. "To find out about a potential investment. I try to do my homework before I part with my money."

"Why this REIT?" Lipscomb asked. "What attracted you to this investment?"

Brandt indicated me. "My friend grew up here. He's been out here visiting and told me about the tremendous growth. Thought it might be an opportunity for me. I came out to see the mall being built down the hill. It looks like it has potential." He shrugged. "Just 'cause a chicken has wings don't mean it can fly. I had Stan Whitaker do some research to find out more."

Lipscomb made some notes. Duran eyed Brandt and tapped

the table softly with a fingertip.

"Would you mind telling us what you learned about the REIT?" he said.

"You mind telling me why you want to know?"

Duran frowned, said nothing.

Brandt sighed, started speaking in his financier's voice, all but a trace of his Texas accent gone. "It's a closed-end fund, meaning only a limited number of shares were issued when it went public. As a result, there are a limited number of investors. There's been no trading activity in the fund since its inception, which tells me it's tightly controlled by very few investors. It's more typical of a real estate limited partnership.

"My guess is whoever set it up decided a REIT would provide more anonymity to investors than a limited partnership. There are a handful of major investors in the fund. All are shell companies. Tracing ownership of the shell companies has been difficult, since each seems to be funded by other shell companies. We were able, however, to find names of some companies that seem to be common to all."

He turned to me, looked apologetic. "I didn't have time to tell you I got a call this morning." To Duran, "One of the companies, for example, is U-Go Discount Gas."

Frank looked up sharply. "U-Go? That's what's-his-name. The camel jockey. Emerson, you know the guy I'm talking about."

Once when we were kids, my sister Elizabeth burst into tears in the middle of an episode of *All in the Family* on TV. When Frank stopped laughing at the show long enough to ask her why she was crying, she said it was because it reminded her so much of home. Frank was no Archie Bunker. He was smarter. Which made it worse. He was no Doug Barrett, either, but that didn't excuse him.

I frowned. "Sarina's dad? Mr. Ahmed?"

"Sure. That's him."

Duran eyed me, calculating. Randy caught his look. I felt his eyes on me, too.

"What's going on?" I asked Duran. "What does Ahmed have to do with this? Why are you really here?"

Duran and Lipscomb exchanged glances. Duran ignored me for the moment, turning back to Brandt.

"You weren't aware of this." He gave a nod when Brandt looked perplexed. "You haven't been entirely truthful, either." He let that hang a moment. "Like they say where you come from, Mr. Williams, this ain't my first rodeo." He pointed his gaze at me again. "Let's say we put our cards on the table, fellas. We show you what we've got, you tell us what you know."

CHAPTER 27

Clouds scudded across a forlorn sky, puffs of pewter racing across a slate backdrop. A lonely ring-billed gull perched on the peak of the barn roof and leaned into the wind, teetering in the gusts. A seagull far from the sea. The kitchen window reverberated gently from the drone of a low-flying airplane, probably headed for the little airstrip nearby. Even the gull knew better than to fly in this weather.

"We're not obligated to tell you anything," Duran said. "You know that."

I turned my gaze from the bleak gray outside the window and tried to read Duran's mind.

Randy broke the silence, his voice low. "Well, I'd sure like to hear it. You know, in the spirit of interagency cooperation and all."

Duran frowned.

"Sounds like it's time I found out what you've been up to, too," Randy said to me.

I shrugged. "Them first."

"Fine," Duran said crisply. "Here's what we can tell you. Lipscomb and I are with CTTF—Chicago Terrorist Task Force. Our job is to prevent, detect, deter and investigate terrorist attacks."

"What do terrorists have to do with a shopping mall?" Brandt said. "In Huntley?"

Duran frowned, irritated. "Not only do we investigate all

criminal activities of terrorist individuals and groups, we also investigate the acquisition of funds used to provide material support to terrorists."

"Follow the money," I said.

He nodded. "We follow the money. For several years we've been looking into a group of Muslim businessmen in northern Illinois we think are sympathetic to terrorist causes. We think they've been using various investment schemes as a way to funnel money to groups like Al Qaeda and Hamas."

"And you think the mall is one of their investment deals?" I couldn't square the image of Pete throwing in with Mideast suicide bombers and Taliban guerillas. Nor with rich businessmen who supported them. It made even less sense if he was pulling off the fraud we suspected. If he knew who he was stealing from, he was a bigger fool than I thought.

"Aazim Ahmed has been on our watch list for some time," Duran said. "It would fit the pattern."

I thought about what Sarina had told me. About losing her brother in Iraq and her father's reaction. Grief can easily harden a man's heart, turn into anger and hate. Huntley had never treated the Ahmed family very well. The country had sent Ahmed's son off to war, to die in a desert fighting people of his own faith.

Faith seems to have little to do with war, really. Wars are about power, property and politics, not faith. Boiled down to their essence, "religious" wars—from The Crusades to the "troubles" in Northern Ireland—are fought over land, or wealth, or power, not religious beliefs. Except to those whose faith defines their very identity. To Ahmed, Al's death must not have seemed so much a patriotic sacrifice as a slap in the face.

"Several years you've been watching Ahmed," I said, echoing Duran's earlier words. "So you haven't been able to follow the money far enough."

"Not yet," Duran admitted.

Lipscomb chimed in. "We've been at this a long time. CTTF, I mean. Since the early '80s. Right after the Puerto Rican independence group FALN took over President Carter's campaign headquarters in Chicago. People forget there are a lot of terrorist groups out there, and they've been around a lot longer than Al Qaeda. But our job isn't easy. Used to be a lot of these groups raised funds through illegal activities—drugs, thefts. It's more complicated now. Terrorist groups have gotten more sophisticated. So are their resources. They're very good at hiding their sources of funding. And we can only go so far.

"Don't get me wrong. Since September eleventh, we have a lot more latitude than we used to when initiating an investigation. But we still have to play by the rules. That means no wiretaps, no electronic or computer surveillance without a warrant."

"Then how'd you know about my phone call?" Brandt asked. "Or Stan's computer search?"

A corner of Duran's mouth went up. "What we *can* do is issue an administrative subpoena for documents—things like phone records. We can even get a FISA order from a judge pretty easily. If we can link you to suspected terrorist activity, that is. It so happens, we didn't have to do any of that. Your banker friend told us about the call."

Brandt's eyes rounded.

Duran waved a hand, went on before he could speak. "He didn't rat you out. A lot of things have changed, even before 9/11. We've had programs in place like InfraGard and the NIPC—sorry, National Infrastructure Protection Center—since the Internet really started taking off back in the '90s. They helped us establish both formal and informal channels with the private sector for exchanging information about cyber threats and use of the Internet for terrorist purposes.

"In the last few years, we've stepped things up a lot. We ask, and get, a lot more cooperation from the private sector regarding information on suspect activities. We now have a real-time information-sharing Web page—LEO, Law-Enforcement On-Line—that provides a resource for federal, state and local law enforcement agencies." Duran looked at Randy. "You must be signed up—you're a member of IACP, right, Chief?"

He paused. Randy nodded. I sensed he was showing off, to let us know how important the war on terror is, make sure we understood the need to cooperate.

"The point is," he went on, "Whitaker was apprised of our investigation because some of this investment group's transactions have gone through his bank. He volunteered to let us know when any suspect companies popped up in the course of financial transactions. Your search request rang bells like a slot machine jackpot. Whitaker called his contact at FBI Chicago, who called us."

The ticking of the kitchen wall clock sounded loud in the silence. The screen door on the porch squeaked and banged shut in a gust of wind.

The notion of a small-town general contractor getting greedy and looking for kickbacks on a big construction job made sense to me. But I had a hard time getting my head around the concept of my sleepy hometown as the center of a fundamentalist Islamic terrorist conspiracy. I still wrestled with the incongruity of seeing two FBI agents sitting at Frank's kitchen table.

Lipscomb leaned forward, set his elbows on the table, tenting his fingers.

"Here's the thing," he said, his deep voice hushed. "For the first time, we think we have a way to trace the money flow. These people are very smart. They're not just funneling money to obvious sympathizers. Like The Mosque Foundation, down in Bridgeview. But they made a mistake, setting up this REIT.

They should've set up a limited partnership, like you said." He gestured toward Brandt then touched his fingertips together again. "Now some of what they do is public, which actually makes it easier for us to make the links. Whatever it is you two are into, we want to make sure it doesn't jeopardize this investigation. We're awfully close on this one. We'd hate to see all that work go to waste."

Five pairs of eyes turned my way.

"I'd say that's your cue," Randy said softly.

I thought for a minute about how to tell it and wondered how much to leave out. I decided to just let it rip. Started with Lou's suicide and went from there. Told them everything I'd learned. Then outlined the theory Brandt and I had come up with, about Pete orchestrating the strike to push Lou out of the deal, and paying off Kolnik so he could cut corners. I told them about George Saunders getting his bank to buy off the construction loan for what we figured must be a substantial kickback. And about Pete's gambling problem, his womanizing, the side loan Brandt had uncovered, and the fact that with Saunders dead, Pete hadn't taken a draw in weeks.

They listened patiently. Lipscomb took notes while I talked. When I finished, Duran asked a couple of questions to clarify some points. Lipscomb read over his notes. Duran stared out the window, gently tapping a finger on the table. As if on cue, they both looked at me. Lipscomb closed his notebook and slid it inside his suit coat while Duran spoke.

"Thank you, gentlemen, for your cooperation." He pushed his chair away from the table, started to rise.

"That's it?" I said.

Duran straightened. "That's it. We appreciate your candor. I'm sure we don't have to tell you not to speak of this to anyone."

Frank's face reddened. "You can't just walk in, tell us these two may have uncovered a terrorist plot, and walk out."

"Watch me." He looked down at Lipscomb to see if he was coming, and saw the exasperation on my face. Put his hands on the table and leaned forward. "You've got a theory that maybe this Anderson is a crooked contractor. What were you planning to do about it?"

I blinked. "We hadn't gotten that far. Prove it, we hope. Put him out of business."

He shook his head. "Leave him be. Just let him do his thing. If this deal goes south on him, okay, we might have to come at the investment group a different way. But if you deliberately rock the boat, you could jeopardize years of work. Can't risk it."

He pushed himself upright and stepped away from the table. Lipscomb got up slowly.

"That's exactly what I'll do," I said. They froze.

Next to me, Randy heaved a sigh. "Aw, shoot, Emerson, don't do this. I gave you some leeway, but don't go messing with these boys."

I turned on him, white heat spreading inside me. "What? You think this is right? Just let Pete walk?"

"I didn't say that." He looked embarrassed. "Look, he's going to end up screwing himself. In the meantime, these FBI guys have a job to do that's a lot more important than putting an over-the-hill high school jock out of business. Don't you think?"

I thought about Lou's funeral, the way Meg looked when they lowered him into the ground, the debris raining from a blue sky when the RV exploded, my conversation with Danny a few days before one of the trains he loved crushed him, and I couldn't shake the notion that all this had something to do with more than a shopping mall. I felt the thumping in my chest, heard myself breathing hard.

"I think there are people in this who matter," I said slowly. "I think Tish Barrett and Meg Brodsky deserve some justice. I think no matter what you thought of Lou, maybe he didn't deserve what he got. I think maybe you should be more concerned about what goes on in this town and let the feds worry about their own problems."

The room went silent. Randy chewed on it. I couldn't tell which way it was going to sit with him, but I was past caring.

"Let's get real here," Duran said quietly. "Our *problem* is amateurs like you who try to play hero and make our job difficult. Fact is, you screw up this investigation and I guarantee you'll spend time in prison."

I turned on him. "Here's what I think. I think this whole thing is about to blow up in your faces. You wouldn't be here otherwise. If a couple of 'amateurs' can figure out what Anderson is up to and stumble onto your terrorist sympathizers, then this thing is already starting to unravel."

Duran leaned forward slightly and looked attentive. Lipscomb slowly lowered himself back into the chair. My mind raced, tried to make the links, sketch it out the way a prosecutor might.

"Pete's getting desperate," I said. "He wouldn't have tried to warn me off if he wasn't."

Lipscomb picked up on it quickly. "Warn you off how?"

"Blew up his RV," Randy told them. "We *suspect*," he admonished me.

"Stay with me here, people," I said. "Pete's tapped out. Everything he owns is leveraged, and no one will extend any more credit to him. His subs are getting antsy because they're not getting paid. He's shorting the building inspector on his payroll. He's running out of cash."

Duran shifted his weight. "Doesn't make sense."

"Sure it does. Hear me out. Look, we know the well's dry. Brandt checked. But Pete's still here. He hasn't cut and run. Even though his banker's dead and he can't get draws. Why? Because he hasn't gotten his money out yet. All this money we think he's taking off the top? Someone else is getting a cut first. Pete's still here hoping to salvage something."

"Or maybe he's too dumb to know it's falling in around his ears," Duran said.

"Maybe," I conceded. "But I think he's smart enough to know he's in trouble. Which means he'll be looking for a way out. This is the perfect opportunity. This is our chance. We get Pete. You get Ahmed, if that's who you're after."

Duran frowned. "I don't follow. How?"

"We make Pete an offer he can't refuse. We buy him out. Hell, we buy out the whole thing. Pete will jump at the chance to get his money out before the bank discovers the scam. He'll take the offer to the principals—Ahmed, whoever—to keep them from finding out, too. If they bite, then you follow the money, see where they put it. If it ends up in some organization that supports Hamas or IPA, Al Qaeda, whatever, you get what you want."

Duran shook his head. "Never work."

Lipscomb put up a hand. "Wait a minute. It might. The banks will cooperate, Mick. They have to. You know these guys will do it all by wire transfer. We get the bank to tell us where the funds are being transferred, and we freeze the account as soon as the transfer goes through."

I waited for Duran's reaction, heard Brandt ask a quiet question instead.

"Follow what money?"

I turned to him, saw that he meant the question for me. Gave him a furrowed brow for a response.

"To make an offer on the mall," he explained. "Where you going to get the money to buy a shopping mall?"

I smiled. "That's your department. You know people."

His jaw dropped. "You want me to come up with, what, a

hundred million or so? That might just disappear into cyber-space?"

"Told you it wouldn't work," Duran said quietly.

"Oh, it'll work," I said. "You just haven't given him enough time to think about it. He loves a challenge."

I could see Brandt already considering the possibilities. I could tell Duran saw it, too. He exchanged a glance with Lipscomb, who nodded.

"Would you excuse us?" Duran said. "We need to have a word."

They filed out, the sound of their footsteps sounding down the hallway. The back door latched with a click. Frank swiveled toward me, thunderclouds in his face.

"For Christ's sake, do you have any idea what the hell you're doing?"

"Shut up, *Dad!*"

He blinked, sat back.

Randy shook his head with a grunt. "You've really stepped in it, Emerson. We're talking feds here."

"You want them taking over your town, Chief? I'd have thought you'd be backing me up on this."

I glanced out the window. Duran and Lipscomb were in a heated discussion. The wind whipped their words away, flapped their coats open and closed.

"What I want to know," I said, "is why Pete would throw in with Sarina's dad. Unless things changed while I was gone, there was no love lost between Ahmed and Pete's dad."

"I'd say that's about right," Randy said quietly. "Doug Barrett was the guy Ahmed had a real problem with, though, not Pete's dad. Ron died back when Pete was in college. Wasn't around long enough for Ahmed to work up a real blood feud. Funny thing is, Ahmed hired Pete to build him a new house a while back."

I poured myself more coffee. Outside, Duran spoke into a cell phone now. Lipscomb stood a few feet away, arms folded, facing the barn. "Why would he do that?" I said.

Randy shrugged. "Pete builds houses. Ahmed probably figured Pete would be cheaper than using someone else."

"What if Ahmed found out all the rumors about Pete are true?" They looked at me blankly. "I'm serious. What if Ahmed had problems with the house? Found out that Pete built it cheap and covered it up?"

"He might be seriously pissed," Randy said. "Expensive custom job like that."

"I'd sue the bastard," Frank said. "Make him fix everything. Or build a new house."

I looked at him. "Sarina said Lou made a point of not inviting her dad to invest in the mall development. You know anything about that?"

"I know he wasn't part of the original syndicate. I couldn't tell you why."

"You could make a guess, though."

He flushed. "Probably for his own good. He wasn't well liked, by several investors."

"You included?"

His jaw tightened. "I've got nothing against him. As far as I'm concerned, his money's as good as anyone's. I think your buddy Lou was an idiot for not bringing him in. Ahmed's done all right for himself. Can't fault his business sense. We might have been able to weather the strike with the additional reserve if he'd been on board."

I nodded and told Randy, "Think about it. Ahmed was already ticked off that Lou wouldn't let him in on the mall deal. Sarina said as much. If he found out Pete built him a custom house that maybe can't even pass code, wouldn't that make him furious? But he doesn't blow the whistle on Pete. Instead, he decides to get even. Tells Pete he'll go public if Pete doesn't help him take over the mall deal."

Randy scratched his head. "I don't know. Doesn't seem like Pete cares that much. Seems like he could just offer to fix Ahmed's house. Say he made an honest mistake."

"What if Ahmed found out all of it? The gambling. The women. I did. It wasn't that hard. He'd have something to hold over Pete's head."

He considered it. Through the window over his shoulder, I could see Duran was off the phone, talking with Lipscomb again. They headed for the door.

"For Ahmed, it's perfect," I said. "He uses his leverage over Pete to get in on the deal. He ends up with a great commercial investment property he and his buddies can use to fund *jihadis* or whatever. And he gets revenge on Lou for what Lou's dad did to him all those years."

The screen door banged, followed by the sound of the back door a moment later. I lowered my voice and gave him one more thing to chew on before they came in.

"People are dead because of this. Lou, maybe Danny, too."

Lipscomb stopped just inside the door. Duran walked over to the table, extended his hand to Frank.

"Thanks very much for your hospitality, sir. We won't take up any more of your time." He turned to me, gestured toward Brandt. "We appreciate your help. We'll take it from here."

"Meaning what?" I asked.

"Meaning that if we decide to move on Anderson like you suggested, we'll handle it."

"Why not let us set him up? I know the guy. I used to play football with him. I know how to work him. Brandt's connected. He can put the right money people in place. Right, B?"

I saw a tentative nod, and the slimmest of smiles on Brandt's face. He was still working the problem.

Duran looked peeved. "Even if I thought your plan had merit, which I'm not saying it does, I couldn't let you execute. You're civilians."

I started to open my mouth, invoke the names of a couple of spooks who'd been grateful I'd helped them bust up a ring of gun-runners. The last time I'd been out in McHenry County, the time that still gave me nightmares. I thought better of it.

"We can handle ourselves," I said.

"We know your reputation, Ward," Lipscomb said softly. "We didn't come all the way out here without running background checks on you two first."

My survival as a kid in the Ward family had depended on keeping a low profile, under my father's radar. The skill had served me well since. I hated to think I was becoming too visible. It would make it harder to get away with some of the questionable things I sometimes did to find answers for people. Maybe Nell was right. Maybe it was time to quit.

"You guys use CI's all the time," I said.

"As informants," Duran replied. "Not as field operatives."

"But you *do* coordinate with local law enforcement, work with police departments like Chief Tate's." I caught Randy's eye. "You can deputize us, right, Chief?"

Randy rubbed his chin, answered slowly. "Technically, sure, I've got the power to do that."

"There you go," I told Duran. "Problem solved."

He hesitated, shook his head. "We'll pass. Thanks anyway."

I wasn't above going behind their backs and doing whatever the hell I had to, but I figured I'd better not get on Uncle Sam's bad side. Maybe it was the adrenaline, or that guilty feeling I sometimes get when I pass a cop on the street even when I'm not doing anything wrong, but my mind had been turning at a few thousand rpm since they'd showed up. As dust settled from the bomb they dropped about Ahmed, things started falling in place, took on a different perspective. Like turning a puzzle piece around and getting a different look at it. A crazy thought popped into my head, and I hung on like it was a life ring.

"What if I can help you get Ahmed for murder, too?"

The words zapped them like a Taser. Brandt recovered first. He scrambled to his feet and hustled over, consternation on his face. Grabbed my arm, steered me toward the door.

"Excuse us," he murmured. "Boy's lost too many balls in the high weeds."

I twisted in his grasp as he pulled me out of the room and waved at Randy to follow. He pointed to his chest, a question in his eyes, and pushed away from the counter when he saw my head bob. Brandt shooed me off the porch and down the back steps like an old woman herding chickens.

"Are you nuts?" he asked, squaring off in front of me on the drive. "First the idea about buying the mall. Now you want to bluff the FBI into thinking someone's been murdered? What the heck you been drinking, partner?"

Randy sauntered down the steps, circled around to the side, amusement on his face.

"Might be a bluff," I said. "Might not. That's why I thought Randy ought to listen in."

Brandt stood up on his toes, stuck his face up close to mine. "What murder?"

"George's."

He blinked a couple of times.

"George Saunders," I explained to Randy. "Bigwig at the bank in Chicago that's financing the mall construction. Loan officer on the project. Shotgunned to death two months ago."

"I swear you're a few sandwiches shy of a picnic," Brandt said.

"It's not so crazy. Think about it. Ahmed got screwed out of the original deal. Makes him mad enough to get even. What do you think he'd do if he found out Pete and George scammed him out of ten million? Worse, what do you think those nutcase fundamentalists would do if they found out?"

I filled Randy in on the details of the shooting. The fact that George's killers kept him alive after they'd blown his knee apart, maybe even a while after they'd shot his arm off. I asked if he could think of a reason someone would do that.

"He's got a point," Randy said to Brandt.

"It just makes sense," I said. "Ahmed forces Pete into a deal. Pete doesn't like it, so he and George put together the scam. Only George takes his cut first, leaving Pete with only enough cash to keep paying people off. Ahmed finds out about the scam. Pete points the finger at George, and Ahmed and his friends send someone to get George to cough up the money. Maybe they didn't mean to kill him. Maybe they wanted to send Pete a message. Or maybe they didn't know that Pete couldn't keep the scam going without George. Anyway you look at it, Ahmed has to be in as big a pickle as Pete. He killed the goose. No more golden eggs."

"It *sounds* good," Randy said. "Chicago P.D. have any leads? Anything to support what you've laid out?"

I shrugged, shivered in the raw breeze. "I don't think so. But I don't think they've got much of anything."

"I can find out." His eyes fixed on something in the distance. In a while they came back, focused on me. "What do you want from all this?" He said it so softly the wind almost took the words away before they reached me.

I shifted my weight, jammed my hands in my pockets.

"The mall's good for this town," he said. "Like it or not, this isn't the same place it was when we were kids. You can't stop the growth. Put Pete out of business and it puts a lot of people out of work. It won't bring Lou back, either."

"I know that." I scuffed the gravel at my feet with the toe of my shoe. "I just want things to be right."

"They'll never be the same."

I looked away. Saw the red Alfa sitting in the drive. Thought of all the times it had been in the shop, all the parts that had been repaired, replaced over time. The time it had been rammed on that farm up on the state line. I could have left it for dead then. Let it sit in a dusty field and slowly turn into a rusted hulk. Instead, I had it fixed.

"That's okay," I said. "Things always change. Sometimes you have to fix them anyway."

He nodded. "I don't like it when people try to go around the law. Guess that's why I became a cop." Smiled. "Besides, I always thought Pete acted too big for his britches. Never cared for him much."

"You'll help us?"

He frowned. For a moment I thought the worst. Discovered I was holding my breath.

"Me an' your brother are friends, and you've got family here. Weren't for that, I might let those two in there chew you up and spit you out. Well, that and the fact I still feel kind of bad giving you that bloody nose when you were a kid." His brow smoothed. "What the heck, considered yourselves deputized."

CHAPTER 28

An odd combination of smells permeated the car. I picked out vanilla, cinnamon, motor oil. All three subsumed by what could only be described as gym locker, but more pungent. As if fear-induced. Or sweated out of bored cops on bad diets. I've smelled far worse in Chicago cabs. Still, it made me long for fresh air.

Randy must have been used to it, but he cracked the windows on both sides without taking his eyes off the road, enough to let in some air but not the rain. He slouched in the seat, left forearm draped on the window ledge, right hand resting on his thigh, and steered with a thumb.

"You okay with this?" I asked.

He lifted a shoulder, let it drop. "Long as you stay on a short leash." He glanced in the rearview, then the side mirror. "Could be the most excitement I ever see on this job. That doesn't mean I like the idea of letting civilians work a case. I should have sent you back to Chicago when I had the chance."

I conceded the point with a nod and looked away.

Half an hour of heated discussion had convinced Duran and Lipscomb not to arrest us for obstruction. Another hour convinced them that Brandt and I were on to something. And one more talked them into using us. They told us all the ways it could go wrong. I countered with a reminder that if it went right, they could wrap up years of investigation. After hammering out possible scenarios, they reluctantly agreed to give us a shot. Randy would be our handler until we were ready to take the next step.

We divvied up assignments. Brandt packed and drove the rental back to Chicago to work on raising money. Duran and Lipscomb said they'd assemble a team, make sure everything was in place to trace the money. Randy had taken them back to their cars at the P.D. After they'd gone, Frank had sighed, said, "Christ, what a mess." I'd reminded him it wasn't my mess, but I was trying to clean it up anyway. He'd looked at me differently after that, as if understanding something about me for the first time.

My job was to make sure Pete took the bait. I didn't feel comfortable coming at him without more compelling reasons than what I had in hand. So I'd asked Randy to come back and pick me up later. Laid out what I wanted to accomplish when he returned. While I waited, I checked up on Bob Kolnik, learned he'd holed up in a Holiday Inn in Dubuque, Iowa, with his wife and kids. Told him that if he was still interested in saving his miserable hide he should wait an hour or two then call FBI Special Agent in Charge Jeff Lipscomb. I gave him the number, wished him a happy life.

Roadside wildflowers bent and shivered under a blustery onslaught of rain as a squall moved through. A fine spray sheeted through the open window. I raised it some. The wipers hypnotically slapped water from one side of the glass to the other.

"You find out anything else about Danny?" I said.

Randy checked the mirrors again before he spoke. "Can't see it as anything but an accident, if that's what you're asking."

"You sure?"

"Ever been inside one of those locomotives out at the museum? Not like driving a car. Controls aren't exactly easy to figure out. You gotta know what you're doing to drive one."

"Just seems awfully convenient. Danny knew something. Now he's dead."

"Pete says he was home the night Danny was killed. You know something different?"

"You checked?" I said. "I thought you said it was an accident."

"Just being thorough."

I considered him, shook my head. Pete *had* been home Friday night, at least until ten. I hadn't hung around any longer than that. He could have gone out later. Or had someone do his dirty work for him like he probably did with the RV.

"Could be he's lying. Wouldn't be the first time."

He glanced my way. "No telling what'll drive a man to kill. I don't think Pete's got the balls. And who's to say what Danny knew? All we know for sure is he and Pete didn't see eye-to-eye." He paused. "Besides, anyone around here you know of can operate a diesel locomotive besides Danny?"

I shrugged, said nothing.

"Air brakes weren't set right," he said. "Looks like Danny just got careless."

We rode the rest of the way into town in silence.

Meg waited for us in the open front doorway, arms folded against the chill. I hunched my shoulders, hustled up the walk to the dry porch and waited. Randy sauntered up behind me, oblivious to the rain.

"Appreciate your seeing us, Meg," he said as she led us inside. He looked around. "Kids at school?"

Her smile faltered. She gave a small nod. "I'm still not sure what it is you want me to do."

"Sorry to be so mysterious on the phone." He paused. "Your friend Sue Ann's in a lot of trouble."

Meg's eyes flicked toward me and back to Randy. Her mouth

tightened as she waited for the rest.

"Pete's mixed up in some bad stuff," he went on. "Looks like Sue Ann's been helping him. I need to talk to her."

"Why can't . . . ?" She stopped as if to think.

"It's better we do this someplace private," he said. "I don't want to show up at the site and tip off Pete. If I call Sue Ann down to the station she might panic."

She nodded, swallowed. Her eyes hardened. "So you want me to set her up."

"I'm trying to give her a chance here, Meg. She helps us, maybe I can see she doesn't go to jail, depending on how deep in this thing she is. We're talking big-time felony here. FBI's in this now. I'm not sure how long I'll be able to protect her, but I'd sure like to try. If she deserves it, that is."

Her gaze hadn't left my face. "This has to do with Lou, doesn't it?" she asked.

"It looks like Pete forced Lou into bankruptcy," I said, "so he could take over the mall project as developer."

Tears suddenly brimmed in her eyes. "Why would he do that?"

"He's running a scam." I sighed. "I think he's already defrauded investors out of millions. With Lou out of the picture he stands to make a lot more."

"We have to put a stop to it," Randy said gently.

She looked away. Didn't seem to hear him. A tear spilled over, left a snail's trail down her cheek.

"I still can't understand why he'd do that to us. Why that would make him want to kill himself. Bankruptcy's not so bad, is it?"

Her plaintiveness was heart-wrenching. I hated to add to her pain. "Lou might have been involved."

"I don't believe you." She sniffed, dabbed at the corner of her eye. "Even if he was, that would have just ticked him off.

He would have gotten even. You, of all people, should know that. You know Lou would never put up with Pete's b.s. You can't believe they did business together all those years without Lou knowing what Pete was up to. And he certainly wasn't involved, whatever Pete's done."

"I don't know what was going through his mind, Meg. That's why I didn't want to do this in the first place. It doesn't matter anyway. Pete's the one we have to stop."

"It matters to me."

"Then help us," Randy said. "We get Pete, maybe your brother can rest in peace."

She brooded, raised her eyes. "What do you want me to do?"

"Call Sue Ann," he said. "Tell her one of your kids is sick. You've got an emergency and need to leave. Ask her if she can come babysit for a while."

Meg hesitated, reached for the phone.

Time ticked by slowly, the silence marred only by the sounds of rain lashing the windows and the whooshing rustle of waving branches in the gusts of wind. Ten minutes later, the *bong* of the doorbell jarred me out of a jumbled daydream. Randy perched on the edge of the couch. He stood as murmured voices at the front door grew louder.

"Why won't you tell me?" Sue Ann said as she followed Meg into the room. She stopped short when she spotted Randy and me. Her face twisted with bitterness, hate and fear before feigning casual disinterest. She turned back to Meg. "What's going on?"

Meg looked at the floor. "Ask them."

Sue Ann folded her arms, looked from Randy to me.

"You better sit down, Sue Ann," Randy said.

"I'll stand, thanks."

"I'm not asking."

She tapped her foot. Stepped over to an easy chair and

plopped down, arms still crossed.

"We know what Pete's doing," Randy said.

Her eyes flickered briefly, but her composure held.

"All of it," Randy went on. "The payoffs. The strike. The deal with the bank down in Chicago. Question is whether you're going to get out in front of this or not. This is serious business, Sue Ann. The FBI's investigating Pete. And not just for scamming a few folks around town. Now if you tell me he forced you into helping out, come clean and cooperate, I'll do what I can to keep you out of jail so's you can still take care of the kids. You keep pretending you don't know why we're here, I can't help you. You'll go down with Pete."

Daggers glinted in her eyes when she looked at me. Her voice was calm, though. "I'm sure this is all a mistake. I don't have a clue why you think my husband's done anything wrong."

Randy glanced in my direction, nodded. I got up and stepped over to Sue Ann. Held my cell phone a foot from her nose. Watched her eyes slowly focus on the photo of her and Bob in the park. Fear flashed across her face and vanished.

She lifted her head, smiled sweetly at me. "So? I gave my brother some money."

"Have you seen him lately?" I said softly. "Talked to him?"

The fear in her eyes returned.

"He told me everything," I said. "He left town. He's hiding out. Cutting a deal with the FBI if he knows what's good for him."

She hesitated, uncertain now.

"The way it works," Randy said, "is there's only so much charity to go around. Your brother tells his story first, the feds aren't going to be as interested in what you have to say. You help us out, though, I can tell them you cooperated. Get them to cut you some slack."

She shook her head. I scrolled to another photo on the cell

phone, Pete this time, a woman on his arm. Sue Ann leaned forward, squinted at it. She clutched my wrist and pulled the phone closer.

"Shit!" She balled a tiny hand and thumped her thigh. Rocked back and forth. "Shit, shit, shit! That prick!" She looked at me, fighting tears. "I have kids, you bastard! Why do you *think* I did it? I didn't have any choice."

Her shoulders heaved and the tears let loose. Meg nudged me out of the way and squatted next to the chair, wrapped an arm around Sue Ann and pulled her close. I backed up and sat. Randy did the same.

She cried it out, heaved a shuddery sigh and told us everything. How one of the girls Pete hired to work reception had asked her why the copy of a sub's invoice they were paying was different than the one going into the file. How she checked the files and found similar discrepancies. Confronted Pete and told him that if he was going to screw up their lives, at least he should trust her instead of letting some bottle-blonde high school cheerleader with the brains of a minnow open her big yap and get him sent to jail. How she made payoffs to the few suppliers who were in on it. Most weren't, she said. Pete just reproduced their invoices, inflated the numbers. Figured suppliers would never check as long as they got paid.

"How long did this go on?" Randy asked.

"I'm not sure." She bit her lower lip. "I didn't find out until about six months ago. Pete said the only way it worked was because of the bank. I just assumed it was this guy Saunders's idea. The banker. So, I guess maybe since the new financing was put together. After they settled the strike."

I considered her, hiding my surprise. "Pete and Lou didn't pull this kind of thing on other projects?" I heard Meg's intake of breath.

Sue Ann looked confused. "Lou? No. I don't know. . . . You

think Pete . . . ?"

"And you believe your brother never took a dime from Pete until this 'arrangement' with the bank? With Saunders?"

"I . . ." She looked at the floor. "I don't know." Her face fell. She covered it with her hands. Sobbed. "I've been so *stupid*. Haven't I?"

Meg patted her shoulder gently, murmured something in her ear. Looked up at me with mouth set grimly, fury in her eyes. I shrugged. Unless Sue Ann was channeling Meryl Streep, she was just a loyal housewife standing by her man.

Sue Ann raised her tear-stained face. Spoke as if she'd been reading my mind. "I gave him everything. Kids. A perfect home. And look at me." She sat up straight, looked down, then at the three of us. "I stay in shape. I'm still pretty. Aren't I?" More tears rolled down her cheeks.

Meg made comforting sounds. Randy looked away.

"I've been such a fool." She sniffed. "I suspected there were other women. I didn't want to believe it. I just looked the other way. But this business with the mall . . . I couldn't pretend it wasn't happening. And I couldn't let Pete screw up everything we've worked for. I mean, the kids . . . what'll happen to the kids?" She gripped the arms of the chair.

Randy put his hands out, patted the air. "It's okay. They'll be fine. You will, too. You'll see. We'll get you out of this." He paused. Spoke again, firmly this time. "Pete's going away for this, Sue Ann. You have to let him go. Make a clean break here. To protect yourself."

She thought for a while.

"Did you keep copies?" Randy asked. "Records? A separate set of books?"

"Of course."

"In the office?"

She shook her head. "In the trailer. The office is just for

show. Pete keeps anything of value on the site. There's security there."

"Can you get them?"

"I'm not sure. Maybe. When Pete's out making rounds."

"Okay, that's good," Randy said. "Now, this is going to be the tough part, Sue Ann. I need you to go back there and act like nothing's happened. I want you to copy the books onto a disc. If you've got time, copy some of the invoices and stick them in your purse. Don't worry about getting all of them. Just a few will do for now. What time do you usually leave out there?"

"When it's time to pick up the kids. Two-thirty or three. Sometimes earlier if I've got errands to run." She flushed. "I'm just helping out part time, you know. The kids still need me."

"I understand," he said. "That's okay. You think you can get everything copied by the time you leave?"

She glanced at her watch, did a mental calculation. "I think so. Then what?"

"That's it. You bring those copies by the station on your way to get your kids. I'll tell Marsha to expect you if I'm not there. And then you sit tight. Just keep on about your business, same as always."

"You're not going to arrest him?"

"FBI's after bigger fish. That's why it's real important you don't spook him, Sue Ann. You've got to act like everything's normal. Can you do that?"

"I don't know. I'm scared."

"That's okay. If he notices, you can always say it's because you're worried about Meg here. Remember, she called you over because she had an 'emergency'?"

She blinked, exchanged glances with Meg. "Are you sure this will work?"

"We'll do our best."

"And they won't send me to jail? I'll get to keep the kids?"

"I can't promise you anything, Sue Ann, except that I'll do my darnedest to see that Pete takes the blame for this, not you."

She took a deep breath. Turned to Meg. "What should I do?"

Meg's eyes shifted to Randy, then me before she replied. "Do what he tells you. It's better than the alternative." She saw Sue Ann's reticence. "Randy's always been good as his word. You know that. Remember the break he gave Pete, Junior, when he got into that accident? Right after he got his license last year?"

Sue Ann chewed her lower lip again and bobbed her head.

"That's good," Randy said. "One other thing, though, Sue Ann. I have to ask. Did you, by any chance, put aside any of that money on your own? You know, tuck it away just in case things didn't turn out so good? Think real hard before you answer. 'Cause if you did, and it gets found out later, then you can be pretty sure all bets are off. I don't think anyone will be able to help you then. You understand what I'm saying?"

She remained silent a long time. "Suppose that was true. What would I have to do?"

"Give it all back," he said. "It'd be a real show of good faith where the feds are concerned." He paused, watched her think it through. "I know you feel like you're getting the short end of the stick here, Sue Ann, but you gotta remember this was *your* choice. Helping your husband because you felt like you had to, to protect your kids, that's one thing. Taking the money, that doesn't look so good. Give it up, they'll probably look the other way. Keep it, I promise you won't like the alternative."

Tears welled up again. She choked them back. "How long will I have to keep this up? Pretending, I mean."

"Couple of days," Randy said. He glanced my way with a raised eyebrow, saw me shrug. "Look, if you have any worries, you call me. I'll arrange to get you and the kids someplace safe. First things first, though. All right?"

"All right." She didn't look convinced.

I stayed with Meg after Sue Ann left. Because she put a hand on my arm when I followed Randy out. She lowered herself onto the leather couch. I sat on the opposite end. She didn't speak for a long while. She reached up and twisted a strand of red hair. Tucked it behind her ear.

"Do you ever think about what might have happened if you'd stayed?" she asked.

"No." It came out reflexively. "Staying was never a choice for me."

A shadow—annoyance, maybe, or hurt—flitted across her face. "No regrets? You don't wonder?"

It took a moment to get at what she meant. "What might have happened between us?"

She offered the barest nod.

I stopped to consider. "I never thought that was an option, either." I didn't know, at this point, if it was a lie or not.

"Curious. I did." She tilted her head. "I wondered a lot. Seems silly now, I know. I followed your football career in college. Lost track of you after that. But every so often, I wondered. Where you'd ended up, what you were doing. Whether you were happy or not. If you were married. I thought of you less and less as the years went by, but even after Phil and I started dating a couple years after I graduated you'd pop into my head from time to time."

"I didn't realize . . ."

"Oh, don't get me wrong. I don't have any regrets. I love Phil. We're good together. And the kids are wonderful. We waited a long time to have them. To give Phil's practice a chance to get off the ground. And to make sure we really wanted them. We did. Both of us. I can't tell you what a joy they are. Well, you know. You have little Emily."

I almost told her that I didn't have Emily anymore. She saw my hesitation and looked at me curiously, but didn't press.

"The point is, I'm happy," she said. "My life is full. But I still wonder. I'm not sure why. I hadn't thought of you in years, but you were the first person who came to mind when Lou died. Isn't that strange?"

"Maybe not when you think about how much time we spent together as kids."

"I was angry with you at first when you came back."

"Why? You asked me to come out here."

A small smile appeared on her face and quickly vanished. "I had this notion that you'd been doing the same thing all these years. Wondering. Maybe settling for less than what we could have had. This silly idea that there was still some spark between us. Not that I would have done anything about it. Just that it would have been a real boost to my ego."

"We went there once, remember? It didn't work out." I didn't want to remember how much I'd wanted it to work out once upon a time, how much my heart had ached when we went from almost becoming lovers to going back to just being friends. I wondered if Jake was right. Wondered if I'd come back because of Meg. Not Lou. To see if she still carried a torch for me. To see if she'd ever had the same feelings I thought I'd had for her. It didn't make any difference now. I had another girl. It was too late for regrets.

"We didn't give it a chance," she said. "But you can't tell me there wasn't *something* between us. Anyway, I realized I wasn't angry with you about that. It was because I was jealous when you never came back from college. Like you'd found some secret key to escape this place that the rest of us missed."

I watched branches on the trees outside the window dance in the wind.

"You and Nell are happy?" she asked.

351

"As happy as can be expected."

"Because you're not together."

I hesitated, then nodded, feeling like my reticence was a betrayal. We sat without talking for a while.

"Lou knew Pete was dirty all along, didn't he?" she asked finally.

"I think so."

"And he didn't do anything about it."

"No. Whether he was involved or just looked the other way."

"It doesn't make any difference, does it? Either way, it got him killed."

Her choice of words made me think.

I called Nell after I left Meg's. No one answered. I didn't leave a message. I tried again after a wordless dinner with Frank at the kitchen table. She still wasn't there. Or she wasn't picking up. Either way, I felt like I wasn't part of her life anymore, like she'd moved on to something else that no longer included me, included us. It made me ache with longing and loss, and my heart felt shriveled and dry and shrunk to the size of a walnut.

Brandt called midmorning and told me he'd worked out the money issues. I asked him how he'd managed, but he wouldn't say more, only not to worry and that he'd be back later in the afternoon.

I put in a call to Lipscomb to ask if he'd heard from Kolnik. He said he'd gotten a call instead from one Jerry McKenna, Esq., from Marengo. Bob sounded eager to cooperate, according to McKenna, as long as an accommodation could be reached regarding a deal. When I asked, Lipscomb said Kolnik wanted immunity. He said he told McKenna that Bob could have it. When I protested, he chuckled. Said all he meant was that Bob could have immunity from any federal charges that might arise. He couldn't speak for county or state prosecutors. McKenna would figure it out sooner or later and have to hammer out more deals.

Ed Jarvis had told me McKenna was one of the original investors. I wondered if McKenna knew yet that Bob was partly responsible for losing him a lot of money. How he felt about that.

I checked in with Randy. Sue Ann had done what he'd asked. He said it made for interesting reading if you liked numbers. They'd never been my forte, which is why I left all the investing to Brandt. Subconscious rebellion, no doubt, all those years of living with a father who'd rather read a balance sheet than a good book.

I'd been circling long enough, picking at weak spots. It was time to try an opening salvo on the main defenses. Nothing like lobbing it from inside the fort. I got lucky and caught Pete coming out of the Anderson Construction trailer a little after noon, sky dark enough to make it seem much later. The wind caught at his jacket, flapped it open. He looked away when he saw me and kept walking.

"You're trespassing," he said. He passed me, stone-faced.

I fell in step, leaned into the wind. "Arrest me."

He waved me off. "I'm going to lunch. Thought I told you I'd rip you a new asshole if I saw you here again. What do you want?"

Dark smudges resided under his eyes, and he looked haggard, like he hadn't slept.

"Actually, I'm here to help." I still hoped to convince him without using what I knew.

He snorted. "Since when did I need your help?"

I gave him a friendly smile. "Not since high school, I guess."

"Not even then, Ward. You caught a few passes. So what?"

I shrugged. "Whatever. I just figured you might be in a cash-flow bind."

His ears perked up, but he didn't take the bait. "What makes you think that?"

"Oh, just some rumblings from subs. You know, rumors floating around the Parkside."

His laugh sounded uneasy. "Can't believe everything you hear. Maybe you forgot what it's like in a small town."

"Yeah, you're right. You know what's weird, though? I was talking with Bob Kolnik the other day about how it's not a small town anymore. By the way, you seen him around lately?"

He slowed, looked at me curiously. "Why're you looking for him?"

"To ask him about the permit process. Frank's thinking of doing some remodeling around the house."

He grunted, bulled ahead. "I don't keep tabs on him."

We rounded the line of trailers and headed out the gate to the lot. Picked our way around the puddles, surfaces riffling in the stiff breeze. Pete didn't do subtle, apparently. I needed to lob something with a little more oomph, quick.

"Sure you don't need help? What with George Saunders dead and all?"

That brought him up short and snapped his head around. "What do you know about that?"

"What I read in the papers. Must be a mess at the bank getting someone to take his place. Curious you haven't submitted any draws since he got killed."

His attempt at a grin twisted his features into a lupine mask. "Too busy to do the paperwork. What's your point?"

"You're probably not interested. Sounds like you've got everything under control. I must have heard wrong." I jammed cold hands in my pockets, turned to walk away.

"That's it? You come here to give me a bunch of crap?"

I paused. "Why? You say you don't need help, I can take a hint."

He eyed me. "Let's say I'm curious. I make no bones about it; I don't like you. Never did. But you want to help? I tell you to stay away from my construction site. Yet here you are. You're like a bad case of jock itch. Whatever you got to say, it has to be worth a laugh. So let's hear it."

"I can make all your problems disappear."

He looked amused. "Magic wand? Pull your dick out of your pants and wave it around?"

I grinned along with him. "Better. I've got a buyer for the mall."

"A buyer?"

I nodded. "Willing to pay a premium."

His eyes narrowed. "It's not mine to sell. Why come to me?"

"A piece of it's yours, unless I'm mistaken. And the other investors, they're in this to make money, right? Maybe they intend to manage it, make money off the leases. But even then, they wouldn't turn down the right offer to sell, would they?"

He looked at me blankly, black eyes flicking back and forth across my face. Shark's eyes, evaluating dinner. "Depends. What sort of premium?"

"I'm sure it'll be sufficient. Like I said, enough to solve your problems."

He looked annoyed. "I told you, I got no problems. What do you get out of this, anyway?"

"Oh, come on, Pete. You think I haven't figured out your scam? I want in on it."

From the look of him, the way he'd let himself go, I never would have thought he could move that quick. He surprised me. Despite the gut, the heaviness around the jowls, the florid face, he summoned the reflexes of his ball-playing days. Snapped his left hand in a lightning jab that I barely saw coming. I leaned back, away from it, but not before it caught me on the point of the chin, clacked my jaw shut and rattled my teeth. Sent me sprawling on my back in the rain-soaked gravel.

Chapter 29

Two pairs of legs appeared in my vision and stepped in unison across a gray sea of gravel. A voice called out, "Everything all right?"

Another voice, nearer, responded. "Yeah. Just got the wind knocked out of him."

The legs were attached to two identically dressed men. They shimmered like a mirage. Slowly morphed into a single body. Bright dots of white pinwheeled around the figure and slowly faded.

"You sure?" the first voice asked.

"I think so," came the response. "He just missed a step and went down. Must've slipped." Pete's face loomed above mine. "Isn't that right?"

I struggled to sit up, waggled my jaw. "Right. Loose gravel."

The man's head bobbed, and he veered off toward a row of parked vehicles. Cold seeped through the fabric of my khakis. I peered up at Pete. Saw his hands hanging relaxed at his sides. Scrabbled back a foot or two as I got up, just in case. Brushed gravel and damp dirt off my pants. Remembered a time in eighth grade when Pete did the same thing to a classmate even though Pete was two years younger. Dredged the kid's face up from the depths of memory. Dennis Swope. Kind of pudgy. Hadn't done anything wrong that I could recall. Just rubbed Pete the wrong way. Wished I'd decked Pete back then, but a bunch of guys had stepped in and Pete had backed off quick.

357

Couldn't push it now.

"What the hell was that for?"

He shrugged. "Whatever you want it to be for. Been wanting to do that for a long time."

"Nice to know you care. I'd have thought you'd turn tail and run by now. How come you're still here?" I rubbed the sore spot on my chin. Wondered how bad it would bruise.

He cleared his throat, spat in the gravel. A gust took it a few inches wide of my shoe. "You know, Ward, once upon a time you might've thought you were better than the rest of us. Turns out you're just like everyone else. You're just a greedy scumsucker looking for a quick score. Well, get in line."

"Guess we're not so different after all, eh, Pete? Like flies on honey, a project like this."

He shook his head. "You surprise me. All that goody-two-shoes talk about helping your old pal Lou. And you're just in it for the money after all. Well, go fuck yourself. You're not getting a dime out of me. I don't give a shit what you think you know."

"You're still here. Must want something. Another swing, maybe. No? Not when I might be ready for it?" I felt my hands clench.

"Fuck you." He turned away.

"You're wrong." I had his attention. "I don't want *your* money."

He faced me and fixed me with an empty-eyed stare.

"Here's what I know, Pete. You're up to your ass in debt. You're bleeding money a couple nights a week at the tables. You're screwing around on your wife. The building inspector in your pocket took off. And your banker is dead. I'm guessing all that makes it next to impossible to pull off whatever scam you had going."

I gave him a second, then plunged ahead before he thought about it too hard. "I can put you together with someone who can buy you out of all that trouble. Someone who wants this piece of property bad enough to pay more than it's worth."

He hung on the words, gears working now behind the flat stare, a glint of something more base than hope in his eyes. I half-expected him to deny it all, obfuscate, protest too much. His silence suggested he was smarter than that. And that I'd gotten it all right. I was emboldened to keep up the pretense, go through with the bluff. Warning bells twitched at the corners of my consciousness, though. His acceptance, other than the quick shot to the jaw, wasn't in character.

"Don't for a second think I'm doing this for old times' sake." I said. "But I'm not out to screw you, either. You've got enough problems. I'll put this deal together, Pete. But I want a finder's fee. A big one. There won't be any commissions involved, so your investors can afford it. Cash. Under the table. Not a dime of it yours."

I held his gaze for a long moment while he seemed to contemplate.

He scanned the lot. Jerked his head sideways. "Come on." He led the way to a big diesel pickup with his company logo painted on the doors. Unlocked it with a remote from several yards away. Motioned me toward the passenger door. I stepped up on the running board, climbed in. The interior felt warmer out of the wind. Pete hoisted himself behind the wheel, stuck the keys in the ignition. Turned the radio on low, but didn't start the engine.

"You're serious," he said finally. The wolfish look returned, lean and wary.

"We know exactly where we stand with each other. You don't like me. I think you're an asshole. Worse, I think you fucked up a really good thing. Doesn't prevent me from seeing an opportunity. Your screw-up gives me a shot at getting in on this deal."

"Table scraps? That's all you're after?" His laugh was short, harsh.

I shrugged. "I don't need much. Enough to buy a new bus, maybe, add to the retirement fund. Couple hundred thousand ought to do it." I saw his eyes widen. "I'm practical, not greedy."

"You really have a buyer?"

I nodded. "You get your principals to the table, I'll bring in my guy."

"Uh-uh. I'll talk to my investors, but I meet your guy first. If he checks out, I'll set up a meeting. How soon can you be ready to go?"

"Anytime."

He gawped in surprise. "We haven't even talked price."

"Let the principals negotiate price. These people can afford it, whatever it is. I know what I want out of this. I assume you do, too."

"That fucking easy."

"Yep, just that easy."

He chuckled. "Seems almost too good to be true. And you know what they say . . ."

"I'd just as soon watch you screw this up so bad you get caught." It was dangerously close to the truth. He frowned, eyes squinting up in suspicion. "But this way, I put a little extra change in my pockets and get to rub Frank's nose in it, too."

His face lightened. "Stick it to the old man? Now that makes more sense."

"So, you're in."

"Sure. I'll play along. See where this goes. What the hell?"

"How about tomorrow night, then? The pub in town. Say, nine-ish."

"That'll do. Now get out of my truck before someone thinks you're trying to give me a blowjob or something."

"Always the charmer, Pete," I said, stepping down. "Fuck you, too."

He stopped me. "Ward, if you're messing with me, I can always see that whoever blew up your RV finishes the job next time."

I caught a glimpse of a leering grin before I turned and headed for my car.

Brandt and I headed down to the tavern a little early, just after sunset. Light faded rapidly in an overcast sky. I drove. A large briefcase and a laptop case rested on Brandt's knees, his hands folded neatly on top. He sat stiffly and stared out the windshield.

"You all right?" I asked. Saw him nod. "What's in the briefcase?"

Duran and Lipscomb, too busy or too important to make a personal appearance, had sent a couple of young agents to babysit us. Collins and Petrick. Interchangeable and nondescript, of average height, weight and looks, they both had brown hair, one a little darker than the other. One had brown eyes, the other blue. They came armed with the laptop and a lot of instructions.

Brandt also had arrived armed, with several letters of intent written on various corporate letterheads. The logos were impressive, the signatures more so. He answered evasively when I asked how he'd managed to get them so quickly. Made me wonder if they were genuine. Knowing Brandt, they were. But I worried that my larcenous side might be rubbing off on him.

Frank hovered while we made plans, but didn't get in the way. I told Collins and Petrick I hoped they'd brought a change of clothes. Otherwise, they'd stand out in their suits like Mormon missionaries in a Vegas strip club.

We were supposed to meet Pete, get him to take us to the principal investors. Embedded with a program that would capture Brandt's keystrokes, the laptop would transmit them wirelessly. Collins and Petrick would follow closely enough to monitor whatever Brandt keyed in. A bank account number, for example, and a password. Also bugged, the laptop would digitally record and transmit whatever was said during the meeting. They told us we could even record video with its built-in web camera. I told them we'd pass. I didn't want Brandt getting self-conscious about trying to aim the laptop to get a decent picture, make people suspicious.

It sounded simple. Brandt's silence now said it had already gotten more complicated.

"What's in the case?" I repeated.

He sighed, knew I wouldn't let it go. I heard the latches pop. Glanced over as he raised the lid, holding the laptop so it wouldn't slide off. I saw the stacks of crisp green-and-black currency. Ben Franklin's wizened visage eyed me from atop each stack.

"Jeez, Brandt!" I pulled my eyes away, put the car back on course. "How much?"

"Two hundred thousand." It came out sheepishly.

"What for?"

"My idea." He sounded apologetic. "I wasn't sure these guys—whoever they are—would go for it without some incentive."

"That's what this is all about. You know that. Wiring a couple million in earnest money to some account somewhere like the Caymen Islands. Tracing it."

"I just thought it would show we're serious," he said quietly. "You know, convince them the earnest money is for real, not some scam."

"Where'd it come from?"

"Lipscomb thought it was a good idea."

Once over the initial shock, I realized that he hadn't

answered, pretty sure, suddenly, why he was being evasive. I slowed the car, pulled it onto the shoulder.

"We're not doing this until you tell me," I said. He looked miserable. "This is *your* money, isn't it? And the money for the electronic transfer?"

He nodded slowly, face that of a kid caught with his hand in the cookie jar and chocolate smeared on his face.

"Why?" I asked. "Is this about the money you lost in the market? I told you, it's no big deal."

"It is a big deal. I screwed up. You wouldn't let me pay you back. I figured this was the least I could do."

"Christ, Brandt, you can't trace cash. And the Hardy Boys back there might not be able to trace the transfer, either. You're risking a lot. You don't have to do this to make up to me."

"I *want* to do it, partner." He set his jaw.

I took a deep breath. Leaned back. "You remember what happened last time we tried something like this? Down in the Bahamas? I'd never forgive myself if this went bad like it did down there."

He considered me and finally looked away. I followed his gaze, watched an oriole preen itself on a fence post in the last of the daylight.

"Why do you do this?" he asked. "Stick your neck out, I mean. It ain't your Type A personality, that's for sure. We both know you'd just as soon soak up sunshine and good tequila on a beach somewhere. You're not the skydiving, parasailing, thrill-seeker sort. I could play shrink and say maybe it's 'cause of all that guilt you carry around. Helping others 'cause you blame yourself for not being there when your brother died. Or not being able to prevent your mom's death. But I don't even think it's that. I think you do it 'cause it's who you are. I keep trying to tell you that."

I didn't know how to answer. I wondered if it was true. If so,

I wondered if Nell had left because of it. I thought of how unimportant that seemed compared to everything else that was wrong with the world. Tried to focus on why a guy like Pete would screw over the town he was born and raised in for a little more money. Why he wasn't satisfied with a smart, pretty wife, nice kids, a decent living. How he'd gotten sucked into helping terrorists.

I felt bad for people like Bob and Sue Ann who had started out trying to do the right thing but got in over their heads protecting their families. I could even understand Ahmed being slowly poisoned by the racial intolerance of a country that professed freedom and equality above all else. The ultimate betrayal of a son who went to war to fight for those principles. How he could let his faith be perverted by hatred.

It all led back to Lou. He must have known what was going on around him. His presence filled the shadowy center of it. What I didn't know is to what extent he'd been a participant. Whether the weight of knowing and not doing anything about it had gnawed at his conscience. Or if it was the fear of being exposed.

Brandt went on. "You ever wonder why I keep trying to horn in on these situations you get yourself into? 'Cause I get why you do it. Sure, it's a thrill. Makes me feel alive. But it's more than that. I feel like I'm doing more good for someone when I take part in one of your causes than in all the other charitable work I do combined."

I waved him off.

"Don't worry about the money," he said. "I've got enough money to burn a wet dog. You know that. Let's go do this."

I studied him, put the car in gear and headed for town.

The tavern was already busy. Friday night partyers began gathering in earnest as the early dinner crowd faded away for an hour of TV before bed. I steered Brandt through the herd toward the bar. Halfway there, I caught sight of Pete back near the door to the kitchen talking to Jake. I frowned. I'd always thought of Jake as one of the good guys. Brandt motioned to me that he'd found a spot. I held up a hand, kept my eye on Pete and Jake.

Pete's normally red face suffused with dark anger, Jake's tense, defiant. Hard to tell, at this distance, what their spat might be about. I shifted my weight, took a step. A knot of people in front of them broke apart suddenly, gave me a clear line of sight. Pete handed something to Jake down low. Jake took it, glanced down. I did, too, saw the roll of green before his hand closed over it and stuffed it in his pocket. They exchanged a few more words and Jake drifted toward the bar, face impassive. I quickly looked away. The whole exchange hadn't taken more than a few seconds.

I joined Brandt at the bar. He'd claimed an empty stool. I stood behind him, leaned over and told him Pete had gotten here ahead of us. Jake slipped behind the bar. Saw me and nodded. Stepped over to take a drink order. I introduced him to Brandt, talking loudly over the din. He smiled, shook hands. Acted normal. Almost made me wonder if I'd imagined what had transpired only moments before. He got us a couple of beers and set them down before he moved to the waitress station to fill an order.

Pete found us a minute or two later. Again I made introductions. Brandt swiveled around, stuck out a hand. Pete ignored it, lifted a beer bottle to his lips instead.

He turned to me. "You said nine."

"We're a little early. We were thirsty."

Pete looked Brandt up and down. "You always meet prospects at night in bars?"

Brandt flashed him a Texas smile. "Anywhere, anytime, long as it's a good deal. Don't your best deals get done over a beer?"

365

"What's your interest?"

"Got two," Brandt said, smile fading. "First, I'm not here as a buyer's representative. I'm here as an investor. I've got authority to speak on behalf of a group of names you'll probably recognize. But I'm in this with them, both as a private investor and a fiduciary trustee of several charitable organizations. Second, this guy's a friend of mine." He indicated me. "I owed him a favor. Seemed like a good way to dig two holes with one shovel."

Pete looked charily at me then Brandt. "I never heard of you. Who else is in this with you?"

Brandt reached down, pulled a manila envelope out of the laptop bag at his feet. Handed it to Pete. He opened it, riffled through the sheaf of letters from Chicago captains of industry. Stuffed them back in the envelope, folded it and put it in his jacket pocket.

"I take it your investors are interested," I said.

He nodded. "Yeah. Mall management wasn't what they expected."

"I'm surprised they want to sell," Brandt said. "This area is prime for growth. The mall will just accelerate that growth. They could always hire one of the big mall development companies to manage it. Sit on it for a few years until it's fully leased and generating real cash flow."

"That was the plan," Pete said. "They don't want to wait that long. You have a good enough offer, they'll consider it."

"I think we can come to terms."

"I'll talk to them, get back to you in a day or two." He turned.

It wasn't what I expected. Panic plucked at my gut. I put a hand on his arm. "Whoa. That wasn't the deal. This is a one-time offer."

He pulled his arm away, looked from me to Brandt. I saw Brandt nod.

"We have another investment we were already looking at," Brandt said. "We like this opportunity, but we're not going to waste a lot of time on it."

"You're really serious? You want to negotiate this deal tonight?"

"I'm authorized to put up earnest money tonight," Brandt said, "and a *cash* bonus depending on how things work out."

I smiled at Pete, clapped a hand on Brandt's shoulder and squeezed. Saw him wince. "Time is money, Pete. You know that."

He hesitated. "This bonus . . ."

"Consider it a token of appreciation to whoever puts the deal together," Brandt said.

Pete mulled it over. "Let me make a call." He pushed his way through milling drinkers and a haze of blue smoke, and pressed his cell phone to his ear as he went out the front door

I turned to Brandt. "Are you nuts?"

"We were going to lose him."

"Now all he has to do is dump you in a ditch and take the money."

"You and the Hardy Boys will be there."

"I don't like it."

"Tough. Now smile, he's coming back in."

Pete shouldered his way back to the bar, towing a young guy in his wake. One of Kenny Miller's kids. I recognized him from the May Day picnic. The oldest boy.

Pete motioned to Brandt. "You're coming with me." He dug a finger into my chest. "You stay put. Junior here's gonna make sure you do. Don't give him a hard time."

"Kenny's kid?" I looked from Pete to Junior and back. "What's he got to do with this?"

Pete grinned. "Nothing. I just offered him all the beer he can drink to babysit you."

"The bonus is in the car. I've got the keys."

"Well, hand them over, 'cause you're not going anywhere."

Reluctantly, I dug in my pocket. Brandt picked up the laptop case. Stood up.

Pete snatched the keys out of my hand and grinned. "Everything goes okay, we'll be back. If not . . ." He shrugged.

Brandt gave me a hopeful look and followed him out. I locked eyes with Junior. Gave him a smile and offered him the stool.

He shook his head. "Uh-uh. I ain't stupid. Pete told me to keep an eye on you. *You* sit."

"Suit yourself." I eased onto the stool with my back turned. Pulled out my cell phone and dialed Randy.

"You saw?" I asked.

"Yeah." Randy was parked somewhere in view of the bar as backup. "What happened?"

CHAPTER 30

Two hours later the only reason my nerves hadn't frayed to the breaking point were the two beers I nursed. They loosened me up enough that I didn't try to plant Junior on his butt on my way out the door. Not that the thought didn't tempt me. To do what, though, wasn't clear. So I sat and worried. Jake was too busy to notice, seemed to have something on his mind anyway. I tried a few times to engage Junior in conversation, make the time pass faster. He wasn't interested. Sucked down beers and kept his eyes glued to the TV.

When Brandt finally showed up well after midnight, I silently wrapped him in a bear hug. Tried not to tear up. Got myself under control, pulled away. Told Junior he could take a hike. Or call a cab. He roused himself and stumbled out. I caught Jake's eye.

"He okay?" I jerked my head toward the door.

He shrugged. "If he's not, whoever's on patrol tonight won't let him get more than a couple blocks." He went back to work.

I turned to Brandt. "I thought I'd go nuts. Spill."

He grinned, amped on excitement. "Worked like a charm."

"You're kidding. What happened?"

"Well, you're right about one thing. Pete'd have to stand up to look a coontail in the eye. We barely got out of town when he told me to open the case and asked me how much was in there. When I told him, he said to take out half and put it under the seat. Said he'd be happy to split what was left with Ahmed if he took the deal. Greedy bastard."

"What'd you do?"

"What he told me. What do you think? Said it was either that or . . ." He drew a finger across his throat.

"He was bluffing," I said. "He'd never get away with it."

Brandt grinned. "I know that. The laptop, remember? I turned it on before we left. Figured I'd let the boys listen in just in case."

"Smart. And the meeting?"

"Went fine. Whatever else he might be, Ahmed's a business-man. A smart one. We talked business. I did my homework, made a good offer. He said he'd have to run it by the other investors in the REIT. I expected that. I'm sure they'll come back with a higher number to give me a chance to make a counteroffer. I wire-transferred the earnest money."

"How much?"

"Two million. Not much in terms of a percentage, but enough to show we're serious. Now we just have to hope our friends at the FBI can trace it to some bad-guy group before these negotia-tions get too serious. I'd hate to have to come up with more."

"More?" I was still trying to comprehend the figure he'd tossed out. I noticed Jake watching us. He looked away quickly when I caught his eye.

Brandt ignored me. "I think we're good, though. Ahmed went for the bonus like a dog on a diet, even though he didn't know Pete had already taken half of his share."

"You are going to get this back, right?"

He shrugged. "Lipscomb assures me I will. Probably take a while, though. The cash?" He shrugged. "Depends on how much they spend and how quick. The serial numbers are all recorded, at least."

I took that in. "Nothing else happened?"

He shrugged. "Other than Pete being ornery and unpleasant?

No, it was pretty uneventful."

"I worried for nothing." I watched Jake wipe down the bar with a towel.

"I wouldn't say for nothing, partner. Makes me feel loved."

Jake worked his way over to us. "You want a round here? You two look like you're celebrating."

We ordered shots of his best tequila, surprised he had a bottle of Gran Patron. Told him to skip the lime and salt. He brought them back, said they were on the house.

"Come into some money?" I asked.

He averted his eyes, laughed nervously. "Yeah, right. I wish. We had a good night. We can afford to give one away now and then."

"Pete owe you some money?" I pressed. "He didn't look too happy with you earlier."

He frowned. "Oh, that. Yeah, he lost a bet on a game. Doesn't like losing."

"Must have been a big bet."

He shrugged, moved away.

Brandt gave me a quizzical look. I let it go. Made him relive every minute he was gone instead. He confirmed the animosity between Pete and Ahmed, but said they'd kept it in check. Told me that the Ahmeds' house was lovely. Big and very upscale compared to the typical suburban homes he'd seen in town so far. Said it didn't look as if Ahmed had made a lot of concessions to his faith. The house, at least the parts he'd seen, had no hint of Islamic influence other than an inlaid mosaic chest, some beautiful rugs, a few other pieces.

"Where's Pete?" I asked.

"Went home to the wife and kids, I guess."

"And the boys?"

"Didn't see them after Pete dropped me off. Don't know if they followed us back or not."

"We'll probably hear from them tomorrow. If not them, Duran or Lipscomb."

We finished our drinks slowly. Talked about summer plans. Projects I wanted to get to around the house. The back steps that needed fixing. Rooms that were ready for a new coat of paint. Trips Brandt said he'd like to take, including a weekend or two fishing and playing golf at the cabin up in Wisconsin. Dates we might get up there together. When we might be able to throw on a barbecue for the old bridge group. Just like old times. Footloose and carefree. Unconcerned that responsibilities might intrude.

We left unspoken all the uncertainties. Whether I'd still be my daughter's caregiver. Or see her on a regular basis anymore. Whether I'd have to work around a family schedule. Or be single and have the luxury, maybe curse, of too much time on my hands.

My business in Huntley would wrap up in the next day or two if everything fell into place. We'd done our part. The FBI would trace Brandt's wire transfer and issue warrants for Ahmed and his group. They'd share information with county prosecutors. With testimony from Kolnik and Sue Ann, Pete would go to jail. I'd done what I could, found as many answers as I was likely to get about why Lou had died with a shotgun in his mouth.

It all seemed too easy, and as dissatisfying as anything I'd ever experienced. Meg wouldn't be happy, either. I felt empty and hollow and aimless, the drink in front of me seeming less and less celebratory by the minute. Brandt sensed my change of mood, got quiet. Let me stew for a while, then gave me a nudge.

"You okay in there?"

I looked up. The bar was nearly empty save a few stragglers. Jake counted money from the till, closing out the register.

"I have choices to make, and soon," I said. "I just don't know how to make them. I keep thinking that if I knew what Nell wanted, I could do something to make her come back. But I don't think she knows what that is. The only thing I'm sure of is that I don't want to grow used to her absence. That would mean letting go eventually. Drifting apart until our connection is stretched so thin it vanishes altogether. I can't let that happen. I can't imagine not being able to watch Emily grow up. Can't imagine her forgetting me. Or seeing her so seldom that I become like some eccentric distant uncle to her and a cordial stranger to Nell."

"You'll figure it out."

"We're good together, Brandt. Why doesn't she see that?"

"She does. She doesn't want to lose it. She'd rather walk away from you than see you taken away from her."

I shook my head. "Won't happen."

"You don't know that."

"You're right. I don't. And maybe that's the point. I could get hit by a bus tomorrow. Who knows? So could she. We can only make the most of the time we have here. We can't spend our lives worrying about what might happen."

Before Brandt could fashion a reply Jake came over.

"I'm closing up, gentlemen. Time to head home."

I relinquished my glass. "Mind if we walk out with you?" I asked him.

He shrugged. "As long as you make yourselves useful. You can put stools and chairs up while I finish the bottle count."

Brandt and I worked our way around the bar stacking chairs upside down on the tables so someone could come in and clean the floors in the morning before opening. Ten minutes later Jake was ready to go. We walked out together. Jake locked the door after us.

The wind had died down to a gentle breeze. A smattering of stars was visible through breaks in the clouds. At the corner

Jake raised a hand in farewell.

He rounded it, headed down the street. We stepped off the curb to cross the main drag. Headed up a block the opposite direction. Almost made it to where I'd parked when the sound of a big car engine at high revs turned both our heads. Heard the squeal of rubber on asphalt, the high-pitched scream of an engine pushed to its limits. Saw twin sets of round taillights fishtailing in a haze of smoke, tires spinning as a car struggled for traction. Watched it leap ahead as the tires gripped the road.

An instant later heard an unmistakable *whump* over the whine of the engine, a sound I'd heard before. The sound of more than one-and-a-half tons of hurtling metal machine smacking into flesh and bone. Saw a dark shape flip up over the roof of the speeding car and tumble to the pavement like a rag doll, roll to a stop and lay deathly still.

I ran without knowing it before the car's taillights disappeared around a corner in another squeal of tires. Sprinted across Main Street. Didn't bother to check for cross traffic, legs churning as fast as I could make them go. By the time I covered two blocks the growl of the engine had receded in the distance. Chest heaving, I pulled up in front of the body crumpled on the pavement, the face dimly lit by the streetlight on the corner—Jake. Knelt down and put two fingers to his throat. Felt a pulse.

"Brandt!" I yelled.

"Already dialing," he called.

I glanced over my shoulder, saw him hurrying down the street, phone pressed to his ear. Turned back to Jake. Looked for the source of blood streaked across his face. Small cuts and scrapes mostly. Forced myself to take a breath, look methodically for other signs of injury. One arm lay at an unnatural angle. Leg, too, bent above the knee. No other signs of bleeding. Nothing I could do. I stripped off my windbreaker and tucked it around his shoulders. Listened to his labored breathing. Raspy and uneven. Froth bubbled at the corners of his mouth, covered his beard. I bent down for a close look. It was pink. Not a good sign. Could be a punctured lung.

Brandt came up behind me. "Jake?"

I nodded. "Tell me they're on their way."

"They're on their way."

Moments later the short bleat of a nearby siren confirmed it. A Huntley Fire Department emergency vehicle rounded the corner from Main Street, lights flashing, siren burping, and gunned down the block toward us.

The noise and lights must have roused Jake. His eyes opened, twitched back and forth, his face a mask of confusion. His skin was white in the headlights, blood like ropes of black disappearing into his beard. He mouthed some words. Coughed and spit up more pink froth.

"Don't try to talk," I said. "Paramedics are here. They'll fix you up. You'll be okay."

The EMTs wheeled a stretcher next to us, assessed the situation. Got busy checking his vitals. Shined a penlight into his eyes. Cut the clothes away from the obvious breaks in his arm and leg. Decided to get a line into him with a morphine drip before they even tried to move him. Even so, perspiration covered his pale face when they splinted his arm. When they started on his leg, he let out a scream. Bit it back and whimpered. Coughed up more pink froth.

"That doesn't look good," I muttered.

The closest paramedic glanced over his shoulder. "Actually that probably is good. Good bet he's got a broken rib or two. Punctured lung and he'd be spitting up red. Look's like only some little capillaries ruptured. We won't know about internal bleeding, though, until they take a look at some films or an MRI."

"But he's going to be okay?" Brandt asked, hovering close by.

"I think so. The docs will be able to tell you more."

More flashing lights added dissonance to the scene. A patrol car pulled up quietly across the street. An officer circled the front of the car and strolled over. Spoke quietly to one of the EMTs before he stepped over to us. He pulled Brandt aside first. I watched the paramedics get Jake ready for transport, heard Brandt answer questions politely in his soft Texas twang. Jake seemed to drift in and out of consciousness.

Another patrol car rolled up silently. Without lights. Parked nose-to-nose with the first cruiser. Randy climbed out of this one, ambled over to the officer next to Brandt, and conferred in low tones. Randy glanced over, motioned me to join them. Weariness hung on him like an old pea jacket, stooping his shoulders. He asked me to recount what I'd seen. I kept it simple. The officer took notes.

Randy looked expectant when I finished. "Something's still on your mind," he said.

I told him about what I'd seen in the bar earlier. Jake and Pete having words. Pete slipping Jake some cash. Randy looked thoughtful.

"The taillights belonged to a Corvette," I said. "Late model, from the shape."

"No plate number?"

I shook my head. "Too far to tell if it even had plates." I hesitated. "Pete owns a Corvette."

He nodded. "We'll check. Anything else?"

I looked at Brandt, shook my head.

"We'll get a statement from Jake later, then." Randy turned to the patrolman, took him aside, excusing us without a word.

The EMTs worked on Jake for a while longer before they hoisted him onto a body board. Brandt and I both moved to help without being asked. The EMTs didn't object. Four of us made easy work of it. We lifted him easily onto the stretcher.

The morphine appeared to kick in, giving him a dreamy look, but fear suddenly flashed across his face. He looked around wildly until his eyes locked on my face. He reached for me with his good arm.

"Emerson," he rasped.

One of the EMTs bent over him. "Just take it easy. Try not to talk."

"Got to." He squeezed the words out.

The EMT turned to me. "We've got to get this guy up to Woodstock, pronto."

"I'll ride with you." I saw him nod and turned to toss the car keys to Brandt. "Take the car." I rattled off some quick directions in case he couldn't keep up.

The EMTs had already loaded the stretcher into their rig and motioned to me to hurry. I climbed in the back, one of the EMTs in next to me. The other closed the doors and ran around to the driver's side. The engine roared to life and the rig lurched forward. A minute or two later, we rocketed through town on the highway, siren wailing. Jake clutched my hand as the rig swayed. On the open road the driver cut the siren. Jake pulled me down close.

"Made a mistake," he rasped. "Big one." He squeezed his eyes shut against the pain. Opened them again. "Henry . . ."

"My brother?" I said sharply. "What about him?" The EMT looked up, turned away.

"Saw Henry killed," Jake said, wincing with each word.

"What do you mean you saw him killed? You were there? At the tracks?"

He frowned and shook his head. He started to say something, got swept up in a wave of pain. Tried again. "Pete . . . thought I could squeeze him. . . . Wrong . . . I was wrong . . ."

"About what? I don't understand." I had too many questions. But the currents caught him, pain buffeting him and drugs sucking him under. I stayed quiet to let him talk.

He gripped my hand tighter, rolled his eyes toward the EMT. Leaned close. "Bat," he said. "I took it. In the shed. Out back. Got to get it."

He leaned back. Closed his eyes. I wanted to shake him, rattle all his thoughts loose and dump them out on the ambulance floor. Make him assemble them into a cohesive picture. Like a puzzle.

"Jake?"

His eyes fluttered open, focused on me.

"Do you know what you're trying to tell me?"

He nodded impatiently.

"You want me to get something for you? A bat? Out of the shed? At your house, Jake?"

He nodded, winced.

"It's important?"

"Yes," he rasped, squeezing my hand hard. "Before . . ." A spasm of pain wracked him.

"Before someone else finds it?" I saw him nod. "Where in the shed?"

"Under . . . under the bench." His eyes rolled in his head and closed again. His hand relaxed, let mine go.

The EMT glanced over at Jake, checked his vitals on the monitor. "Better let him rest," he said quietly.

The ER seemed quiet for a Friday night. A mother and three children ranging from five to eleven took up one corner. One on the floor with a coloring book. One sitting with a magazine in her lap, feet swinging back and forth. The smallest asleep on her mother's shoulder. The room empty otherwise. Brandt walked toward me slowly, a full cup of coffee in each hand. He passed one to me. I blew on it, sipped carefully. Made a face at the burnt taste. Jake had been poked, prodded, sent to radiology. No word.

I wondered if Jake had any family. Whether I should call someone. Remembered he was an only child. Thought he'd said something about his folks passing away. Didn't think he'd ever been married. Realized how sad it must be to be truly alone in the world. Made me miss Nell and Emily—and appreciate Brandt's presence—that much more.

The phone in my pocket vibrated, startling me. I pulled it out, answered.

"Tate here," a voice said. "Any word?"

"Not yet," I replied.

"You're at the hospital?"

"We'll stay until we know more."

Randy was silent for a moment. "I drove by Pete's house. Car's in the driveway. Not a mark on it. Didn't see the need to wake him up. I'll talk to him tomorrow."

"Okay." I tried to keep the disappointment out of my voice. Wondered now if Jake had been confused by the morphine. If he'd mixed things up in his head. A sports bet with Pete and a bat in the belfry. Nothing made sense anymore.

"You there?" Randy said.

"Yeah, sorry. Thanks for telling me."

"Go home. Get some sleep."

"Soon as we know something."

An hour passed before a trauma nurse came out to tell us that Jake had been taken to surgery to repair the damage done to the broken leg. He'd been lucky, though, she said. Three cracked ribs, a broken arm, but nothing life-threatening.

Brandt and I drove back to Frank's in silence, exhaustion sapping us of the energy to speak. Inside, he headed for the kitchen to get a glass of water. I followed, quietly rummaged through cupboards and drawers. He watched me assemble a flashlight, phone book, short pry bar, paper and pencil on the table. I remembered as a kid Jake had lived in town, checked the phone book to see if he was still in the same house. Jotted down the address.

"What's up?" Brandt said softly.

I told him about the ride in the ambulance, what Jake had said. Told him I had no clue what was going on or what Jake's ramblings might have to do with Henry's death, but it had sounded important. Important enough that I should go find out what he was talking about.

Brandt gave it some thought. "You think the hit-and-run was deliberate. Something to do with Pete?"

"Randy says it wasn't Pete's car," I told him. "But Jake was scared. Said he made a mistake bracing Pete in the bar tonight, bet or no bet. At least that's what I think he meant."

"Can't it wait until morning?"

I glanced at the wall clock. "It is morning. Jake seemed to think somebody else wants what he's got. Might be too late already."

"Then go."

"Don't wait up."

The hour before dawn is always the most peaceful part of the day. A time when even creatures still awake in a twenty-four/seven world are still and drowsy. The four-square house on Grove Street was dark, silent. It sat across the tracks from an asphalt lot next to the milk processing plant that housed dozens of semi-trailers. I drove slowly past and stopped in front of the next house. Parked and killed the lights. Waited and watched for a few minutes. I saw no sign of life.

I turned the car around, drove back across the tracks and onto the frontage road that ran parallel. Pulled onto the shoulder and killed the engine. I waited a moment or two, got out quietly and made my way back to the house on foot. A streetlight blinked, casting dancing shadows on the walk up to the porch. I went up the steps and froze when I saw the front door ajar. Listened, but didn't hear a sound except the thumping in my chest and the rustle of leaves in the breeze.

I stretched out a hand, pushed the door open, pry bar ready. The interior yawned blackly. As I stepped inside I saw the splintered jamb around the latch. I swung the door shut the way I'd found it. Let my eyes adjust and looked around. Felt my way into the living room, using the pale squares of windows as a guide. Covering the flashlight with the palm of my hand, I switched it on, let a little light bleed out. The room was trashed, furniture overturned, cushions ripped, pictures pulled off the walls.

I held my breath, listened for sounds of someone in the house.

CHAPTER 31

Every room in Jake's house looked the same—torn apart by someone doing a quick, but methodical search. Nothing moved on the dark street outside the front windows except shadows as tree branches gently swayed and settled.

I walked to the back of the house, found a door from the kitchen leading to the backyard. Eased it open and let myself out. A dark shape squatted in a back corner of the lot. The shed. I glanced around, saw no movement. Walked across the yard to the shed door. Used the same trick with the flashlight to give me just enough light to see a hasp with a padlock turned to look closed, but still unlocked. A statement, maybe, about the changes Huntley had been through since I'd left. A place where you wanted to trust your neighbors, but didn't anymore. Judging from what I'd seen in the house, Jake had good reason not to trust someone.

The door creaked softly as it opened, revealing a tomb-black interior. I eased inside, closed the door behind me. Used the flashlight sparingly to get my bearings. The shed was full of what looked like fifty years' worth of tools and lawn care equipment. Two gas mowers and an old hand push reel mower crouched, toad-like, on a wood floor. A couple of rusted bikes rested in a corner on flat tires like old folks in wheelchairs. A skeletal crew of shovels, rakes, axes, a hedge trimmer, leaf blower and other tools lined one wall, some on hooks, others propped against it haphazardly. Just to the left of the door was an old workbench covered with hand tools, half-empty paint cans, oily rags, loose nails and screws.

A dusty canvas tarp was thrown over a charcoal grill sitting next to the mowers. I pulled it off. Draped it over the corners of the window frame, working by feel and the dim light coming through the dirty glass. I thumbed the flashlight on and went back to the workbench. Bent down and peered beneath it. I found only dirt, spider webs and some scattered junk. Jake had spoken with certainty, despite the drugs and the pain. I grabbed one of the rags on the bench, used it to brush aside the dirt and junk on the floor. Shined the light on the wood planks, looking for a crack to wedge the pry bar in. Jammed it in a joint where two planks met end to end and put some weight into it. The board cracked and splintered with a loud snap. I stopped to listen, afraid the noise might attract attention. Hearing nothing but my own shallow breathing, I wrapped the rag around the jagged end and pulled up the rest of the plank, nails groaning as they pulled loose. Shined the light into the space between the floor joists.

Packed dirt lay only a foot or so below the floor. The light reflected off spots of some shiny black surface. A layer of grime covered an old plastic garbage bag. I pulled it out of the hole. Untied it and opened it wide. Wrapped inside, an aluminum baseball bat, well used and dirty, just like Jake said. I panned the light slowly from grip to end. Wondered why it was so important that Jake had hidden it away. I noticed that some of the dirt flaking off the end of it was lighter in color. More of a rust than the grayish-brown of dry topsoil. Dried blood. *Whose?*

I tied up the bag. Jake could clear it up later. With some story about accidentally giving some kid a bloody nose, no doubt. But the uneasiness in my stomach said something different. I shrugged it off, chalked up the jumpy nerves to lack of sleep and the late hour. I blearily checked my watch—nearly five. I stood and stretched, put the flashlight in my jacket pocket. Tucked the pry bar under my belt in back and pulled the jacket over it. Grabbed the garbage bag and slipped out the door.

The sky had lightened. Enough to make out details now, not just shapes in the dark. A few early birds twittered, signaling that dawn wasn't far off. I stepped away from the shed and rounded the corner toward the house. Cold metal caught me in the soft cleft under my chin, snapped my head back and stopped me in my tracks. Pete stepped out into the open holding the other end of the shotgun pressed to my throat. He smiled in a way that wasn't comforting.

"Worse than jock itch, Ward," he sneered. "You're more like a case of the crabs. Or gonorrhea."

"Big word for you, Pete." I tried to breathe slowly and think.

"So, what's he got?" another voice said behind me. A woman's voice.

Startled, I tried to turn my head, but Pete held it in place with the shotgun muzzle. A light came on, played around my feet. She came up behind me and took the bag out of my hand. Backed up a step or two and circled around until she was standing next to Pete. Shined the light at my face, then aimed it at the ground, giving me a better look at her. A tall blonde, hair pulled back into a ponytail. She wore a black nylon warm-up suit with white piping, jacket zipped halfway up over a white tank top, white athletic shoes. She looked amused.

My mouth went dry. I had to work to get the word out. "Tish?"

"What do you think, baby?" she said to Pete, her eyes still on me. "Think he found whatever Jakey was talking about?"

"Just open it." There was anger and impatience in his voice.

She laid it on the grass, stooped next to it with the light and looked inside. She frowned. "Oh, for God's sake, it's a baseball bat. Who gives a rat's—"

She looked up and saw Pete go rigid. "What's wrong with you?" she said.

Her face followed his glazed look, tipped down at the bat again, stayed there a long time. When she looked at me, her face had changed, hardened, as if someone else had taken control.

"So why did you come looking for this?" she asked calmly.

Pete prodded me with the shotgun.

"Jake asked me to," I said.

"He tell you why he wanted you to get it?" she said.

"Only that he thought someone else might try to take it. I didn't think it was that important, but he insisted. Obviously, he was right."

She nodded. Stood up and leaned close and shined the light at me for a better look. "But you don't know what this is or where it came from? Or why Jakey hid it in that shed?"

I moved my head a fraction of an inch, felt the metal barrel dig into my skin. "Nope."

She sighed. "That's too bad."

"What'll we do with him?" Pete said.

"What do you think?" she snapped. He recoiled as if slapped. "We'll take him out to Kenny's. Keep him here. I'll look for some rope."

She disappeared into the shed. Pete pushed harder on the muzzle, backing me up against the wall.

"Jesus, Pete," I said. "You and Tish? After all these years? What, you see a chance to move in now that Lou's gone? Ditch Sue Ann?"

He smiled grimly. "Now that Lou's gone? That's rich. Tish and me? We never broke it off. Been seeing each other all this time."

I stared at him. "Is that it? Lou found out? Couldn't take that, too, on top of being put out of business by his partner?"

His laugh was short, humorless. "You are so far off base,

Ward. It's a wonder you can find your pecker in the dark."

Tish stepped back through the doorway. "Shut up, Pete."

"What?" He turned and glared. "I didn't say shit. Christ, I'm tired of you telling me what to do. We wouldn't be here if it wasn't for you."

She glared back. When she spoke, her voice dripped icicles. "We wouldn't be here if you had any fucking brains and the sense to keep your dick in your pants and your money in the bank." She aimed her stare at me. "Turn around."

Pete grabbed me roughly by the arm and jerked me so I faced the wall. He jammed the shotgun up against the base of my skull. Tish pulled my hands behind my back and wrapped a length of rope around them, pulling it tight.

"Let's go," she said.

Pete yanked me away from the wall and gave me a shove that nearly sent me sprawling. I caught my balance and followed Tish. Pete stayed close behind, giving me little reminders of his presence with a nudge of the shotgun between my shoulder blades. She led the way down the street, across the tracks and into the processing plant lot. They'd hidden the big SUV I'd seen Sue Ann driving among the semi-trailers.

Pete popped the locks with a remote. Tish opened the front door and motioned me in. She threw the garbage bag in the back, took the shotgun from Pete and climbed in behind me. Kept the muzzle leveled at my head. Through the windshield, I could see the walkway up to Jake's front door in the narrow space between two semi-trailers. Pete got behind the wheel and drove out of the lot, winding his way through town out to Huntley-Dundee Road. The eastern horizon was tinged light gray.

Neither of them spoke. Exhaustion crept up on me in the silence, made me feel sluggish and dull. I opened my eyes wide, forced my thoughts back to the center of all this. Lou, who had always taken what he wanted, I now realized. He'd expected it all to fall in his lap—the homecoming queen, the football scholarship, the great job. None of it had come easy, so he'd taken shortcuts, as if it was his due. I thought of all the people he'd bulldozed on his way. People who probably weren't all that unhappy he was dead: Sarina for the way he'd treated her father; Ahmed himself, who got cut out of the original mall deal and had his business torched by Lou's father years before; Bill Caruthers, Jr., who watched his father disintegrating before his eyes; Danny DeHaan, the traditionalist who'd hated what Huntley was becoming; Frank and all the original syndicate members who'd lost millions backing Lou's ambition to be more than a small player in a small town.

Pete had always been obvious, clumsy and transparent. Lou was worse, had this polish, this veneer that hid his intentions. Acted the gentleman while he played the rogue. Like the way he stole Tish.

Tish and Lou. Pete and Tish. Tish and Hank. Henry . . . Jake saw Henry get killed. Hank had died in a stolen car stuck on the railroad tracks. So why was everyone so interested in a baseball bat that Jake had hidden away? We were already a couple miles out of town. I had to do something. I rolled my head on my shoulders, pretended to stretch while I pulled against the rope around my wrists. Felt it loosen a little.

"I thought we had a business deal, Pete," I said quietly.

He shrugged. "Things change."

"What deal?" Tish asked.

"He didn't tell you?" I glanced at Pete, saw his jaw clench. "He's selling out. Getting his money out while the getting's good."

"What does he mean?" she said sharply.

"Just what he said." Pete's voice was short.

"I want to hear it from you."

Pete fumed. Slowed and turned south on a side road. Eventually spoke. "Ahmed and his people want out. They screwed up with Saunders, trying to get the money back. Ward, here, found a buyer willing to pay a big enough premium it more than makes up for what Saunders took out."

"Shit, Pete," she said, "you think this is for real?"

He answered defensively. "The buyer's legit. Has a bunch of big investors behind him. Came with two hundred thou' in cash and wired a couple million in earnest money to Ahmed's offshore account."

"And you bought into it? From this piece of crap?" She jabbed the gun into the back of my head. Pain shot through the back of my eyes.

"Take it easy," I said. "I'm in it for the money. What the fuck's wrong with you? You think you're the only one who wants a taste of the good life?"

"You had your shot," she said, giving me another jab. "You blew out of here like you couldn't wait to get the stink of this town off you. The rest of us made something of this place. And now you want to come in here and take a piece? Like you deserve it or something?"

She reached over the seat and smacked a hand against the back of Pete's head.

He cringed. "Ow! What's that for?"

"You dumb fuck. First you let Saunders in, and he just about sucks you dry. Then you gamble away what you have left. Now you want to let some other outsider come in and take it all away from you?"

"It's the only way out, Tish! With Saunders dead, everything at the bank's got to be on the up-and-up from now on. We just gotta pray they don't do an audit. And hope that little shit Kolnik keeps his mouth shut."

"Shut up," Tish said, her voice low.

"Why? Because of him?" He jerked a thumb at me. "He figured it out."

"Shut up!" she said again. "Just don't say any more, okay?"

"He's right," I said. "What difference does it make? I don't care. I don't live here, remember? Like I told Pete, I saw an opportunity. I get my finder's fee for this deal, I'm gone."

"You never should have come back in the first place."

"That's what everyone says."

"Well, everyone's right. Now you're going to regret it."

I was beginning to think she was right. Sweat trickled down my sides. I put a little more effort into loosening the rope. The SUV slowed again as Pete took another corner. He looked pale, nervous.

"Are you sure about this?" He glanced in the rearview mirror.

"Yes," Tish said. "Now shut up."

He brooded. Did as he was told. Less than a quarter mile later he turned onto a long gravel drive. I remembered the weathered clapboard farmhouse that slowly filled the windshield from a lifetime ago. Lilacs in front grown tall and bushy over the years just now beginning to bloom, their scent filling the early morning air. House dark now, but once filled with sunlight in which a little girl in a dirty dress played.

The drive curved left before it reached the house. Pete followed it a hundred yards past the house and pulled up in front of the barn, now grayed by sun and wind. They climbed out. Tish opened my door, waggled the gun at me. I swung my feet out, slid off the seat onto the gravel. She pointed the muzzle at the barn. I led the way through an open side door into the dim interior, the hard steel of the pry bar in the small of my back small comfort. Not much of a defense against a shotgun.

Something felt wrong with all of this. I smelled fear, panic, and it wasn't just mine. They'd overreacted. Or Tish had. If she benefited from Pete's scam, then she had nothing to fear from me. I told her so.

"You know, this deal I helped Pete put together is a good solution for all of us."

"Shut up," she said. She put the muzzle between my shoulder blades and shoved me ahead.

I ignored her. "You two walk away with millions. Start over somewhere. My finder's fee doesn't come out of your cut. No skin off your ass."

"Shut the fuck up!"

"You can take the girl out of the country . . ." I said softly. "I thought you left all this behind, Tish. You know, with the fancy house, fancy clothes. You said you never wanted to come back to this. But you've still got Roy's mouth."

"Fuck you!" She raked the barrel across the back of my skull, setting off an explosion of lights in front of my eyes. I staggered and fell to my knees, pain pulsing through my head.

Slowly the world came back into focus, the whirling lights faded and winked out. I found myself staring at a tractor parked just inside the big double doors at one end of the T-shaped barn. My eyes slid to the low, squat alien shape next to it. The pointed front end and sloping hood of a Corvette, headlights closed as if asleep. Right front bumper caved in, the fiberglass hood above it cracked and splintered.

Tish and Pete. His-and-hers Corvettes. Tish had run Jake down. *To protect Pete? From Jake?* No, from what Jake had. A bat. An old, bloodied bat. I swung my head around, looked up at Pete.

"Jesus!" It came out a whisper, as if fear wouldn't let me voice the thought. "You killed Hank."

He pasted a sneer on his face, too late to cover the fear.

"Meg said he got into a fight with you that night," I said. "He came back, though, didn't he? Tried to take your car, or maybe just key it or something stupid like that. And you killed him. With that bat. That's what Jake knew."

He shook his head, kept on shaking it as if that would make it all go away.

I wouldn't let him off that easy. "You killed my brother. Put him in your car and rolled it onto the tracks to make it look like an accident. You sorry son of a bitch. All these years we believed it. Thought he screwed up. But it was you, you prick!"

Fear and guilt built on his face until he looked about to burst. "I didn't do it!" he said.

Tish turned on him, swung the gun away from me. "Shut up!"

He ignored her, wildness in his eyes now. "It wasn't me. It was her! I swear."

"Shut the fuck up!" she barked.

"Hank did come back. We were hanging out in Diecke Park. He rode in with some friends."

"I'm warning you, Pete. Don't say it. Not another word."

He looked at her, eyes pleading. "Enough. It's got to stop. You want me to shut up, then let him go. We were just supposed to scare the crap out of him, not kill him."

"You stupid idiot!" she screamed. "You think he's going to let it go? Just walk away and forget about it?"

Confusion played across his face. I strained against the rope, loosened it some more, but held still when Pete turned his gaze on me again, eyes dull now.

"Hank was drunk," he said in a monotone. "He tried to get into it with me. Got in a couple good punches that put me down. I'll give him that."

Tish pleaded. "Shut up. Please, just shut your mouth."

Pete kept on going. "He had me on the ground, started punching me. Wasn't much in him at that point. He was too drunk. Tish came up behind him, hit him with the bat. Knocked him off me. He just lay there." He shook his head again. "It was Tish, not me."

She was crying now. "You are such a dumb fuck, Pete. You never listened."

She pulled the trigger, the blast deafening in the close space. Pete's eyes widened in surprise as he staggered backward, red spreading out across the front of his jacket as blood welled from his chest. A second explosion put him on his back, his face thankfully out of sight. One shoe twitched, then he lay still. The sound of the shotgun's pump action, ejected shell hitting the cement floor with a hollow clink, pulled my eyes away.

CHAPTER 32

"Shit, Tish. Did you have to do that?"

She turned her tear-streaked face to me, swiped the back of one hand across her cheek. "I never loved him. I've never loved anyone. I'm not sure what that's supposed to feel like. But he was about the closest thing to a friend I ever had. Because he understood me. You know? Like he knew how I felt. We were a lot alike, I guess."

Her eyes focused, hardened. "You know I had to do that. If he told you, then he would have told someone else. I'd go to jail. That wouldn't be good."

"I won't tell anyone, Tish. I promise."

Her mouth turned down, hatred distorting her features. "You're all the same. Promise a girl anything so you can get into her pants. Say you won't tell a soul. Before you know it, story goes through the locker room like athlete's foot—'Guess who I fucked last night?' "

I shook my head. "Hank was never like that. Lou neither."

She laughed mirthlessly. "You've got to be kidding. You're right about Hank. He was sweet. You know why he tried to fight Pete that night? For my honor. Hank knew it was over between us. He knew I was going out with Lou. He was trying to protect me from Pete. For Lou's sake. But Lou? I was his biggest conquest. He just didn't realize I was using him as much as he used me."

"Lou never talked about you that way. Not that I heard."

393

"But he wanted me just as bad as any boy in high school. Worse. Would have done anything for me. Anything as long as I fucked him, that is."

"I don't believe it. I think he really loved you."

She snorted. "Who do you think came up with the idea of making Hank's death look like an accident?"

I stared at her, open-mouthed.

She nodded. "He was there that night. With me and Pete. Pete wasn't thinking straight after getting punched in the head. I was scared shitless. Lou told us what to do. Heaved the bat into the bushes. Helped us get Hank into the car. Followed us out to Seeman Road. He helped Pete push the car onto the tracks when we saw the train coming."

Like trying to move an arm that's fallen asleep, I heard the words, but my brain didn't want to comprehend them. My best friend growing up, the guy I would have stepped in front of a bus for, had been an accomplice to my brother's murder. I saw Tish Miller as clearly then as I had the first time I ever laid eyes on her. I just hadn't understood it at ten. She was something primeval, malevolent, dressed in pretty skin. A she-wolf in a lamb's-wool sweater. She and Pete were whelped from the same pack, but Pete had been weak. Tish turned out to be the alpha male.

Anger ran hotly through my veins, throbbed at my temples. I took a slow breath. "You're not a very nice person."

She shook her head. "No, I'm not."

"No wonder Lou wanted out. Fucked by his partner, screwed by his wife. Did he know you and Pete were trying to ruin him?"

Her grin appeared more like a grimace. "He outlived his usefulness, lost his drive. Pete still had it. Still wanted more. So did I." She shrugged. "When Lou lost it all, I figured the only thing he was good for was his life insurance."

I looked at the shotgun she held. I didn't think I could be

surprised again, but the horrible truth rolled over me like a tsunami. "You killed him."

She shrugged. "What do they call it? Euthanasia. He was depressed. Suicidal. Everybody knows that. I just helped him along. He was having second thoughts. Started to get pissed about what Pete had done. Got really drunk one night and rambled on about how he was going to turn Pete in. Said it didn't matter if he got dragged down with him. I couldn't let him do that."

"He didn't lose it. You took it away from him. You and Pete. When he had nothing left, you killed him. How much did you get?"

"Life insurance? Two million."

"And Danny? He figured it out?"

She nodded. "Like I said, you're all alike. You think with your dicks. That's all you want. Some hot piece of ass to put out for you. Danny? He loved those trains. So did I. I used to go out there when I was a kid, pretend that those trains were going to take me far away from here. Danny taught me how to drive them. I let him cop a feel now and then, batted my eyelashes at him. God, he was pathetic."

"It has to stop, Tish. Pete was right. It's too late to try to fix it. It's all falling apart."

"One more," she said softly. "I'm not over my budget yet. Funny, it gets easier after the first one." She paused. "They'll figure Pete ran out, split before he got caught. You? I doubt anyone in this town will miss you. Those who might will just figure you went back to the city. And who's going to suspect me anyway? I'm still the grieving widow. I had nothing to do with Lou's business. Certainly not with Pete's. Why would I?"

She had it all figured out. And I was on my knees in hay and cow manure getting a real good taste of how George and Lou had felt staring down the yawning black bore of a twelve-gauge.

Follow the money, Brandt told me. *Follow the money,* Duran and Lipscomb said. Look where it had gotten Lou, and Pete, and Saunders. And now me. Death on a budget.

I pushed my wrists together, put some slack in the rope. Curled my fingers up and felt for the knot, worked it.

"You think Kenny and whoever else is in the house is going to sleep through that shotgun going off? Come on, Tish. It's over. Can't you see that?"

She shook her head. "Kenny's away for the weekend. Took the family up north. It's just you and me. Nice and romantic, don't you think? Just what you always wanted."

"I've got my faults. But you? No, I never wanted you, Tish. Henry did, though. Loved you with a purity that's rare in this world. Probably the only kid in school besides me who didn't want to get in your pants, just into your heart. He never saw the rotten core inside you, the emptiness, never realized you don't have a heart. And you killed him."

She tipped her head, considered me. "Get up."

I froze, afraid she'd see my fingers had loosened the knot. Her brothers taught her to swear like a sailor, but not to tie knots like one.

"Get up!"

I slowly got to my feet and stood facing her. "What now?"

She motioned with the gun. "Through the barn. That way."

I started walking, twisted so I still half-faced her. Side-stepped so she couldn't see my hands behind my back and jabbered to distract her.

"You know that part about no one missing me? You're wrong there, Tish. My friend Brandt will miss me something awful. He knows I went to Jake's, knows what I was looking for. And Jake will miss me, too. He's going to pull through just fine. You'll have to figure out another way to keep him quiet. Where we going, anyway?" I felt the rope coming loose.

She grinned like a gargoyle. "Hog pen. Out back. Save me some trouble."

The words chilled me. Frank always got a couple of piglets in the spring when we were kids. Let us fatten them up over the summer and put them in the freezer come late fall. We fed them everything, even table scraps. They'd follow us around like dogs if we brought them steak bones. I knew what they could do to a carcass in a couple of days.

"You don't think I'm gentleman enough to drag Pete out there first before you shoot me?"

Her grin widened. "I'll handle Pete. I always could. You, I don't trust."

Feverishly, I worked the knot harder and felt it come undone. I put a hand up under my jacket, got a good grip on the pry bar. The double doors at the end of the barn were close now. I remembered the day Frank had talked to Tish's dad down near the doors while he milked a cow, sunlight framing him in the doorway, cat brushing up against his legs, waiting for a squirt of milk from one of the cow's udders.

Tish motioned me to the side, came around me cautiously. She held the shotgun in one hand, kept it leveled at my middle. Didn't take her eyes off me while her hand fumbled for the latch. She put her shoulder to the door, gave it a shove. It rolled open on tracks, hit the door stop and bounced back a foot.

"You know, I own this place," she said softly. "I made Lou buy it for me. Years ago. My daddy rented it. Kenny, too. They never could afford to buy it. Just barely made enough to raise their families. I told Lou it would make a great investment, that he'd build a subdivision out here some day. It was the one piece of property he couldn't sell when Harry called in the loan. He begged me for it, to mortgage it at least, and help him out. I told him to screw himself."

She waggled the end of the shotgun at me and nodded toward

the gray daylight. I moved forward, closing the gap between us. Now or never. In one motion, I stepped toward her, pulled the pry bar out of my waistband and swung. She was quicker than I expected, almost as if she anticipated me. Maybe she acted on instinct, as primal as her messed-up psyche. She jerked backward, out of reach. Instead of bone and flesh and bone, the pry bar clanged against gunmetal, sending a jolt of numbing pain up my arm. The gun went off, fire and smoke and a black wad of metal pellets exploding from the muzzle. My left side erupted in flames, searing pain stopping me dead in my tracks. Tish took a step back, ejected the spent shell. She raised the gun and leveled it at my chest, her lips twisted in fury. Pulled the trigger.

The silence was deafening. My ears rang. I wondered if my eardrums had ruptured and I just hadn't heard the blast. Or maybe I died and didn't know it yet. Dead men couldn't hear, could they? Tish dropped the gun. Turned and ran. The shotgun clattered on the cement. Soft-soled sneakers thudded on it, too. I heard them.

I ran after her, felt like someone pressed a branding iron to my ribs. Slowly gained on her. She darted left at the top of the "T." I followed. She grabbed a wooden handle sticking out of a pile of hay. Whirled and stood her ground, waving a pitchfork at me. I pulled up just in time to keep from impaling myself on the tines. Tried to backpedal. She didn't hesitate. She lunged and thrust the pitchfork at me. I sucked in my belly, shoved my ass back and curled my arms over the advancing tines. Lost my balance and fell backward. Started scrabbling with my feet almost before my butt hit the cement trying to back away from her and the deadly points of the slashing pitchfork.

She attacked relentlessly, thrusting again and again. I twisted from side to side, avoided being stuck by fractions of an inch each time. I saw her eyes focus, anticipate my next move. I rolled the other way onto my stomach and brought one knee up under me. Felt my feet find a purchase on the cement and exploded like a sprinter off the starting blocks. I felt her fury envelop me like the blast wave of the exploding RV, knew she was right behind me, about to attack again. I could feel the thrust of the pitchfork in the air behind me.

I did what she'd done—stopped and turned, swinging the pry bar in front of me like a shield. It clanged against the tines, knocked the pitchfork aside. Her momentum sent her tumbling into me and we went down in a tangle of limbs. She scratched and clawed at my face. I tried to catch her wrists in one hand but she flailed wildly. I hacked at her arms with the pry bar to knock them away. The bar smacked her in the side of the head instead. She squealed, hands flying to the point of impact. I bucked her off and scrambled to my feet. By the time I turned around, she'd retrieved the pitchfork.

I moved in swinging. Instead of attacking, she parried, twisting the pitchfork to the side. My arm met the slashing tines, flesh no match for sharp steel. I grunted in surprise as my forearm slid onto the two middle tines, speared like a fish. Then snorted in pain when she tried to yank the pitchfork away. The pry bar fell from my fingers and clanged on the cement. Tish's mouth opened when the pitchfork didn't budge. I didn't give her a chance to consider a next move.

Fearful from the sudden pain, I stepped toward her and put some momentum into a right cross to her jaw. Her head snapped around. I grabbed the handle of the pitchfork and snatched it out of her hands. Held it tight and jerked my arm loose, tears springing to my eyes as a river of fire ran up my arm, joined the inferno burning along my ribcage. I turned and heaved the pitchfork across the barn. Swung around to face Tish. She was breathing heavily, shaking her head like a tired prizefighter. She looked at me cross-eyed, tried to focus. Backed up warily when

I advanced.

My left arm hung uselessly now, pain from my side forearm shooting through my brain like lightning bolts. My throat was dry. Dust from the hay filled my nostrils along with the pungent scent of manure. Wearily, I considered my options. Took the phone out of my pocket to call in the cavalry. Tish's eyes widened, darted wildly around the barn. I looked down at the phone to see the numbers, started to press them. In an instant, Tish leaped to one side and headed for one end of the barn. *The Corvette.*

Too slow, I whirled in her direction, but missed as she went by, my arm refusing to take directions. I took off after her. The sound of a door rolling open brought us both up short. A square of daylight over the tractor and the car widened into a bright expanse of gray sky. Voices shouted, and three figures rushed inside around the vehicles.

"Stop right there!" a voice said.

Tish froze a few yards ahead of me. Beyond her, Randy stepped away from the tractor, gun drawn but pointed at the floor ahead of him.

"You all right, Ward?" he called.

I glanced at the spreading red blotch on the side of my jacket. "I think so."

He nodded. "Time to give it up, Tish."

She came to life then. Burst into tears, spoke hysterically. "Oh, thank God you're here! He's trying to kill me! He killed Pete! Just shot him. Oh, God, it was horrible, just h . . . horrible! Thank God you got here in time!"

She put her hands to her face. Her shoulders sagged, and she staggered a few steps to her right. Randy looked confused. Another officer stepped out from the other side of the tractor for a better look. They both lowered their weapons, uncertain now.

"I'm bleeding here, Randy," I said. He glanced at me. "Don't tell me you're going to listen to her crap."

Suddenly, Tish spun and bolted in my direction, keeping herself between me and them so they wouldn't try to squeeze off a shot. At the last second, she veered away, no recognition in her eyes now, just wildness, an animal running on instinct. She headed for the milking stalls, the open doors that beckoned from that end of the barn.

Randy shouted before she'd taken three strides. "Hold it right there, Tish!"

She turned at the sound of his voice. Kept on going, her stride crablike while she kept him and the gun in view. She didn't see Pete's body. Hooked the toe of one shoe under his leg and sailed over him, arms and legs akimbo. She landed on her side and slid on loose hay toward the wall. Then came to an abrupt stop that widened her eyes and made her gasp. Her look of surprise turned pained. She looked at me. I saw something accusatory in her eyes, then precatory, as if beseeching me to do something for her, help her somehow.

I frowned and took slow, heavy steps toward her, my wits dulled by pain. Randy approached from the side, gun extended in both hands. Her breath came in thin and thready rasps, and her eyelids fluttered. The pitchfork handle stretched out on the floor behind her, blood slowly staining the wood. The end of it had jammed up against the cement footing where the floor met the wall. I watched helplessly as her eyes took on a glassy look just before her eyelids closed.

CHAPTER 33

They dressed the ugly, burned swatch of skin grazed by the shotgun blast, patched up the holes in my arm, and gave me a tetanus shot. Said I could go. I went looking for Tish instead. They'd taken her to surgery. Brandt waited for me in the lobby, but I wasn't ready to talk yet. I pestered a nurse at the desk outside surgery, but she stonewalled me. She said she couldn't and wouldn't tell me Tish's condition. There was no sign of the Millers, and I wondered if they'd been told. Wondered which they'd take hardest, her condition or the fact that their daughter had killed four people.

I gave up and went to find Jake instead. They'd moved him into a semi-private room. He lay asleep in the bed nearest the window, the other bed empty. I dragged a chair next to the window and looked out at a cheerless ashen sky. Brandt found me there half an hour later. Sat down wordlessly and let me think it through. Some time later we both turned at the sound of the door opening. Tate strode in quietly, looked over and shook his head.

"She died on the table," he said. "Feel up to talking?"

Before I could answer, Jake opened his eyes. Turned his head side to side. "What'd I miss?" he said, his voice hoarse.

I told him. About finding the bat. About all of it. Randy took notes, even though I'd already told him some of it while we'd waited for an ambulance for Tish. Moisture threatened to leak from Jake's eyes when I finished.

"Sorry, man," he rasped. "I should've said something a long time ago."

"You saw what happened the night Hank was killed?" Tate asked.

He nodded. "I was a scared kid back then. I didn't think anyone would believe me if I told what happened. And I was afraid Lou and Pete would come after me if they found out I'd seen them. So I took the bat. Figured I'd turn it in at some point." He paused, looked at me. "The Army changed me, man. Made me grow up quick. By the time I came back, it all seemed like ancient history. Your family was long gone except for your dad and your sister, and I didn't have the heart to stir it up again. Not after all that time."

"Why brace Pete?" I asked. "Why now?" I saw Randy grow more alert.

Jake looked uncomfortable. "I didn't do it for the money. Honest. I saw what you were trying to do for Meg. Even though Lou didn't deserve it. I don't know. I figured it was time to take Pete down. Thought I could come at him from a different direction. Get him to confess, maybe."

He sounded sincere.

I turned to Brandt. "You called in the troops." I saw him nod. I moved on to Randy. "How did you know where to look?"

"I had my suspicions," he said simply.

"The shotgun?"

He nodded. "That and some other things. Ed Jarvis told me about the life insurance policy. I knew Tish had a Corvette, too. I had patrols out looking for it, but she was smart enough to drive it straight out to Kenny's and hide it."

Brandt's eyes never wavered from my face while Randy spoke, his expression peculiar. Finally, he turned to Randy. "What about the shotgun?" he asked.

Randy told him about how Lou's gun had been loaded for

bird or clay, not deer.

"You're a lucky man," Randy said to me. "That Remington holds only four shells. Tish never bothered reloading after getting it back from the crime lab."

My luck had held in more ways than one. Luck that Brandt cared enough to call for help instead of succumbing to exhaustion and tumbling into bed. Luck that Tate still knew a lot of people in this town, a lot of their habits. He couldn't get to know all the newcomers—not eighteen or nineteen thousand of them—but he still had his fingers on the pulse of the place where he'd grown up. And luck to have found love, to know the joys of being a father. With all that luck, I couldn't figure out why I felt so bad.

The FBI arrested Ahmed the next day. Randy came out to Frank's to let us know. He said Duran told him the investigation had come to a fruitful conclusion and his services, along with those of his department and staff—meaning us—were no longer needed. I'd taken a chance and given Sarina a heads-up about her father's involvement after leaving the hospital. Decided she deserved to hear it from me, since I helped set the whole thing in motion. Figured she wasn't likely to alert him. She didn't seem surprised, but I could tell she took it hard.

Brandt and I drove back to Chicago the day after that in separate cars. I left without seeing Meg or even saying goodbye. She'd have to get her reality check about Lou from someone else. I wasn't ready to tell her what he'd done, the lies he'd told, the sins he'd helped cover up. I wasn't sure if that was because I didn't think she'd believe me or I wouldn't be able to contain my anger. My instincts had been right—I stopped being Lou's friend the day we graduated from high school. I don't know when he stopped being my friend. Maybe Frank had spoken the truth. Maybe Lou had never been a friend.

Summer took hold in earnest. With Chicago's second season well under way, construction projects all over town snarled traffic and generally inconvenienced people. Both temperatures and tempers flared. I vowed to stay cool, didn't venture out much. Stayed within walking distance of home when I did go out.

Duran and Lipscomb had used the threat of the death penalty to persuade Ahmed to roll on the fundamentalists who'd killed George in their zeal to recover the money he stole. Memorial Day weekend, both Brandt and I got form letters from the Special Agent in Charge of the FBI's Chicago Field Office thanking us for our cooperation in an ongoing investigation of "vital national security." We chuckled about them over good tequila and cold Negra Modelos on my patio.

Brandt produced a small package wrapped in brown kraft paper and held it out. I hesitated. Took it against my better judgment. Wrapped inside were two slim volumes—a copy of J.D. Salinger's *Catcher in the Rye* and Shakespeare's *The Tempest.*

"What's this?" I held them up.

"Mitzi was going through George's things and found this box of books in storage. Funny thing is, they all had the wrong dust jackets on them." He paused, an air of triumph on his face.

"I don't understand."

"Those two books?" He pointed. "Together they're worth about twenty grand. They looked old, so I had a guy I know appraise them. That Salinger? A first edition. Most of the books in the box are worth five or six times that. That's where the money went. George was buying up rare books."

I turned the books over and studied them. "And these two?"

"For you. Thought you'd appreciate them."

I handed them back. "I can't accept these."

"Why not?" Surprise registered on his face.

"Filthy lucre," I said. "I know I'm usually okay with that, Brandt, but it just doesn't sit right this time."

He squirmed uncomfortably.

"Look, B, you don't owe me," I said. Firmly yet gently, the way you'd explain something important to a child. "You and I, we're good. Your friendship is more important to me than the money. You know that. Those . . ." I gestured at the books in his hand ". . . those could cost you everything. Turn 'em in. Maybe somebody'll give you a reward. You can split it with Mitzi."

He looked shocked, then suddenly grateful, like he hadn't thought it through.

I raised my glass. "Friends?"

He saluted with his own. "Family."

"Family," I murmured.

Two days later, I stood in line at O'Hare waiting to board a plane to Seattle. I'd been given an incredible gift when I met Nell, a gift to be cherished, nurtured. I had no plan, no expectations, just an overwhelming need to see the woman and child I loved.

ABOUT THE AUTHOR

After stints as a manual laborer, dishwasher, bartender, restaurant manager, commercial photographer, magazine editor and public relations executive, **Michael W. Sherer** decided life should imitate art. He's now an author, freelance writer and marketing communications consultant. *Death on a Budget* is his sixth novel in the Emerson Ward series (*An Option on Death, Little Use for Death, Death Came Dressed in White, A Forever Death,* and *Death Is No Bargain*).

Mike's also the author of *Island Life,* a stand-alone suspense novel, and *Night Blind,* the first of a new thriller series set in Seattle.

Mike lives in the Seattle area with his wife and family. Please visit his web site at www.michaelwsherer.com.

DATE			

BAKER & TAYLOR